THE
AMATEURS

LIZ HARMER

Vintage Canada

VINTAGE CANADA EDITION, 2019

Copyright © 2018 Elizabeth Harmer

Published by Vintage Canada, a division of Penguin Random House Canada
Limited, in 2019. Originally published in hardcover by Knopf Canada,
a division of Penguin Random House Canada Limited, in 2018.
Distributed in Canada by Penguin Random House Canada Limited, Toronto.

Vintage Canada with colophon is a registered trademark.

www.penguinrandomhouse.ca

Grateful acknowledgement is made for permission to reprint from the following:
Lyrics to "Goin' Down South" written by R.L. Burnside.
Published by Mockingbird Blues. Publishing, Ltd. (BMI).
Administered by Wixen Music Publishing, Inc.
All Rights Reserved. Used by permission.

Library and Archives Canada Cataloguing in Publication

Harmer, Elizabeth, author
The amateurs / Liz Harmer.

ISBN 978-0-345-81125-7
eBook ISBN 978-0-345-81126-4

I. Title.

PS8615.A7433A82 2019   C813'.6   C2016-906011-X

Text design: Kelly Hill
Cover design: Rachel Cooper
Cover images: House © Uliana1997o/Dreamstime.com;
Deer © Nick Jio/Unsplash; Pool © Ghost Presenter/Unsplash

Printed and bound in the United States of America

2 4 6 8 9 7 5 3 1

Penguin
Random House
VINTAGE CANADA

To Adam

Although necessary, it was absurd and cruel,
reasonable in intent but botched in particulars,
a task for professionals bungled by amateurs.

— Paul Fussell,
"The Romantic War, and the Other One"

Nature is pathetically willing. . . . The flowers
growing in the desolation of Mount St. Helens
testify to what in human beings we would call a
lunatic hopefulness, the optimism of the amateur.

— Frederick Turner,
"Cultivating the American Garden"

There is a world of created things, of living beings,
of animals, of entelechies, of souls, in the minutest
particle of matter. . . . There is, therefore, nothing
uncultivated, or sterile or dead in the universe, no
chaos, no confusion.

— Gottfried Leibniz, *La Monadologie*

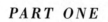

PART ONE

THE

AMATEURS

THE COLLECTORS

L ooting was absolutely *not* frowned upon. One of the happier aspects of this new era was that everything was up for grabs. You would never again go without a pen. You would never come to the end of plastic sandwich containers. In a reversal worthy of a God with more humour than vengeance, the people who remained were outnumbered by every other thing. There had been a time, parents told wide-eyed children, when humans were a cancerous growth upon the land. Ten years from now, if you wished to shock a thirteen-year-old, you would tell her that people had once been so populous, so resourceful, so filled with greed they had begun to eliminate the other species. How was such a thing possible, the child would say, thinking of the raccoons and cats that moved in sea-waves, too numerous to count. The trick had been, it seemed, not proliferation but longevity. People didn't reproduce like rabbits, or like spiders with their hundreds of eggs, but despite incredible odds, they'd managed millennia of dominance. And then it had all changed.

The odds were against them, yet here they were, down to forty-two, not including pets. Here they were, gathering in an Anglican church in the city's core. Marie refused to live with the others in the huge brick houses near the escarpment; instead, she stayed in her apartment above the art shop near the abandoned mall downtown.

But even she came every day to the old stone church where they held meetings. Every afternoon a meal was prepared, and the remaining people gathered with an air of gentle gravity. They gathered on land the way now-abandoned satellites that had once choked the atmosphere with signals did in the sky. They gathered the way debris did in the unthinkable sea.

Perhaps it was not surprising, then, that some of them, these orphans of the age, had become collectors, specializing their hoards. Rosa, twenty-nine and unable to leave the group because of her stubborn mother, had begun to accumulate stringed instruments. She took borrowed cars up to the music store on Upper James, or down to the one on King, searching through the basements and garages of former teenaged guitarists who had lived in wealthy townships. The group had some gasoline left over, kept in one of the garage-caches near the church, but there was always the worry that the gas gauges of these cars did not read true. So Rosa planned for the possibility that she'd have to walk or find a bicycle to get home, and was careful to remain inside an invisible perimeter. Even so, she had amassed enough cellos, violins, ukuleles, banjoes and guitars to fill two rooms of one of the houses where she and her mother were squatting.

Sometimes, Rosa took Marie with her. Without traffic, and without other people, it was easy for them to traverse the city as though they were giants. They took their few large steps from the lake, which buttressed the city's northerly side, and rode under overpasses and over bridges, past the smokestacks that had once fumed sulphurously and through the half-crumbling sights of a mid-sized city: parks, parking garages, a hundred small shops and homes, restaurants and cafés, all reduced to square footage, to the skeleton of their meaningless parts. The city was greener now, Marie thought, except for those streets atop the hill sacrificed to commerce and its billboards and lots. You could breathe easier now.

Inside the car, Marie felt calmed by the fine lines of digital light, numbers arranged into bright slivers of neon green or red. She had become used to the emptiness of the streets, as though hollowed out by some terror. Happy in the cocoon of their small or midsized cars, windows rolled down, Marie and Rosa played music to match the heat and talked about the men. Rosa had taken a liking to Mo's ass; Marie insisted that he hardly had one.

"It's not his ass so much as the way he walks with it," Rosa would confess, black hair whipping in the summery air.

"The way he walks with it!"

"He's very poised, you have to admit."

Marie would never say so to Rosa, but of course, Mo was the most eligible of the last men on Earth.

Today, they had driven past parked cars and through unlit intersections to retrieve yet another piece for Rosa's stash. One of the satisfactions of the new era could be had in the smashing of windows, so Marie was not shocked at the sight of Rosa in long wild hair and sunglasses stepping through a broken window with a baseball bat. And she knew that Rosa thought nothing of the Berretta peeping its black handle out of the waistband of Marie's shorts.

"We should bring Mo along next time," Marie said. "How could he resist you?"

"Shut up," Rosa said, grinning.

"He can take you back there," Marie said, pointing to the hardwood stage where amps were still plugged into walls, their black wires like severed rat tails.

"Stop." Rosa was eyeing the space with head tilted, an interior designer trying to visualize.

Both women were, despite their jokey bravado, scanning the empty store for a port-sized gap, craning their necks to listen. Ports were everywhere, an invisible multitude. Most stood in living rooms; almost all were privately owned. Sometimes it seemed that you could hear them humming, as refrigerators once had. No one knew where their source of power was, but when you found a port, at first mainly because of the space cleared around it, it would seem to shimmer in the light like a spider's web.

There was a rustling, a faint clinking, and in the time it took for the chills to register, Marie had whipped around with her handgun aimed, arms out straight. Facing her was the stupid beauty of a full-grown deer. Its ears flicked, and Marie's chest heaved with adrenaline.

"Holy crap," she whispered.

"People so jumpy shouldn't carry guns," Rosa said. She had put up her arms in surrender as soon as Marie yanked out the weapon.

"You and your guilty conscience," Marie said. "What I really need is a hunting rifle, clearly."

The deer stood still, staring.

"This is why a person should always have a dog," Marie said pointedly. Rosa had forbidden Marie to allow her German shepherd-cross to hop into the back seat of the car.

"What good would Gus do at this point?"

"He would have been keeping watch. First line of defence."

"That's the vocabulary of war."

"*That's* the vocabulary of Mo."

Rosa reddened and dropped her arms.

Marie held hers rigid and pulled the trigger. Once, twice, the sound enough to deafen them for several ringing moments. Two tiny wounds opened in the deer's chest, black and then spurting blood. It attempted to bolt, then fell, first to its knees, then to the ground.

"Can you help me get it into the car?" All of Marie's kills had thus far been theoretical or tiny: for months she had been perfecting her aim and had never hit anything larger than a raccoon. Only her dog knew that she'd been unable to eat the raccoon, that she had instead let Gus tear at it until all that was left was inedible, its prison-striped tail, its bandit face.

Rosa followed Marie to the body, and the women knelt to hoist it. "We killed it," Marie said.

"Oh, but it was alive, and it was so pretty," Rosa said, knowing that this would make Marie roll her eyes. She laughed when Marie did.

"Stupid deer," Marie said. "There's a forest full of yummy bark and berries, and it comes strolling up to this wasteland on Upper James." The street was mostly parking lots, billboards, five lanes of asphalt. A car dealership across the way still boasted a dancing wind figure, faded from black to grey. A wind machine would once have filled it with air, bending it at the waist, making its puppet arms perform a frantic dance. Now it whipped up once, lethargically, painted face grinning.

"Creepy," Rosa said.

They lifted the deer's body onto an old emergency blanket and then waddled sideways, each holding two corners. Proud as two hunters could be, they drove back down through the escarpment, bouncing on roads full of potholes.

"This drive is getting sketchy," Rosa said. "If the road gets much more cracked up, we won't be able to use it. And who's going to change the tires? Fix the engine?"

"When we can't drive, we'll just walk. We'll hike." In a previous life, Marie would often climb the three hundred metal stairs built into the side of the cliff at various points in the city. When she did it now, she felt the ghost of that former self climbing ahead of her, felt the ghosts of all her fellow fitness freaks. Those who had left water bottles dug into the dirt, who had numbered the steps with permanent marker.

Hot wind flew through the car's open windows. Marie felt for the gun and reached into the back seat for her camera, which she hung around her neck. From this spot on top of the escarpment that locals had always called "the mountain," they could see the city through the weave of trees. It spread silent and still below them, grey and brown buildings, puffs of green, emptied highway bridges over the blue of the bay beyond. The car bounced along that curve of road, and Rosa eased off the gas, pressed lightly on the brake.

A Janis Joplin song was playing, a hoarsely sad "Summertime." Marie's favourite thing to find in a house was an old mix CD, preferably without labels; this song came from one of those.

"When I was in high school, my best friend started dating this really weird guy. He used to pull his penis out, like, while he was driving," Marie said.

"What?" Rosa laughed. "Just for you guys to stare at it?"

"Pretty much. It just sat there in his lap." Had it really happened that way? Marie squinted out at the lush oaks and ash trees and maples on either side of the road.

"Who does that?"

Old habits were unbreakable. Rosa still signalled her turn. "He was crazy. My friend kept breaking up with him for the penis thing, and then he'd do it again when you weren't expecting it. Must have been compulsive. Like a flasher. Anyway, we used to drive all over the place on the weekends in this van—I'd sit in the empty back of the van like a kidnapped child, no belt, no windows—and we'd drive through the city looking everywhere for Pez dispensers."

Rosa laughed in her throaty way. "That is not where I expected this story to go."

Marie went on. "There was this holy grail of Pez for him. But I hardly remember any of the details. Was it a Darth Vader Pez he wanted? Maybe Bugs Bunny? Something rare. And I have no mental picture at all of his penis."

"Sounds like your friend was dating Pee-wee Herman."

Marie leaned back and closed her eyes. Joplin's voice was raspy and full of emotion. "Man. Remember Pee-wee Herman?"

The cityscape reminded her of the heavy garbage days of yore, those days when people put bookcases and old lawn mowers and defunct computers on the lawn, and anybody who wanted their junk could take it home. Or maybe it was more like this: Marie as a child rooting through her grandmother's attic, crawling into cupboards and behind the dummy doors at the back of closets, which she'd believed were secret passageways. Now the whole world had the complicated architecture of a crumbling mansion. This last year she had done the things she'd never dreamed of doing before: camping out on the Bruce Trail, sleeping on the ridge over the gorge they called the Devil's Punch Bowl, smashing battery-powered alarm systems to spend full days in the art gallery surrounded by shadow-darkened Alex Colvilles. But unlike everybody else, she had not relocated to one of the huge houses south of Aberdeen. She still slept in her cheap IKEA bed in the apartment above her store, where she still dusted and maintained inventory. Even during the cold months of January and February, and even during that awful March when they'd all huddled together in shared rooms, Marie maintained the pretense of living elsewhere. The shop was only a fifteen-minute walk away, but both Rosa and her mother, Bonita, continued to insist that Marie was too far from the rest of their people. Marie knew what they were thinking: Far enough outside of their mass, Marie was liable to be sucked into a black hole.

"How long before the deer starts rotting? It needs to be dressed, right?"

Marie shrugged. "We'll be at the church in ten minutes, so ..."

If she were melted down and remodelled in plastic, Marie would have the following accessories: tank top and skirt, heavy analog camera with lens and film rolls, handgun and bag of dog treats. Plus dog, Gus. She and Rosa stopped in front of her store. In the same fit of whimsy that had made her open an art supply shop ten years earlier, Marie had named it Frankincense & Myrrh. She had been in a lighting-incense-to-mask-the-reek-of-pot stage. Plus, she'd reasoned at the time, lonely and stoned, it was a place she wanted people drawn to from afar, a place they'd come to buy gifts. She'd painted the large gold star on the sign herself.

Rosa stayed in the car, which was now blaring "Smells Like Teen Spirit." When, outside the store, Marie looked back, Rosa waggled an ironic rock and roll hand sign at her. Gus was in a part of the alley Marie had sectioned off with fencing; he was panting and appearing to smile. He followed her out, and as they approached a view of the PINA billboard, Marie reflexively reached for the camera now sagging at her neck. Every day for 356 days, Marie had been taking photographs of this particular image, this billboard perched on its steel frame like a bird of prey on the edge of an apartment building across the way. Every day Marie unfurled her store's awning with the hand crank and then went into the road to take the picture. Once a roll was filled, she'd develop it in a makeshift darkroom she'd set up in the vacant top apartment, which she'd been planning to rent out in the days before vacancies were everywhere. She'd made the light she needed for developing the photos by applying red film to a large flashlight.

Sometimes an image would be over- or under-exposed, would be clouded or haunted. The images were not meant to be anything other than her record of decay, her monument to post-reality, each the same and with its minor variations, just as Monet had done with his lilies.

In the store the photos hung by clothespins along a length of twine that had turned into two lengths, and now had so many turns that the photos were nearly covering the back wall. To Marie, the billboard itself was detestable now, omnipresent as an unloved spouse. In its centre was half of the world's most notorious silhouette: the pineapple. In art school she'd read about this graphic: simple but cheeky. It did not take itself too seriously; sometimes it was sliced into yellow chunks, sometimes it was striped with rainbow colours. At Christmas, from its spikes a single ornament would appear to hang. Here, on the billboard, it was made to shimmer against a blue background. Beside the glassy halved pineapple, one word: *port*.

The billboard's face would never again be slicked over, never again hold a new message. Marie had taken her first photo of it on the day, not quite a year ago, that she'd realized this, the first day her WiFi icon had searched frantically, spinning around and around like a dog chasing its tail, seeking a connection.

She reached for the camera and lifted the lens, then stopped short.

"Rosa!" she hissed.

But Rosa couldn't hear her over the angry blare, the mosh-pitting, head-banging song they both loved. Gus went up to the car and nosed at Rosa through the open window.

"Oh shit. Holy shit." Marie's vision blurred as she stared through the tiny window of the camera, as she focused the scene by clarifying gradations, as she clicked, rewound, clicked, rewound, clicked.

She had to stop to wipe her face.

Rosa finally noticed something was wrong. She got out of the car and ran to Marie. "What's wrong? Why are you crying?"

Through the fluttering camera's eye, Marie stared at the billboard, daring it to change again. "What does it mean?" Someone had painted an enormous red *S* in front of the word *port. Sport*.

Marie's mind cast around for explanations. Click, crank, click. Someone had climbed up. Merely out of poetic impulse? Merely for fun? Someone who, like her, relished the wet slap of paint or its sizzle coming out of a can. A prankster. Or—click, crank—it was a message to her. It was a message from someone who knew she took the picture every day. The hairs lifted on the back of her neck.

She came to the end of the roll.

"We should get to the church," Rosa said, gesturing back with her thumb to where the deer weighed down the trunk. They would begin to attract hungry animals or, maybe, lose the meat to decay.

"But what does it mean? Who did it?"

Both Rosa and Gus looked at Marie as one would at a beloved but delusional family member.

Marie allowed herself to be led back to the car. A thought was slowly taking form. What if there were other people in the world? Maybe there were others.

She tried not to think his name, but then it was the only thing in her mind: *Jason, Jason, Jason.*

Chapter

2

THE SUPPORT GROUP

Forty-two people were left. Philip, their self-appointed leader, had a ledger and took daily attendance. There were always absentees: groups taking hikes or canoe trips, couples newly in love. Once they'd nearly lost Donnie, who'd fallen down a flight of stairs at the library and lay unconscious with a broken leg and then conscious with a broken leg for the three days it took the rest of them to find him. The attendance ledger was their salvation. The attendance ledger and its law: after twenty-four hours without checking in, you were considered missing. The most recent losses had happened during the hard months of winter, and who could blame those who had disappeared? One couple had driven south with their four children; five others had gone out through port to nobody knew where. Before that, they would lose dozens at a time. These last surges of travellers (or *quitters*, as some zealots preferred to say) were like those final kernels in a bag of microwave popcorn. The kernels drew heat and popped, leaving only a handful of their remaining kin at the bottom of the bag.

It had been nearly a year since those who had stayed found their way to the church. Philip lived there still, at least officially, though lately he had been sleeping on Bonita's couch. Marie had been a late joiner, arriving for the first time last fall, in mid-October. "I'm just here for the soup," she'd joked, the sort of joke that nine months ago could still separate people into opposing camps: those sympathetic to cynicism on the left, zealots on the right. She'd been uncomfortable with the religiosity of recruitment. For months people would spot each other on the street and come towards each other with arms lifted and hands open.

"Hey, there's this place—have you been?" one person would say to the other. "I've never seen you at one of the meetings. You should come."

Marie was wary of this sort of shy, shrugging coaxing, which she felt masked a deeper manipulation, the reverse psychology of a cult. Eventually she realized that this group of people was unthreatening precisely because of their disunity. Overwhelmingly, they were secular humanist and slipshod; they included several children, a handful of seniors, one girl in a wheelchair, Donnie with his crutches—each of them more needy than conniving. The only person among them who seemed to have any religious belief was Mo, whose ritual of pressing head to ground several times a day was cross-fertilized by the Rastafari anti-materialism he'd picked up from his bygone friends. Philip and Bonita had once been parishioners in the church, but assured everybody—as apologetic as any anti-gun super-tolerant lefties—that they had not been fundamentalists, that this church had been as liberal as they came.

The group's attempts at organization were ongoing and, Philip claimed, crucial to their survival. He with his ledger. They had inventoried the hospital, and went on frequent trips to the library, sorting through whatever might prove useful. Their lifted collection now contained books on edible plant identification, urban gardening, solar power and quantum physics. Bandages and antibiotics were accessible to everyone, while pain meds were locked away with the batteries. They took turns poring over old newspapers, clipping anything they could find that mentioned Albrecht Doors, his company PINA, or port.

Rosa screeched to a stop in front of the church, jumped out, ran up the stone steps and disappeared inside the building. Marie and

Gus lagged behind. The heat was sapping Marie of energy. Her face was slippery, arms and shoulders sticky. Gus, trotting beside her, licked her hand.

The big church doors flapped open, ejecting Philip and Rosa alongside Steve, a big Dutch guy, formerly a greenhouse worker, whose wife and three kids were part of the group, too.

"Should be all right, still," Philip said. The hooves of the dead deer were hanging out of the trunk, the slender and demurely crossed ankles of a beautiful woman.

"Even with the heat?" Rosa said. "We really came as quickly as we could." She shot a look at Marie. In the car, Marie and Rosa had discussed the red *S*, briefly, Rosa insisting that the likeliest culprit was one of their own. They had agreed to keep its presence to themselves for now.

Marie loosened the bungee cords and opened up the trunk. "What do you think, Steve?"

"Nice shot, ladies," he said.

Steve, Rosa and Philip worked to inch the doe out, and Marie took a fourth corner of the blanket. Blood had soaked through the wool, was warm and sticky in her hands. They carried the bundle to their makeshift slaughterhouse, a garage in the backyard of the house next to the church, and laid it on the cold cement floor.

Inside the church, the rest of the group was eating loose greens and a soup made mostly from boiled and mashed beets. They were calling it borscht. Several wood-burning stoves had been carted into the church foyer and duct-taped with complicated tubes for ventilation, and here meals were served as though by do-gooders at a soup kitchen. People wore hats and aprons, sneakers and smiles. The two women who had put themselves in charge of food prep actually had been just those sorts of do-gooders, so they knew some tricks. For example, if you mix up a variety of canned soups into the same pot—chicken noodle with cream of mushroom even—it all tastes fine in the end. And if you've got hot sauce and garlic and salt, you can make anything palatable.

"This is not the best place for us to be," one of these cooks was saying to Donnie, as Marie ladled herself a cup full of soup. The group used paper coffee cups for everything, as these could be repurposed as seed pots, and they had no running water for washing. "The summer's too hot, and the winter's too cold."

Such admissions always came out warily. Most of the group had grown up in this city. Some of them had seen the city change from booming steeltown to a place abandoned by the steel industry. Some of them had seen it go from depressed to slightly less depressed to renewed. Some of them were still annoyed about the gentrification of Locke Street, of James Street. One of them had grown up on an orchard in an eastern township that became a strip mall that was itself then abandoned and boarded up. They felt, some of them, like underappreciated spouses who hung around even after affairs with flashy new mistresses had been exposed. The one thing they all had in common was attachment to place.

Donnie sat with his crutches leaning against the column next to his pew at the back. He turned toward the serving table, and grunted his assent.

In the pews, with legs drawn up or crossed, with faces held in hands or heads bowed; or not sitting in the pews at all, but milling around the aisles and in the front and back of the church, were most of the people in the world that Marie now knew. The stone ceiling soared above them, collecting their separate conversations so that one voice could not be made out from another. Whispers echoed harshly. Gus trotted away to sniff the backside of a yellowing Yorkie. A cat meowed violently and jumped off a high windowsill onto the red carpeting at Marie's feet before bounding away, and several children ran shrieking down the aisle after it. Candles fat and thin, tall and short, scented, unscented, beeswax and aroma-therapeutic, burned along the steps and sills, the tables and altars. The effect was somewhere between a séance and a bad date.

Philip had washed his hands, as Marie had, beside one of the rain barrels outside, sudsing up with organic dish soap and pumping water over his blood-rusty palms.

"Nice work," he said now, sidling over with his own cup of soup. A drop of it was caught in the thicket of his beard. "You were made for summer."

"Thanks," she said, eyeing him.

"You always seem like you're sizing me up," he said.

"That's because I am."

One night around Easter, Marie had too much to drink and let Philip kiss her. His beard had been so full that his mouth had seemed to hide, his wet warm tongue and lips as shocking as the whiteness of his teeth when he smiled.

"I like skepticism in a woman," he said now.

"I know," she said, resting her hand on Gus's head.

"And I like a woman who can hold her own in a shootout," he said.

"I'm sure you do."

He laughed, grabbing at his beard, and then dropped the smile. "Well, I guess you know what I think about you," he said.

She smiled. "I do," she said, but as he walked away, she wished she'd waited to hear a litany of her traits, herself as refracted through the affections of another. It had been a very long time since anyone had stayed up late with her, had told her what she was like.

"Enjoy summer," she heard him saying to someone else now, and the words gave her a brief chill of worry. She found an empty pew to sit in. Sometimes the church was like a party filled with people you knew only superficially. She supposed eventually they would become more like family. True rifts would form, and factions.

Vocabulary of war.

Mo had come in; Marie heard him laughing. Many of the men had chosen to grow beards, but Mo still shaved his face clean. His dreads were tied into a huge knot on the top of his head. Marie watched him talking to Rosa and two other women, one of whom took off her hairnet to shake out a greying brown bob. Mo's magnetism, his princely aura, was such that despite the fact that he'd been a busking pothead in a previous life, they all wanted to impress him, to be seen by him. It was because of a kindness in his eyes and smile that could not be faked, and it was his good looks, the youth and health connoted by his broad shoulders and neatly muscled arms.

She sipped her soup. It was a little too sweet. A lone kernel of yellow corn floated to the magenta surface.

"All right, everybody!" Philip's shout signalled that they were about to get started. "Steve is still in our underused slaughterhouse dressing some venison kindly foraged by our very own Marie Desroches, and"—he was interrupted by whoops and clapping—"yes, that's right, and we are fortunate enough to have everybody present and accounted for."

Mo picked up his djembe and came to sit beside Marie. "Hey," he said, nodding.

She was embarrassed by how special this made her feel. She gave a slight nod in return and then took what she hoped was a casual sip from the cup of soup.

As she looked at Philip, she became aware that on the raised portion of the chancel behind him, something was different from usual. There was something new sitting there: a thick phallic dome-shaped thing covered over by one of the old dropcloths she had contributed to the group when they were winterizing every wall with layers of draperies. Paint-gooed and splattered as if it were an imitation of a Pollock, the covered dome stood a few feet taller than six-foot Philip.

"You think?" Mo said, glancing at her.

"I don't know what else it could be. But I don't know why he'd risk bringing one in here," she said. "Or how he'd manage it."

Mo shrugged. "But we're talking about Philip."

"Still."

Rosa sat down on the other side of Mo, and their whispers melded with those of everyone else. Marie listened, eyes on the stage, pressing down her irritation by cultivating the same remove she once would have felt watching any television show.

"Enjoy summer," Philip said to the group with foreboding. He pulled at his beard. He was gearing up for a speech.

Marie clenched her jaw.

Now Philip was standing behind the pulpit, now walking up the aisle. He pushed his glasses up the bridge of his nose, and they slipped back down. Marie, Mo and Rosa were in the pew second from the front. Rosa's mother, Bonita, in the pew ahead, turned around and gave Marie and Rosa a reassuring smile. Bonita was only ever approving and never mean. Her body, despite the whippling of age, revealed surprising rounds of muscle. Like Marie, she was sinewy and hard.

"Enjoy summer, but—" Here Philip walked to one set of maps taped on the wall between two tall windows.

The stained-glass windows glowed blue, yellow, green, and told stories Marie didn't know or couldn't remember. Black glass arranged into medieval calligraphy gave them titles: *The Good Shepherd. Suffer the Children Unto Me*. Her mother had been a lapsed-Catholic and then anti-Catholic, but Marie as a young woman had considered converting; she had been, and still was, attracted to the idea of cathedrals. Now, in the windows of the smaller-scale majesty of this church, she saw through the depictions of Jesus and his disciples to the cuts of stained glass in which they were wrought. The faces of the men in the scenes were finely detailed, with eyes and hair. The sheep had black noses. She had done some research, and discovered that this church, though old, had replaced these windows in the last few decades, that the black joints holding the jewelled glass together were almost certainly not lead.

Layered over and beside these windows were maps of all kinds, road maps, historical maps, maps of the constellations, novelty maps. A few days ago some people in the group had argued over whether the maps of the universe had been incorrect all along—if what was needed was a paradigm shift—or whether this universe remained intact, and port was somehow interacting with alternate versions. Marie, ever agnostic, preferred the idea that all maps were destined to be incorrect, but there was no convincing Donnie or Philip, both of whom thought understanding the multiverse would make a difference, would have some effect on their predicament.

Marie struggled to pay attention as Philip continued. "But I think it's time we think about migration. Somewhere we might go for winter. I'm thinking southern U.S. No need to go much farther than Virginia. Maybe North Carolina." He pressed his index finger to a map of the world. The word *migration* was heavy with meaning.

"We've got it good here, Philip!" Bonita said. "We're setting things up. Numbers have settled."

He nodded, seeming to consider. "For some of us, it's hard to envision, though, just how good the future could be. As you know, I think we should all consider a fresh start." These arguments had been ongoing for months. During the winter they'd all agreed: once spring came they'd make their plans for relocation. But then spring had been busy, and summer had arrived and obliterated their previous commitments. Philip wanted badly to leave—we can always come back, he said—while others, like Marie, believed they should stay, that they were stewards of this place and time. The unspoken question for many others, Marie knew, was whether or not leaving through port was a viable option; the fantasy of doing so had been the only way some had made it through the bone-deep frigidity of winter. This rift had allowed smaller arguments to arise. Steve and his wife Regina thought Philip didn't have it in him to lead, and were questioning his self-appointment to that role. The argument had opened a wound, still raw, so that Marie remembered it well:

   —Why should this guy be in charge?

   —But he's not in charge.

–If I were calling the shots we'd have left by now. He's not a strong leader.

–No one's calling the shots. It's a democracy.

Steve and Regina made it clear they thought that Philip's attachment to Marie, and his fear that she would be left behind, was keeping him from thinking straight. Philip had frequently discussed with Marie his dismay over her habit of opening the store every day as though expecting customers, but she was tired of Philip's obsessive care over what he deemed to be an unhealthy habit. *Go ahead and leave, see if I care,* she thought. Even now, from his pulpit, he was looking at her meaningfully. He finally broke her gaze when she took a loud slurp of the lukewarm, overly sweet soup-goo.

"We all agreed that this past winter was miserable. If we end up with another harsh one this year, we'll be sorry we stayed. Winter can be a matter of life and death, which some of us may have forgotten."

"I don't think any of us could forget that. Sometimes I have nightmares where my teeth are chattering," Bonita said. "But by winter this year we'll have some generators up and running. We'll have the solar panels sorted out."

Philip pulled at his beard. "I believe we'd be better off without having to depend on electricity at all. We're not exactly experts in the re-establishment of the grid. And time is not with us. Sooner or later the gasoline won't be usable, and we'll be stuck."

Philip claimed not to consider himself a leader. In his past life, he'd been a librarian stationed on the arts floor of the Main Library, and had been known by his colleagues to be overly attached to the collection in his charge. He was supposed to cycle the books more. Nonfiction was becoming obsolete, they said, as the Internet age advanced. The twenty shelves sorted into the 800s of poetry, prose, speech-writing, Shakespeare, et cetera had contracted first to fifteen, then to ten and then to eight. But Philip had refused to weed out books that were still in good condition, and this made him a fossil. The librarians were unionized and he couldn't be fired or reassigned, so younger library assistants were tasked with tossing out books behind his back. His natural setting was in a dusty place, alone, oriented to the past. But in the new era, no one else in the group had wanted the job of speech-making and organizing. No one else had seen the importance of having a central location, regular meetings and an agenda. And Philip had learned to like giving speeches.

"Look, I'm not the kind of person who would suggest doing something rash just for the sake of it. I have really been thinking about it, and I've been talking to some of you—and you know what?" His question echoed into the crowd. "You know what?" Again he paused. "I'm pretty sure life is short, and we might as well be comfortable. That's all we've got now. I mean, why not live on the beach?"

The crowd sipped soup, remained silent. The stillness was punctuated only by the occasional scream or laugh from the small children, who were situated in farther-back pews with their parents.

"Well, think on it, pray on it, do what you do. I think if we're going to go, we need to be on the road by September. Let's say five weeks or so."

Philip moved his hands over his head and face, first ruffling his hair, then removing his glasses, pulling at his beard.

A few people tentatively raised their hands.

"Philip?" Bonita said.

"Hmm?"

"There are questions."

"Okay. Well?"

He pointed at one of the raised hands—Donnie at the back, bad leg splinted and set down, good leg tucked under him in a half-lotus. "What's under the sheet?"

Marie realized she was clenching her hands so tightly that her bones seemed about to splinter. "They can all leave," she whispered to the dog. "I'm not leaving." She was a child with an overpacked suitcase threatening to run away. Her mother would have enfolded her, while Marie cried, *I can live without you!* That phrase had always come too easily to her lips.

"Before we get to what's under the sheet, let me just say, in support of my argument, that we need a longer growing season. This isn't just something we can choose to do. Stay in this city, that is. We'll freeze, or we'll run out of food."

"This is not a dire situation, pal," Mo said softly, tapping his hands on the taut skin of the drum. His words weren't loud enough for Philip to hear. Mo spent most days in the garden and greenhouse, and he was convinced they'd soon be growing too much food. He had spent many winter days on the streets with his friends and did not fear the cold. "We just gotta gear up again."

"Normalcy is sanity," Bonita said.

"And novelty is loss," said Louise, another older woman. Marie recognized these phrases as slogans that people had once used in an attempt, unsuccessful, to counter those spread by PINA, who had proclaimed: *The present is over!* And, *Why only live once?*

"You will all have a chance to voice your concerns. I've set a date for voting on it, and the results of the vote will be unassailable. A week from today."

Marie looked at her clasped hands. She knew—they all knew—such a vote would not be final.

There are no rules! PINA had once told them. *In the new universe, there are no rules.*

"We don't know what's out there!" a male voice shouted from the back of the church. Everyone shifted to see who the speaker was.

"A very good point," Philip said. "Thanks for that, Marcus. It's why we need the five weeks to get ready. We should probably have guns, just in case. We need to all be on the same page. But let's move on now, to—" He swung around and gestured at the covered dome. "Consider this. If we do decide to stay for the winter, which

I strongly urge us not to do, I'd like to start work on our information-retrieval project."

Now Philip, who was walking backwards as he spoke, pulled down the dropsheet, and for a moment, it seemed as if he'd done a magic trick. There appeared to be nothing there. Then Marie's eyes adjusted, and she saw the slight shimmer in the air, like wavering heat. She saw the small silver tattoo printed in the corner of the shimmer: *port*. And then, of course, even smaller, the logo, the machete-split graphic of half a pineapple.

They'd all seen one before. Most had stumbled upon one, still humming in the naked corner of an abandoned living room. None of them understood how port functioned, how their batteries still worked, where their batteries even were. Everyone left behind was hopelessly backward: Luddites or late-adopters or conspiracy theorists. Outsiders, outliers, outcasts. Yet they had all lived through the history of this product, from the rumours of its existence first trickling in, to the explosion of its popularity, to this, now, this newer and lonelier Earth. None of them understood the point of its creation. Unless it was simply this: the extinction of humanity.

Marie had watched it all. At first, plenty of journalists and academics and politicians had contested the buoyant claims of PINA's spokespeople, and especially of its founder and CEO. His name was Albrecht Doors, as though from birth he had been foreordained to produce openings to other realms. Doors always seemed to be fitted with a thin mic in the ear, had always seemed to be doing TED Talks about why children should not go to school, about how reading literature was more important for his programmers than learning to code. But soon there were no experts to weigh in, no experts to dramatically examine the ports like monkeys perplexed by a new toy dropped into their cage, like dogs surrounding and sniffling them.

Now, by all accounts, Doors too was history.

A breeze whistled through the cracks around the stained-glass windowpanes, and the candlelight flickered. Chin resting on the floor, Gus curled his lips and growled.

"You can't just bring a port in here!" someone shouted.

"Why would you do that without consensus?"

"Goddammit, I'm leaving. Fuck this."

But no one left.

"Please, please," Philip said, raising his hands palm-down as though addressing a room filled with second-graders.

"He is out of control," Rosa whispered to Mo and Marie. "I can't believe this."

"How'd you get it all the way over here, Phil?" Andrea asked. "I mean, without getting sucked into it." Andrea was young, and to Marie she seemed silly and therefore an unlikely holdout. She was a frequent object of Rosa and Marie's gossip.

There were no ports in any of the houses where they were squatting, since the army had removed them the summer before. They had rumbled through the city with canned and dried goods, motivating them to clear up grocery stores and cafeterias until they left in openbacked trucks, in their camo and helmets. That had been a harrowing time of accidental burns and paranoia, of too many men with too much armor. It was then that most of the remaining people had decided against carrying guns, though Marie thought this had been foolish, and her own insistence on being armed was another reason some of the others in the group were frustrated with her. There was a greater proportion of bleeding hearts in this crowd than she was used to. The artists and anarchists she knew saw beauty in violence and struggle.

"It's not a *vacuum*," Philip said, pushing his glasses up his sweatslicked nose. "It's not going to just grab you up and out of your seat."

This did not satisfy Andrea. "But they always had to be installed by a portician."

"There are ways to move them," Philip said. "Before he left, Lionel showed me how to unstick the bottom layer from wherever a port was located. I can de-install, and I can reinstall. And they aren't heavy—you just have to be careful."

"Anyway, we're not supposed to take them," said a woman from a pew farther back. "What if whoever owns it needs to come back?"

Unlike the PINA people—unlike almost everybody else—Marie and all those left behind were overly scrupulous. They had not forgotten how to shudder. They were superstitious about what you should and should not do regarding the machines, which seemed not quite really to *be* machines. So despite their prodigious looting, every one of them feared taking a port, or even touching one—the way one wouldn't touch a baby bird lest it be rejected by its mother. Had this bit of bird lore ever even been true? Fifteen months ago, Marie might have asked PINA for the answer, but now they were left to their bickering. Above all, no one wanted to interfere with any traveller's ability to come back, if coming back were possible.

"There are no rules, remember?" Philip said. He pulled out an envelope full of what looked like business cards.

"But, she's right—what if the others try to come back?" said Regina. "We agreed we wouldn't touch the ports until we know for sure."

"How are we going to know for sure? How long will we wait?" Philip shouted. "Forgive me." He lowered his voice. "But it seems like people can't just come back," he said, pacing now. "I mean, clearly. Surely we've learned this much."

Marie frowned. This wasn't exactly true. Although they had proof that a person who went into a port disappeared, some of the group thought it was possible that the travellers were frequently re-emerging and sinking back into the world: perhaps they just couldn't yet be seen by those left behind. The world might be overrun by people again someday. That perhaps the port was a mouth that could spit you back up as if from the belly of a whale.

Marie looked at Rosa; Rosa looked back at Marie, and nodded.

Marie stood up. "We saw something today, on my billboard, and I think, Rosa and I think, maybe there is someone who has come back."

Philip looked at her impatiently, with irritation, and she found his posture vaguely attractive. Blushing, she continued, "Someone painted a big red *S* on the billboard so it looks like it says 'sport.' And I think—"

"You think what?" said Philip. "That it's proof of something?"

"I think it could be."

"It was just one of us, surely. Someone who knows about your project was trying to prank you. Someone trying to get your attention."

Marie turned around to look out at the others. "Well, was it one of you?"

A few people shook their heads.

"Marie, we'll talk about this later," Philip said.

"But if there are others . . ." Marie paused.

"Later," Philip said.

"Yeah, we *will* talk about it later," Steve shouted from the back of the church, thick arms crossed over his tarpaulin-aproned chest.

But Philip had already moved on, his hand on the port just at the spot where they all knew the zipper pull to be.

At first, the public had been told that port worked like a revolving door, that it went both ways. PINA quoted people who reported that they'd evaporated and come back, and that the experience was glorious. *Carpe diem*, they said. You haven't lived! Someone claimed to have been among the Arawak people before Columbus. Someone claimed to have witnessed the cave painters in Lascaux.

Marie had snorted in disbelief, sitting in front of her TV with the chopsticks in her hand hovering over a bowl of noodles. These so-called travellers had been in the Bahamas before Columbus, and they'd gone prehistoric, and *yes*, they were wearing appropriate costumes and had unruly facial hair, but they didn't give any information about those times and places. What was it really *like*? Marie chewed sardonically, pointed her chopsticks at the screen. No. It was not believable. These people were awestruck and dumbstruck, but they knew nothing at all. Or they were manic for environmentalism. "You have no idea what it's like with all the trees!" they said. Green so green it made your eyes hurt. Green so green it will make you grow leaves and buds. Contagious green.

This talk of colour had come close to tempting Marie. It was pathological to not be tempted at all. People around her had acquired a missionary zeal. "I want to see *everything*." Marie's sister Claudine's eyes had gleamed. "I want to see the Mayans! The ancient Egyptians!" Gasp. "Shakespeare!"

So time and space was just an enormous sponge cake you got absorbed into? PINA—through Doors or his favourite mouthpiece, Brandon Dreyer, who was said to be the source of the corporation's weird poetry—claimed that this new tech had broken through the shell of perceived reality, which was like an egg they'd all been fertilized in. Now they ought to—had an *obligation* to —poke their heads through and look around. "The present is over!" PINA proclaimed.

Claudine had gone, and not come back. Marie imagined her—when she felt optimistic—walking around Elizabethan streets in rags.

"The present is over!"

One by one, sometimes in groups of two, sometimes whole families together, the people disappeared. The slogan was meant to persuade them that it was passé to live in the here and now, but it had ended up being prescient. This present, this reality, the original reality, was kaput. All things had ground to a halt. You didn't notice people disappearing until one day the streets seemed hollowed out, the space between one person and the next walking down the sidewalk had grown too long. The gaps were everywhere. Marie's shop door stopped chiming its happy *heave-ho*. The newspaper in the stand outside was three days old. Then four days. Then five.

Everyone in the group had reasons to grieve. At first the gather-ings at the church had been like AA meetings. Hi, I'm Marie, and I've been left behind. Today I was thinking about how much I miss the smell of street meat. Hi, I'm Lillian, and I've been left behind. Will I ever get another letter in the mail? Hi, I'm Bonita, and Hi, I'm Philip, and Hi, I'm Rosa, and Hi, I'm Mo.

Philip unzipped the machine. Everyone knew about the zippers, which were like long slits into empty space, so nearly invisible that one had to strain to see.

"If I didn't know better," Bonita said, "I'd say that the emperor has no clothes."

"Philip, come on, what the hell?" Donnie had already been, in his rotund middle age, perpetually annoyed. He was huffier and scoffier now that his leg was broken, possibly beyond proper repair. But he was not alone in his fear. Portophobia: it was like an allergy, or a genetic adaptation.

"What I want to know is why the present isn't changing furi-ously." Marie didn't bother looking in the direction of the voice; it was Andrea who had said this. She was hung up on the belief that people were time travelling, which the rest of them had established was impossible.

Philip stopped his delicate unzipping and stared at Andrea, this small, thin twenty-something girl with limp brown hair. He put his hands through his own greying hair and frowned, then held the back of his neck, elbows drawn wide. An aggressive gesture, Marie thought, to mark his dominance.

"We've been through this, Andrea. Clearly things don't work the way we thought they did."

"I don't feel like you've adequately answered my objections." Andrea had a stack of books, all of them popular accounts of physics.

Philip pointed a finger at her. "Do you know any physicists? Got any physicists lying around?" He went back to the pulpit, where he leaned over his own arms in the prayer-posture of a fervent preacher.

"A physicist really would come in handy," Rosa said.

"It's just that if everyone who's disappeared was, like, in the past, we'd all be dead, or buildings would crumble before our eyes, or something," Andrea said.

Donnie cough-scoffed. Mo tapped his fingers on the drum, hit it softly with the side of his palm.

Philip returned to the port to complete his theatrically slow unzipping. "It doesn't matter if I can't answer your objections, because here we are."

Marie thought of the word *yawning* and then the word *gaping*. It had been a very long time since she'd seen a port wide open like this. Obscene as an open mouth. Or worse: the opened body of a surgical patient, skin curling away from the incision.

"It *is* a vacuum, Phil," Bonita said, then put a bony knuckle between her teeth.

Philip stepped back a few feet. "I need someone to go. Preferably a team. If we're staying here for the winter—although I still do not think it is necessary for us to do so"—he stared pointedly at Marie— "I want us to at least make a little progress on the information-gathering front."

Steve stood, opened the back doors and propped them, letting in a gust of hot wind to make the candles flicker again. His apron and sleeves were still blood-soaked from his work preparing the meat from the deer in the shed, and he wiped at his arms and hands with a cloth. He watched Philip, shaking his head. Only then did Marie realize how hot it was. The church was hushed, as though in prayer. Even the children and animals were quiet.

Philip stood calmly, waiting for volunteers. The business cards, he said, would act the way a rope around the waist works for a person lowered into a well. Something to catch them. Marie put her hand on the coarse fur of Gus's back and felt those steady breaths come in, go out, come in, go out. The expression on his grinning dog-face seemed to say, *Don't worry.*

"We all need to contribute," Philip said. "I'm developing a theory that you can come back if you can only remember where you came from. I'm calling it the amnesiac theory."

"So, it works like an addiction," Marie said. "They're like lotus-eaters."

"Right," Philip said. "That's what I'm saying. They forget."

"It's not *just* that they forget," Marie said. "I think they must be unable to think straight. Even when they had the remotes, way back, those remotes that were supposed to work to bring people back, even then nobody did."

"How do *you* know so much?" Donnie said, then coughed viciously into his gardening glove.

"I don't know anything!" Marie's shout boomeranged back to her, hard and cruel. Rosa put a hand on her shoulder, and she shrugged it off. "But just think about it. Anyway, it's *very* risky. And so is leaving town. We don't know what's out there, and I think we have a really good thing here. There's lots of us, and Bonita and Steve and Mo have done so much on the greenhouses, and we know our way around. I don't see why we need to leave."

"Then we're stuck at the same impasse. What is the point? There's got to be something better out there!" Philip said. He paced, shaking his head. "So it's up to me. I'll go. It's gotta be me."

It wasn't clear to Marie whether he meant he'd go to Virginia or into the port. He stood there, his eyes big and panicked, like a trapped animal.

"I don't think anybody should go," Marie said, lowering her voice. Sweat trailed slowly down her chest and back. "We need to just stay put. Wait awhile."

"Wait for what?"

"At least we should find out who painted the *S*."

But what she really wanted was for every day to stay the same. To open the store, take her photo, drink her one instant coffee out of a tall white cup. Bicycle through the empty city. Congregate here at the church. She had to stay. Otherwise the world hadn't meant anything. It had been nothing but a circus, now all folded up and gone.

Philip stepped inside the port.

Instantly, Steve and Mo raced up the aisle and onto the stage. They pulled Philip out with difficulty, as though the port had its own gravity. They heaved him out by his armpits and waist as they would a drowning man and zipped the thing back up. Mo tried to kick it over, but it was stronger and less pliable than it appeared and did not budge.

Marie got out of her seat and made her way to the chancel. Philip had psyched himself up to jump off a cliff; now, pinned down, his breathing was huge and fast. "I don't know if I can take it anymore. I want to go out there. I want to see if there's anyone else. A scientist. Anyone."

"Why?" Mo was pushing moist hair back from Philip's face.

"I just need to know. I need to know." Philip was crying now. "There's no future anymore. I need to know this isn't it. I need life to be more than this."

Mo was shushing him as a mother would a child. He pulled Philip closer so that his head was lying in Mo's lap. "You don't want to go out there, man."

"But—"

"It's okay. It's all right."

The church filled with the smell of melting wax. Marie felt an itch like guilt, its source inaccessible. The others began making their way to Philip's side, proceeding in lines up the aisles.

"If this were a movie, some of the doctors and scientists would have stayed," Philip said. "We'd have a proper cross-section. We need someone with some expertise."

"Let's just get ourselves sorted out, Phil," Bonita said. "It might be a good plan to go. Maybe it's a good plan. We're not saying don't go. But I think we need to figure out our next move together."

"Let's eat," Steve said, turning away from Philip. He tried to lead the others outside. They shrugged, nodded, shook their heads, but slowly a consensus took hold of them. The smell of cooking meat had been wafting in for a few minutes now, and hunger was everything. Soon most of the others followed Steve down toward the garage where venison was being barbecued and smoked by Regina.

Marie waited on the stage with Philip and Mo. Philip was sitting up now, leaning over his bent knees.

The port loomed out of the space behind her, a giant pointed finger. Where the light caught it, it dazzled. Marie held her breath and tried to listen. The humming, the low electric buzz seemed to change gears. It, too, seemed to be catching its breath.

"Maybe we broke it," Marie said. She scanned the sanctuary out of long habit, searching for an on-off switch she might toggle. "How are these things still running," she said.

She was careful not to put her back to the port and its uneven buzzing. The sound was too much like human breathing. Her skin crawled. She picked up one of the business cards Philip had left piled on the pulpit.

On each, he had written: *You are not at home here. Remember port and the place you come from. Come back, come back.*

THE DREAMERS

Long before most of the world had drifted away in lifeboats, long before port was anything more than a theory of Albrecht Doors, Marie and Jason had been newly married and living in romantic squalor. Just downtown and near the church where Philip now held sway, their apartment on Caroline was partitioned within a larger building that had once been called Home for the Friendless. The ceilings were high, and next to their working refrigerator was an icebox that might have worked, too, if they'd known what to do with it. The clawfoot tub in the bathroom was stained grey where it wasn't chipped to reveal charcoal-hued metal underneath. Its late-addition shower nozzle always pointed in a direction that invited mould into the crevices where no mop could reach. From outside, the red brick building was stately as a manor. For awhile Marie believed that her artistic fantasies of a place like this had been so strong, she had conjured it.

Both Marie and Jason were still students, and most of the time when they were home they walked around half dressed. Marie kept her fingernails short, and always had blue and black stains on her finger pads. She had set up folding tables in the living room where she listened to singer-songwriters or riot grrrls as she made her prints and hung them along the many rows of twine stretched across every wall; these served as the apartment's only decorations. Romance had confused her. She had believed in the saddest Leonard Cohen songs, that a song was enough, that art was enough. She would sing along, pulling a squeegee through a silkscreen frame. At regular intervals, Jason would poke his head out of the second bedroom—his office— to admire her in her paint-stained shorts, her thin bra. To make more coffee, he unplugged the refrigerator. Otherwise the fuse would blow.

They'd had a registry at Sears for their wedding guests, at her mother's insistence, but had no idea what stuff they needed to build a life together. "Building a life together" was the kind of phrase used by the sort of people who liked to have a set of good china. Marie and Jason had approached the registry at Sears with the same whimsy with which they treated the marriage itself, wandering around, scanning things at random. Jason held up an electric mixer: "I guess we need one of these?" Everything he said seduced her. So they had a workbench without tools in the living room, which they used as a counter for their appliances, because there was only one outlet in the kitchen.

In his white T-shirt, thin enough to show his nipples, and his white boxers, Jason stood with two mugs of weak coffee and watched her work. "I like that one. What is it?"

"It's the view of Montreal from the room where we stayed," she said, clipping it up and leaning against the couch. He handed her a coffee. "But it's in negative," she said. "All the shadows are inverted."

"Everywhere you turn there's an inversion," he said, pausing to drink. "I think I need to switch to Philosophy."

Marie was accustomed to his non sequiturs. "Can you just switch to a different PhD?" she asked.

If Marie could now go anywhere that she imagined, as PINA had promised, it would be to that apartment, to those thousand perfect days she and Jason had together. She would lie on the couch and bask in that time. He'd been very nearly a boy then, and if she ever met his new wife, the horribly named Maria—as though an imprecise doppelgänger of herself—she would lord those days over her unrepentantly. *I knew him when the world was going to be ours, I knew him when he was ageless and sweet, I knew him when everything was perfect.*

In the afternoons, no matter what the weather, they'd go for walks in the neighbourhood and fantasize about the future. The same walk under an umbrella, the same walk with flakes of snow catching on their hoods. A sign of the uniqueness of their love, a sign that it wouldn't go ugly or stale the way everyone else's did, was that they never tired of each other. Presence made the heart grow as fond as absence did. The rest of the world shimmered around the edges of the clam they'd shut themselves into. It was love, as though they'd invented it, and the fact that so many artists had felt this sort of thing before did not puncture Marie's unlucky certainty.

Jason had liked to walk toward the escarpment where the mansions were, where single houses were bigger than the twenty-apartment Home for the Friendless, and pointed at them like Satan to Jesus: *All of this could be yours.* He'd say to Marie, *I'll be the philosopher, and you'll be the artist, and our babies will have picnics there, out on the lawn.* On the way home, they would stop at the corner store, where they bought all their fuses, and for dinner they ate whatever was available: lunchmeats or pickles, ice cream cones or bowls of cereal. Some of those boxes of cereal had come infested with brown flour-moths, and these flew around their pantry, leaving grey dust on Marie's fingers when she killed one.

She'd thought he was a visionary; she didn't know that he really did want wealth and fame, that he wanted children who'd play on an expansive lawn. Maybe she should have understood that he was driven, that he had the focus required of ambition, by the way he scooped up grants and scholarships, by the way his professors spoke about him, by the careful way he chose words, even by the way he took out library books only one at a time. He did a thing well, and then he did another thing well. He was so unlike her. His charisma was a line that ran up and down his body, holding it still and symmetric. She was the sort of person who took twenty books out of the library at a time and only got through a single one, who bounced between sentences and ideas the way she bounced between art projects.

She'd fallen for him when he was a patron at the public library where she worked the desk part time, and he would take out a book from the 100s section, about aliens creating the world, or ancient reptile overlords, or interplanetary conspiracies. He was too handsome for such nerdy subject matter, with eyes beautiful because they seemed intelligent and calm, and when he got through all of the books in the 130s, he started reading Dostoevsky. She came to anticipate his arrival at the circulation desk, where he would return his book from the week before, and take out the next one. Week after week, she watched him, his face seemingly both unconscious of being watched and deeply controlled. Unlike most patrons, who wanted to engage her in long discussions, and told her random things that came into their minds, like why they named their children after Greek goddesses or the awful temperature of their apartments, like why the library should not stock this thing or this other thing, Jason didn't speak to her at all. Their transaction did not require it. She longed for him to have an overdue charge or any kind of message she could use to speak to him. *He's beautiful,* she told her friends—the very friends she stopped seeing later, in her obsession with him. *And I think he might be even smarter than me.* This was her schtick: ironic self-aggrandizement that had worked to attract men to her before, that always made her girlfriends laugh. But what could she say to Jason? She took his plastic card to scan the barcode, and after he left with the single book in his hand, no receipt necessary, symbol of a clean life, she read over his file and tapped his name into the PINA search bar. She knew his phone number and address near the university, where she then made a habit of walking more often to increase the odds of running into him. She knew that he was a star student, a scientist, and that he did not have a social media account at all.

"Do you believe in all this stuff?" she said at last one day, her curiosity and her desire indistinguishable, two waves that refused to break.

"What stuff?" he said. He was not in a hurry, and there was no one behind him in line.

She looked down at the book he was returning. A paperback it was amazing that they hadn't weeded, binding broken and taped and retaped, yellowing pages. Seventies-style font and a grainy photo with a white saucer in a black sky. The story of a Tennessee couple who had been victims of alien abduction. "In aliens?"

"Don't you?" he said.

"In aliens?" she said. "In alien abductions?"

He watched her with indifference bordering on impatience, or so it felt. It turned out later that he'd been as attracted to her as she was to him, an improbable ending, a fantastical conclusion to the story of her desperation.

"Agnosticism is healthy," he said. "I feel the same way. But the stories are interesting: either for what they tell us about psychology or about the universe."

A week later he wandered into fiction, his first foray. She left the desk and approached him in the stacks. He was contemplating a ratty copy of *Notes from the Underground*. Soon he would read *War and Peace*, and *The Brothers Karamazov*, and all of the Russians one week at a time, and she felt that she was going to ruin his life of clean, careful choices. "Jason," she said to him, standing there in the stacks. She moved as close to him as she could, because he was too slow and she knew how to be fast. "I'm Marie."

"I know."

"Can I take you out for a drink some time?" she said.

On their first date he talked about the evolution of flirtation, and about whether flirtation could be taught to a robot, and he argued that it could, precisely because humans were so responsive to flattery and interest. Marie understood that this was a method of flirting, too, and she told him about the world of art, she told him how she made an effort to go to new galleries without planning what she would think or see beforehand, to avoid placards or leaflets, to avoid all the famous paintings, and to stand in front of a painting to discover what she would feel. Sometimes a painting would disturb her—she had used the word *disquiet*, she remembered now, because this sort of attraction woke up your dormant language and gave you new words—and it would turn out to have been painted by a person who'd lived in a lunatic asylum in Nazi Germany, perhaps Poland. But, she told Jason, she also liked to see up close a glob of paint, a clear paint-stroke on a famous painting, the proof that Van Gogh had been as near to that same canvas she was now. She liked, too, what Rothko tried to do with colours, an obliteration of narrative and language and thought, the attempt to approach something deeper than feeling. Blabbering, drunk, she had smiled into his face and said, "I think you like robots and aliens, and I like humans, and . . ."

And he touched her arm, her hand. She felt the calculus in his touch.

"I like humans too," he said.

When she and Jason weren't walking along the road with mansions, they were driving to the outskirts of the city, toward its orchards and greenhouse-dotted expanses. They would leave their dirty dishes in the sink, forget to plug the fridge back in, and climb into the old Nissan, with its broken speedometer, that his father had given them. Jason would already have packed the car with a thermos of hot chocolate and a flask of bourbon, and the binoculars would shudder lightly on the blanket in the trunk while he drove through the city, oblivious to his speed. On these drives, Marie would push a cassette into the car's player. The library had been throwing away cassette tapes in heaps. They didn't waste time trying to donate or sell them, and since Marie had been tasked with inking out the barcodes and deleting their records from the catalogue, she didn't see the harm in sometimes tossing them into her purse instead. She had purloined Cat Stevens and the Beatles, but also George Michael and Michael Jackson. Christmas songs and books on tape—self-help and Agatha Christie and spiritual encouragement—were piled in their tiny reels in their little plastic cases on the back seat.

Their ritual became a deep groove. She believed that he'd never done these drives with any other woman. She was the only one who wouldn't laugh at him for hoping to see a UFO, to see something strange in the sky.

Each night was like the others. They parked in a church lot. The dome of the world invisibly held them; the atmosphere was a window through which they could see all of the universe's possibilities. She had felt as if she was a child under that dome—and this was what she'd lord over that wealthy Maria if she ever met the woman. (Bitterly, secretly, Marie called the new wife "Ave Maria," rolled the r in *Marr-rr-ea* until it barely resembled Marie.) *We lay on a blanket together, and we believed.* Mostly it had been quiet. The occasional struggle of car tires against gravel, and once in awhile, the whooting of a train. Sometimes she was silent, and lay there having sensations, seeing on the inside of her eyelids constellations that mimicked the ones out there. Jason had told her he didn't believe that silences were awkward, and even now she would not have added a single word, would not have wanted another person. In those days it had been true that anything was possible.

"A thing in the future determines what happens in the past," he told her, putting his hand on her navel, leaning in to kiss her. "And not the other way around."

"Is that right?" she said. "That doesn't sound right."

"We don't know all that much about time's direction, only that we perceive it to be linear," he said.

He had told her already, and so did not repeat, how the universe holds billions of stars, billions of star systems like their own, and so must house many other Earth-like planets with beings like themselves. He found this consoling. And she had believed, as she lay there, that she in turn wanted his clean lines and logic, his calm, his sparse belongings. She had believed she truly wanted there to be less of everything, and also that he wanted what he saw in her: more company, more words, more versions, more ideas. She had believed that he was starving and that he was lonely for more.

In addition to aliens and A.I. and time travel, one of Jason's obsessions had been lucid dreaming. It was easy for him to wake while dreaming and walk the streets of his unconscious. Marie could not do it, even when using all the tricks he'd taught her.

He'd set his watch to go off every ninety minutes, and each time it did, he'd ask, "Am I asleep?" And while he was sleeping and the watch chimed, the sound would reach him deep where he was, and he'd see through the gauzy confusion and know that he was dreaming. At first Marie wore foam earplugs to bed, but soon the distant chiming didn't wake her either, instead reaching into her dreams where her dream-self barely noticed it.

In the mornings she would make coffee, forgetting to unplug the fridge when she started the machine, and so he'd run out to the grimy corner store to buy new fuses. Eventually he had a large stash of them on hand, said nothing to demean or correct her, laughing instead, kissing her on her neck, her shoulders, her chest. He had been happy. He was not prone to happiness, but he had been happy with her.

"I dreamed that I had a lucid dream," she told him once.

"That *is* a lucid dream," he said. "When you become aware that you're dreaming, then you're lucid."

"But I wasn't lucid. I just thought, *Oh, I'm having a lucid dream.* But it didn't feel any different than any other dream."

Even his eyebrows were fair, like a small child's. "Well, I don't have access to what you're experiencing," he said.

Another trick to induce lucid dreaming was to toggle a light switch whenever you saw one, so that you'd be inclined to toggle one while sleeping. Cause and effect only behaved themselves in waking life, and these habits could help trigger lucidity. In the morning when they sat to drink their coffees and eat toast, for the sake of romance—*I'm so happy, I must be dreaming*—Jason would get up and flip the light switch. The golden light in the hallway flared on and off, on and off, on and off.

Marie was able to pluck from her memories the angst that was otherwise always with her, and remember only those days when they'd been together in the apartment, Jason at his screen sorting out the mysteries of the universe into formulae to describe strings and particles, and Marie rolling sticky ink over a carved piece of lino. She would find pages and pages of scrap paper covered in numbers and equal signs and squiggles of pi in his tiny scrawl. She collected them for some future art project. They were as beautiful to her as cave drawings, or—more so—fossils.

Now she could see that their good fortune foretold its own undoing. Not only the world but their love was like an egg destined to break.

In the clammed-shut innocence of their marriage, she'd been working on a series of prints that connected fetuses with universes. It happened by accident. She carved a third-trimester fetus housed by a thick uterine wall into a fat block of linoleum. Each of the veins in the cross-sectioned uterus was a little tick-mark. She printed blue on white and black on blue, and then she printed white and blue on black and saw that the uterine tissue surrounding the fetus was the night sky lit up with stars. By then, she and Jason were deep into discussions about when to start a family. Marie believed they should wait until Jason finished his doctorate, which would also give her a few more years to launch her art career (although she did not use the word "career," and despised the concept of "professionalization").

Nothing had ever come of these or any of her other prints. Among friends, on patios, over wine, she claimed not to have ambitions, saying that she worked on her art because she loved it, and nothing could take that away. If she were never recognized, she said, never paid, that would be okay. Art would hang not only on the walls but from the ceilings and draped from curtain rods and over the backs of sofas. Art would be not artifice but integral to life. She may even have quoted Oscar Wilde (this was how full of shit she'd been): *Your life will be your art.*

The friends were all Jason's. She had by then abandoned her college pals, or they her, drifting apart, they told each other, or moving to New York or L.A. Who needed people? She hated everybody but him, wanted the world to be nobody but the two of them. When they did go out, the people surrounding them at a large plastic patio table in Hess Village, a trendy cobblestoned area near their apartment, thick with bars and clubs, booming with music, were grad students and professors from Science and the Humanities. These were the people who invited them to poker games and to smoke weed. How was it that Jason and all the nerds were somehow less socially awkward than she was? Jason, despite growing increasingly agitated about his work, remained beloved and not the least bit eccentric in this company. Beauty was a warrant, she thought. Jason, with his kind eyes, his naturally lean, broad-shouldered body, was an aesthetic object. His looks were as much a fluke as his intelligence: rare, and a ticket to the admiration of others. On one of these days she realized, from across that plastic patio table, that it wasn't only that he *wanted* wealth and fame and a perfect, beautiful family. It was that the world would give those things to him. It wasn't envy she felt for him in that moment, but fear. *I won't be one of the fools to give in to you*, she thought. *Between the two of us, everything will be different.* He lifted his hand to order another pitcher of beer.

So later, when the first miscarriage came, and then the second, she knew that she had, by wishing, caused them.

Jason was telling a philosophy grad student that he was tiring of physics. "At first it was just that I wanted the puzzles, but now I want to find a way to look underneath the puzzles."

"There aren't enough collaborations between science and humanities departments," said a woman, a young history professor whose name Marie never bothered to learn. "The future of all of our professions depends on it." When they were drunk, these academics slipped into generalizations that otherwise would have embarrassed them.

"It isn't like the relationship between the maths and philosophy isn't already belonging to a rich and storied tradition," said a heavily accented Eastern European man.

"With physics, at a certain point," Jason said, "you get so far from describing reality that you don't even know why you're interested in the puzzle anymore. It's a puzzle for its own sake, like any puzzle. Physics can't answer the questions I'm asking anymore. It can't really even ask those questions." He looked over at Marie. She was still capable of flooding with feeling for him then, his eyes on her, his good looks. In bed that very afternoon, moving his finger slowly up her waist, over her breast, he had told her that she was the only one who could ask the questions. She was always saying what came into her head—observing ant life, for example, and wondering about the stories ants told themselves, how they interpreted their existence. He would tell her to go on, go on, go on. "Maybe artists can ask the questions I'm talking about," he said to the others.

"How romantic," said the Eastern European professor. He had always appeared to detest Marie.

"For example," Jason continued, "Marie is always zeroing in on shapes and textures."

The others ignored this. "But even in philosophy," someone else said, "you're hardly engaging with anything urgent or pressing. I think what's happening is you're just finding the real limit of what we can know. We don't have the vocabulary or the framework to understand most things."

"Nah. I don't believe that," Jason said. "You find a way to build the vocabulary. And it's not that science can't do it, it's only that the powers-that-be won't let me. If it doesn't sound plausible to a grant committee, it doesn't get studied."

"But who wants to know everything anyway?" Marie said suddenly. She pictured such knowledge like a room suddenly lit with over-bright fluorescence. She knew that Jason *did* want to know everything. He wanted a god's vantage.

Everyone turned toward her, silent. As always, they treated her with polite condescension.

"Beauty would increase. With every scientific advance, our awe increases," Jason said. "Like Darwin. Copernicus. The world doesn't get smaller because we know it better."

Jason's father had died only a few months before, but looking at him then, she had perceived in him no additional despondency. She had felt only distrust in his belief in his own specialness, no matter how much proof there was that he was above them all, an anomaly.

"You treat math and science like they could tell us everything. I think that's reductive," Marie said. "You're acting like one of those people who would explain love chemically."

"Of course I am," Jason said. "As well you know."

As well you know: one of his favourite phrases. "Well, I'm not," she said. "And I don't think you are, really, either."

She picked up her beer from the scratched and grimy table, waiting for someone to move the conversation elsewhere. Someone cleared their throat. They were all of them kinder than she was.

Jason, she saw much later—too late—was suffering, and drinking too much. Nothing had meant what it had seemed to.

Marie was never paid for her art, but for her entrepreneurship she earned a kind of fame in their city. She opened Frankincense & Myrrh after the divorce, just as the artists began to arrive, tired of the cost of living in the capital on the other side of the lake, and converted the vacant buildings to galleries, the dime stores to vintage clothing shops, and the convenience stores and markets to cappuccino joints.

She was solvent by thirty, consoled by a growing savings account, the shop's view of York Boulevard from the wide north-facing window, and by chitchat with the artists and activists who came daily through the door. Her store was local and idiosyncratic, and she was beloved for her good brushes and paper as much as her appearance of being slightly scattered, a fledgling too soon dropped from her nest. The activists came for poster-making supplies and a place to pin signs, and they saw in her one of their own: a person unattached to any status quo, a person willing to make sacrifices. Most days, she woke up thinking *heave-ho*—the sound of the shop-door opening so constant it became seared into her brain. She became, to her surprise, a person of commerce. As an artist she was too critical, too sarcastic, too skeptical. She loved making art but did not believe in the idea of art. Just like she had loved but not believed in marriage.

She'd had no friends during this time, only customers—and that had been plenty of company. Now that it was gone, she longed not for any person from that period, but for the feeling of life in the store, for her old playlists and the grids and buttons of ordering pages, for the cleanliness of a well-inventoried existence. She longed for her old routine, how it felt to watch the street cycle through the hours, from early dark to midday shine and busyness, to the lighted streets of evening.

And for Jason, his shadowy presence.

One year after the divorce, on Marie's twenty-eighth birthday (and even though both she and Jason had agreed that all dates were arbitrary, and all birthdays meaningless in the face of infinitude, occasions more grim than gladdening), she began to dream about him. She dreamed about him as he had looked at twenty-three: her first sight of him standing in line at the library with a single book in his hand. What if she'd never spoken to him, and all had been only potential? In the dreams his mouth opened to reveal first their solar system and then the whole Milky Way, until it had opened so wide that she could see everything, every star, every system in the known universe. She woke terrified. Even the bedding she'd embroidered herself in a medieval style, unicorns and greenery and gold leaves, seemed sinister.

She had phoned him, asked him to come back, and he came. He told her that he understood hormones and grief, the loss of his father and then of those possible babies, had crushed them both. She remembered how she had stopped talking to him, left him alone in the apartment in the middle of fights, refused to smile, forced him out. "You weren't in your right mind," he said then, standing in the shop after she'd closed it up and locked the door behind them, although anyone could see through the windows on every wall. "I know it wasn't your fault."

"It was a mistake. It was grief," she repeated, filled with the ease of another future arriving to solve the past, him coming upstairs to spend the night and then the sounds of him above while she worked the next day, his familiar weight a creak on her floor, the whoosh of him showering. But it was by then already too late, and she'd known it. He'd so quickly managed to be scooped up by the biological imperative of this other woman—thirty-six-year-old Maria and her *fascinating* brain and her feminism and her parents' wealth and the fact of her pregnancy. Maria could afford to support him through to the end of his doctorate and into post-docs or while he flailed for a job. She'd been his professor, once. And now he was going to have a child, and he was going to raise it.

Had Marie any choice? "You can love two women," she told him. "Maybe the universe is infinite, and there are no rules."

"I'm different with you than I am with her," he said, heavy with sleep on her mattress on the floor. "I am two people."

Without her, he'd have the family she couldn't have, and he apologized to her with his mouth on her body. Whatever had gone wrong between the two of them, the many babies that grew to the size of pebbles and apricots and then shook themselves loose to be found in grievously bloody clumps in the toilet, whatever would not take hold, would not take hold because of her.

It wasn't his fault, it wasn't her fault—and so they carried on together, despite Maria and the baby. The single year apart would be only a blip in their long lives together, she told him. He tried to leave her; he came back to her; they had one-night stands; their one-night stands became an affair. "I shouldn't come back," he said. Then, "How am I supposed to live without you?"

"You'll never leave me," she said.

Marie found out about the wedding from a friend of a friend and then posted a few regrettable things about it on her feeds before shutting those accounts down for good. "Nothing weird about your ex-husband marrying a woman with almost the same first name as you. Puts a lot of pressure on that one vowel," she'd written. The paltry recompense she'd received for this was a little thread of WTFs and frowny faces and "who needs men like that" and that sort of thing.

Jason was the love of her life. As though she had been fore-ordained by some god with a dark sense of humour to constellate herself around this man, and to never, no matter how much she fought its gravity, be free of him.

Poor *Marr-rr-ea*, Marie thought, mocking her with the rolled *r*, beyond good and evil by then, beyond good manners, and beyond grief. What mattered was that he always came back.

By the time they'd watched PINA's demonstration video, the affair had gone on for years, but Marie hadn't seen Jason in a month. She tried to reach him at his office phone as he preferred, but he didn't return her messages. The world was not fair but nepotistic, favouring the beautiful and wealthy, and so Jason had a job in Maria's department. The PINA video clip passed from status update to status update almost as quickly as the man shown on stage slipped into the invisible tube and disappeared. Evaporated.

Everyone Marie knew expected news that the video was a hoax. It was the only thing people talked about at the store, when they weren't wondering whether she carried oils in Sap Green or silk-screening kits or a certain ironic tote bag everyone else seemed to be selling. "I hope I get this series finished before the world ends!" they joked, many different versions of the same joke. Customers were always thrusting their phones at her, to show her new videos and tweets. The original PINA video was followed by months of public outcry, by concerned journalists asking concerned politicians how it was that something that rearranged your molecules and *moved you to a completely different place and time!* (people always dipped into an exclamatory tone here)—how something like that could be safe and ethical? There were no rules; the rules had changed. But what about the epistemological and ontological implications? The bloggers, the academics, and everybody's grandparents had their panties tied in knots. Who were we now?

PINA's port campaign rolled out more slogans. They argued for curiosity. They argued for fun. They said: Did curiosity *really* kill the cat? Don't let Big Brother tell *you* what to do! But by then the slogans were unnecessary. Everyone was pooling resources, tapping out bank accounts, buying ports the way people stock up on bottled water at news of an approaching hurricane.

Marie wanted to see how things played out, to be sure about side effects and unintended consequences. Meanwhile, Albrecht Doors went from billionaire to trillionaire in a matter of months, beaming out his neat and toothy smile from YouTube and TED and *The New York Times*—even though, all too soon, no one was watching.

"You don't do it for the money." This had been one of Doors' many soundbites. "You do it to *feel* something."

And it was weirdly true: All of those trillions were worth nothing now.

One day during this time, Marie had gone to a party thrown by a local celebrity-artist who'd bought a port. She decked herself out in a tight black dress and gold jewellery, in case Jason happened to be there. The celebrity, a man who called himself Salt Peter, had been the first in town with a PINAphone and, before that, the first to have a blog. He'd been one of the first artists to move from the expensive capital around the other side of the lake and into Marie's once-depressed, now-trendy, gallery-ridden neighbourhood. Technically, he did not even live in her neighbourhood but had purchased an enormous house near the escarpment, one of the houses that Marie and Jason used to wander past, admiring. At the front door, stacked turrets loomed over her. Salt Peter and his husband had completely restored the place.

"It's a bitch to heat, that's for sure," Salt Peter's husband said to a small group who toured behind him. He was a shirtless man buffed to a shine. Marie, carrying a glass of wine procured from a full-service bar in the front room, followed the husband along with a couple she'd never met, both of them agelessly shining with plastic-surgery. The house boomed with music that sometimes lowered to breathy voices.

"Do you like this music?" their host said on the winding oak staircase.

"Sure," she said. It was some kind of electronica mixed with sound effects (moaning, whispers, a scream).

He nodded, approving.

"You produced this one?" said the man next to Marie.

Their host nodded again.

"If I'd known that an artistic career could buy all this," Marie said, gazing at the many chandeliers she could only assume were tasteful. Around the corner were more people she recognized only vaguely draped on leather chaises and sofas, vaping fragrantly.

"What do you do?" the woman inquired.

"I own the art store," she said.

"The art store," said the woman. "You mean the one with the gold star?"

"Yes."

"Oh, but we don't live here," the woman said. The "oh" seemed to be a disavowal: *don't think we're like you.* Her lipstick was wine-dark, her eyes heavy with liner. "Salt P. is trying to convince us that this is the place to be."

"I used to live near here," Marie said. "It's a beautiful neighbourhood."

"Seems like you can get a big old Victorian for barely a nickel," the man said.

"Seems like it."

"Where do you live now?"

"I have an apartment above my shop," she said.

Their host had by now left them standing alone in the cavernous upper room. Smoke wafted around them.

"The city doesn't seem to smell as badly as it once did," the man said.

"I guess because it's not a steeltown anymore," Marie said. "They shut one of the factories down. There were a lot of layoffs. And the other one got bought out by an American company. More layoffs."

"Doesn't seem like it has hurt anybody," the woman said. "Still a bit depressed downtown, from what I hear, but things are improving, right?"

Marie stared at her. "I'm not sure about that," she said, thinking of the teenage mothers and young fathers and the tweakers and otherwise bedraggled men and women she saw down there every day. "The bars are nicer now."

"You grew up here?" said the woman, whose name Marie would never know, because the man was tugging on her sleeve. "You'll have to excuse us," she said, then. "We want to do a few lines. You could join us . . .?"

But Marie declined and headed back downstairs, where Salt Peter was pacing in a large room with paintings hung top to bottom of each wall, salon-style. Most of the paintings resembled Caravaggios, realism plus dark emotion, realism plus pain; they were unlike the paintings Salt Peter himself did, which roared with energetic paint strokes, which lacked all control. His hair was long and greasy, in the manner of the homeless, in the manner of grunge, the counterpoint to his beautiful husband, whose hair was neatly pompadoured.

Salt Peter called everyone to join him in the living room, where he pronounced that the Internet age was over. His husband came around with a glass of wine, handed it to Salt Peter, and stood back as Salt Peter climbed, glass in hand, onto the back of the leather couch.

"It's time to enter a new era!" he said. "And one of you will come with me!"

He climbed down, still balancing his own glass, a tightrope stuntman from a silent film, and took a woman Marie knew, Larissa, by the hand and did a little dance with her. She was dressed in skirt and corseted blouse, like a bar wench, and Salt Peter twirled and dipped her and kissed her hand.

Marie stood with her arms over her chest, wineglass in hand, frowning. Behind the couch the port had been standing all this time. Though she'd heard Salt Peter owned one, she hadn't really believed they existed—not until she saw it shimmering there. She had only ever seen them on screens.

"A new era!" Salt Peter said, laughing loudly.

The port was already open. Marie could perceive its tall slit hovering in space.

Salt Peter turned Larissa around three times and then shoved her into the thing. He went in after her, pulling the flaps closed with a zipper so small it was like a knife's slit through an amniotic sac. A roaring white noise she hadn't registered was silenced.

"How does it work?" Larissa's shouting voice was muffled. She and Salt Peter were still wavering, visible as objects viewed through still water.

"It knows your thoughts, sweetheart! It works Dorothy-style."

"Dorothy-style?"

"You click your heels three times."

She must have tried to click her heels, for Salt Peter said, "Not literally!" and laughed, big and loud, and then: nothing. All was silent; they were gone.

The husband lurched toward the port.

Marie realized she had stopped breathing. She began unconsciously fanning herself with one hand.

"This is getting out of control," someone whispered.

Then Marie began to choke, gurgling; she ran to a bathroom to throw up. She looked at her thin face in the mirror, ripped out her huge gold earrings and gulped water from the tap. She turned the light switch on and then off, on and off. Watched her face disappear in the mirror, then reappear, disappear, reappear.

When she returned to the party, people stood around as if at a performance, waiting to know what their expected response was in order to deliver it. The port was, in its emptiness, a gleaming mirage. Salt Peter's husband was standing next to an old record player, sobbing into his hands. Another man had come to stand with him, was rubbing his shoulders as he cried. "He said they can come back," the husband said. "They can come back, right?"

"Of course they can. He hasn't left you. You just had too much to drink. Come on," said the friend, leading the way toward the bar, toward the people there.

The husband looked up and directly at Marie. "It doesn't feel right, though. Does it feel right to you?"

Economists and other experts appeared on TV and radio shows to predict enormous shifts in population. "Chances are, if you don't have a port, you know someone who does," said a prominent techno-statistician, before she became unavailable to be interviewed, as did her replacements, one by one. The airwaves teemed with reruns, the news channels recycled the same information again and again. The *New York Times* filled the Sunday paper with investigative reports, photos of abandoned buildings and stories of lost employees, charts predicting collapse. The numbers were reminiscent of predictions about climate change; if we go over this threshold, flooding and refugees. If we go over this threshold, catastrophe. So, said the *Times*, here's what will happen if we lose 5 percent of our population . . . here's what will happen if we lose 10 percent, and so on. By the time this report came out, the worldwide loss was estimated at 10.8 percent.

"Why isn't anyone coming back?" a reporter asked Albrecht Doors.

Doors smiled into the camera. "Because they don't want to come back."

"Why would anyone believe the CEO of a company about their own product?" Marie asked Leroy, a sculptor who came into the shop every day. He'd been at Salt Peter's party, too, had seen Salt Peter and Larissa disappear.

"People are easily fooled," Leroy said. "That's, like, the deepest truth about human beings. Plus, they *never* know it. You can invent a religion and wave your arms and say, 'Hi, I'm creating this religion to make enormous sums of money,' and you end up with thousands of devotees. You can tell your people to murder people and also that they won't have to be murderers, and they'll go around with machine guns, doing as they're told."

"Yeah," Marie said absentmindedly, hitting the keys on her 1980s vintage register, which whirred and dinged like a child's toy. "Only $8.50 today," she said. "You still working on the miniatures?"

"But imagine," Leroy said, looking past her and into the street framed in the window. "What if you could go to a place and time where, say, things hadn't been monetized yet. Meaning, like, pre-money. A place where your wealth was measured out in goats."

"Tempting," Marie said, thinking Leroy must be making a joke about the heavy bag of change he was handing her.

But that was the last time she saw Leroy, who could never have afforded his own port. Maybe he had gone into Salt Peter's house to use his, which is what Marie had already decided she would do if the catastrophic conditions predicted by the *Times*—starvation, violence, random explosions from unattended chemical plants, some other country invading—should come to pass.

Another month passed; still she had not heard from Jason. Finally she drove around the lake to Jason's new home. Stood knocking and ringing at his door, then sat for an hour on the front porch of the Edwardian he shared with his Maria. How old was his boy? The child must be five already—proof that Marie's life with Jason, like Jason himself, had disappeared. The family he had now was so intact and beautiful, it was like he'd found them clamshelled in plastic at a store. She sat for hours on the porch that might have been hers, until the sun began to set and she saw with creeping awareness that the streets were too still. When a person did pass by, they were distracted, lost in thought. People who weren't leaving were holing up. Those who remained on the streets were madmen, muttering to themselves.

That day she had gone to Jason's house, Marie had wrestled a window open in the back and pulled her body through its crack. He had left no message for her. A stack of mail sat in a tidy pile on the kitchen table, and the dishes in the rack were long dry. A pile of apples was rotting in a basket on the counter, smelling of vinegar, so thick with fruit flies that they were like rising ash. An inert PINAphone sat on the counter, a dead PINA laptop on the table. A barely humming sound came from the port—inconspicuous in the living room behind a leather armchair. Fucking bourgeoisie. She resisted the urge to put knife wounds into the thick hides of canvas paintings of bird's-eye Venice, and Rome and the Toronto skyline. She thought of Salt Peter, of his sobbing husband. *They can come back, right?*

She left a note for Jason on the table and another on each door. *I'm at the store. Come say hello.*

She could not bear to write the word *please*.

Chapter

4

THE NEIGHBOURS

Marie cornered Rosa outside while everyone except the few strict vegetarians ate the juicy, amazingly fresh meat. Even the few aging hippies and longtime vegans ate some celebratory softened apples from their stash.

People came up to Marie with tears in their eyes—as though by killing the deer, she'd healed their firstborns. "I guess I need to go hunting more often," she said to Rosa.

"If it's admiration you're after," Rosa said, a slight edge in her voice. Mo was standing next to her.

"Excuse me?" Marie said. "I think we could all stand to learn how to hunt."

Rosa squeezed her lips together impatiently.

"What the hell, Rosa?" Perhaps, thought Marie, it was that not everyone had the cool nerves and steady shot to kill animals. Any accomplishment in this group invited envy. Any trait, even. Marie envied Rosa her youth, the six years between them a chasm of loss; she envied her black hair, her full, arched eyebrows.

"Don't worry about it," Rosa said.

"This is pretty fucking aces," Mo said to Marie.

"Thanks, Mo."

Smoke escaped the garage through seams and gaps, stinging their eyes and throats. Philip was seated in a nearby folding chair, a blanket around his shoulders. Bonita stood behind him, rubbing his neck.

Marie tried to keep her voice down. "Phil was so strange about the sport sign thing. Don't you think?"

"Not really," Rosa said. "I think you're being strange about it."

"Hey, hey," Mo said. "What are you arguing about? The billboard?"

"First, we'll figure out if it was one of us," Rosa said. She crossed her arms over her body, and spoke with such evenness it was clear she was fighting to sound calm. "And after we do that, we can think about more wild theories."

"Why is it a wild theory, Rosa? Nothing is normal here, right?"

"When you are grieving you don't think straight, and added to that, none of us are grieving properly. You're like a mother whose child disappeared, but clings to hope while everyone else can see that the child is dead."

Mo squeezed Rosa's shoulder affectionately.

"And now we're all kind of coping with the fact that no one is coming back. Everybody has left, and not one single person has come back."

"Not yet," Marie said, trying weakly to be funny.

"Oh my God, Marie. That's like saying that we should still hold out for a unicorn sighting, when no one has ever seen a unicorn."

Around them, people were eating and eavesdropping on each other. How could you trust anybody, thought Marie, any of these strangers? Not one of them had been untouched by what had happened. So not one of them was thinking straight.

"You can cling to the past or you can face what you see," Rosa said.

"I don't know why you're yelling at me," Marie said.

"Nobody wants to leave without you," Mo said. "That's why she's upset."

Rosa made a sound and hit him gently.

Marie's mother had paid for a few therapy sessions after the divorce from Jason. There she had been told that she needed to have boundaries, was permitted to make her own decisions just as others were permitted to make their own. Now she thought: Maybe the framework for such things had changed? Perhaps the truisms of therapy were useless now, had been developed for psychological survival in a heavily-populated super-mobile world, not for a circle of forty-two who needed each other in ways more literal than not.

"That makes me wonder, actually," Mo said, looking around at the others. His large hand touched Rosa's for a lingering moment. "It makes me wonder if the red *S* was intended to keep us here. Keep us wondering and paranoid instead of moving on."

Marie knew, but did not say, that she'd never move on. Never.

"Why don't you come to the fire tonight?" Rosa said, though to Marie's ears the invitation sounded half-hearted.

The group in its small cliques was already beginning to disperse. They had wood to chop while there was still a little light. Philip might go to fiddle with the inert solar equipment, like the young boy he'd once been would have taken apart a radio. The rest would start passing around bottles of hard liquor and wine.

Rosa's hip was now resting against Mo's leg as though by accident. Marie's stomach lurched. But she said casually, "Maybe for a bit."

"Probably it's just unintended consequences," Bonita said to Marie. They were having their usual, ongoing conversation about what had happened and why it had happened so quickly. She heaved an axe down through a hunk of wood so that it stuck into the surface of a tree stump. Bonita contended that PINA could not have counted on everybody wanting to buy a port; they could not have known that the desperation to get out would be so strong. The ports were chinks to break open dams. People were like water, in a hurry to rush.

Not being much on the Internet in those early days, Bonita had heard everything a little late, either through the newspapers or from

Rosa over the phone in her kitchen. Rosa was like her other children, Marcos and Camila, buying up new phones and new computers and paying for PINApps and tossing out their carcinogenic-ridden old electronics to be picked over by desperate children in developing nations. Bonita, who had been a poor child, understood the abjection of poverty better than the others, who were merely economically depressed. She thought the ports might be benevolent, even if such benevolence were an accident. Families in the developing world could go through some unguarded port to a space-time before capitalism had destroyed the possibility for their self-reliance, before their self-reliance was sacrificed to enable the self-reliance of the wealthy. A poor child would climb into one as he might have climbed into a dumped refrigerator, or, better, the poor would take over the abandoned homes of the too-rich and novelty-seeking, just as they were.

In her insistence that some of what port had accomplished had been good, Bonita was the most optimistic of the group, and she had quickly learned not to say such things to the many who did not know where their loved ones were. Even her own Marcos and Camila had jumped off a cliff with the other sheep. Rosa was the only stone of familial loyalty. "I won't leave without you," Rosa had said to her mother. Bonita felt that now, at least, you knew who people were and what they were made of.

Bonita threw the axe down into another hunk of oak, which splintered and split. She split each half into half, and Marie would carry these piled quarters of fresh, slightly piss-smelling wood to the tarp-covered shelter near the woods, while Bonita readied to split another.

"Hey, take a break," Philip called from several feet away, where he sat at the fire. "You're almost out of light, anyway."

The kerchief over Bonita's short mess of grey hair captured her sweat, and she pulled it off, wiping her dewed upper lip, her forehead, before folding it away in the back pocket of her jeans and heading over.

Marie and Bonita sat in matching Adirondack chairs, and Bonita moved straight into her list of reasons for Marie to move in here, to the Robenstein-Williams house, where she and Rosa lived, since there was plenty of room for Marie and Gus, and even for all of the art supplies, if Marie wanted. They'd set up the sunroom with lines on which to hang Marie's photos. They'd turn one of the bathrooms into a darkroom. All but Marie had claimed these homes and back-yards of the city's formerly wealthy. They'd connected the lawns by pulling down fencing, which they'd used to cordon off a large vege-table garden near a retiree's hobby greenhouse.

Marie kept her eyes on Rosa. Her friend's pretty round face on the other side of the fire beamed up at Mo. Marie knew that radiance like this was a matter of hormones. It was also the play of firelight: eyes were bigger, blemishes did not show. Mo put his hand on Rosa's knee. Mo, the other optimist, respectful and kind. His djembe stood behind him on the grass. On the other side of Bonita, Philip and Donnie were arguing. Andrea was picking inexpertly at one of Rosa's guitars.

The few young families had gone back to their homes. The group needed to keep small families, especially, in the fold. A community needed builders, and builders were people who had a stake. People left through port for the same reason they stayed in their hometowns: for the sake of nostalgia. So you had to manage nostalgia most of all: *The past looks better but it is only the longing that makes it so. Do not trust your desires, nor your memories.*

Every night, the group kept this fire blazing, big enough to be visible from the air if anyone were watching. Sometimes they danced. Once the children had gone yawning off to bed, carried limply in their parents' arms, flip-flops dangling from small toes, the smell of marijuana would punctuate the heavier smell of burning wood.

Through the winter, they had burned what they could find. Chairs and small tables they attacked with axes; wicker items were easily bro-ken by hand; baskets and hampers and paper were thrown on the flames. After the thaw, though, Bonita and Philip became concerned about the chemicals that might be in the smoke, so now they burned only trees.

"I still think it would be a better use of resources if we burned all the extra stuff here," Donnie said. He was sitting next to Philip in one of the Adirondack chairs with his bad leg lifted onto a tree stump. Donnie was one of the ones who thought no one was coming back; he was also a loner who had lost no one close to him—mostly because no one *had* been close to him.

"And when we all get cancer from inhaling fumes," Bonita said, "who's going to cut out our tumours?"

"But think of all the other fumes we aren't inhaling anymore," Philip said.

"True. But we have no idea how much radiation the ports give off," she returned.

"Bonita, you are a cancer conspiracy theorist," Donnie said. "You think everything causes cancer."

"Everything does cause cancer. But you're one to talk," Bonita said, swatting at his good knee, "since you're a government-agency conspiracy theorist and a PINA truther."

"You only apply words like that to diminish the possibility of their being true," Donnie said. "People just say 'conspiracy' when they want to make you seem paranoid."

"But you're the one who said 'conspiracy,'" Andrea said. She was always listening in, poor lonesome frightened one, thought Marie. Andrea continued plucking shyly at the guitar. "About Bonita!"

"Well, we are a bunch of potheads," said Bonita. "That much is for sure. And anyway," she said, pointing to the wilted left side of her chest, "cancer is *not* theoretical."

"And we can't deny the former existence of government agencies, whose actions may or may not have caused human near-extinction," Donnie grunted. "I know you all don't remember what PINA was up to just before port launched, but there were a lot of secret meetings with Albrecht Doors. Doors was buying up the rights. To *all* the tech."

"Yeah, yeah," Bonita said. "But we need to focus on immediate concerns. At this rate, we're burning through trees too quickly."

"I don't think that's possible," Philip said, putting his hands palm out toward the large fire.

"That's what everyone says. Famous last words."

"We should make a tally of famous last words. We could, like, find all the notes people left," Andrea said, looking up from the guitar and into the fire.

"Next on the agenda: an endless and meaningless project," Donnie said.

"Endless, maybe. Meaningless, no. Is poetry meaningless?"

Donnie let out a scoffing laugh, a cough. "Yes! It is!"

A bottle of rum came around, then a joint. Marie let them pass. Rosa and Mo were kissing, counting on the privacy of the ignored.

"What about that one about the road less travelled by. 'I took the one less travelled by, And that has made all the difference,'" Andrea said. "That poem isn't meaningless."

"You *would* quote Robert Frost," Donnie said.

"Collecting famous last words would be something to do, anyway," Andrea said, glowering at him. "We're not animals."

"We *are* animals," Philip said. "That is precisely what we are." He got up and moved to a seat closer to Marie.

"You know what she means," said Bonita. "But most people didn't really leave notes, right?"

"There's a T. S. Eliot poem on the tip of my tongue, here," Donnie said.

"Anyway," Bonita said, "the point is, everybody thinks they won't run out of resources. That's what the pilgrims thought, and look what happened."

"Wouldn't have happened to the First Nations. They were here for a thousand years, not destroying the Earth."

"Maybe. What do you think, Donnie?"

Donnie was one-quarter Ojibwe.

"How should I know? For sure at least I know that they never had all this mass-produced junk lying around. Goddamn industrial revolution."

"Well we're pre-industrial again, I guess," Bonita said. "And that is not so romantic. People were dropping dead from the plague all the time. There were many, many ways to die."

Through the tall licking flames, Marie saw Mo's hands on Rosa's face; he was pulling her toward his mouth like she was something delicious he would eat.

"We probably do need to start getting smarter," Marie said. "We have enough time on our hands."

"Here's the thing," Philip said, slurring a little, listing toward her. She gently pushed him back to sitting. "If things get bad," he said. "We just leave."

But Marie shook her head. She wasn't going anywhere. And she knew that Bonita wouldn't leave either. This place, maybe, if necessary, but not these people. Bonita had always held on to hope for a community like this. This was what she would have called heaven. Or if not heaven, some blessed place. To Bonita, this was, in all the important ways, the hereafter.

Shortly after Mo and Rosa had gone, leaving the drum on its side like a discarded toy, Marie got up to go home. Her loneliness was sharpened by Bonita being high and by Philip being drunk, as though they were two negligent parents.

Philip had leaned close to her before she left and said, "I think I went through."

"What? You mean the port?"

He made a moaning sound of assent.

"But you didn't. You didn't disappear even for a second. You didn't go through." She felt a chill then. "Probably wasn't a great idea to bring one into the church, though. Without consulting anybody."

Philip lazily nodded. "I felt a tugging. Do you think part of me went through?" His eyes had closed. "The pressure was incredible. Like jumping from a plane."

"Okay, bud. But I need to get home before it's completely dark," she said. "See you tomorrow."

"Home," he said. "Homeward bound."

"Yup."

She snapped her fingers for Gus.

"Wait," Bonita said. She ran to her house and returned a moment later with a heavy flashlight that she forced into Marie's hand.

Calculating that she still had half an hour until sundown, Marie made a detour west to her favourite place: the bridge over the highway. She wanted to feel the full force of its emptiness, the overwhelming expanse of asphalt, lanes winding through the landscape like fine charcoal ribbons. In the distance, if she waited long enough, she'd see packs of deer, the consoling beauty of muscled bodies on thin legs. The dappled fawns were like a negative image of herself, white spots on tan hide. But it was getting too dark to see much now, and coughing into her hand to break the eerie quiet, she nudged Gus, and they walked back down toward her apartment.

She flicked the light on and off to notice how dark it was getting. So many of the things she owned had lenses now: binoculars, flashlights, cameras. The barrel of a gun, too, that was a kind of eye, and she swung the flashlight as she walked, contemplating what paintings she might make of these repetitious circles. Or prints, maybe, silkscreens. The streetscape in its hollow silence was like a Chirico painting Marie had loved as a teenager. Long shadows, black on grey, empty space. His paintings evoked a creeping awareness that something was coming, something was right around the next corner. Her past love of Dadaism and Surrealism had gone along with a teenage obsession with the bon mots of Dorothy Parker and the habit of wearing cloche hats she bought secondhand. Now a Dali made her remember her naïveté, made her mouth dry up with shame.

Far away, there was a clanking sound, a rattling: raccoons hoisting their quivering fat bodies into Dumpsters, knocking over long-emptied cans. She could feel the presence of dogs, too, other animals, prowling and slow, nervous and careful as they led their bodies down alleyways. Once in a while the quick thin movements of a cat. Rarely was there barking. Silence was what she'd always wanted. For there to be fewer people and less to do. Jason had wanted company. It was the central conflict of their marriage. In those days, she had felt in her body how the world was bloated with beings.

"Be careful what you wish for," she told Gus, scratching him aggressively behind the flop of his black ears, as they walked down James Street. Power used to force its way through wires into bulbs and lamps, swelling them with light, controlled distention. Now twilight deepened quickly, the sun blushing behind bluish clouds. Moonlight made a quilt-like geometry of the shadowy shapes of buildings against the starry panorama. She hurried, knowing darkness lured out things she feared. Cockroaches would spill out of sewage drains like pennies overfilling a jar. Armies of rats would stare at her, eyes aglow.

She had to strain to see the corner of the store emerge in the darkness, the watery moonlit sheen of the windows on all sides. Gus raised his head, lifted and dropped the feathery end of his tail. She didn't know how old he was, would never know. Could you discover such things, if you had the right training and equipment? Perhaps mammalian age was recorded in the liver or the joints, evident only after death. Could you discover age by examining DNA?

She shone the flashlight up at the billboard where *Sport* now seemed to be an urgent, encoded message just for her. Meaning: *Be a good sport*? Or: *This is all just a game*? She moved the light up and down the street, searching for shapes, movement, the flash of eyes, raccoon or cat, caught and frozen. But the darkness swallowed up the weak stream of light.

Three hundred and fifty-some days ago, electricity had ceased flowing, and water no longer rushed through the pipes when you commanded it. There was no longer any way to do most things she had known how to do, so every small habit of life required more energy output: to shower under waterfalls or bathe in murky lakewater, to cook and to keep warm, to keep away the many smells that were everywhere. Musks of various kinds, body odours, the shit stink of death. In the spring, when everything had begun to thaw, the garbage-rot smell grew.

The winter, while awful, had temporarily neutralized certain smells outside, though indoors, smells were trapped along with whatever heat peoples' bodies and burning wood could make. Everyone had lived in the few rooms they could insulate with heavy drapes. Someone had come up with the one bright idea to raid the sports equipment stores for sleeping bags and down-filled jackets and weatherproof materials. Marie had sealed up her shop and apartment, taped windows with thermoplastic to keep air out, and stayed there on all but the worst nights, huddled under layers, beside Gus. During the day, the group had travelled the route between houses and church on stolen skis and snowshoes through a blinding, sparkling cityscape that seemed enchanted because it was unrecognizable. Most of the group had not known snow to be so white, to so obliterate and soften the shapes of things, though Mo had spent a winter in Yellowknife, and Marie had been to northern Quebec, and Jack had lived for two years in a commune in Vermont. They could agree at least that they had never seen snow this white *here*, downtown. Real snow like this had a function, which had been lost by all those years of salting and plowing: it would soak into the ground and melt down into the lake. They were convinced that in these ways the ecosystem would eventually reboot, maybe even in a few years. The worms and maggots and increasingly apparent legions of mice would no longer seem disgusting but merely elemental to the processes that had always kept the world clean.

The day it all went dark, Marie was at the small Chinese grocery across the street from the store. She and the others had known this was coming. News no longer arrived via paper or TV. Each day the holdout shopkeepers and artists came into the street to find out: Had anyone seen Charlene? Bob? No one had seen Evan, who owned the Cranberry Café, for a week. People didn't give word that they were leaving. They were just gone, as though sheepish, as though they knew their departure was shameful. "If you won't dignify your leaving with goodbyes," Marie had said to Min, whose elderly grandparents owned the grocery, "then you have proven that you are wrong in leaving."

Min was distracted that day, or perhaps she disagreed. Their orders weren't coming in; they couldn't contact their distributors; the customers were gone. Min's grandparents acted as though this were a crisis they would weather and then defeat. They'd sell food even if they couldn't sell citrus, even if they could no longer sell fresh fish. They'd sell whatever was bottled or canned. They'd always opened the store, and they always *would* open the store. But then Min and her grandparents, too—poof—were gone. Marie found a note on the unlocked front door: *Help yourselves*. It was meant kindly, an invitation, but the phrase haunted her.

Help yourselves.

People were behaving as though drugged, she thought. This was her first theory, that the idea of port was like opium to an opium-eater: what if, without dying, you could just *go*. A different form of curiosity had kept her here. At first she had wanted to see how bad it could get, how few people there could be, whether she could be the one to outlast. She had wanted a test of her endurance, a way of discovering for herself what the marathoner wants to know. And then one day she had looked down into the solemn street, and it was so beautiful. Reality had become the dream, and she was awake for it.

That March, they'd all worn masks over their mouths and noses. The big grocery stores were the worst, bacteria of decay making the air a swamp. They took what they could, cans and more cans piled into grocery carts. The bottled water most of them had once considered an unnecessary evil of capitalism was now a godsend. Donnie had jokingly put an empty bottle on a stick like a totem.

How had they survived that first winter? Canadians had always felt this way in spring, but that first year was something else. *We're still here*, they said to one another. The worst is over. *Help yourselves.*

Marie and the others had gone through houses and apartments in a fever of inventorying, carrying the stiffened carcasses of pets to backyard graves, or, finally, because there were so many, to pickup trucks that could transport them to bonfires on the beach. This way at least some of the streets would be clear and clean. Even if she hadn't seen this happen, Marie would have known how alone she was now. It wasn't only the darkness and the silence, the way echoes returned sounds to you, everywhere, the lack of movement in the channels and tubes behind walls and underground—it was even in the taste and feel of the air, the buzz of it. You could sense that there were fewer people sharing oxygen.

And yet, most days she still went home alone. It was at one of their fires in the spring that she'd got drunk and kissed Philip, letting him inch his meaty hand with its fat fingertips up her shirt, and it was at one of these fires that she'd told everybody about Jason. Several months later, the thought of these revelations still made her cringe. She had sat on one of the log benches, leaning in (it was awful to picture her own intensity), and recounted everything. Rosa teased her later that she'd talked for forty minutes straight.

And after nights like that, she only felt lonelier, or lonely in a different way, and realized she preferred the dignity and decorum of life above the art shop. Through her bedroom window she could see the uppermost tip of the gold star on the sign, its backing of unpainted wood with a few gold brushstrokes feathering over the edges. She could see the windows of stores and apartments, now empty, that used to punctuate her life here: the grocery with its bins packed with fruit and nuts, the homes of neighbours who were also her customers, who sometimes walked naked past translucent or ill-fitting curtains. The printmaker's studio space, the specialty shoe store, the Italian café and the independent coffee shop. Normalcy, she had come to believe, is sanity. Marie knew this was a conservative view, but she could now also see that the time of upheaval and transition in her own life had been the most tragic for her. Abandoning one's marriage was not an artistic gesture. Whether or not one should reject the status quo depended a great deal, it turned out, on the content of that status quo.

Gradually, through minor shifts and adjustments, she had found a new routine. The pleasures of before were replaced by new pleasures: the discovery of guns, the companionship of a dog, the ability to walk up a street without fear of traffic. At first she missed things like buttery croissants that melted wafer-like on her tongue, and dark-roasted coffees, and the feel of possibility, as she unfurled the store's awning every morning, of conflict or intrigue or even love among the people she knew.

Last November, when she'd been shivering alone in the apartment, chewing on jarred olives and pickles until a layer of skin peeled from the roof of her mouth, she realized that she'd been, all these years, enacting other people's lives. Hollywood lives—televised lives. When she had thought she was dreaming of being an artist, she had really been dreaming of the approval of an audience. When she'd wrapped her hands around a full cup of coffee, it had felt large and full of import because of all the crime dramas she'd watched in which beautiful women held such cups along with their promise, their whip-smarts. So she, like everybody else, has been a victim of advertising. She had been curating herself, in the same way she curated the store. Once she realized this, she was okay. But she also knew that the only way forward was to commit to living her life among the church-haunters. It wasn't only the roof of her mouth becoming raw and raggedy.

Now Gus jangled next to her as they walked. On a heart-shaped glint of metal his former address and phone number were engraved, but no name. His meaty breath, the soft sounds of his paws on the sidewalk, the damp coarse heat of his body—all this provided comfort. She'd always wanted a mutt like this, loyal and smart, and this too felt vaguely familiar, as if from a dream or a movie she couldn't recall.

For months she'd had to remind herself that no one was watching her from the windows or the streets or the CCTV cameras (which, though powered down, still seemed pointed and vigilant), or from the PINA satellite camera system, the PINA maps, or any of the PINA projects that many had suspected were surveilling more than was precisely legal. Despite the cold and telling feeling on the back of her neck, the certainty that she was being watched, she'd told herself over and over that her paranoia was mere residue—left over from a habit, like the fresh coffee smell she was convinced, every morning, she could catch whiffs of.

Looking at the billboard now, she wanted to feel what she had that afternoon when she'd first seen it. But the sensation had faded. Her first foolish instinct—that it was Jason come back for her—was as improbable as the idea that any of those stars above were the UFOs he'd once believed in. And now she longed to be the person she'd been then, ten years ago—twenty-four, twenty-five years of age—on her back in the grass, wanting to believe in anything. She wanted that Jason back, shouting, pointing, wild: "There! Don't you see it? Don't tell me you don't see it!"

The day when the door to the store no longer signalled its opening with the chiming *heave-ho*, it had seemed an unbearable loss. But all was loss, so she locked her door behind her, and she and Gus went upstairs to bed.

Sometime later, Marie woke up in total darkness. Gus's eyes, regarding her from the end of the bed, were glints of reflected moonlight. Faint lines and pricks of light also dazzled on the glass frames of her art prints, and on her watch's face, which she slanted toward the open window. Ten past three. Without the light of passing cars or street lamps, without neon signs and twenty-four-hour Laundromats, the intensity of the darkness was unwavering, as though this were a still point around which everything else turned. And nothing was so unchanging as the middle of the night.

Something had woken her. She quieted herself, held her hand out to Gus, and they stared at the window, listening. Had it been a bang or a shout? The darkness seemed to smother sound. She heard a distant clattering, that was all, the raccoons in the midst of their ongoing and unending mission to scavenge.

Gus jumped off the bed to the floor and stiffened his body so that it seemed to point.

"You heard something?"

His body remained rigid, trained on an invisible target. She climbed down beside him, peeping out the bottom of the window. The only other sound was a kind of scuffing. Footsteps? It might have been litter pulled down the street in the wind.

She reached her hand back for her binoculars beside the pillow and stared through them out the window. It was useless. There were only shadows and deeper shadows, the few reflections of light too small and faded to make a form. She willed the clouds to open.

There it was again, outside in the street. *Scuff, scuff, scuff.*

She stood as slowly as she could and, unclipping Gus's collar, led them both through the kitchen to the back door, thinking to go down to the store, where she might see better from the wider windows. She got as far as the door. Stood with her hand on the knob and then slid the chain lock closed and double-checked the deadbolt.

People had managed to survive before central heating, before central air, before cars. This was how the argument went in their group. There was a certain courage and creativity in facing the lonesome largeness of the world. But at this moment she deeply regretted the lack of a phone. With a phone she might have called a police force; a phone would have meant there still *was* a police force and that she wouldn't need to be so brave, need to have the gun. With a phone, she might have called Rosa to bring everyone and come get her.

Why? Rosa would have said.

I'm scared, Marie would have pleaded.

She went back to the bedroom with the heavy gun held in one shaking hand. She comforted herself with the sharp metal shucking sound as she pulled on the top to reassure herself that a gold bullet lay inside. She sat up on the bed with her head resting on her knees, while Gus sniffed out some small moving thing she couldn't see. There were no lights to send away the vermin.

Why did she think she had to do everything herself? Another question from her ruined marriage. Why couldn't she *let* him? She'd given him everything after the divorce, forced boxes of books and CDs and all the cassettes into his arms. Later he brought things back to her, hidden in the pockets of his pants, carried in one grocery bag at a time. The only piece from that old Sears registry that remained with her was the workbench, upon which sat her long-unused paints and brushes.

Hysterics were pointless, she reprimanded herself, and she needed to think. Whoever was out there with cans of spray paint was potentially menacing. Like a big clown smile or a snake, the red *S* could as easily be horrific as friendly. Whoever was out there might be the same person who had scuffed his feet, who would again scuff his feet.

They had been living in a dream world, a bullshit utopia. All utopias were bullshit. They had believed they were the only ones, as though this city were the centre of the universe and these forty-odd its most special denizens. They thought something had selected them—if not a deity (they'd never agree to one), then an evolutionary force, some teleology. They, with their haplessness and innocence, with their decency to each other, would rebuild this world.

But a few months ago someone had raised the question of the psychiatric hospital, where inmates must now be unmedicated or overmedicated and no longer restrained by gates or surveillance.

"And what about the prison?" Donnie had said.

"We have to look behind every door," Marie said.

"All the doors were automatic," Mo said. "All the locks were unlocked when the system went down."

"That seems unlikely," Marie said. How could everything be so fragile? "Aren't there failsafes?"

"Don't forget about Y2K," Donnie said, and they all laughed.

"Maybe some kindly officer unlocked everyone. Some kindly nurse," Bonita said.

"Or else shot them all," said Rosa.

Before they got to the bottom of this, the discussion had turned ideological, had turned to a dispute about statistics: you were more likely to be killed by your own father than by an undermedicated schizophrenic. That criminals were only criminals because society had deemed them so, and not because there was such a thing as real evil. Philip had assured her they'd investigate, but hadn't followed through.

She should have been stockpiling weapons and training dogs. She should have done it herself.

They had thought that in this world everything was perfect, because anytime you wanted to, you could just leave. The port was always going to glow with that possibility, and that was how you knew you wanted to stay, since every day you chose to do so. But right now, there was no getting out. There was only a long night and its darkness, and she would not be able to sleep.

Gus jumped up and let out two loud barks.

"It's alright," she cooed. But then she heard it. Too close—*clink, clink, whoosh*. And this time, glass shattering.

Chapter

5

THE LOTUS-EATERS

The daily work, even in these extreme circumstances, was mundane. First: food, shelter, hygiene. The incredible labour involved in fending off decay. Then: information. Just as people, in leaving, had revealed something about the nature of humanity, so too the world they left behind was revealed as something new to those left behind. Without its disguises of commerce and ambition, of self-important news stories and distractions, the Earth was stark.

The wall of maps the survivors had made included pictures of the Earth from space, that glowing Gaia of blue and green, its billowing clouds like sheets hung outside on the line. But it wasn't this beauty they were conscious of daily; it was Earth's hostility to man. Water eroded. Vines, trees and weeds aggressed. Things smelled of mildew. Clothes washed by hand and left to dry in the beating sun quickly faded or greyed. Vegetation and rot were enemies now. Raccoons gazed at you slant-eyed and chattered ominously all night.

And yet, despite the robust vegetation, so little was edible. Those who remained learned things they had never before needed to know. How to make a seed poke its little mole-head out of the ground to take a look. Which wires led where. How to dry out food to make it last. That a stain often could not be removed. The physical cost of sugar and coffee. The unknowable subsystem of pipes and sewage.

The conveniences of the modern age, which had once held humans aloft in a hammock, now left them splayed on the ground.

People behaved in leaving as they had in life. A man would leave without finishing his leftover lasagna or unplugging his fridge, and the pasta would go hard, then soft, its rot eventually indistinguishable from ricotta, the cheap plastic container buckling as the bacteria grew. The situation became worse when the power went down, smellier, organic matter turning fecal where it sat, then neutralizing again when the bacteria, having done its job, moved on. A woman, before leaving, would make sure everything she owned was unplugged and that a window was cracked for the cat. Such a cat would be long-neutered, declawed—easy prey. Biological cycles meant more than news cycles once had.

To those who remained, it seemed that there was a spectrum of leaving behaviour, containing every variation you could imagine. The only thing the travellers had in common was that they had gone.

And now, despite how everything had changed, there were so many good reasons to stay. There was no one around to watch the survivors. No one to accuse them of idleness, of not doing their jobs. After all, how many buildings and roads could forty people be asked to maintain? They took breaks and did as they pleased. In the rash, chaotic early days, they had broken many clocks. There was no one to measure their credit ratings. No one to demand taxes. The long list of things that seemed to have ended were wars, poverty, marriage, careers, capitalism, the Internet, television, hospitals.

The problems of greed were now abolished. Perhaps someone's child would one day say, *But there must be more to life than this.* History would begin again. Perhaps ambition lay like a spark inside each person, waiting for the right fuel, for a bit of tinder.

Still, there was not much ambition in this bunch. These survivors always settled on *stay*.

Marie could see nothing from the upstairs window, even when the faint light of dawn brightened to day. She would have to go downstairs. Gus had given up his vigil, but when she rose, he stood up anxiously. For a while in the night she had lain in bed certain that she'd hear steps coming up her stairs, or a pounding on her flimsy door, but eventually she had dropped off. Sleep had not been enough to soothe her shattered nerves. She was sure what she'd heard was her storefront window being destroyed—possibly by a member of another group as bored and fearless as her own. Perhaps the act was not malicious, but she could not reason away her worry.

Now it had been hours since the noise; it must be safe to go down and assess the damage to the store, to count what had been lost. Worst-case scenario, the intruders had interfered with the photographic record of the billboard, whoever they were—not monsters but men made menacing by darkness and mystery. Men—or maybe women—just like she was, she thought reasonably. People who had a desperate need for specialty art supplies. She herself had done the same thing yesterday with Rosa at the music store. Yes, people with guns and baseball bats were people exactly like her.

She loaded the gun, enjoyed its weight in her hand, then inched down the stairs with Gus beside her in her best imitation of a TV cop. Back to the wall, hand on gun, thumb on lip and ready to aim. Her breath came out choked and wavering. The wall was cool on her back as she moved down the stairs.

At the bottom, she nudged the door open and stared into the gaping maw of the store. All the paint pots were where they belonged, shining like gemstones. Red, green, yellow, blue. Not a single canvas was awry. Stacks of paper in every shade of white, black, grey, beige, ivory. Brushes, pencil sets, clay, pastels, tubes of watercolour, markers with their sampling pages still inscribed with the curlicues of long-gone strangers. On the back wall, the rows of photos still hung on their twine. Finally, she came to her water-dulled and fingerprint-streaked

panes of glass. The decalled letters she had designed: FRANKINCENSE &
MYRRH: ART SUPPLIES. Her now unnecessary chalk A-frame leaning
against the wall. She had spent the night imagining the floor littered
with glass icicles and floes, her gorgeously cared-for window ruined
forever. She touched the glass, then burst into tears. What if she had
lost this? This last good thing from before.

Her arms went limp, the gun now loose in her hand. "Gus? Come."

But then she paused. She *had* heard something last night. Scuffing
like footsteps, the whoosh and shatter of glass breaking. She unlocked
the door and went out into the street. Hot wind whirled the debris
that was always present now, the leaves and papers and bits of plastic
recycling. Outside the Chinese grocery, glass glittered on the sidewalk
and in the long-empty bins. So her prowler had been hungry and had
not noticed the unlocked door. In the dark, the now faded invitation
for visitors to help themselves would not have been visible.

Inside the grocery, the empty shelves were cast in darkness. She
knew without a doubt that there was no port inside the grocery, but
as she stood there she felt certain that if she were to turn her back on
the store, one would appear. She could almost hear the loud humming buzz of it, like a low-hanging telephone wire. So she did turn,
and felt it—the certainty that something was pursuing her, watching
her, and that she and Gus were not alone. She'd felt the same thing
in the church the day before. But there was nothing to be done.

She left, grabbed a metal pan and stiff broom from her own
store, returned to sweep up pebbles and shards, and poured everything into her wagon, which she tugged to the Dumpster in the
alley. Her arms and legs hurt, and twice she sliced a finger on a piece
of glass and had to run home to bandage herself, but out of loyalty
to those she'd known in the neighbourhood, she went through with
this laborious project.

Finally, she went down the street to gather cardboard at convenience stores she'd long ago jimmied open, and carried off the few

boxes that remained. She sealed the grocery behind this cardboard, though she knew the barrier wouldn't last.

Returning the duct tape and box cutter to her own shelves, she again felt a warmth on the back of her neck, as if she was being watched. She looked up at the small brick apartment building upon which her billboard perched. *Sport.* She went in for her camera, came out again and took her photo. Then she wheeled her bicycle out from behind the counter, whistling for Gus.

In the morning, the survivors were like bears coming out of their caves. People sat around the fire and boiled a mixture of cloves and cardamom and cinnamon and different kinds of tea, which they pretended to love. They passed around jerky and berries, and observed how much like cowboys they were. Like pilgrims, like settlers, like cavemen. And this was another point they frequently made to each other: they were doing their own kind of time travel just by staying here.

There had been discussions early on about relocating to a farm out in Binbrook or Jarvis, but however reduced, the group preferred the feeling of being close to an urban setting. They preferred, they told themselves, a little haphazardness, the adventure of disorganization. Even Philip, the ex-librarian. "Librarians," he would sometimes explain, "are neither quiet people nor necessarily organized."

But this morning, Philip said nothing. Marie noticed he was pale and sweaty, as though he were coming down with the flu. She parked her bike and walked over to him.

"You okay?" she said.

"I think so," Philip said.

She picked up a stick and tossed it into the woods for Gus. Watched as Bonita ladled out some of their improvised chai—admittedly, the spices were growing stale—and took a cup to Philip. "Hey. You feeling alright?"

"Why is everyone asking me that?" he said gruffly. "Just hungover. Getting old."

"Is that all?" Bonita put the back of her hand to his forehead and then sat down and blew on her watery tea.

Almost everyone was here now. The kids were running around in dizzying circles behind people's seats, whooping with their hands hitting their open mouths, while Donnie, from the back deck of a house, shouted, "That's racist! Hey! Tell your kids to cut that out! That's racist!" They did not cut it out. Marie noticed that one of the boys had even tied feathers to his head. Yasmin was behind Donnie on the same deck. Her husband, Joe, was helping her to get her wheelchair over the lip of the ramp Philip had constructed, somewhat awkwardly, using a wooden plank. Tiny six-year-old Zev—Jack's grandson—ran with the others. Zev hadn't had an asthma attack in months.

Marie glanced around for Rosa and Mo. "So you had a rough night?" she said to Philip.

"I dreamed about *it*." Philip had taken the cup from Bonita but had not taken a drink. His eyes were fixed, it seemed to Marie, on nothing.

"It?"

"It. Port. It was really strange. I dreamed about it the way you dream about a woman."

"The way you dream about a woman."

"Something happened to me in there."

"Okay."

The jerky came around, and Bonita took some for herself, plus Marie's and Philip's shares, and then passed it on, toward Andrea and Regina. The kids screamed and whooped. Donnie yelled. The wind changed and blew smoke into Bonita's eyes.

"Steve and Regina are taking a few families on a farm scouting mission. Apparently Lulu saw a chicken cross the road," Bonita said.

"Lulu saw a chicken cross the road?" Marie said.

"I kid you not," Bonita said. "Want to go with them?"

"I have something I've got to do at the church," Philip said.

"Like what?"

"I'll go with you," Marie said.

"No."

"Geez, fine. But maybe at least try not to fall into the port again," she said. The jerky was hard and difficult to chew, like plastic.

"Well, maybe Marie and I will go do some target practice, then. Or I'll work in the greenhouse. I've got plenty to do." Bonita's tone was defensive, and Marie looked at her and Philip quizzically.

"Steve, control your children!" Donnie shouted.

Steve smiled and waved at Donnie, pretending not to hear.

Mo came walking out of the last house on the block. No Rosa. He nodded briskly at Marie, nodded more shyly at Bonita, grabbed a small bag of jerky and a handful of blackberries, purple juice dripping, balanced two sloshing cups of tea in one arm and then wandered back to the house. Bonita and Marie watched his body grow smaller.

"Well, I guess they've finally gone and done that," Bonita said.

"Uh huh," Marie, beside her, agreed, her mouth tight.

After breakfast, half their number drove off in a fleet to a set of farms, hoping to find animals or people. Such outings were practically vacations; a rumored chicken sighting was only an excuse to break the usual routine. Marie instructed Steve on how to use his gun properly, which annoyed him, though he listened, but she stayed back with Bonita to work the garden and greenhouse.

Then, finally, Mo and Rosa came out of Mo's house. "We're going foraging," Rosa said cheerily. There was no invitation to Bonita or Marie. "And maybe fruit-picking too. Or is fruit-picking also foraging?"

"I'm coming with you," Marie said.

"Oh," Rosa said. "Okay. Ma? You wanna come too?"

Bonita, had she been born to different parents or in a different age or in love with a less domineering man, might have held a managerial position, might have run a business. She was commanding, and she knew everything. She knew at all times where each of the eighteen women in the group were on their cycles, and who was pregnant, and who was no longer giving off the reek of fertility and lived in the same calm post-menopause that she did. She knew even before a couple did that they were about to break up. She'd been the one to tell Rosa, a week ago, that Marie was also interested in Mo.

"First of all," Rosa had said, "how do you know I'm interested in Mo?"

"Oh, mija, I think you're in love with him."

"What?"

But you couldn't fool this woman.

"Don't lose your friendships over men."

"Marie's still in love with her ex," Rosa had said. "She doesn't get to own every man she likes the look of."

Now, Bonita eyed all three of the younger people. "Nah. I'm going to hang back. But you guys be good to each other," she said, turning her gaze on her daughter.

Marie found it calming to be with Rosa and Mo. And she found she wanted to set all three of them free of whatever tension existed amongst them. She wanted to say: Have sex, fall in love, leave me out of it. She felt ordinary, not being the object of Mo's attention—but so what? All that told her was how much she relied on male attention. They walked down the hill together, under the tree canopy of Caroline, past the red-brick Home for the Friendless she'd lived in with Jason, past street after street of narrow two-and-a-half-storey houses with their pointed attic lids, like rows of sharpened pencils.

"I guess all the astronauts are gone too." Rosa sighed. Now she and Mo were holding hands. Grass, with slow determination, was overtaking the sidewalks, winding its long way out from under weights of concrete and asphalt. Ants piled their homes everywhere.

"Yeah. I dunno," Mo said. His ropey dreads hung loose, and sometimes one would drag across Rosa's arm.

"Astronauts would be the first to go, wouldn't they? They're not even committed to being on Earth in the first place," Marie said.

"I guess. But we don't know how widespread this thing is," Mo said. "That's why Philip wants to head south. Think about, like, I dunno . . . Mississippi or wherever. These Bible belt states: you think these guys are just going to take off through something just because the government approves the technology? And what makes us so special? Nothing. It can't be just us. I know this city is full of self-haters, but still."

"Do you ever think about where you'd go?" Rosa said.

Marie felt that they talked about this too often. It wasn't really a game, when there were no rules. Many consequences, no rules. People pretended to several fantasies. Of course, in theory they could go anywhere at all, so PINA said, anyplace real or imagined, past or future. But most people said predictable things. There was talk about ancient Greece, ancient Egypt, the Mayans, the Aztecs, though they knew that in such places they were likely to be enslaved. ("I wouldn't mind a shorter lifespan," Marie had said once, and Bonita told her she'd better sleep off that morbid exhaustion.) Marie always gave the obvious answers: the twenties in Paris was a favourite. Andrea liked the idea of living in Hollywood in the fifties, since she secretly believed herself to have a Marilyn Monroe quality. Steve and Regina refused to say where in front of the kids, but otherwise confessed they'd travel to 1993, the year they'd met. They'd go to Nirvana and Pearl Jam concerts, follow the bands around in an RV. But they would only go if they knew they could come back again, and so they wouldn't go.

Marie thought the game dangerous precisely because each of them did in fact have in mind a particular place and time. Each of them knew exactly where they'd go, down to the minute and hour, down to the precision of what one of Jason's philosophers had called a *time slice*.

At first Marie had thought she would go back to the apartment on Caroline, a year after she and Jason were married, exactly eleven years ago. But then she reasoned that she could enter only as an observer, watching her old life without inhabiting it. Instead, she knew, she'd really go to wherever Jason and his new Maria and their children had gone, though this was a crime in several ways, an intrusion on their portal fantasy, their portal dream lives, as well as an intrusion on their marriage. She was not yet ready to commit a crime against the fabric of reality, whether or not everyone else was doing it, even if she had been willing to commit other crimes.

A stronger deterrent than her scruples was her doubt. The port was just supposed to know where to take you. People trusted PINA as if it was more reliable than God. They believed that wishes could come true, that they deserved this. They did not heed the old slogans, forgot about *Be careful what you wish for.*

People had always been stupid and full of hope, thought Marie. Despite their cynicism, everyone believed in magic.

The quiet of the downtown was a kind of bliss, at least during the day, full of warm shades of red brick and trees. The streets had been stripped of categories and priorities, and buildings that had once seemed awful for being untended or turned into halfway houses filled with bedbugs, now could be seen as they were, as sturdy, even kindly shelter, as gifts to those who might need them.

"Remember all the poor people who used to live down here? All the beggars. Where'd they go?" Rosa said.

"I *was* one of those poor people," said Mo, pretending outrage.

Marie laughed.

"I used to busk on the corner of Hughson and King."

"You mean when you were a teenager. You weren't really poor."

He didn't answer this. "Decimation would cut the population to a tenth, right? That would leave us with fifty thousand, give or take, and here we are with, like, one ten-thousandth or something. So this is an extinction. We're the mutants. We're the ones selected out. We're the ones who will survive and reproduce. The fittest for this."

"But we're not the fittest for this," Marie said.

"Proof's in the pudding." Mo shrugged.

"But none of us knows how to do anything," Marie said. "We're the least efficient possible group of people to be working together." None of them could reconstruct anything with their makeshift archives, agree on anything or plan ahead.

"And I don't know if Darwin can really apply anymore," Rosa said. "It's like trying to use Newton to explain Einstein. Our lives are happening at some other level now. I'm not even sure that I believe in the genome anymore." She stood with her face scrunched up, thinking, until Mo laughed and kissed her.

They were standing outside the once-horrible basement-dark mall at the corner of King and James, only a few blocks away from Marie's store. Marie followed Rosa's gaze and stared up at the old bank tower. It was one of the only glass towers in the city, its skin a mirror reflecting the blueness of sky floating with clouds, no longer explosive with helicopters or planes, and below that the squat mall, and then just the three of them and Gus. Stick figures, barely visible. Mo and Rosa started walking again, but Marie didn't move.

"There's something extra sad about a bus stop where the bus will never come," Mo said. He turned around. "What's the hold up?"

"Where are we going?" asked Marie.

"Down to your shop, first, to get the wagon. Or that's what I assumed."

Marie told them about the noise in the night, about the broken glass. "I don't know what I'm afraid of. I just—I looked into the grocery—and I checked it months ago, there is no port in there—but the whole thing felt both bleak and kind of alive. I feel surrounded by *them*."

"But there's no port there?" Rosa said.

"It's not just the grocery. It's—Philip's been acting strange. He was talking about the port like it was alive, a person. And yesterday— I don't know—I know there's no port in the grocery but I felt, yeah, just surrounded."

"The ports aren't alive. That's just projection," Mo said flatly.

"How do we know they're not alive, though? They don't have engines. What makes them hum?"

"I lived with a port for awhile, when Yasmin and Joe and a couple of my old pals were living here too. I mean, it was in our house with us for two months. One of my pals jumped through. Last summer. We still had electricity then, and my pal Jamesie knew a guy who was moving the ports on the black market. He'd figured out on his own how to take them apart. Maybe he'd watched a portician, I dunno. You know how it is. Opportunity is the mother of invention. Yasmin and Joe and I, and Jamesie, we were squatting in this place but some of the other neighbours were still around. They knew what we were up to, but nobody said anything. Bigger fish to fry by that point. So this guy came over to take the port out. We tipped him off to the other houses on the block that had one, and he did his pirate thing. But just before he could take it apart, Jamesie was gone."

"Why did Jamesie go then?" Rosa said.

"No clue," Mo said. "That's the thing. You cannot predict who is going to go through, and people don't really give you clues. It's like with drugs. I don't know if you've known any junkies. They're kind of thinking about them all the time, though they don't tell you that."

"That story doesn't at all prove your point, Mo. It makes the ports sound more dangerous."

"I'm saying I lived with one for two months."

"I think we have to go back to the church," Marie said. She felt close to panic. "We have to go check on Philip."

They hurried along the streets, Marie feeling more paranoid the closer they got to the church. She could tell Mo and Rosa thought she was unhinged, while she felt that they were two lovesick weights she had to drag along. She was urgently, now, afraid for Philip. Despite everything they'd witnessed, people were always full of doubt, always saying, *How can you believe that?* Marie could hear the disbelief in Rosa's voice. "It's not crazy to be afraid," Marie said. "It would be crazy to say we're safe and that nothing's ever going to happen to us. There's only so many of us and too many jobs to do. All it takes is someone getting an infection, a year from now, two years from now, when there aren't any antibiotics left. Don't they go bad? We don't have a fucking doctor. Not one nurse. All we have is Philip and his fucking CPR training."

"Hey, man, don't worry. I'm learning all I can from the MERCK Manual," Mo said.

Marie laughed weakly. "We shouldn't have been smashing windows all the time. So wasteful. We need to pool info. We need to weapon up."

"But no one is living anywhere near the stores we smashed."

"Do we know that? Do we *know*?"

"Maybe this is good," Rosa said, putting a hand around Marie's arm, trying to calm her. "If the ports are really as dangerous as you're saying, then you can stay with us instead of returning to the shop. There's power in numbers."

"*If* they are?" Marie found Rosa's optimism wearying, a hard sun and no shade. It had begun to seem like stupidity. "Philip would have stopped that chicken expedition if he were okay."

"But you never know. Chickens could help eat the bugs in the garden and fertilize the soil." Rosa looked helplessly, nervously, at Mo, seeking reassurance. "We have sunlight and water, but we need an ecosystem, right?"

"How could any chickens have got through winter?" demanded Marie. "We've been really stupid. It's a waste of a morning, chasing after a chicken. Delusional. There are no chickens without people to take care of them."

Mo nodded gravely. "No chickens where there're wolves."

"Are there wolves?" Rosa said.

"Probably. If there are coyotes and wild dogs, why not?"

"And foxes," Rosa said.

The world was enormous, thought Marie, and here they had been, pretending it was small. The trees and buildings on all sides, as if through the magic of CGI, seemed to thicken, grow longer and larger and leafier.

At last, they neared the church.

"The ambitious have set out to sea," said Marie, as she rushed towards the concrete stairs leading to the big red doors, Gus whining behind. "We need somebody with a little drive. We need to get properly organized. We need to sort out what we have and what we need and what we know, and figure out how to *do* stuff. We need to anticipate problems."

"Let's get our five-point plans," Mo said.

But Marie knew Rosa had only ever wanted love and ukulele songs. And Mo just wanted to be high. Marie could feel them dragging their heels as she marched them up the church steps.

"Everyone's a coward! Us included! We're the lotus-eaters! We are! We need to start acting like fucking human beings! Human beings should be *resourceful*. We should have our wits about us." She held the doors open wide for the others, and Mo and Rosa sheepishly entered. Even Gus hung his head.

"No one wants me to shout."

"Marie. You've been through—" Rosa tried.

"Your reactions are, let's say, a little over the—" added Mo.

"What Mo's trying to say is just—"

Marie turned away from them, her eyes alight, her muscles tense, the adrenaline from the long night driving her into a fury. "Philip! Philip!" A tabby jumped off a sill and meowed loudly, leaping past her and out the open door. Avoiding the sanctuary, but not quite aware she was doing so, Marie went down into the cold concrete basement where they stored anything perishable, where they kept baskets of squashes, and where Philip could often be found, counting and inventorying. She rattled on the locked doors of cabinets and closets, shouted his name. The other two followed quietly for a time, then broke away. Marie exhausted herself and slumped down in a corner, let her skin cool against the contact with the stone wall. Wiped sweat from her face onto her shoulder the way professional tennis players once had.

She heard Rosa calling her name, and so she heaved herself up again. "What?"

Her name rang out again. "Marie!"

She found them at the front of the church. Hands held in a wedding pose, which they dropped when they saw her. They stared at her. She wanted to spit at them, *Spare me your concern.*

"The candles are lit," Rosa said.

"So Philip's here?"

Mo shook his head.

Behind the happy couple was the glimmering port. Uncovered and beating like a heart. She had the urge to hold it in her arms, the way one cradles a hurt kitten, a lost child. Big-eyed and alone. She wanted to reassure it. She stood, staring, and took a step.

"We've been walking around in a stupor," Marie said, unable to break what felt like a gaze. "We're spending too much time taking stock." She felt as though something was reaching toward her. With a great effort she continued, "We can't afford to be so indecisive."

Mo took three big steps to the stage, jumped up, and with a surge of energy, threw a dropcloth over the port. On the carpet nearby were business cards, scattered. Each of them bore Philip's thin cursive, the same message, telling its holder to remember and to come back.

"What is it?" Rosa said. "What's happening?"

"You didn't feel it?" Mo said.

"What?" Rosa said. "Do you think that Philip went through?"

"It seemed like a person," Marie said haltingly.

"It seemed like a woman," Mo said. "We gotta get out of here."

"Oh my God," Marie said. She had the urge, an urge she hadn't had in twenty years, to cross herself.

"What? What?" Rosa said.

Mo's voice was cooing and sweet. He held Rosa's hand and turned to put his back to the port. "We gotta get out of here, babe. Marie's right. It's worse than we thought."

"It's seducing us," Marie said. There was a light at the end of the aisle from the open door, the light beyond the foyer: all they had to do was get there and close the door behind them. The light felt very far away.

"We haven't been strong," she said. "We've just been lucky."

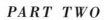

PART TWO

THE

PROFESSIONALS

Chapter
6

THE OPTIMISTS

Doors was the kind of guy who would start by telling you something that offended every single one of your sensibilities, yet by the end of the conversation, you were nodding. Brandon's mother would have called this dangerous.

But if I'm aware it's happening, Brandon argued with her in his head. *If I am just reexamining my preconceptions.* Sometimes it's wise to rebel, and other times it's better to listen.

All that zen stuff, Mom would probably say. Then: *If your friends jumped off a cliff . . .*

Pretty rich, Brandon thought, coming from one of the people who had, in effect, jumped off a cliff.

"Dreyer, are you getting this?"

Sometimes you could hear the squeak of Doors' German accent like a rusty hinge. *This* sounded like *sis. Getting* lost its final *g*. Doors was an invented last name, legally applied decades before young Albrecht could have known that he'd be the one to create—no, *discover*—portal technology. The name was meant as a metaphor for the American Dream, for doors that everywhere swung open when you nudged them with your knee. Portal technology had been fantasy back then, time travel laughable. All this was part of the official story. Brandon knew that the press's appetite for rumor and conspiracy

where Doors was concerned had no basis in reality. There were insinu-
ations of Nazi sympathies, concerns that Doors was not a true
American. By the time Brandon joined the company, the press was on
to complaining that Doors owned too much of the market, and PINA
was an unhealthy monopoly. When Brandon, early in his tenure,
explained to his boss that the word *schadenfreude* had become common
English parlance, Doors had laughed scornfully. Of course, he already
knew that. People want to see the mighty fall. This was why he lay on
so thick his immigration Dream story. Even so, Brandon knew that at
bottom, journalists and politicians had for Doors the feeling that most
of them did, the feeling one had in the presence of a movie star. They
were overawed at his daring, afraid of his power. Doors was not like *us*.
Doors wasn't associated with tech so much as with glamour and the
creation of mystique "That's what one does in America," Doors
explained to Brandon, who then gave the quote to the news outlets. "In
America, one learns to be savvy or dies. We Americans, we do not
reward good hard work—how boring!—we reward the naughty boy,
the little Huck Finn, the good troublemaker."

"Dreyer?" Doors said now. "Your notebook looks peculiar in that
you are staring at a blank page."

Brandon nodded. Then he smiled, shook his head. "Was just
thinking about how I might word it," he said. These meetings with
Doors were sporadic, and Brandon had never been a person to take
notes with pen or pencil. His hands still wished to clutch and thumb-
tap, or to pose clawlike over a keyboard.

"Just get it down, for chrissakes," Doors said. He wore his longish
black curls slicked back, his salt-and-pepper beard nearly shorn but
with just enough stubble so that it really did resemble a sprinkling of
salt and pepper across his wide jaw and its famous cleft, a period to
punctuate his face with certainty. Brandon knew that he himself was,
by comparison, goofy and unsure, with his slightly crossed eyes and
crooked smile, his body lanky and a bit clumsy. Whereas everything on

Doors' person was calibrated to give the appearance of certainty, each trait recognizable from its repetitions in the old media. A man such as Doors had been made for TV; but was he unable to thrive without his elephantine ego being fed by the endless straw bales of media representation? Apparently not: Doors was as energetic as ever.

Brandon stopped fiddling with his notebook's elastic tie and cracked his knuckles. Some of his colleagues around the table lifted their arms to check retro Timex wristwatches, all gifts from Doors four years ago when they were celebrating the failure of a smartWatch one of their competitors had introduced. The risks the other company had taken, much like the risks PINA had once taken with their phones, were useful; the smartWatch was bait thrown into battle to show whether there were any guns trained on your target. It had bombed, because, Doors believed—and the rest of the company with him—the public was tired of gadgetry. *You don't give people a thirst for novelty*, Doors said, in a refrain written by Brandon, *unless you have something novel to give them.*

There were, at the table, six men and six women, all between twenty-five and thirty-seven, a carefully haphazard assortment of backgrounds, the sorts of kids who'd been scouted from the Ivy League, mostly, with one college dropout named Benji, who had a form of slow-moving genius Doors recognized, and Brandon, who, while he'd gone to Yale, had met Doors through a friend at a party. Doors had, ahead of his peers, corrected for the overabundance of men in the PINA workforce in policies enacted a decade ago. The Ivy League was gone now, Brandon realized with a pang. There was no longer a well of elite talent from which to draw; the people left at PINA, and whatever children they'd manage to bear, were *it*. They'd all grow old together. "Loyalty is more profound than any other influence," Doors was saying. He'd been holding forth on the virtues of loyalty for forty minutes. What was Brandon supposed to write? "Loyalty" with an arrow or an equal sign pointing to "good" or "profound" or "powerful"?

He knew the point wasn't Doors' words but whatever they were being primed for, the punchline they were all awaiting.

"The fact that blood is thicker than water is irrelevant. We create our blood ties; the bonds of loyalty are a kind of magnetism." Doors stopped talking abruptly. Brandon was struck, as he often was, by the seeming innocence in his boss's gaze. People who didn't know better thought this was one of his affectations, like when Doors reached for a word he knew only in German. The deer-in-headlights look was not an indication that he was stunned, just sincere. Just this side of warm. Sometimes over a drink, Brandon would try to explain this to someone. Last night, it had been Suzanne. She'd asked, "What's it like to be in the inner circle?" And he'd said, "Let me explain something to you about Doors." He never gave away much, even after drink number three, drink number four. He might say *Albrecht* with too much throat, but mostly it was nothing he wouldn't say in front of the man himself. One took care these days to be transparently kind, as one had in the days of PINAphones, since you were always one hack away from exposure, and you knew how much of your life was being recorded and held aloft in a cloud. It felt as if everyone might be wearing a wire—an effect of the solar-powered cameras planted all over the place, with their full audio and video. There were wires underfoot and in the walls. In any case, everything he told Suzanne (or Rachel or Riya or Jenny) meant *He's like a father to me*. But this Brandon would never actually say, because there was a necessary line between sincerity and telling all.

Last night, Suzanne had been teasing. "Twelve, huh? So, who's Judas?" She had been nursing a whisky drink with maraschino cherries (the supply run several weeks earlier had been entirely focused on bars). The bar's design had been modelled after Ten Forward, the bar in *Star Trek: The Next Generation*—down to the glowing melamine bar top and the tiered chess sets only the nerdiest among them knew how to play.

"Who needs Judas in a world without Romans?" Brandon wasn't entirely sure what he meant by this, but Suzanne smiled and breathed out a smoky, dragonish laugh, and with her mouth pursed around the cherry, she had her desired effect on him. "The thing is," Brandon said, "without being a revolutionary, Doors did completely change the world."

"But he is a revolutionary, then."

Only smart, ambitious women here, and sometimes even Brandon, who considered himself a good guy, tired of them.

"You know what I mean," he'd said.

Now, in the boardroom (not really a *board* room, as there had never been a board), Doors was looking thoughtfully at his notebook. "I'll get right down to it," he said.

The room was silent, respectful, and Brandon thought it was amazing that after a year of these bogus meetings—since PINA could not be said to exist anymore—none of them had stood up to Doors. There had been, would be, no outrage. They were loyal to Doors, ready to listen and obey his command. The group was making Doors' point. They wore their neutral/pleased expressions, affect-free but not quite indifferent, even those who knew they could never go home, since home was outside the continent. All except Zahra, who was biting her lip and glaring down, and Brandon, who couldn't stop his finger-fiddling and knuckle-cracking.

"I want you to know how important it is to me that we all remain loyal to each other. You to me, yes, but also me to you. I don't ask something of you that I would not do myself. I cannot do it myself, though, as—I'm sure you'll all agree—I'm needed here, on deck."

Once in a while Brandon felt a brief stab of paranoia. It was the closed quarters, even if the quarters weren't close. It was his own doubts about Doors and Doors' sanity, and his feeling that he was the only one to harbor these doubts. Was this group becoming a cult, their leader's charisma replacing thinking? His peers looked too quiet, too still, sitting around that table. Were they, like him, disheartened? There was no reason to hold these meetings, and no one would say so. Or maybe there was a reason; maybe the meetings were held to make the rest of the population think that there was someone in charge, a group of elites making decisions, and not this: a lecture on loyalty, an exercise in obedient listening.

Even he, Brandon, Doors' closest ally, the one depended on for spin, would not ask the question. He glanced at Zahra. She continued to glare.

There was a long silence during which Doors seemed to expect a response. When he got none, he went on. "I am going to start sending out teams of four. The first team will head north. We need to go out farther than a supply run and beyond where we can communicate with each other, because we need to know what's out there. Think of it like—you'll be nomads with better facial hair." A few of them laughed weakly. "I've selected the first four of you already, but I want you all to be ready to go. All of you must have your bags packed and be ready to leave the instant I tell you to."

Yes, definitely, the group had become much more loyal and obedient since moving in here, most of them more than a year ago, since they were merely happy to have survived whatever it was that had happened. Brandon struggled to remember how pissed off and disrespectful they'd been before the move, struggled even to remember his own perpetual feelings of panic and distraction. All of that had been exchanged for this peace.

"You could just tell us now," Zahra said, her eyes on the ruddy tabletop, which gleamed with varnish. She seemed to be speaking to herself. "We need to pack a car with enough batteries and chargers, make sure the car's working . . ."

Brandon watched Doors react to this. He had spent thousands of hours with the man, stood beside him while he groomed new recruits, as crisis after crisis hit, while he watched his own face on news reports. He had even watched Doors waving his hands over touch-free keys so that the inputting of code was exactly like a conjurer's trick, though for years Doors would only code in private or not at all. Brandon had spent so many hours with Doors that he had been called by *TIME* magazine "the man behind the man." So he knew, before it happened, what would:

Nanosecond #1: Doors' face would go tight as though in pain.

Nanoseconds #2–6: Doors would smile.

Nanoseconds #7+: Out of that smile would come a Buddha-like glow of warmth and good humour.

"Yes, Zahra, everything is under control. We'll have a car ready. You have nothing to worry about, because each team will stick together." Doors stood and walked round to where Zahra was sitting, put his hands on her shoulders. (Brandon knew how those strong shoulders felt, hard as fresh tennis balls.) This forced Zahra to look up at him. Kindly, Doors said, "Any reaction you have to this demand is normal. You have nothing to worry about. We're still in our grief steps."

Then Doors glanced searchingly around the room. "Brandon," he said, calling him by his first name for the first time since the meeting had started, warming them all up, "Why don't you stay behind and talk to Zahra."

Brandon was a good pup and never said no. He tried to give Zahra a Buddha-like smile of warmth and good humour. She narrowed her eyes. The rest of the group filtered out of the room—"Hold your questions, pack your bags," Doors said in parting, with a joviality that felt off-key—and left Brandon with Zahra in front of the large bank of windows overlooking the quad.

Already the festivities outside were booming through roving speakers. Kites in magenta and green and blue—a kite shaped like a dragon, a kite shaped like a rocket ship, kites emblazoned with variations of the PINA logo—set the blue sky aglow like a stained glass window.

"It's reckless to consider the worst," Brandon said, settling next to Zahra. She was like a punished pupil, folded in on herself and facing the table. "Optimism is our greatest strength; worries are our weakness."

Silence. Those round shoulders exposed by the halter tops Zahra always wore bowed more deeply forward. She, like everyone Brandon knew here, did a lot of yoga.

"Or, if you want to play naughty student, I can be game for that too," Brandon said, putting his hand on hers.

She lifted her head. "Don't give me this bullshit. You of all people."

Brandon was aware that women liked to believe they had found something deep in him that no one else knew. Even Suzanne, for all her performances of invulnerability, believed he had revealed himself especially to her. But in fact, he had no secrets from anyone. That was the second greatest weapon: transparency. No one could uncover what wasn't covered.

"Me of all people?" he said. "Why should I be different?"

"God. Stop talking like a fucking yoga robot."

"I don't see why you would be angry with me."

She suddenly uncoiled and shook out her arms, stretching back. "For a marketing genius, you can be pretty thick-headed."

"If everyone's a genius," he said, "then no one's a genius."

"Aren't you humble."

"Look, do you just not want to go?" Brandon could not imagine this, since he himself was hoping to be one of the chosen four. "What's the matter?"

"Do you think Doors really has our best interests in mind?" She said this and looked at him cleanly, unblinking.

Doors had planned everything. Even the glitches and hiccups, which were necessary to let the air in. Each of the twelve had been selected not for their techno-wizardry but because of their control over their emotions and reactions. Brandon recognized this in Zahra's ability to calm herself: her face quickly became expressionless, her mouth unpouted itself. She could scare off tears; she never cried. Brandon met her eyes neutrally.

"If you are beginning to question whether Doors has our best interests in mind—I mean, he's not our parent," Brandon said. "We're all adults, and we're all in this eyes open."

"I guess I'm just reexamining my commitments," she said. "Checking my premises. Worry isn't weakness. Just because you or Doors says a thing doesn't make it so."

Zahra still had the slight lilting accent of her Pakistani girlhood. She had not grown up obsessed by Jean-Luc Picard and wouldn't like it now if Brandon laughed at her accidental emphasis on *make it so.* He didn't laugh. He was warm.

"Do you know that proverb? Or maybe it's a beatitude? 'Consider the lilies which neither toil nor spin and even so-and-so in all his splendor wasn't clothed as beautifully as these. Even your father in heaven.' I forget the rest. But the gist is: What do you have to worry about?"

"What's that? Jesus?"

"I think so."

"Why are you telling me about Jesus and beauty?"

"I'm not."

"We've talked about this."

"Forget it, Zee." In one high dark corner of the room beat that flashing green light. "I'm telling you there's no point in worrying."

"Maybe the point is"—she dropped her voice—"the point is that worrying makes you do something. Forces you to act."

"And what action should we take, Zee? We're only afraid of the outside world because we aren't sure what's out there. But there's no evidence of danger or malice. It's just the ports, ports that we already know so well."

"I haven't seen a port in almost a year."

"You can go and visit the one in port-hall anytime you want," he said.

She slowly shook her head, with something like disappointment.

Brandon felt sure there was something she wanted to say to him but wouldn't say. "Worry is your enemy," he repeated. "Questions are not your friend."

"Right." She'd been like this even in bed. Never stopped appraising, never loosened control. Was perpetually moving through the poses of a yoga routine. For awhile, it had been his mission to give her such an orgasm that she'd forget herself, but this had proved impossible.

She leaned in to him now and lifted her eyes. "Why is Doors asking you to reassure me? Why is it your job to ensure that we are all unquestioning? Isn't there value in thinking for yourself?"

"What?"

"Why are you sticking by him so dogmatically?"

"But this isn't dogma."

"You are just reciting platitudes, Brandon. Are you going to go pack a bag now?"

"Of course."

She gave him another hard look. She got up to leave, and Brandon moved toward the window, out of her way. A volleyball game had broken out in the quad; a white ball popped gently up, then fell.

"Let's just see," she said, eyeing the camera. "Let's see what your good friend Doors does if he thinks he's got a skeptic in his twelve. Maybe I'll disappear under mysterious circumstances."

"This is paranoia," Brandon said.

"I hope I survive it."

"You don't know when to stop."

"I guess that's the difference between us." She had said something like this while in his bed, lanky brown limbs drawn deliciously against his white sheets. *That's the difference between us.* But Brandon couldn't remember what that difference had been.

"What does that mean? I *do* know when to stop? I'm not dogged enough? I give up too easily?"

It was Zahra who left the boardroom first, door closing behind her with the programmed force of an airlock. That wall had its share of windows, too, facing the cleanly white hallway, which was empty now that Zahra had walked briskly away. Outside rose the volleyballs, the beach balls, the kites. Blue skies clear.

There would be no mysterious circumstances, Brandon thought. Up in the corner, the green light blinked off.

Air travel was no longer possible, but you could jump through a void to any time or place that you imagined. All the wealth this had brought PINA was worth nothing now; these were the contradictions of their time.

You couldn't see people disappearing, inking out, one light at a time, so everything darkened imperceptibly, turning from a city to a countryside in little over a year. He had watched it happen from the roof of his old condo, and from his once-office-now-apartment at PINA, on screens, in the data. He and Zahra had fallen in love on PINA's roof, quietly fearful and a little bit thrilled as the world ended in a million whimpers. Even at PINA, the number of employees was way down, down by nearly 90 percent from the peak, so that the main atrium was too large and cavernous and mostly abandoned, and it was possible to walk down this long hallway and run into no one.

The feeling of being alone again in a room with Zahra was like a layer of sweat on Brandon's skin, a glaze he couldn't shake as he walked toward the archive. Zahra used to like to pretend she was flailing from one affect to another, speaking to him with anger and contempt and then faux-crying and then giving him that knowing smile, as though she could hide herself beneath these thick coats of expression. And in fact, she did hide.

Maybe even she didn't know what her feelings were. Brandon knew what that was like. After all, Zahra's parents and her brothers were gone forever, and she would never find her way back to them. Just before her family had disappeared, she called her parents and spoke to them urgently in Urdu. They were wealthy, they would be okay, they would be protected from the violence hitting the streets in Pakistan, the demands made by those who thought ports were apocalypse machines, more efficient than nuclear weapons, the hostage-taking that Zahra's mother kept comparing to the French Revolution. "She keeps saying it's a guillotine," Zahra told Brandon. "I told her, of course, it's not a guillotine. She says people are being forced into it against their will. I told her it was no tragedy to go into one. She says, 'Why haven't you gone into one, then?' She says people she knows bought one and were stabbed in their sleep."

This all sounded improbably dramatic to Brandon, who had trouble fitting these hysterics into his idea of Zahra's aristocratic-seeming life. Brandon reassured her that PINA had reached peak port and the bubble would soon burst. But they were out of their depth; none of them had foreseen what port would do to the world, although their colleague Benji had believed that it would follow the same surging trajectory as had personal computer use, social media, the PINAphone, and that pretty soon everyone would adopt it. The rest of them had been skeptical even about this. The stakes seemed too high, not to mention the expense; the cost of a port installation was a few months' pay for most middle-class people.

But money kept coming into PINA; and people had disappeared so fast, there was no time to plan. While they were figuring out what to do with their wealth, airlines had died, competitors fell away, and people providing amenities, like their own personal catering company and personal barbers, stopped showing up at PINA. The morning talk shows, the evening news shows, had hammered PINA with questions about what would happen to the economy if people were leaving. *It's not American! People don't just take off to some other space-time instead of coming into work.*

"This is bigger than America," Doors had scoffed. "Is your job your life?" He had been trying to convince people that port was countercultural, anticapitalist, even antifascist, an expression of freedom. "Are you really not going to find out for yourself?"

"You perfect a thing, and then it dies." Doors had said this to his employees, and then to CNN, to the *Times*, to "The Daily Show"; Brandon had tweeted and retweeted this mantra, had managed the feeds as he always did, until nobody bothered to watch TV or write updates anymore.

"Leave San Francisco to the hippies and deadbeats again," Doors had said finally, at the meeting where they'd agreed to live on the PINA campus until it blew over. "*Fuck* Stanford. *Fuck* Berkeley. Sanctimonious elites." This was during what they began to call the third wave of disappearances. Brandon had watched the city falling apart in those final days. *You perfect a thing until it dies* was graffiti-scrawled on the refurbished factory-turned-condo across from Brandon's window. "Even the hippies won't last long without electricity or plumbing," Doors had said.

The reporters who remained demanded to know: why weren't people coming back? Everyone knew at least one or two people who had gone into the ports proclaiming that if they didn't return within a week something should be presumed to be very wrong. But still, people could not resist going. Lawsuits were filed, and Doors easily settled them, his kingly riches making him untouchable. Then subpoenas arrived, with court-dates unwisely set for many months in the future, by which time there was no court.

"Why aren't people coming back?" Brandon asked then.

"Would *you* come back?" Doors answered.

Zahra had said, "Oh, no," when Brandon had told her all the planes were grounded. It was his only clue to her grief. But he knew: grief was desperation, was chaos, and there was a Zahra with real feelings locked away.

He reached the door to the archive but kept walking. There were six bends in total, all around the half-mile mark, so that the building from above was a perfect hexagon. Suzanne, last night, had said he had a reputation for pacing. Pacing was a gesture of genius; a genius brooded and paced. But Brandon wasn't pacing out worries or mathematical problems. He was walking because he could not run. Six months ago, jogging, aerobics, Zumba, kickboxing, CrossFit and anything else that produced more than a normal amount of sweat had become taboo. He had persisted for a brief while, but when he went to get his ration of water, he was met with head-shakes and frowns. Nothing would be forbidden outright, but the feeling that he had let his comrades down was stronger than any law. He didn't want that look from the waterers.

"It's okay. I don't need any extra," he told the girl pouring out his share into bottles.

"But look at you. You'll get dehydrated."

"I'm acclimated."

"You are sweating like a pig."

These were the grandmotherly manoeuvres he was dealing with. Exertion that led to extra laundering, showering or thirst became impossible. Two decades of a near-daily running practice and all efforts at being as lean and strong as the former track-star version of himself were shot. Now he walked, a little briskly, as his mother had done in the nineties with weights Velcroed around her wrists and ankles. Walking and gentle yoga: that was it.

At bends three and six were wide windows overlooking the inner campus as well as the outer. He stood there and fantasized about a long, hard run out as far as the ocean, and then maybe a swim. He'd be happy to feel the scorch of cold water. What was freedom worth if you couldn't at least run? Another contradiction: running had been his false outlet for freedom in a circumscribed age, and in the nearly absolute freedom of today, he wasn't able to run.

Over the quad, kites caught wind, whipped against their tethers and flew.

The question of whether the group—the 996 souls who remained at PINA—would stay here permanently had been settled a year ago. A vote had been taken, though Doors pointed out that every democracy was a democracy in appearance only, controlled in ways more subtle and less transparent than any other kind of regime. Which was not to say that this democracy, here, in what Doors was now calling "Stable," was a farce; it was, he pointed out, more transparent than any other system they'd ever known, and because they knew it well, they could see its contradictions rather than be secretly influenced. It was theirs.

"There are no market forces here," Doors told them, though at that time everyone, including Brandon, was still bewildered by the fact that creating the perfect product could somehow have collapsed the economy. Often, now, Doors spoke not into mics or through filmed projections but through the buzz of gossip. He would give information to the twelve, and each of them would go out into the crowds and pollinate. His words became their constitution: *We are united in our desire for a good life. Life without want, without war, without suffering. Life enriched by good food and conversation and books and art.*

There were plenty of dorms and offices where people could sleep, so everyone had voted to stay. That day had been marked by celebratory kite-flying and drink-guzzling. In the vast atriums, auditoriums, and the bowling alley where people sometimes gathered to read poetry or sing songs, everything needed to sustain the 996 was stored. Bottled water, compostables of every shape and function, canned goods, birdseed (for the poultry garden), toilet paper, writing paper, soap, tampons, gauze, et cetera. An enormous cache of survivalist gear. People were slotted into roles that suited their skill sets and desires, although each job was temporary. You could rotate out of kitchen and garden work, as long as you took your turn, because such work dirtied the fingernails or parched the flesh. No one considered himself oppressed.

Rain barrels were positioned to catch moisture, and solar panels were attached to batteries and wires. The giant swimming pool, filled with rainwater, they used to irrigate the gardens. But anxiety about drought never left them, and was the only reason anyone gave against staying there. Arguments over time spent bathing and laundering broke out occasionally, and people hated the outhouse situation. Water was their only problem, but as Doors pointed out, and Brandon agreed, a good problem was better than a flawless machine. "Problems keep us human, and they keep us innovating," Doors said. "We need work to do."

PINA's techies knew a lot, but not so much about infrastructure. They had dozens of porticians and zero mechanics, few plumbers, few civic engineers. Now, a year in, having consumed 59 percent of the bottled water supply, people gathered in bathing suits around old water features and sponged themselves with collected rainwater. Flush toilet use was forbidden. Beside the existing group of port-a-johns outside, holes were being dug.

Thirst would not drive them mad, Doors claimed, sending out staggered search parties in a widening circle of supply destinations, to find bottled water in gas stations and convenience stores and private homes and spas and grocery stores. The searchers were instructed to be on the lookout for desalinators and plumbing supplies.

"All we lack is information," Doors had said, peering at the screens in Brandon's archive with a wistfulness that mirrored Brandon's own. "It is the only thing we lack."

The archive couldn't tell them what they needed to know: Where were the other people in the world of here/now? And what was happening in the millions of pockets port had made? But it could tell them a little. After lapping the building once more, Brandon settled into the room buzzing with machines and piled with binders, notebooks and newspapers. He had come to crave this white noise.

He sat down in the leather desk chair and went straight to the screens he'd left sleeping a few hours earlier, tapping "Nellie Young" into the search bar. The name of this writer had slipped into Brandon's mind suddenly, just that day, and he could not say what had triggered it except for a vague but increasing doubt about Doors. Long ago, before port's launch, he'd had a conversation with Doors about this writer, who had leaked some information about port that was potentially damning. "She's going to make it sound dangerous," Doors said. "Everybody's looking for an angle." But after that, Brandon had heard nothing more about it. Doors continued to insist that if people were leaving, it was because they wanted to, and if they weren't coming back it was their choice, and that the result—this good life at Stable—was wonderful. Win-win.

Results hammered in: screenshots from one of the VPs (gone), and a string of e-mails with the misleading subject line "RE: NY," which at first glance seemed to mean "RE: New York," and which Brandon normally would have ignored, assuming it had to do with their New York offices. Now he realized that NY, of course, stood for Nellie Young—this thirty-something Brooklyn novelist who'd been commissioned to write a *New Yorker* article about port. Brandon had met her once, at one of the parties Doors liked to throw for people he deemed influential. She'd been sent a pre-release port model and had written the first third of a long article, before her notes abruptly ended. PINA had acquired this work-in-progress, as well as several of Nellie Young's personal e-mails and PINAphone pics of her notes.

TIME MACHINE IN MY LIVING ROOM

Not exactly a Maytag repairman, my port-installation
technician looks fresh out of college. Acned, thin and
glaring, he tells me his name is Kevin and waits while
I move furniture in my tiny studio apartment to clear
the sixteen-square-foot area he'll need. I've dated men
like this. Smarter than me, far less interested in the out-
doors, and physically bowed by having done too much
gaming. Doesn't think to help me shove the couch out
of the way.

"Is *portician* your official title?"

"Yeah, I guess."

"Who came up with it? Is the relationship to the word
mortician intentional or accidental?" I'm on edge for some
reason. He looks at me as though I've tried and failed to
be amusing, and he won't pretend to laugh.

The port comes in a box so thin it resembles an envelope.

[The text goes on like this for several paragraphs. Nellie
and Kevin continue to have a stilted conversation, proof that
her gifts are for fiction and not journalism. Where did he go
to college? How did PINA recruit him? He installs the port
using tools she's never seen before, pulling up a fine gauze
like a curtain. She compares him to a mime.]

When I ask Kevin how—and whether—I can return
to my apartment from wherever I go, he hands me a little
remote that has since been discontinued. It has several
unlabelled buttons. He says they are working on remote
designs that users can wear like jewellery. Kevin does not
appear to share my giddy amazement, and he continues
to install this time machine.

"What do the buttons do?"

"Once you're over, you'll know how to use them. Once you've gone through."

"Have you gone through?"

Kevin looks down at his phone, perhaps taking a measurement. I can see his furrowed reflection on the glittering surface of my terrifying new possession. "This part's tricky," he finally says, and he explains to me how the port works once I'm ready to use it.

It sounds like magic, totally unreal, and it's not until after he leaves that I realize he hasn't answered my question.

Brandon only vaguely remembered the remotes, which had been presented to PINA engineers right before the launch. They had been Dawn-the-designer's idea, quickly snuffed out. Why had they been discontinued? How else would people be able to come back?

He knew that, like most PINA employees, he only knew part of the story, and very little about how port *worked*. Doors had offered explanations in his hand-sweeping way—it is highly developed A.I., it has its own power source, the *multiverse*—but Brandon did not himself know who was trusted with the essential details. The engineers, maybe, some of whom were also porticians, and whom Brandon thought of as two-dimensional, the skinny nerds who mostly kept to themselves even now at Stable, eating at their own tables and looking at others with sociopathic contempt. Probably they at least knew more than he did.

The search results that followed the article on his screen were Nellie's piecemeal, jotted notes. From what Brandon could see, Nellie had begun to feel about the port the way a person feels about a beloved pet. She compared it to the volleyball from *Castaway*, and to a childhood stuffy, and made several other pop-cultural and personal references to illustrate her point. Her final note, dated three months after Kevin's visit, read, *I think I have fallen in love.*

Peering at the pictures of her paper-scattered desk and living room, Brandon realized that someone had broken into her apartment, but he couldn't tell who, because he couldn't find the original e-mail. Who had she fallen in love with?

NY: mentally unstable? Find psychiatric history.

Has anyone found any more notes?

Last heard from NY end of March. Presumed gone.

Finally Brandon found the e-mail from Doors that spelled everything out. Hidden at first because it began a new chain, with a transparent subject matter. A surge of familial pride warmed Brandon's face. Hiding in plain sight was a classic Doors manoeuvre

Subject: Discovery by Miss Young
Friends and family,
I have found myself thrilled by the unfinished article
called "The Time Machine in My Living Room." Is there
anyone anywhere not beguiled by the prose of young
Nellie? What interests me most is her discovery that port
is likewise alluring, and the question is whether this is an
integral feature of the machine or a viral element. We all
know that even the common cold conspires to spread in
this way. Keep me abreast.
Yours, with warmth and admiration,
AD

The formal diction and lack of abbreviations were signals of Doors' seriousness. He rarely sent e-mails in those days, called himself post-text. Brandon counted seven cc'd names, five of them among the twelve, including Zahra. His own lack of addressee status drained the warmth from his face. None of the others had ever been mentioned by *TIME* magazine, let alone featured on its cover.

Brandon scribbled in his log until he was nauseated and thirsty.

It occurred to him that Doors had been encouraging him to work on this archive and must have known he'd find this e-mail. Now he recalled with dull shock how he had sometimes asked if port might have some power, like a magnetic force, that drew people to it. Doors had, again and again, assured him that everything was consensual. Brandon had felt reassured by Doors' vehemence. But now it seemed that several among the twelve had *known* that port acted on a person like a common cold. And it seemed that Doors, who'd claimed that port was only a thing he'd stumbled upon and not truly designed, had known this—Brandon glanced at the time-stamp—at the beginning of the second wave, when the U.S. population was stabilizing at around two-thirds its previous size. Which meant that Doors had done nothing to pull port off the market or to warn anybody. Nor had he apologized, just as he hadn't with other scandals that had dogged him: the factory conditions in Cambodia, in Thailand. Doors had been careful with his words, but never really apologized.

Brandon reeled, nauseated, still scribbling, until the door boomed with three knocks. He moused the windows closed, one by one, and stashed his notebook in a nearby drawer.

Doors stood in the hall. Slight smile. "Come out. Join the festivities." He put his hands on Brandon's shoulders. "We need you."

To mark the end of Year Zero, this first year together at Stable, Doors did not get up on a stage to make a speech. This was not a time for tragic heroism or ambition. What it was time for, finally, was the good life. So Doors mingled in the crowd and ate his small portion of turkey meat just like everybody else.

Brandon thought: at least they aren't depriving us of protein. Then he thought: *they?*

Tables had been placed over the turf and decorated with low-energy lighting, giving the gathering the feel of an enormous wedding. Suzanne, who was helping to distribute little Mason jars of beer, whispered to Brandon that they should start the dancing. He frowned at her, and she shrugged and sashayed with her tray over to another crowd.

Brandon had been instrumental in creating the presentation that was now projected onto the white wall of Wing One, the image wavering where it hit window glass. "The good life," said his voice over the speakers. The jumbo image of his face caught all its flaws: slightly crossed eyes, asymmetrical jaw, bald spot in the stubble. He took a big swallow of beer as the image of himself said, audio one half-second behind his moving mouth, "We hold no things to be self-evident." Big flirty smile.

Beside him, Dawn, another one of the twelve, moved so close that her arm pressed against his. "We believe in good food and smart tech. We believe that creating new tech has never been about money but has always been about making life better and easier. We believe in a clear view to past and future, to stars and to mitochondria. We believe in flexibility and optimism. We believe in changing our minds. If it doesn't work—" His image paused.

"Melt it down!" returned the crowd. People raised their Mason jars full of amber liquid.

"To us! To our health and prosperity!"

Brandon accepted the hearty clinking of jars from those standing near him on the Caf-Wing side of the quad. His face was replaced with the frozen projection of a retro PINA pineapple sporting an outrageous number of spikes.

"The problem with that old logo is that it has too much detail," Dawn said, gesturing at the screen. Five years ago, when Brandon met her, Dawn had worn a springy blond corporate bob and heavy red lipstick, but her hair now fell limp over her protruding ears. She put a tiny bite of greens into her thin-lipped mouth. "What you want," she said, "is broad strokes and outlines."

"For simplicity," Brandon said.

"Well, for simplicity, yes. But also for imagination. You want people to fill it with their own desires. Desire is the main thing."

People's faces were lit bluish by the moon- and LED-light. They were now rising from their seats at the many tables, dancing on the soft artificial turf. During the droughts of the years before port, real grass had become more taboo than smoking or gas-powered cars. This turf was already marred by dents and scratches, coming apart like an old carpet, and they had nothing to replace it with. Soon some of them would probably be enlisted to lay tile.

"Desire used to be the main thing we wanted in a good design," Dawn said. "But what is desire being replaced with here?"

There was no logo for Stable. It was only a word in a person's mind or mouth.

"With stability," Brandon said. His thin slices of turkey were complemented by a salad of dandelion greens and balsamic vinegar, and its sharp savour filled his mouth. The scent of manure wafted towards him, but they had got used to the smells of life near poultry, and without indoor plumbing or frequent showering.

The compostable plate was sagging in Brandon's left hand, so he sat down cross-legged on the turf and tried to balance the plate on his knee.

"I guess so. I haven't figured out yet what the design principles of stability would be, this sort of stability, or how one would make a logo for it," Dawn said. She laughed half-heartedly. "A few years ago, you know, I would have said, 'Who wants stability? Give me chaos any day.'"

"We're part of a corporation in the true sense," Brandon said. "From the Latin *corpus*. We're all parts of a living body, despite our stability. Stability is not unchanging."

"Latin, huh?"

Despite himself, Brandon felt a swell of emotion. He could hear in the endless night sky the whipping of wind against fabric.

He recalled an old thought experiment by the stoics to do with the question of the universe's infinitude: go to the end of the known universe and reach out your arm. Either you find no boundary in which case the universe is bigger than you knew and you must move further out, or you do find a boundary, something to contain you, which means there is something beyond the boundary. Either way, there's more to the universe than you can imagine.

"I studied Classics at Yale," Brandon said, trying to explain himself, but the words came out like an awkward brag. At a nearby table Zahra sat, still and serene, as several men he barely knew jostled nearby. They were as obvious as male birds puffing their feathers. She glanced over at him and smiled.

"But you probably knew that already," he said, returning his attention to Dawn.

"Oh, yes," Dawn said. "The whole Brandon Dreyer mythology. Doors used to tell us that you were an ideal PINA employee, because you knew so little about tech. That you came here not because of ambition, but because you were following your college sweetheart. All very adorable."

"Hmm," Brandon said, used to this, the sarcasm, the teasing, the tinge of resentment. He could feel Dawn moving away from him with a nearly indiscernible tilt.

"You're the great romantic," she said. "For me it was prestige and money. But mainly money."

Brandon didn't bother to mention the irony of all these young techies magnetized by money now finding their millions worthless: the irony was too obvious.

Dawn took a big bite of her soggy greens. "Well, in any case," she said. "I'm not like you guys. You virtuous boys in the boys' club. Higher calling and all that. It's easy to be an idealist when you aren't the one getting your hands dirty."

Brandon felt wobbly. "Getting your hands dirty?" he said.

"When we did the Testifiers campaign, we were thinking that, at best, we'd make a billion dollars, and only lose a few hundred thousand people. Not that we thought in terms of losses then. Anyway, here we are, and I'm not entirely thrilled that the world has ended."

Brandon tried to sound casual. "We really didn't do adequate testing. . . ."

"Of course we didn't! You write up the legal disclaimers and you set your product out on the open sea. See how it does. You know, all the nautical metaphors Doors loves. Sea legs, et cetera. The launch was the test."

"And here is the result," Brandon said.

"Exactly," she said.

Doors was half a field away, smiling at a few of the drink servers. He sensed Brandon's eyes on him and turned, then nodded as though giving a command. Brandon raised his glass in Doors' direction and took a sip.

"Doors loves you," Dawn said. "Doors *adores* you." She had removed her body from all points of contact with his. "You two have this completely intimate understanding. Whereas he's always testing me. Always trying to get to me, to make me crack. Years of this bullshit. And there you are with your bromance. Goddamn misogyny."

Brandon had believed—had thought they all believed—that in marketing and distributing port, Doors had only been capitalizing on a strange situation. Surely Doors couldn't have known *everyone* would buy in. He couldn't have known—clearly he didn't know—that people would not return. And now that they hadn't—except for the single alleged returnee, Kate Generato—Doors had doubled down, claiming that this made perfect sense. Why would you stay in this time of our planet's dying? Why would you come back here? Not even Benji or Dawn, the most opinionated of them, had answered these questions with the obvious: Maybe you want to see your family again? Maybe you miss your life? Maybe you feel homesick? The odds were against no one coming back. Doors would never admit guilt. Had never admitted guilt in his whole questionable life.

But, Brandon thought, telling himself to calm down, maybe people just weren't returning to anywhere near where those who remained were cloistered. People might be returning all the time, finding an empty world, and going back in.

Also: *We* are staying in this time of dying. Why are *we* staying?

The good life! The good life! This was the apparent answer, these words projected onto the building. Who knew how good life could be? How sweet?

Kate Generato was the only person they knew who had returned, a woman haunted and drunkish, stumbling to the security entrance by the lavatories, swooning into Stable like a mysterious stranger who arrives at a fairy-tale castle. They'd grilled her, and her answers had been thrilling at first—she claimed to have gone to a place utterly unlike our own, in some other galaxy, with different planetary bodies in a long night—and so they had relaxed. Brandon had relaxed. Now they need not doubt that their loved ones had gone somewhere else in time and space. Not only that, but Doors had been right: people could return if they wanted to. "How did you get back?" they had asked Kate. "How did you end up here?" But she seemed spooked, and at times claimed that she was inside her own dream. After a few gentle interrogations, when they took turns getting her food and drink as well as warm blankets, since she was always shivering, Kate Generato stayed in a room for months recovering, rarely leaving her bed. The room was right next to Doors' old office, where the first port had been—almost accidentally, according to legend—designed.

Doors' reaction to Kate Generato's appearance had been puzzling. He did not seem surprised or relieved. There had been an uptick in meetings, and in them, Doors was frazzled. Sometimes he would whip around and scream in someone's face. Benji, and then Joni, brought up the question of the test subjects (in reality, actors hired by PINA) who had become known as the Testifiers, famous for their awe and excitement, part of the enormously successful marketing campaign when port was first launched. Doors dealt with such inquiries by ignoring them and then, when Benji pushed, shouting "I don't answer to you, do I, meat-man? Why don't you find your way out of here if you don't like it?" Benji had threatened to leave, but, as Doors had predicted, came crawling back instead. Benji wanted to talk constantly about the remotes, the return technology that was supposed to be given out to all original purchasers of ports. Why hadn't we made sure—ourselves—that they worked? Even though we couldn't have predicted or controlled the unauthorized port-hopping, some people at least would have been capable of returning. There were rumors that one of the Testifiers really had gone and returned, not merely pretended to, like the others. Benji wanted Dawn to track down the Testifiers, but Dawn had told him not to be ridiculous. It was impossible! Everyone knew they were actors, they had signed complicated contracts, the legal department was shredded, the Testifiers were gone. Benji was becoming paranoid, as they all were, knowing so little.

Brandon thought of the woman he had seen walk into a port on a stage. How much trust everyone had then, the way you trusted a magician not to saw through an actual body.

And now, thought Brandon, there was the Nellie Young e-mail, the one suggesting that port is like the common cold; port influences people's behaviour; port is therefore, somehow, alive?

The clues had been there, waiting for Brandon to put them together. Maybe it was irresponsible to release a product when its creator didn't really understand it, but that was the sort of irresponsibility that made the consumer world go around. Upsetting Brandon now was that Doors did not tell him what he suspected or what he knew. Brandon was not in the inner circle; he only believed he was. Did Dawn know this? Did Zahra?

"It's practically a marriage," Dawn said.

"Huh?"

"Brandon plus Doors equals . . ."

Brandon had drunk too much beer. The walls were tilting, his senses dulling to a pleasant blur. Around him people were rising from their seats as though about to float beautifully into the sky. They gathered in the middle of the quad, dancing and jumping and singing and shouting. Music floated out of synced robotic sound systems cutely built into sunglass-wearing teddy bears that buzzed around on the turf like fuzzy little R2D2s. Someone had replaced the retro PINA logo with old videos of pop songs, preceded here and there with ads for defunct companies. Everything was defunct; there was no Internet; the video cache was infinite.

"Even if Beyoncé is still out there somewhere, there will never be another album," Dawn said with exaggerated wistfulness. "Wanna dance?"

"Nah," he said. "No thanks. I'd rather watch for now."

He took her sagging plate and she spun her reedy body out into the crowd. There was a higher than average number of nerds and wall-flowers in this group, and the dancing was stilted, but Suzanne and Co.'s magic moonshine helped. The stars above gridded into constellations Brandon could no longer identify. During his Canadian boy-hood, his parents had taken him camping and given him names. The dippers, of course, and Orion with the three-starred belt. But no longer were the moving lights of airplanes overhead, as there had once been, as there had always been.

The breeze cooled his sweat-beaded neck. If any satellites were still picking up signals, if anything still surveilled, perhaps it would see this warm and lit quad as a haven in a darkened world.

"Quite a night," Doors said, sidling up to Brandon. "I still regret the Mars failure, of course, as I—as you know—regret all failures. But to end up here in this place of great welcome and hospitality that we created—well, it seems right and fitting, doesn't it? It seems poetic, doesn't it, Brandon?"

"It's poetic," Brandon confirmed.

In all interviews, Doors gave the same cryptic answers to the same questions. If someone suggested that "DOORS" was what he should have named the company, he had a ready response. Why name it for a sweet fruit? the interviewer might press. Why choose such an un-tech biotic shape to represent the most advanced silicon tech available to man?

—Exactly, Doors would say. Precisely. [At which point, the reporter would refer to his Cheshire grin.]

Q: Detractors have claimed that the name PINA did not come to you in a dream but in an adolescent drug-induced haze. Detractors have claimed that when you arrived in Los Angeles, you saw the palm trees and believed they grew pineapples.

—Who are these detractors? [Laughter.] I want their names and addresses.

Q: Where did you come up with the name?

—Let me say this. Have you ever examined a pineapple? Have you ever taken a pineapple in your hands and lifted it to the light and given it a good, strong look? A close look?

Q: Is that a real question?

—Let me just say these two things. One: there are no accidents. Two: a person who cannot look closely cannot invent. A person unwilling to fiddle will fail. Everything is discovery, and nothing is invention.

Doors followed Brandon around a crowd of maniacal dancers to another table, where, after dumping their compostables in the wheelbarrow, they tore off hunks from one of the enormous bread loaves made from the nearly extinct bags of flour. Zahra was still within view, watching them with her big eyes.

Doors smiled at him. "I'm proud of what we've done here." In lieu of a speech, Doors would often give his remarks to Brandon, counting on him to spread them around. "This really is the start of something."

"I'm hoping you'll choose me for the mission—or the voyage," Brandon said abruptly. "What are you calling it?"

"Ah, is Mr. Dreyer getting restless? Does Mr. Dreyer suffer from wanderlust?"

"A little. Yeah, sure. Of course," Brandon said. It was difficult to meet the man's eyes. What would he do if he suspected Brandon was having doubts?

"You talked to Zahra this afternoon?"

"She's got questions, and, frankly, so do I."

"I love it when you are frank," Doors said. "But don't forget, also, that curiosity killed the cat."

Did curiosity really kill the cat? had been one of Doors' favorite slogans, one of his own additions to the ad campaigns. Brandon's face was warm, his feet prickly with discomfort. "Did it?" The man didn't mean a thing he said. "Curiosity built the world."

"True. Okay. We'll agree to disagree." Doors spoke casually, as though nothing were at stake.

A series of shrieks and hollers rang out, then a conga line formed and began to snake around the table.

"This is fucking beautiful," Doors said.

Brandon nodded. Zahra, at her nearby table, nodded back at him, as though to encourage his conversation with Doors.

"I'll go in the next group," Brandon said. "You'll put me in the group."

"What if I need you here?"

"I want to see it for myself."

"You want Zahra to see you as a hero."

"Maybe."

"We'll talk about this later," Doors said. "Get up. Get up." He raised his hands in his conjuring way, as though a touch-free screen were within range, and a few more people lifted out of their seats. Suzanne broke from the conga line and took Doors' arm and the two of them cha-cha-chaed away.

Back when Brandon still had some influence over Zahra, she had told him that thirst was the reason people believed in God. Desire doesn't go away. And thirst was more primitive than any other desire. You can't make water.

"Doors' worst nightmare," Brandon said. "To imagine that there is anything he cannot reproduce."

"Doors doesn't have nightmares," Zahra said. "It's what makes him dangerous."

"Doors knows his limitations."

She had snorted at this. "You can't create a thing like port and not have it go to your head. His ego is untrustworthy now, if it ever wasn't. Every great leader, inventor and CEO has been a little psychotic. Certainly delusional."

Brandon resisted her ideas about Doors, but a germ of suspicion was worse than a seed. It spread before you could root it out or deprive it of water.

"Doors probably thinks," she said, "that he *could* make water."

Brandon had shaken his head. One of the first things you asked if you were studying Classics and Philosophy is how to be certain that anything was real. "Maybe we're brains in vats," Brandon said, referring to a famous thought experiment. His favourite, the problem of not being able to know whether things were real. This was also the favourite of his *Matrix*-loving, then *Matrix*-hating geek friends at Yale. Brandon had always thought people *were*, sort of, brains in vats: brains seated in the fluid of the body, joysticking the limbs and face around from some deep and inner place that couldn't quite see itself. Doors had said that eventually tech would come full circle and return to biology, and that what we thought of as biology was just some other nerd's sophisticated tech from a far-gone past.

Zahra was, in those days, still inclined to kiss him. She did so, luxuriously, and he put his hand on the fine smooth line of her jaw. The kiss, the fact of her body: had they been lies, too? "The question is," she had said, "are we safer with Doors or through the port?"

"Do I want to be here?" he asked himself now, after midnight, the party still booming and chugging its muffled way through the layers of glass as he made his way back to the archive. Going over the notes again would surely confirm that he'd overreacted, seen nothing at all. There would be no mysterious circumstances.

In the darkened stairwell, Brandon knocked into Suzanne. Silvery moonlight coming through the outer windows illuminated her fetal-curled body pushed up against the wall of the third-floor landing.

"Why aren't you at the party?" He sat down next to her, awkward and unfamiliar despite their several nights of intimacy.

"I don' party," she said.

"Kind of seems like you do."

"Immalacholic, Peter. Peter, I don drink."

"Brandon. And I was drinking with you yesterday. And you're drinking right now."

"Onedayatatime."

Darkness surrounded the buildings. The outer glass was soundproof, but he put his ear to it anyway, thinking that he might hear the hoot or howl of something out there in the ever-expanding wild.

"I'll help you to your room," he said.

She grunted. He lifted her by the armpits to standing and then hoisted her over his shoulder.

"Yerstrongerthanyoulook, Peter," she moaned into his ear, as he lifted his heavy feet up one stair and then another.

"Brandon."

"BrandonBrandonBrandon. I bet you like it. Like this. Caveman."

He flopped up a stair, up another stair, Suzanne's dead weight pinning him down. Was there a woman in Stable who wasn't pretty and fit and of reproductive age? Was that, too, part of Doors' plan? He finally got her to her room and tapped it open with the card he found in her back pocket.

No, not all the women. Sandra, he counted, Becky and Georgia: all grandparents. Plus married couples, dozens of children.

"Thisprettymuchexactlylikecollege." Suzanne slumped into her bunk.

"Only nerdier." Brandon went to the window and winked her blinds closed, though no one was out there. "It's like some nerd's wet dream."

On the bed, Suzanne muttered and moaned. "Kiss me," she said. "Caveman."

He stood above her. Her eyes were closed, her mouth moving soundlessly. "Good night, Suzanne." He shrouded her in a thin blanket and then stepped into the hallway, ensuring the door was locked behind him, just like a gentleman.

Chapter

7

THE INVENTORS

Port was never supposed to succeed.

It wasn't even supposed to make a difference to the decline of the age. But the last breaths of the gasping economy had been accompanied by a sudden surge in product development. This was mainly because of funding from a government that was finally terrified. The climate had once again become an enemy, as though a pantheon of angry gods had arrived to punish man for his—not hubris, but stupidity.

PINA had been trying to buy rights to any technology that might save the world. Technologies to make Mars livable were the most exciting ones. More depressingly, many people had concluded that the world could not be saved except by drastic cuts to population. Some fanatics had reintroduced the language of eugenics, but this was forbidden inside PINA. Famous for his humanitarian-environmentalism, Doors had his employees' e-mails and phones tracked, and people were fired or given sensitivity training upon discovery of keywords like *weed out* or *sterilize* or *higher IQ* or *better genes* or even *overpopulation*. That this process of selecting the bad seeds in the PINA population resembled eugenics in analogy (though not in fact) was not, according to Doors, ironic. Praise poured out in media headlines: "Albrecht Doors Heroically Stands Up Against Eugenics" and "PINA Helmsman Cares About Your Future" and, with less flourish, "Company Not Population, Says Famous CEO."

Doors was reluctant to be called a CEO, with its almost universal connotation, by then, of corruption and laziness. He protested that he had not grown slovenly with success; there were no concubines feeding him grapes. His still-sharp genius was behind early prototypes of the CarbOskin, designed for plugging your PINAphone or knockoff directly into your skin, where it would use stored caloric energy to charge; and the BioBark, which inhaled carbon dioxide and converted it to energy. In retrospect, Doors said, the apocalypse could have happened a hundred different ways: aside from the many climate-related possibilities, people in their abundant stupidity could have replaced trees with BioBark. Or the overproduction of CarbOskin, instead of solving the obesity epidemic might have caused people to drastically over-farm. What had happened with port had been the best of all possible outcomes. This Doors proclaimed with practiced optimism.

And what had happened happened only because of that optimism. Not everyone in those days believed in the multiverse. Not everyone, not even the physicists, agreed that overlapping universes or dimensions, or whatever you might call them, explained quantum behaviour. And physicists sometimes got tangled up in the names for things, the precise definitions; this is what allowed Doors to step in. Doors didn't just think; he acted. He tried things before the math was worked out. He was not concerned with nuances, such as whether to designate certain masses as planets or debris. So he took what little he needed to know about quantum particles and dazzled with ideas. He was known to wax on about how quantum particles, these smaller-than-microscopic furballs, behaved so strangely: they seemed to communicate with one another from enormous distances; they could be in two places at once. When delivering a talk he raved over the possibilities that these paradox-exploding particles represented: everything was random, and nothing was.

"The other scientists are in a childish snit, wringing their hands, Brandon," Doors said backstage, after he was done. "But I know we can *make* a quantum computer. Everyone wants to *prove* things. But the more interesting question is what this might mean about reality. What it might mean if the quantum world is real, and we are a projection. If it is real, and *we* are not."

Unlike so many others, Brandon had never feared the blaze in Doors' eyes, or the obsession that led Doors to live at the PINA offices instead of in his mansion on the coast, where he might have been throwing Gatsbyesque parties with all the luminaries of the time.

One night, as the story went, alone in his office in the expanse of buildings that was very much like a compound, Doors was conducting an invisible orchestra with his touch-free keyboard—("the *elegance* of it, Brandon!")—and had taken several hits of high-grade ADHD meds, when the meaning of his name hit him. *Doors*. He was surrounded by prototypes, by a thin arch shaped out of CarbOskin and BioBark that he had, a few days earlier in a fit of whimsy, combined. At first the three-foot high arch had throbbed a little, as an aroused body does, he thought, responding and rising to touch, and then not much had happened for a while. Doors sat in his office, baroque organ music pounding out of speakers, until he noticed, suddenly, that the prototype was communicating with him. He was confronted with an ancient problem: Was it inside my head, that voice I heard; or did it come from without? He dwelt on this even as he considered the command, the urging idea: *So lay another screen along it*. He sat there with the touch-free screens at his bidding, awaiting input for the commands he'd been building toward all afternoon—and those screens, too, were throbbing expectantly, in their way. *So we lay another screen along it*, he thought, dropping commands into the touch-free keys. Doors had always been the kind of chef to mix first, measure never. *Doors*. He was thinking A.I. He was thinking biotic A.I. He was thinking: here it is, maybe, here it comes, the singularity. The A.I. is beautiful, and it can speak, and it will be our glory. And then again, he was thinking *doors*.

He went to one of the labs with his not-yet-fully-formed-thought (Doors, Doors, Doors), humming, singing, jumping down the stairs three at a time. He grabbed mice and rats from the experiments, thus ruining those experiments. Running back to his office, box of rodents under his arm, he pointed at the surveillance cameras blinking at him on their thin necks. "We're not scientists, we're inventors, dammit! Science has gotten us exactly nowhere! I'll get us somewhere. Doors will bail you all out!" He said these words aloud, maybe, or maybe he thought them. Thoughts were streaming through his mind, now. He had fucking *solved* the problem of energy use, and he *knew* that the universe was multiple, even infinitely multiple, and so of course, of course! Now the machine had the ability to generate its own power, the converting adapting power coupled with the quantum knowledge, and all you had to do was make the machine biological—already it knew how to think—and what was a person but a member of a cognitive system who obeyed algorithims and believed in its own uniqueness—here it was, the solution to all problems—

Mouse 1 scurried around in circles under the arch-shaped prototype for a few minutes.

"Ah, you are confused, my good rodent?" Then, while Doors was watching, it disappeared. Vanished. No trace. He touchlessly tapped in commands, searching, and got the same result. Mouse DNA: zero. Mouse DNA: zero.

No trace? "Speak to me," he said, and heard nothing. Tried another mouse and a rat, and then, faced with the enormity of his discovery and his certainty about what had happened, he stood up and went to the window. Moonlit greenery spread out endlessly toward the far-off lights of the city. The universe was so vast that the ocean was by comparison a puddle, a droplet, nothing. He looked back at the shimmering skin-thing he'd sculpted. A tree in some new and wonderful garden. He nursed his high and turned it over in his mind. Being alone with knowledge no one else had was the best thing there was.

He had made a *door*.

"But it doesn't make any sense."

Doors called his (then) group of nine together for an emergency meeting the next morning. He was still wild-eyed, pupils barely points, irises oceanic in their blue. He was dishevelled and smelled of the splash of mint cologne he'd used to poorly mask his body odour, and now he swung around to stare at Benji, the one who'd spoken. Benji with his builder's body, biceps and pecs swelling pouch-like beneath his thin v-neck tee.

"It doesn't make sense, Al," Benji said.

"Al? Is that what you're calling me now?"

"Pardon me, um, sir. But how could the COs and the BB combine with TFT to make, well—what? A portal to another universe?" Benji gulped.

"My God, Benji! My God! You want this to make sense? I am telling you the *singularity*—I am telling you that what you think of as sense is already obsolete!" Doors collapsed into his chair and buried his face in his hands for a full five minutes, during which the others attempted to communicate via barely audible whispers, shrugs and nose-wiggling.

"I've never seen him like this," Brandon whispered to Zahra. They all worried about his drug use and his delusions.

Zahra widened her eyes.

Benji shook his head, then shrugged.

Finally, Dawn, in one of her power-suits and power-bobs of yore, said hesitantly, "Well, if this is true, it could be the invention of the millennium. I can't think of another thing more potentially world-changing."

"The wheel, fire, mathematics, air travel, rocket ships," said Benji, counting on his thick, squat fingers.

"Glad you mentioned those," Doors said, finally lifting his head. "Because fire and mathematics, those weren't inventions, right? Those were discoveries. Did not a god named Prometheus come out of the heavens and hand the fire right to us? If you think of a door to another universe being an accidental discovery, then it makes perfect sense. If you think maybe this is a gift? If the universe is a multiverse, perhaps there must be access points? Reality is flimsy."

"But we're not saying," said Benji. He and Dawn were the only two willing to contest Doors back then. ("That's Benji's value," Doors had said to Brandon on more than one occasion.) "Surely we're not saying that this portal just happens to be in the middle of your office, right? It can't be place-dependent, if—if—we're saying this is happening. Because the odds of that are staggeringly small."

"How do we test it?" Dawn said.

"I did test it. I tested it fifty times last night. Mice, rats and then a raccoon vanished whole."

"How'd you find a raccoon?" Brandon laughed.

Doors winked at him.

Brandon had the feeling of being at a museum after closing. Most of the programmers wouldn't be in for several hours. There were long shadows on the still-dewy turf of the quad.

"Then all we know is that they vanished, right?" Dawn said.

Doors stared at her. Brandon knew he hated her getups, the high-heels and blazers, which he thought too prim and old-fashioned for PINA "Yes. And?"

"Well, we don't know where they went."

Doors walked to the window. "We have our best guess."

"Other worlds is our best guess?" Benji said.

Doors glared at him, a look that Brandon knew, from experience, meant, *I'm the genius, remember. Don't fuck with me.*

"Another possibility is that they were destroyed," Dawn said.

"Destroyed as in killed? Are you suggesting that I murdered fifty innocent mammals last night?"

"Fifty?" Joni gasped.

"He's hysterical," Brandon barely whispered. They stood around the table, bodies still, as though worried that movement would catch the eye of a predator.

"Listen, you fuckers. Without me, there would be no PINAphone, no CarbOskin. I mean, there are some problems with the CarbOskin. So it needs to be retooled. My point is: You need to trust me when I say I can see what is happening here. Vision. This is about vision. Which you either have or you do not."

Brandon couldn't help his laughter. Doors was a drunk uncle, or he was a genius. It was contagious, and soon they were all bent over, chuckling and giggling, squeezing out tears, cramping in the gut. *What if! What if this were true!*

"Listen, you fuckers," Brandon said in his best imitation of Doors' accent. Part of Brandon's role as good puppy was to keep things fun, to keep them light. Doors' eyes alighted on each of the nine in turn, but he did not correct them as they grew more hysterical.

"I can't stop laughing," Dawn gulped, whispered. "Why can't I stop?"

Doors left the room with a wave of the arm that meant they were to follow, which they did, falling into line behind him, still aftershocking with laughter, which died into strange somber quiet as they stood silent in the elevator, Doors' odour filling that small space, daring them to wince. They marched silently down the hall to Doors' office and piled in, surrounding his immense worktable.

Doors barked at Benji to move.

"What?"

Doors peeled what looked like a film of dried glue off Benji's triceps. "Stay away from the prototype! Sometimes I wonder how I hired such a meathead."

Benji rubbed at the spot on his arm and slinked around to the other side of the room. Zahra was now closest to a barely visible archway.

"Dawn, you come with me. The rest of you, stay here and wait."

Later, Dawn told the others that this exercise was an example of Doors' cruelty, but none of the rest agreed, because none of them liked Dawn's super-corporate, serious-suit deal either.

They waited for several minutes, long enough for most of them to pull out their PINAphones to take a photo or thumb in a quiet notation—and while they had the phone out anyway, to check e-mail, feeds, clips. They were hunched over these little screens when Dawn and Doors returned. Dawn was struggling to hold an enormous mammal— a fat beige body—which scratched and tore at her blouse like an infant trying to feed. When it finally scratched her across the clavicle with a little black paw, she screamed and let it go. Then they saw the bandit face.

"You've got a raccoon trap out there?" Benji said. He was the only one who hadn't been thumb-scrolling. He'd continued to feel around on his arm like a child who'd been slapped.

The raccoon stood frozen on its hind legs, blinking at them rather humanly, and, as though it had a nervous tic, running its fore-paws over its snout again and again.

Doors shook his head. "Look at you idiots on your phones. You just proved how successful this could be with only the barest amount of spin. All right, little guy," Doors said, scooping the animal up. He and the raccoon looked into each other's faces, and the creature calmed—slowed its blinking, stopped its pawing, did not struggle against this forced embrace. "Let's make history."

Doors deposited the animal onto the floor in front of the shimmering arch. It only took a few seconds to step, gingerly, under it. "Consensual, I told you," he said, turning back to Dawn.

All eyes were fixed on the space there; all hearts pounded.

"Three, two, one," Doors said and snapped his fingers. The raccoon was gone.

Brandon slept until noon. Sometimes he thought he still smelled Zahra's musk in his sheets and on the pillows. This was not impossible, since the group laundered so infrequently and used only the thinnest, most biodegradable scent-free detergents. Zahra had called his admiration for her puppy love, so perhaps he was like a hound for her, nose trained on the alluring balance of her pheromones. Of course, by "puppy love" she meant to demean, to tease, and to keep him in his place.

"I'm thirty!" he had told her. "Eventually love is just love."

"Software engineers never fall in love," Zahra said. "Neither do programmers."

"I'm neither of those things!" he said. It was only later he understood. *She* was a software engineer. *She* was a programmer.

He was still staring at the white ceiling with its huge vent, which marked its previous existence as an office, when there was an urgent knocking at his door. He answered, and Suzanne nearly fell into his foyer.

"Hello," she said, steadying herself and then curtsying.

"Why were you pounding like that?"

"I'm a very energetic knocker." She walked in and plopped into his red faux-leather chair, a copy of the red chair they all had. "I really wanted to thank you. I know you could have taken advantage of me last night, and . . ."

"Oh, come on, Suzanne."

"But really. I appreciate it."

He turned on the console to start some water for the coffee beads. "Are you really an alcoholic?"

She stared at him.

"But why would you work in the moonshine department?"

"Moonshine department!" She threw her head back, laughed. "You guys have no idea what we do down there." When she said *down there*, he pictured the coal ovens of a ship. "I work on the kitchen side of the garden. I'll give you a tour if you want."

The water sounded a ding, and he poured two cups of what tasted almost like an Italian espresso.

"Listen, B." She was wearing a long skirt slit up to just below her hip, and it fell open to reveal a luscious thigh. "I need to know if you're into me, because if not, I've got to find someone else to waste time with."

"I'm into you," he said.

"But you know what I'm really asking, right?"

He squinted at her and took a sip of his coffee. He thought of this as his Marlboro Man affectation.

Suzanne said, "You are so weird-looking. I mean, you're a catch, sure, you're a good guy, would make a good partner and father and all that, but you're not, like, you're not a movie star or anything."

"So this is your land-a-man strategy, phase two: insult the meat?"

She had taken a big sip of coffee but, forced to laugh, spit it all back into the mug. "I guess we should talk about this later. You've got lots of good things going for you. Not a bad body. Good teeth. Witty."

Brandon reddened and turned away from her toward the window, which, thankfully, was not currently reflecting his expression. "Some things you don't say out loud to a person's face, Suzanne."

"Oh, explain it to me."

"Hey, you're the one who's all about honesty this and transparency that."

"Fine. You're right. Doors wants us to, like, settle down. Have babies. Plus couples are a better use of space. Frees up rooms."

At the mention of Doors, Brandon bristled. "We have more than enough rooms. He's just into symmetry. And about three-tenths of the time, he's full-on bullshitting."

Suzanne stared, startled. The door was still wide open, and the possibility that someone had heard these words made Brandon's stomach lurch.

Suzanne stepped back and kicked the door closed. Then she grinned. "Three-tenths of the time?"

"He just likes the idea of people settling down, because this is supposed to be a new age of stability! Rah, rah, rah!" Brandon gestured like the lead baton-twirler in a parade.

"You've gone bananas. Two days ago, you were singing the man's praises. The man who'd changed the world."

"Listen. I just found something in the archive, and I'm still digesting it. If you'll—" He was going to ask her to leave, but in a few sharp nanoseconds, he saw her face register intense curiosity and arousal, until she rearranged her expression to look simply flirtatious.

What move now? She would want to hear what he had to say—for what reason he still did not know—and to appear indifferent to it. As though she was just some girl from the moonshine department! Really, she wanted to hear those deep secrets, his secret resentment of Doors. Possibly only because it was excellent gossip. Her only move would be—yes—here it came:

"You just need to relax, Brandon. You've been working too hard." Closer, closer, touching his leg.

"You ever have sex with Doors?" He could see the answer in her face. "What do you call him in bed?"

"I don't kiss and tell," Suzanne said, pouting obnoxiously, a hand still on his thigh.

The difference between them—he and Suzanne, himself and Doors, himself and Zahra, himself and 98 percent of the population—was that Brandon couldn't lie. He was transparent. He had no gift for intrigue and could not now ease into some kind of fake sex where they would both use each other, making power moves, making knowledge moves.

Should he also be suspicious of sweet Suzanne?

He pushed her hand away.

It must have seemed like contempt, because she said, "Well, fuck you, then," and left the room.

Chapter
8

THE PERSUADERS

A few days after port's release into the wide world, with first-round launches happening simultaneously in the major cities of Europe, North America, and the Pacific Rim, Doors had barged into Brandon's office. He opened an article on his phone, handed the phone over, and sat on the couch, eyes squeezed shut. Outside, the sun was coming up on the bluish horizon, orange bleeding out from behind the wall of mountains.

Brandon stood by his desk; he had already read the article, but he took Doors' phone and glanced down at it.

"No publicity is bad publicity," he said.

Doors opened his eyes. "This is not about publicity. This is far beyond publicity. I'm not just some hack with an app!"

"I know."

"This is my life's work. This is my legacy. It doesn't seem to matter what I give to these people! Press releases and speeches and glad-handing and donations. All the fucking philanthropy, and still they hate me."

"Uneasy lies the head that wears a crown . . .?"

"Don't try to placate me with your allusions, Brandon, no matter how apt. I don't want you to talk me down. I want you to fix this. People don't understand port at all! They're afraid of it! They think it's—What's the wording she uses?"

"Ethically questionable?"

"No. Yes, but what's the other one?"

"Possibly evil?"

"Yes." Then, "Possibly evil, Brandon? Possibly evil?"

"People will always think what they want. You can't stop them thinking it. But their behaviour's another thing, right? Just like with the PINAphones. *What are they doing to our brains? Are they killing the bees?* And yet everyone bought one, right?"

"But then we're the ones who are ethically accountable. Since we know better than they do." He moaned again.

"Doesn't matter. Can't change it now. Can't put a rabbit back into a hat."

"Is that really an idiom? Of course you can put a rabbit back into a hat. That's all the magicians are doing. Pulling rabbits out, stuffing rabbits back in."

"Hm. Yes." Brandon handed back the phone. "You're right. That made no sense."

Brandon went to the counter, spooned some espresso grounds into a metal filter and began making two cappuccinos. "We make things. We devise things. It's not our job to ask the ethical questions. So now the politicians are doing their job. The reporters are doing their job."

"They are incensing the public, that's all. To get clicks. It's sickening."

Brandon sighed. For years he had been working Doors' persona. Doors did and said things, and Brandon disseminated the spin. When the documentary *Behind Every Door* came out, when rumours arose that Doors had impregnated and abandoned a princess from a small island nation, when people suggested that he was criminally hard on his employees, and of course, when factory conditions in developing nations were exposed, it had been Brandon's job to face the media, to show the world that Doors was, while not a softie, a great leader who inspired the loyalty of those who knew him. He did not say that this loyalty was mostly due to the fact that Doors took so many risks and made his company so much money. It was Brandon's job to call the public puritanical or to insinuate that reporters were shallow or had done poor research. It was his job to subtly discredit the filmmaker who had claimed that the intensity of Doors' eyes was the result of a severe dependence on amphetamines.

"Port is not about ethics—port is neutral," Doors said. "PINA is neutral, at worst."

Lifting his cappuccino to his mouth, Doors was at his most vulnerable. Like a small animal at a dish, big-eyed and thirsty.

"We don't need to worry about it," Brandon soothed.

"But this journalist is calling for a full investigation! She says the Testifiers might have been lying. And you know we were sloppy. We got caught up in our own enthusiasm."

"Our enthusiasm is our greatest asset."

"People are pouring money they don't have into buying ports."

"Too late in the day to feel guilt about that sort of thing."

"The protesters have already started gathering, Brandon. Look out your window."

"Okay," Brandon said. "I see only two or three."

"Two or three at six in the morning. This is not a good sign."

Doors took a dainty sip of his drink, while Brandon stood staring through the lenses at the world beyond them. Security had thinned, and the smooth outer walls near the road were not climbable but not barbed with wire either. "We should get some men on the parking garage entrance," he said. "Or they'll be inside."

"Oh, let them come if they will," Doors said.

Brandon watched an old yellow school bus full of protesters pull up to the gate. Other lives went on all over the world without Doors, without him.

"You need to contact her," Doors said. "That writer. Rebecca What's-her-name. Brandon. You must."

"Okay," Brandon said, though he knew that she would only ask for an exclusive interview, a chance to see the grounds, and that whatever she wrote would change nothing.

"We might have done more testing. They're right about that." Doors sighed again. "We need to start thinking about getting off-grid *now*. While we still have a choice. Who do I contact about that?"

"I'll find out."

It occurred to Brandon that he had never known the man outside of enormous wealth and fame; Doors was already a phenom when they met. It was impossible to see in him the boy he'd once been, to imagine him as anything other than his present self. Fame and power created a mask; nobody, not even Brandon, could see under it.

Doors leaned over, wincing. He put the cup down on the smooth, modular table in front of him. "Do you know that I spent weeks with a port in my bedroom, in my office, that I rarely left its sight?"

"Its sight?" Brandon and his colleagues were used to Doors' personification of port by now; they gently mocked it. Doors ignored this.

"Have you ever had a vision before?"

"You mean like a hallucination?"

Doors frowned. "Let me tell you what I am fully confident about. I want you to listen carefully, Dreyer. The ports are not evil. They are not annihilating human beings or any creatures. How could that happen so quickly, with no trace? How could the ports, without the aid of radiation, do such a thing?" He stood up and walked to the window, picking up the PINoculars Brandon had left on the sill and putting them to his face. "The problem is the lack of a way to communicate once you get through the port. If not to come back, at least to send word. It's the only thing we need to iron out. Ian in research has the remotes all ready to go. We have some time, right, we have time? If there was a way to haunt your family members or whoever you left behind . . ." He laughed in a way that invited Brandon to laugh along.

"You spend some time with a port," Doors said, "and you realize that you aren't reading it. It's reading you. Who would we be to get in the way of something so incredible?"

For a moment, the reality of the room seemed to waver. Brandon could see through the scene, through Doors—into what? Madness?

Doors clapped a hand to Brandon's face. "Well, thanks for this. This was helpful. We did all we could, right?" As he stood and readied to leave, he reassembled slowly into the public face Brandon knew so well. His eyes bored into Brandon's.

"Right," Brandon said.

Now Brandon splashed himself with water, dabbed on a little mint cologne and left his room. There was no one in the high-ceilinged hallways. Along the way, he saw a few empty jars left on the bamboo flooring, and in the quad, one teddy-bear-speaker remained, shuddering its way around the tables. He picked up his pace, emboldened by the fact that people were still in the process of rising, that there was no special reason to rise. Only New Year's yoga at two, and the commencement of a fast for those interested, a diet of greens and beets to announce to one's cells that a new year had begun. He walked quickly to the first stairwell and pushed open the door to the second floor with unnecessary vigor. He found room 222, knocked, jiggled the handle and knocked again. When there was no answer to his several attempts, he flashed his key over the lock and let himself in.

He had seen the inside of this room only in the surveillance videos. Doors had shown him the footage: Kate Generato, who never left her bed. Kate Generato who claimed to have seen the other side and to be ill, who could not tell fiction from reality. Brandon and his colleagues knew nothing whatsoever about this woman. Her name sounded fake, that was for sure. She might have ties to any number of organizations, and she might have a history of mental illness. There was simply no way to know. They'd agreed, many months ago, that it was best to proceed as though she were a CIA operative and to keep her locked in. She'd be well fed, watered, cared for, but until they could figure out who she was and what her presence meant, she'd be a kind of captive.

Brandon had seen her on screen, not long ago, her auburn hair the only colour in the frame; she was under white blankets and between white walls. She tossed and turned in a perpetual restless sleep.

Now he opened the door quietly as a would-be thief, afraid that she would try to attack him and escape, but the room was empty and silent, even along the wall it shared with Doors' room. Brandon presumed Doors wasn't in. All the better, he thought, because Kate Generato's empty room smelled not of bleach, not of recent urgent cleaning, but of disuse. He tried to remember how long ago, exactly, he'd viewed her on Doors' screen. Two weeks ago? Three? Was that long enough to erase the smell of a living body? The bed was stripped, sheets folded crisply and piled with two pillows on top. The various tabletops were gleaming and bare. He knocked gently on the bathroom door, but there was nobody in there, just the usual warning tape over the toilet and sink, the many signs reminding people not to defecate or urinate or wash their hands.

He opened drawers, hoping to find some proof of her, some answer to the question of what had happened, but the drawers were empty. Mouse droppings in the bottom one—his stomach lurched. No stains or hairs on the bedding, even. Nothing.

The camera was pointed at the bed. The green light still blinked: go. He stood in front of the camera and shrugged theatrically, since it didn't matter now, since Doors would know, if Doors cared to know, that he'd been in here. He pulled out his log and wrote *Kate Generato* under *Nellie Young*. Then he left the room.

What he needed was to get at the archive of footage, to find the tale it told, but he'd have to develop a tidy reason for why he needed access. It shouldn't be too hard, but he was a little unnerved, lacking his usual calm. He could see this reflected in the curious expressions on the faces of those few early risers who passed him in the hall.

Brandon lifted his hands to his cheeks and scratched at his growing stubble. So he'd head to the port-hall, instead, and find out for himself what was going on with the machines.

Because Nellie Young must have been wrong. And Doors was always exaggerating. Brandon had been around enough ports to know that they were inert. They did not interfere with your free will; they could not suck you in as a black hole would. Those who left chose to do so. Consensual. The zippers could not unzip themselves. He'd go find the port, and he'd confirm.

He put the little Moleskine log in his shirt pocket and walked quickly, his long arms stiff pendulums at his sides. A couple of guys wearing security badges nodded at him as he passed. Why did PINA have so much security anyway? At the gates, fine. But why were these security guards stalking the living quarters like armed hall monitors? He broke into a slow jog and then began to sprint (the floor caving gently with each step), and nearly smashed into Simon, who was also wearing a security badge and a holster at his hip, with a heavy-looking handgun. Its snap-on cover was unsnapped.

Brandon saw Simon noticing that he had noticed the gun, and coughed to hide his surprise. Who would guns be for? It was just *them*.

"You heading to yoga?" Simon asked.

"Uh, yeah," Brandon said. "I was supposed to meet someone."

Simon nodded. Brandon resisted the urge to say more. Simon did not ask, *What's the hurry?* Instead, he grinned and said, "That was some party last night."

"Huh. Yeah," Brandon said, walking on past with an apologetic wave.

The green lights along the hall flashed with a faux-friendliness. *We're watching. We'll keep you safe. We're watching.* He resisted the urge to knock them down, and when at last he reached the outer door, he burst into the quad.

The tables from last night had been collapsed and stored, and over the turf was a rainbow-colored brickwork of yoga mats. Hundreds of Stablers were already arranged like origami: bent at the waist in the curved triangle of downward dog, or folded into lotus flowers, foot over knee, or balanced on one leg, in tree pose. He scanned for Doors, who was sure to be looking for him, about to pop out of nowhere with a fatherly clutch on Brandon's shoulder. Maybe by now Suzanne would have talked to Doors, warned him that Brandon had discovered something and turned disloyal. Or perhaps Doors had already watched the footage from Kate Generato's room, or tracked what Brandon had been searching for in the archive.

Brandon circled the bodies, daring Doors to appear. People folded and unfolded. Children played in a corner, some of them also trying out their parents' poses. Brandon knew exactly what Doors would say: *It's a beautiful thing we've created, Brandon. Don't take beauty for granted.* He would point at the cloudless blue above. And he would be right. Clear skies could be read as cosmic approval.

Brandon made it to the other side of the quad and reached the innovation wing without spotting Doors. Or Zahra, whose tree pose he would have known anywhere, whose long arms and legs gave deeper meaning to the word *limb*. He would stop in at port-hall, and after he was done there, he'd find her. Maybe he'd get on his knees, pose like a hopeful knight. A gesture to mean: *You are the love of my life. Come with me.* "Don't you want an adventure?" he'd say, and she wouldn't be able to resist. Doors' imagined words to him and the proposal to Zahra both ran through his mind now, long lines. *You are the love of my life, come with me. We have a long road ahead of us. You are like a son to me. Don't do what you imagine you should do. Darling. Daddy. Do what I tell you, good boy.*

He continued on, robotic, efficient, not yet feeling in his mind the urgency pounding in his chest. Finally he entered port-hall. Even now he expected that Doors would be standing inside waiting for him, but the hall was as hushed as an empty cathedral.

The port stood in the center, nearly invisible, opalescent on its stand.

Brandon laughed. It was phallic. A vibrator. A joke. The sound echoed, shrill and unmanly. He felt, as though he were a hound sniffing out a trace, that someone else had been there recently. He walked up next to the port, as close as he could get.

There was one coppery hair on the pedestal. He picked it up.

People had left in trickles. For a long time, their leaving had barely been noticeable—until things began to collapse: workers not showing up to clear debris on the highway, police not coming when called. What PINA called "the first wave" had included a flood of think pieces and blog posts and interviews and rants, and an unholy number of tweets about the merits of leaving or not, comparing the act of leaving to suicide. Protesters had surrounded PINA, like the Israelites marching around Jericho, hoping that by their will, the walls would fall. Some of them had camped in the surrounding woods for months, but none managed to get inside.

One percent of the population left and you hardly knew it. But the so-called "second wave" was more frightening. The grip of society fell lank, like the hands of a patient whose anesthesia was taking effect. Even close to the PINA campus there was, along with the clicking of crickets and the howls of god knew what—mountain lions, bears?—a nightly chorus of gunshots and squealing tires. Then came the third wave: the grid went down and darkness expanded in every direction, until only Stable had power and light.

PINA folks tried to make the best of the situation. New couples formed out of grief.

"We did this," Zahra had whispered to Brandon, only once, in the middle of the night.

Brandon stood next to the port in the great hall, thinking of his last year of high school, when skinny, pale Brandon had lost his father. The man had gone into hospital for routine gall bladder removal and come out septic. His shivering and the protrusion of his wide eyes made him look like a person who had seen a terror from which he could not recover, and then, just as the fever seemed about to subside, he developed pneumonia. Brandon's mother, after witnessing her husband dying in this crude and accidental way, just around the time Brandon was receiving his acceptances to Yale and Stanford and Princeton, took a leave from work and began a daily bourbon habit.

"I'm in mourning!" she slurred on the phone.

"Don't look at me like that, you bitch," she yelled at her sister, Elaine, who came over to the house with casseroles.

"I can talk in front of him however way I want," she said, clutching Brandon at the waist from her near-permanent seat at the kitchen table. "You don't get to tell me."

Brandon floated through those days, unable to feel anything. He didn't notice rain until it was dripping down his nose. One day his aunt Elaine picked him up for a drive on a Sunday morning. "You need to get out of that house for awhile," she said. "It's not healthy to be around that kind of grief."

That kind of grief. No word about his own grief. Unspoken between Brandon and his aunt was the concern that his mother's mind would run off a cliff, into depression, into mania.

Aunt Elaine took him to a place called Cross of the Fire, which turned out to be a church.

"Mom wouldn't like this," he told her.

Aunt Elaine wore her hair short and butchy, and she smiled at him in a way that resembled his mother's, but with less sincerity. Meanwhile, Mom was alone at the table with her mug of acid. Aunt Elaine's cheeks were like hamster cheeks, swollen with something hidden. She said, "Your cousins and your uncle don't want to come to church either. But it's wrong to dismiss a thing you haven't tried for yourself."

Beware of religious zeal, his mother had told him. He said this to himself under his breath as he entered the building, a hex to counteract the manipulations of the usher in the suit who was smiling and shaking his hand, to counteract the effect of the poetry of the bulletin's heading: *Zeal for your house will consume me.*

"Do you think you are not worthy of God's love? Who told you you were not worthy of God's love?" This was all he could remember of the handsome preacher's words. He argued in his head: *My worthiness is not the issue.* Chanting and swaying began. Beside him his aunt was sweating insanely, embarrassingly, as though she'd been poured over with oil, face slick, chin dripping, eyes squeezed shut. A man in the bank of seats ahead of them had turned around and they were clutching each other's hands, talking in a language he didn't understand. Later he found out this was speaking in tongues. The Holy Spirit was a flame that burned invisibly above your head, giving you powers. At the front, the preacher touched a woman on the forehead, and she fell down. It went on for hours. Heat emanated from Aunt Elaine's body, and Brandon recoiled when she tried to take his hand.

In the car afterwards, she acted as though nothing out of the ordinary had occurred. But he didn't want to see her chubby-cheeked, overly familiar face. It was as though he had witnessed her doing some exotic sexual manoeuvre he hadn't yet discovered in the dark and horny backrooms of his brain.

"See, Brandon," she told him as she shifted the car into gear, "God just wants to love you."

Through his years at Yale and into PINA, Brandon got daily e-mails from his mother. She told him always how proud she was, but he saw, too, how lonely she'd been since Dad died. Most of the time there was nothing new to say, and the e-mail was just a virtual wave of the hand. Rarely did they speak on the phone or in person.

> B,
>
> I don't begrudge you for going to Yale, of course you had to go, I don't begrudge you for taking the PINA job. I miss you a lot, though, and sometimes I think I should have come with you. Dad always said I was stubborn. Uncle Peter bought a port with god knows what financing, and of course Elaine is off sweating and praying and gibbering. What's PINA not telling us? Do you know what's going on with these things?
> Love, Mom

Even with his own mother, he'd had to be careful what he said. He knew as well as anybody how not-private e-mail and phone calls were. In an early TED talk, his first viral one, Doors had proclaimed, "Privacy is the costliest, deadliest aspect of the American experiment. Good riddance!"

So Brandon told his mother that the ports were very new and expensive, and it wouldn't hurt to wait, and he hoped she understood what he meant.

She wrote a month later.

> B,
>
> I miss your dad worse every day. Started working out and getting facials. You can probably understand why. You plant an idea like time travel in a grieving person's head . . .

I know it's been eleven years. I'm stuck. I don't know how
it's been so long. Visit soon.
Love, Mom

That e-mail sent a flare of anger up Brandon's spine. His mother
needed a proper friend and confidante. It was inappropriate for her
to lay her pain on him. Later, guilt would take the place of rage; guilt
would deflate him.

B,
I'm losing my resolve. Your Uncle Peter took off either
through port or with that dental hygienist he's been boff-
ing or with the hygienist through port. Anyway, he's gone
and Aunt Elaine is blaming everybody but herself and
God.
What a strange time to be alive. I'm going to come out
to see you, if you can't get away. So proud of you. Hope
you're okay.
Love,
Mom

PINA's front atrium had once been a source of pride, the first face any
important visitor to the campus would see. Light poured in from
three storeys of glass, and commissioned works of art—pineapple
sculptures in bronze and silver and glass—were arranged near expensive groupings of couches and chairs. Huge colourful canvases hung
from the only wall, over the elevators. But around the time of that last
e-mail from his mother, the atrium was peopled not with loungers
but with guards—undertrained guys Doors had dressed in security
uniforms. Sometimes Benji even took a shift. It was becoming difficult to leave or to come in uninvited.

Brandon thought the security was paranoid, but he had needed to leave so he obediently flashed his badge and his key, gave his details, waited while the guard called Doors directly to confirm permission.

He hadn't heard anything from his mother in a couple of weeks, but the silence didn't necessarily mean anything. She had said she would come out to see him, and he had urged her to follow through, suggesting travel by bus and train. The last e-mail he'd received was her ticket confirmation. Phones were down, Internet was increasingly unreliable, the late-in-the-day promise made by one company never to stop providing signals clearly broken—but at least he knew the ticket had been bought. So he drove out to the train terminal, alarmed by the quiet of the streets. At the terminal, pigeons hopping and loudly flapping were the only evidence of life.

Clearly, at PINA everyone had been protected from the news. The Internet was an intranet, and nobody could find a newspaper or a reliable anchor on what was left of the intermittent broadcasts. Fox News was the only holdout, the only group still publicly frightening anybody. There was a joke at PINA that Fox News holding out only proved that to resist port was to be backward. Brandon had an image of he and Zahra and the rest of the twelve as the final crew of the *Titanic*, although things were of course not as catastrophic as that. There were ports aplenty, plenty of lifeboats to go around. Brandon had thought, back then, that they were just awaiting Doors' word.

He walked along the sidewalk up to the terminal, trying to trigger the automatic doors, which, it soon became clear, were not going to open.

"Where the fuck is everybody?" The word *everybody* dangled, unheard. He ran around to the other side of the building, looking for a door to pull open here, or here, or here. He nearly tripped over a man with a suitcase curled up against a wall.

"Ain't nobody in there, man."

"What do you mean?"

"Just that."

"My mom bought her ticket, like, a couple of weeks ago."

The man shrugged. "A couple of weeks is a long time." He did not otherwise move. Sunglasses concealed his eyes, and the red cords of a first-gen PINAplayer trailed from his ears.

"How did I not know about what's happening here?"

The man sized him up lazily. "Ain't my job to make you believe."

Brandon reflexively pulled out his phone (ask PINA: *Where did civilization go?*). But of course there was no signal. In the rafters, the pigeons sat in a row, darting their heads. He tried to figure out how long it had been since he'd last left the compound. He'd not gone home to sleep in—holy shit—weeks.

"Can it all change that quickly?"

"Weren't quick at all."

Brandon became aware of the man's sour smell. "Are you okay?"

The man smiled, revealing black teeth.

Brandon felt around in his pockets and left a few dollars in the man's cap. As he drove away, it dawned on him with hot embarrassment that the money was worth nothing to anybody anymore.

Zahra was beside him when, days later, Doors gave his last public speech to the remaining 10 percent. "Welcome to a new, better, more optimistic age. For all of you who have stayed with us, I congratulate you on your intelligence and foresight and good luck. To us!" People leapt out of their seats like worshippers in that Pentecostal church. Tears were streaming, arms raised, and there were even a few frenzied screams.

Zahra's thin fingers were loose in his hand, and he absently pressed on them one by one. He had felt numb since his return, without his mother, from the terminal.

"You have not been abandoned!" The people's excitement fuelled Doors. "You have persevered!"

Brandon realized suddenly, as though startled into waking up, that his hand was on the port's zipper. Small nub, like a clitoris. His finger and thumb squeezing it. He thought: *You want to go home. You can go home. Back to the place where you belong.* With detachment, he watched himself unzipping the port, slowly, erotically.

All the people everywhere, they had simply gone through it. It was so restful; it was so easy. His mother had found peace there, perhaps, had slipped into one and gone away. His aunt, his uncle, his cousins, his first love, Cecile, all his later loves, everybody with whom he'd played dodgeball, sat in labs, opened up the cavities of dead animals, tried to write code, read poetry. Every single incidental player in his insignificant life. Even the man sweating with his aunt in the church, maybe even that preacher with the high forehead. Had the Fox News anchors resisted, in the end? Would he ever know if they had?

The philosopher Berkeley had believed—preposterously—that things existed only if they were perceived. But now this idea didn't seem so preposterous. The people he remembered had only existed when his gaze was on them; he had removed his gaze and—no— no—now he was thinking like a megalomaniac; now he was thinking like Doors. Still, it was as hard to believe in the existence of the sweaty man in the church as it was to believe in the existence of strangers.

Do not be afraid. The sentence seemed to hold him there, his finger and thumb on the zipper's nub. A port had never tempted him before, and now it was hypnotic, nearly irresistible, the edge of a cliff on which he barely had a toehold. With great effort, against a current, he pushed himself to walk to the other end of the port-hall and out.

Once he'd pressed the door closed, ensured that the light on the lock was blinking red and put the key into a back pocket, he found there were tears in his eyes, that his heart was pounding. Sweat pooled at his armpits and lower back, sticking his shirt to his skin.

He ran from the hall and into the quad, over the soft turf and past one triangular contortion and another, until he found Benji attempting to pull his muscled body farther than it could go, lunging and reaching.

"Inhale. Exhale." A woman was speaking into a mike from some unseen spot. "Now re-e-e-each back into downward dog. Take your time. Hold for five breaths. Breathe."

Benji spotted him and stood. His round, clean-shaven face hadn't broken a sweat. "Hey, Dreyer," he said.

"You seen Doors?"

Benji appraised him coolly. "He's not somewhere out in the quad?"

"I can't see him."

"Did you check Zahra's room?"

Brandon took his meaning, but barely, and told Benji he'd do that. On his way back down the hall, he nodded at security-badged Gordie, and then at Simon, receiving indifferent smiles in response.

At Zahra's room he knocked. Waited. Knocked again.

"Yeah?"

"Zee? It's me."

She was in a thin tank top and tight shorts, the sort of thing she liked to wear to sleep. Her expression was sober. Later, Brandon would obsess over this: Had it been tinged with wistfulness or guilt? Had it held regret, or longing? Or perhaps, he would think too late, she was feeling trapped, and that thing like shame flicking through her eyes had been a cry for help.

Her room was more austere than it needed to be, everything a shade of tan or off-white, nothing on the walls. Even the lamps appeared uncomfortable with their small decorative flourishes, their resemblance to Ionic columns. Shirtless salt-and-pepper Doors with his white linen pants blended into all this muted monochrome, bent over his notebook at the kitchen desk. He looked up at Brandon, beamed a smile and looked back down. "Good morning," he said.

"Good morning," Brandon said. He was perfectly in the moment, not thinking ahead, not reflecting. He took Zahra's two thin elbows in his hands. "I have to talk to you," he said. Port's tug remained a confusion at the back of his mind. He put his lips on her cheek, knowing it was a desperate move, knowing she couldn't stand a show of feeling.

She pulled back from him and smirked. That flicker of something like fear, or shame, had disappeared from her expression. She backed up toward Doors.

"I need to talk to you," he said again. "Can you meet me downstairs?"

"What is it you need to talk about, Brandon?" Doors turned his attention to him. A flashlight held to the eyes.

"If you don't mind, it's just that—"

He saw that Zahra was waiting for him to realize what she and Doors were up to. Maybe that was what had been in her eyes: Zahra, braless in her tank top; Doors, shirtless and barefoot at the desk; the rumpled sheets. But he was not going to be theatrical, was not going to give them anything, was not going to shout like someone on a lowbrow television show, was not going to say *What the fuck* or even *What the hell*, was not going to betray how betrayed he felt. Maybe he was a person of feeling—so what? That didn't mean he was going to ask questions whose answers were plain.

Later he would comb through each second of this encounter, each more horrible in retrospect, more heartbreaking and full of questions he didn't think to ask. Later he'd wonder if Zahra's fear—it was the electricity of her fear that had charged the air—was directed at him or at Doors. He'd wonder how much of what she'd told him about her life was true. He knew everything, or so he'd thought: her early immigration, her ability to detach as though selfhood were a raincoat you snapped on and off, her ability to leave her friends on the playground if they bored her, her fear of abandonment, her desire for him, Brandon, her knack for statistical analysis, the poker tours she'd played in and won, always winning, in love with being loved, fully aware of the effect her long body and cool regard had on men. And women too, sometimes. Thus, she and Doors were made for each other. Thus, perhaps, she had some control over the flickering in those brown eyes, and maybe he was caught in a liar's paradox. ("I'm a born liar," she'd told Brandon once. "Your body can't lie," he'd said, feeling her flesh respond to his touch, his mouth, the arching of backs and limbs, the hardening of nipples. "Of course it can," she had said.)

But in the moment, Brandon felt none of the things he would feel later. Doors put his pen down and came to stand next to Zahra. He put his hand on Zahra's back. He towered over them both and smiled.

"We're not together anymore," Zahra said. "You and I."

This poise and serenity was exactly what made him want to take her with him.

"We're all adults, here, free to make adult decisions," Doors said.

For the first time, Doors seemed to Brandon like a revenant of his own father, who might have said just such an inane thing.

"We're all adults here," Brandon mimicked in a growl. "So why are you sneaking around?"

"We aren't. We're being perfectly forthright," Doors said. "I knew that you would feel betrayed by this relationship, but I also knew that you would find out sooner or later. We weren't trying to hide anything, only to have a little privacy. Surely you can understand."

"Privacy!" Brandon said. "Oh, yes. *Surely*. I understand."

"Brandon, my old friend. You are a lover. You are a romantic. The way you see the world is beautiful, and it has been an asset to our corporation for these many years. But your feelings are not entitlements. You do not own the things you love."

"Ownership, privacy." Brandon's tone was still sarcastic, but he felt helpless and weary. "Look, pal. I'm going to stop you there. We've got bigger things to worry about than me and my feelings for Zahra."

"Pal?"

"*You've* got bigger things to worry about, anyway."

"We have some business, do we?" Doors said.

"We do." Underneath his bravado, Brandon chastised himself. What did he think he was going to do? Expose Doors' evil or ineptitude? Go into the quad, demand the yoga teacher's headset and rally the people into a new and better democracy?

"Why are you so . . . tousled?" Doors cocked his head.

"I've always admired your diction," Brandon said, attempting a sarcastic imitation of the German accent. "I'm tousled because I have recently made some surprising discoveries about the port."

Doors gave a big Buddha smile of peace and goodwill. He tented his fingers into a triangle. "Yes, I know," he said. "You found the information about Nellie Young. You are very disturbed about the possibility that people are leaving against their own will. You are disturbed that Kate Generato seems to have left us again through port."

"Are you surveilling me?"

"One doesn't need surveillance when one can intuit with a high degree of accuracy. And what could he mean, do you think, my Zahra? What could he mean 'against their own will'? How old-fashioned, what a fascinating belief about *free will* our old friend seems to have."

Zahra sat on the bed with her legs crossed and hugged a white pillow to her chest. Doors was calm and patient, wearing a zoned-in look Brandon recognized, the look he had only rarely assumed in the days before the grid went down, but which now persistently plastered his face. Doors had changed so utterly at the beginning of Year Zero— "You have not been abandoned!"—that Brandon had forgotten the volatility he'd witnessed in the years before then. How many times had it been Brandon's hard work to calm him, to keep him quiet or seated, to balance out his intensity with jokes, or to counterbalance the mania for invention with the easy air of logic and coolheadedness?

"What did you do?" Brandon said.

"I don't know what you mean, Brandon. Zahra, do you know what he means?"

Zahra shook her head.

"What did we do? Did you know?"

"You are my dearest friend, Brandon."

"I thought I was. I thought you were." Brandon, too, sat on the edge of the bed.

"You needn't be afraid of me," Doors said.

"I'm not afraid."

"It's written on your face: pupils, beads of sweat. Your bottom lip is quivering."

"Fuck you, Doors."

"Yeah, yeah. Let's have it."

"What?" Brandon was exhausted. Gravity was stronger in this room. Doors was a weight, a force.

"About time you stand up to me. I knew you had it in you."

"I thought you couldn't take this garbage," Brandon said to Zahra.

"A couple things, Dreyer. A couple of things you need to consider. First of all, I have been telling you since the beginning what I believed about the ports. I told you on *day one*. This is not and has never been a conspiracy. We are and have always been transparent. People knew what they were getting into, pardon the pun."

"I was just in port-hall," Brandon said. "People did not know *that*. People did not know that port was inciting them to unzip and jump in. I didn't know that it was so strong, that it could *lure*. If I didn't know, how could the masses have known? I don't think people were knowingly buying a fucking manipulation machine. A rapist. And we need to acknowledge that what happened with Kate Generato was an anomaly, that she was very sick. *People can not come back.*"

Zahra's eyes told him to calm down.

"Brandon, I've always found you to be one of the most guileless people I've ever known. It is the source of my deep trust of you, but it is also a thing that keeps you from seeing."

"Don't change the subject."

Doors unlocked his intense gaze. All three of them were now sitting on the bed.

"You don't need to be afraid," said Doors. "Not of me. So we knew that port was more than we understood it at first to be. Sounds insane, sounds dangerous, but it wasn't. Port can sort. Port can think. Do you hear what I'm saying? It's a beautiful thing when consciousness arises from an unexpected place, and we must attune. We must attune."

Normally, Brandon ate up this shit: it was just like his long monologues about yoga and mass meditation and what such practices might affect on the quantum level.

"We've attuned. Haven't we, Zahra," Doors said.

Zahra nodded and gave Brandon a tight smile.

"You've attuned," Brandon said to her. Then, addressing Doors, he said, "What about Kate Generato? She was out of her mind."

"Oh, Brandon. I need you to think a little harder. Go outside of your own limited humanism. What is it exactly that makes a human life so valuable?" Doors put his hand on Zahra's bare shoulder. "I would have hoped that after finding this Nellie Young data, you would come to me. You would have seen that just because a port can—what would the word be—*induce?*—desire—you would have seen that I am still the Albrecht Doors you've always known and trusted. That nothing will have changed. What do we have if we don't have loyalty? I expected more from you, Brandon Dreyer."

"What does that mean? This was a test? Of my loyalty?" Brandon put his hands to his cheeks and scratched. "Did Nellie Young really write what I found in the archive?"

"Everything you discovered was real," Doors said. "But the more important question is whether you are loyal to me, your friend, your good close friend, or whether you are loyal to your idea of me. How easily you gave up trusting me."

"I didn't. I did come to you."

"You went to the port. You went to Zahra."

"We must attune?" Brandon said, looking to Zahra, who looked away. "I can attune."

"You ought to have," Doors said. "But it's a bit late for that now. Wouldn't you agree?"

Chapter

9

THE GUILTY PARTIES

So, he was a fool. The only thing Brandon had not divulged before Doors ushered him out, though it was likely Doors knew it anyway, was that he was going to leave PINA, with or without permission.

Zahra's pity was on him like a sweat stain, spreading as he bolted from her room to his own, where he mashed things into his backpack. Batteries, compass, and above all, water were his main concerns. He'd find maps later, in gas stations along the way. He left the room and stopped for more water, filling steel canteens and clipping them onto the hooks on either side of the bag. He used up every last ration coupon, even the ones he'd been hoarding, and when the woman at the dispensary clicked the tap down with an eyebrow raised at him, he gave her the stupidest smile he could manage. Didn't say *Been so thirsty lately* or *Just stocking up for a not-so-rainy day* like some kind of amateur.

Then he went down to the latrine access, a long hallway leading to a door at what had once been the back of the building, several floors directly below the boardrooms. It was the only point of exit to the wilderness outside the compound. He walked past the guards, pretending his bowels were cramping, though they weren't anymore. He nodded his way past them—Jedi mind trick; they nodded back—and out to the back forest, where dozens of port-a-johns had been set up on their deeply dug holes, far enough out and downland so that they could not interfere with the groundwater of the wells.

Because he could not think what else to do, he stashed his backpack behind a tree and went inside one of the vacant blue pods and closed himself in with the dim air, with its excretory smells and heavy chemical air freshener that seemed to singe the nostrils.

For the time it took to do his business, but no longer, he put out of his mind the way it felt to be this far from the security of the compound, whose sleek walls were unclimbable, whose doors were thick and impenetrable. And manned. After, hiding like a frightened child, he saw the truth of the situation. If the world was gone, if people had disappeared like Doors' experimental rodents and raccoons walking into what looked like total annihilation, then they—*he*—had done it. They who remained were here because they were in on it, even him, Brandon, Brandon-the-guileless, Brandon-the-fool. And what they'd done had made it so that their compound was free-floating and lonesome as a space pod, and the world outside as vast and indifferent as deep space. Doors had stepped up and become what he now was— false source of calm and happiness, supplier of endless platitudes—precisely because others were inclined to terror and worry.

How long could things remain stable? What happened when they ran out of resources, ran out of booze, or of water? They'd have to expand outward, and for all their technical knowledge, they knew nothing at all about how to do that. With the clarity of desperation, Brandon saw that they should have been working hard all this time, should be planning to send out more than four people at a time. Especially since the world outside was filled with ports, magnetic sinkholes aglow with whatever one most deeply desired.

Brandon knew that Doors must have called a decisive emergency meeting of the twelve by now, but it seemed that no one had come out to the johns to find him. No one came rushing out, calling his name, banging on doors. When he finally left the pod, the only people he encountered were a few other bathroom users. They were vaguely recognizable, like those people he used to see at the same transit station, way back when. You could be homesick for anything, he thought. Even for the rush of trains, for the urine stink of a station's concrete floors. None of these other latrine-users noticed when he ducked behind the rows of potties and into the thicker woods.

Once hidden in the trees, Brandon swung his pack around, rummaging. Weaponry, of course, was the thing he'd forgotten to find and pack. He could use a stainless steel water bottle as a bludgeon—that would be his only hope. Doors had allowed no access to guns for the twelve, allowed them no weapons training, had waved away every such suggestion in meetings. Only the security detail had received guns. "Democracy has always been a farce." Prick.

The days of going online to ask PINA for help and instructions would never return. He'd have to go back and arm himself. Clearly, his escape had needed more careful planning. Or, maybe he really did have free will. Maybe if he went back, Doors wouldn't detain him. Maybe he could go back and leave again later, in good faith; or he'd insist on manning the rescue mission and leave that way.

But it was beautiful out here, trees reaching for sun as though in salutation, all neck and torso, all reach, the smell of pine like air you could actually stand to breathe. And at least there were still redwoods, ancient trees to outlast everyone. He jogged a little, just to feel how his feet could lift off the needle-covered forest floor. As he drew close enough to see cracks of light between the trees that revealed the rows of plastic johns on the perimeter of the compound, he heard rustling. His heart flew in panic, and he tried to shush himself, the beating now in his ears, so he could assess the danger.

It wasn't a bear. It was voices, three distinct male ones. He crouched behind a tree and listened.

Deep bass: "Yeah, three."

Southern drawl: "And you got it all packed up?"

Bass: "Right-o."

Drawl: "Sourced out the old stations, ready for a fight."

Bass: "Yup."

There was a silence, and then the third voice said, "There doesn't need to be a fight if all goes well."

Bass: "How are the numbers looking?"

Drawl: "We're at about fifteen. Seven women, three children, us, plus two other guys."

Bass: "Holding steady, then."

Third voice: "Safer that way."

After this came a long pause filled with the idyllic sounds of birds and their chirrups, coos and caws. A chipmunk peeped out of a hole in the trunk of a nearby tree, rose on its hind legs and gazed at him. Just sounded like escapees or something, too small to be a rebellion. There was the shirk-shirk sound of a knife whittling wood, and he swiveled his head towards it.

Three figures came into view. They were making spears! He recognized the man who must have been the Southern drawl, an older guy who had always seemed a little wobbly on his legs and whose voice resembled Morgan Freeman's. He was an old-timey software guy whom everyone called DOS. The other two Brandon recognized but could not name.

He chanced another look and saw a gone-cold firepit, a pile of logs covered by a tarp, bungees, and some boxy cages that might have been animal traps. Brandon had heard about a group of PINA survivalists who'd been worried about some kind of political uprising, but no one he knew had been involved with anything like that. Instead of gluing his eyes to screens, he should have been learning this—survivalist skills, outdoorsy stuff, how to pitch a tent, talents other than data analysis and PR that might keep him alive.

"We see you, Brandon Dreyer," came Deep Bass. "Might as well show yourself."

Then again, perhaps PR skills would always be necessary. Brandon stood up and wiped dry dirt and brown needles from his hands. "Hi," he said, putting his arms up, half-shrug, half-surrender.

All three guys were older than him. They didn't have beards but might as well have. In their flannel shirts and trucker hats, they looked like what they were: nerds pretending to be manly men. Two of them were burly white guys, and then there was DOS, thinner but not fit and strong and geared-up the way the others were. Inside, they'd have stood out like red tulips in a field of short grass, and Brandon wondered why he hadn't noticed them more. He tried to picture them in white button-ups or loose yoga gear.

"Put your arms down," said Deep Bass, the burliest white guy, shaking his head. "We're not threatening you."

"It's nice out here," Brandon said, unsure what to do with his arms now that they hung limply at his sides. He slipped his index fingers through the little hooks on his backpack, feeling like a four-teen-year-old trying to appear casual.

"You look like you're packed up for a little trip," said Deep Bass, low and accusatory. "You abandoning your shipmates? Or maybe the captain sent you out here, wants to know what we're up to?"

If Doors knew about these guys, he hadn't told Brandon. "You guys planning a coup, or what?" he said, deflecting.

Deep Bass took a step towards him, but DOS waved a hand at him calmly. "Nah, nah. We're just practicing living in the woods. Kind of a hobby, right?"

Ignoring this, Deep Bass grumbled. "There's some of us who think things aren't quite as 'stable' as they once were. In fact, let me tell you what we really think. We think that everyone else that *used* to be on this planet is *fucking* dead."

"No," Brandon protested. "Not dead."

"Oh, you gonna tell me that everyone is alive and thriving, living out their time-travel fantasies like they're off to Club Med? What we've got

here is some fucked-up sci-fi nightmare!" The spear Deep Bass had been
whittling he now grasped in his hand. "Did you ever see Kate Generato?
I don't know anyone who actually saw her, except on a screen."

"Billy, don't lose your shit," said DOS. He turned to Brandon.
"Billy lost his wife. Came home from work, and she was just gone.
Didn't leave a note, nothing."

"They go into those machines thinking they can come back,"
Deep Bass—Billy—said. "Do *you* think they can come back, Mr.
Right-Hand-Man?"

"To be honest—" Brandon cleared his throat. "I don't know what
to think. I mean, yeah, I did see Kate Generato. I met her." He put
his arms up again, mollifying, instinctively deferring to the clutched
spear. "I don't think the people who disappeared died."

"You think they vanished to some other space-time? Some other
time-space?"

"And what about the Testifiers?" Brandon said, shame flooding
his body. "They came back."

Billy scowled. "Everybody here knows that the Testifiers were
actors. *You* know that. And anyway, they are long gone. You've watched
that footage, right? It's creepy as hell. Those smiling actors, the joke
time machine that turns out to be real? And even Kate Generato, I
mean, she's only one person. Even if you count the Testifiers, that's just
four people who claim to have gone in and come back. There are *six
billion* missing people."

"To be fair, we don't know the numbers," Brandon said. "I guess
there is a question, if they *are* vanishing to another space-time, if that's
what's happening, whether they'd still be themselves on the other side."

"The other side!" Billy shook the spear. "That's a euphemism for
heaven."

"What I mean is, if their molecules got sucked up and rearranged,
as they'd have to be, you know, wherever they end up, then I wonder
whether a person would still be themselves anymore."

The three men gaped at him. "Is that what Old Albrecht is saying?" Billy asked softly.

Brandon shrugged. "Doors said something, like, um . . ." Unconsciously, he took a few steps backwards until he was against the smooth muscled trunk of a eucalyptus. He was telling more than he wanted to. "He said that port can sort, port can think."

The three stood quietly then, eyes cast down at the needles and leaves on the hard-packed forest floor where it snaked with roots.

"So, you guys are planning, what?" Brandon asked again. "A takeover? Or just taking off?"

Eyes turned up at him, wary. The smaller white guy, the young one who hadn't yet spoken, cleared his throat and shot a gob of spit onto the ground next to him. "We know you trust Doors. We know you think you know everything about the man and all that's gone on. But the problem has always been that people put their heads in the sand, hide from reality, distract themselves. Before, everything was about having fun, while the planet filled with poison gas, basically."

"Let me just stop you there," Brandon said.

"Let him finish," said DOS, holding up his hand.

"Anyway, there's a few of us who wonder if maybe this isn't the good life. Maybe what we need to be doing is to go and see for ourselves if we can live out here, in the world."

"But why are you doing all this in secret?"

They stared at him.

"Do you think Doors won't let you leave?" Brandon shook his head so hard that the bottles on his pack clanged and rattled. Loyalty for the man he'd wanted to betray welled up in him again. "He's powerful, but he's not evil. He's not a monster."

"What kind of evil is this, though?" The youngish guy rubbed the stubble on his face, studied Brandon. "Think about it. Port can sort, and port can think, yeah? It isn't just housewives or thrill-seekers, it's not just the upper crust or the middle class, not just lemmings or followers or even addicts. We are talking about, basically, total annihilation."

The guy was at least forty, but he spoke like a millennial, wrinkles around his eyes and mouth mismatched with his adverbial flourishes and his baseball cap. "What's left of us? I mean, we're on the endangered species list. *We* are. Okay? And so everybody's taking off. We're talking Buddhists and Christians, immigrants from India, immigrants from Russia, indigenous people, prisoners, pedophiles, street kids and hookers and addicts and astronauts and politicians. The fucking president of the U.S. of A. Responsible people and desperate people and bored people, and, I mean, think about the scale of this fucking thing! We've been hiding from it. Cowering in our giant beehive like Nazi criminals. Except our trial's not coming. Civilization has dis-a-ppeared."

The clear air, the tree bark, the words like shots. It was dizzying. Eucalyptus mixed with the pine-sap smell, stronger now, like a chemical. Brandon tried one more feeble protest. "We're not hiding out in Stable. We have plans to spread. Doors has things under control."

"Yeah?"

Brandon nodded.

"To be honest, we've lost our faith in Doors. And if his plans don't work?"

"Melt it down," Billy and DOS grunted quietly.

Through the trees was the far-off building Brandon knew so well, its white length as pretty as driftwood beyond the blue flash of johns.

"If the disappeared people don't come back," Billy said. "Then, Brandon Dreyer, we have all bitten off more than we can chew. And even if they do come back. The scale of this thing! The disaster of it. A change like this is absolutely unprecedented."

"Not entirely unprecedented," Brandon put in, retreating to rationality, to fact. "We live on a planet where the continents all used to be attached." His scientific knowledge was embarrassingly foggy. "We live on a planet where we and the apes share a common ancestor."

He could see they were disappointed in him. DOS shook his head. "This is real, man. This is reality." He turned and spoke to the other two. "If he's confirming that port is *thinking*, then we are talking about a giant nervous system. Ports are neurons, and they're communicating along pathways, right?"

"What?" Brandon said.

"The ports are a web, we think. A giant spiderweb with its own neural-system."

"Leaving theory aside," continued the younger guy, "what's indisputable is the collapse of civilization. Our money's worthless, and that's hardly the worst of it. Think about the future! Five years, ten years, twenty . . ."

Brandon sensed irritation in the older two. They'd heard this speech before. "When you guys say 'melt it down' . . .?"

"We're speaking metaphorically. Of course," Billy said.

Brandon pulled the pack off his shoulders, which were now sore.

"Anyway, we're going to try something new," Billy said. The spear was still clutched in his hand and now he pointed it directly at Brandon. "Just to try it."

"Hey, I'm not going to fuck this up for you," Brandon said. "But you don't want to go out there, do you?" He gestured at the deepening woods. "Are you planning to hike, or what? If we're talking about"—he gulped here, unable to take the words seriously, unable to pretend to do so—"an A.I. spiderweb, why the fuck would you go out there?"

The younger one glared at him. "We're not going to tell you anything else."

"I swear, I won't say a thing. You see my pack, right? You can see what I'm doing." He sank down and leaned against the tree. "I've lost people too. We've all lost people." He bent his head back against that smooth bark, which was cold as a stone.

"I'm with you guys," he said. "I know what port can do. I swear it. I swear."

✠

By the time Brandon left the men in the woods and returned to the building, creeping back past those guarding the latrine access, he didn't know exactly what he was going to do. Just as soon as he left them, the woods in all their splendor excluded him. The ecosystems of worms working through decay, the many furtive creatures making homes in nests and burrows, had nothing to do with him, and, for all its flaws, Stable was humane and safe. The doors going into the main hallway that closed behind him were secure and well-engineered, did not need melting down.

Better here than out there in the great unknown, he told himself, forced to eat insects, possibly, forced to resist the powers of port everywhere he went.

The men had not been surprised when he explained port's allure, the way it seemed to interfere with one's thought processes. They were scientists, after all, or nerds at least, and had already come up with those theories. Apparently Brandon was the last to know; certainly he was the last to suspect malice. He muttered to himself as he paced toward the archive, where he would, he knew, become a person obsessed with putting the puzzle together, a person who would never really act. That's when he saw Suzanne standing near the executive rooms with a tray braced around her neck like a retro cinema waitress. All she needed was a little cap on her pretty head, a little more piping on a red uniform. On the tray were rows of jars full of amber liquid.

"Why aren't you in there?" she said. "They started twenty min-utes ago."

Brandon tapped his key on the lock and pushed a boardroom door open, even as Suzanne tugged at his elbow, hissing at him to get cleaned up first. But it was too late. For the first time, he was aware that in an hour and a half he'd gone from slightly tousled to dirty and sweat-soaked, as though he'd been hiking through the woods for days. Stress was making him sweat and stink.

At the long, glistening table were the other eleven of the twelve. Everyone wore tight yoga shorts, and the women had bamboo halter tops in colours ranging from bubble-gum pink to teal to heather grey. Zahra was sitting between Benji and Dawn, three chairs away from Doors. As Brandon moved to sit at the last empty chair directly across from Lena, a broad-shouldered woman with a throaty Dutch accent, another four got up and walked to the door. Sebastian, Peter, Joni and Kelly.

"Wait a moment," Doors said to the four. "Have a drink before you go." He nodded at Suzanne, who offered the tray and came around to distribute jars.

Doors stood and raised his drink. "To the four of you! To Sebastian, Peter, Joni, Kelly—and the sacrifice you are about to make! To the good life!"

"Hear hear!" A chorus of clinking.

Suzanne met Brandon's eyes, mouthed the word *sacrifice*. He shrugged, and she left behind the four with her empty tray.

Then there were only eight of them left, plus Doors, who was exempt from any count. An old PINAtalkie sat in the centre of the table, its mahogany so shiny that the white device was doubled by its mirror image. Doors picked it up and put it to his mouth, staring at Brandon. He pushed the button.

"Testing, testing. Come in, Sebastian."

"Roger. Sebastian here. Over and out."

"Thumbs up," Doors said. "Over and out." He held the talkie but let one finger hover over the button. Then he turned the volume dial way down.

"So. Dreyer," Doors said. "Even after your little display earlier, you've decided to come back and encroach upon the inner sanctum."

Everyone but Zahra turned to look at him. He said nothing. Doors' slight sneer had made "inner sanctum" sound moist and intimate, sexual, even wrong. The room had its own personality, its own smell and feel: the chairs that seemed to hold you as if in a giant hand; the wood and leather that sometimes had the scent of old tobacco, sometimes of sweet rum; the view out the window of the blue or grey sky and the opposite side of the building with its long crisp white line. There were the times they'd come here at Christmas, the one time it had been lightly snowing; the shared thrill of seeing before anyone else in the world the things that would change the world. For years he had come to this room, in some years every day, on some days more than once. Always at his boss's side, watching as one by one each of the others was replaced and replaced again. Dawn's face, Lena's face, Benji's. Each of them was good and kind; as a group, they were a better arrangement of humans than any other he'd known.

So, yes, he'd been a puppy, imbuing this room with meaning and calling it home, imprinting on each of the others his own affectionate scent. It made him want to cry now, but he wouldn't.

Instead, he said, "I had been hoping you'd send me out with that pod, Doors. I'm ready."

"We're not convinced that you are ready. We're not convinced that you can be trusted. Our emotions"—Brandon cringed at the paternalism in Doors' voice—"can be guides, but often they are confusing."

Dawn's eyebrows were halfway to her hairline. *Are you going to let him talk to you like that?*

Silence was his best chance here, Brandon knew, since Doors would not be moved, just as Zahra would not be moved. He was out of the inner circle now, forever. So he said nothing, while Doors waited for him to beg or to cry.

At last, Doors spoke again. "You have something you'd like to tell everyone."

Brandon remained silent, collected himself and remained collected. He stared back at Doors, returning his best imitation of those intense eyes.

"Why don't you tell everyone what you've found out?" Doors said.

Always, home was somewhere else. Thirst was unquenchable; Zahra had been right. People were nomads, but they were designed to be trees, meant for deep root systems and long lives lived in the same spot. Later, on the road, past the initial thrill of escape, Brandon would find himself pulling over to catch his breath. It was this room he'd long for.

"Brandon," Doors said, with an unguarded expression. "Brandon, remember how little we know."

But Brandon had formed a hard case of silence around himself that could not be penetrated. In his mind, he was already tracking the route that would take him to the meeting place the men in the woods had agreed on, before they'd known he was listening. He imagined himself pushing the accelerator down hard as he drove up one hill and down another, the lap-lap-lap of the sea if he stopped by the beach to sit and think. To breathe.

"If you weren't using this childish silent treatment, I know what you would say," Doors said. The German accent had thickened, which Brandon knew to be a sign of stress. "You would like to ask me what it is that you don't know. You would ask me to educate you. Yes?"

Doors had always been gentle with him. He'd hired Brandon during a short-lived phase during which he went incognito to art gallery openings and local parties and approached strangers with comments like "I believe in the power of intuition, don't you?" Brandon was the only person who remained from this period. Now he was like a child encountering a parent's temper for the first time. He resisted the urge to blurt: *But you're afraid, Albrecht, of what I know.*

Doors began to move around the table, from one to the next, touching a shoulder here, the back of a neck there. This seemed to be a message, even in its vague hostility, of love for Brandon.

"You don't need to ask, Brandon. Do you think we released these ports on humanity without understanding what we were doing? What power we wielded? Do you think we are eliminating people?"

Brandon saw Dawn flinch as Doors came near her.

"And you must know that even if we *were* eliminating people, that it would be for the best? You know we weren't doing that, but that if we had been, it had to be so?" Doors' eyes still somehow radiated calm and kindness. Their twinkle indicated that this performance was an elaborate joke. "The Earth can breathe again. Do you know how beautiful is the creation of such a thing? That time and space, they shimmer, nebulous despite their apparent solidity?" This string of questions seemed to Brandon like hard exhalations filling up a balloon. Doors went to the window. The swaths of colour there— oval of green, stripe of white, expanse of blue above—appeared to form a kind of flag for PINA. "What we've made here, yes, it has a mythic quality, doesn't it? This place is no more real than any place anyone has ever dreamed up. What is your reality test now? How can you be sure what is real?"

Brandon nearly spoke then, but again resisted. Doors came around to the empty seat at the head of the table, sat in his chair and rolled himself on it around to where Brandon sat. He pushed his knees up against Brandon's.

If Brandon started laughing at this—laughter began filling his head like the onset of a sneeze—he knew he would never be able to leave.

"Here is the climax to the scene. Here is what you want to know. You all want to know why I would stay behind if port is so wonderful, right? If I trust it? That's what the papers want to know and the interviews and all the reporters and the scientists and all the fucking ethicists too. 'Why did you send the Testifiers in, Mr. Doors?'" His imitation of an American accent sounded like Homer Simpson. "'With all due respect, Mr. Doors, shouldn't you send yourself?' 'Where's my mommy?' 'Where's my daddy?'" Doors laughed. "Brandon, you, you of all people. I know the rest of you have put it together. Welcome to your mind being blown. Welcome to your betrayal."

Dawn, ordinarily so unflappable, let out a cry. "We thought it was for the best," she said. "What could we do?"

Brandon looked up into Doors' eyes, with their gaping pupils. Then at Zahra, who stared back, stony. So. Doors was nothing but an asshole.

"And it is for the best! The old liberal myths are dead. Humanity—the concept—is dead." The heat flowed from where Doors' knees touched Brandon's, and it seemed to Brandon as if Doors might be about to grow enormous, to extend hugely into space, magical and demonic, to loom above them, taunting them. "You're too attached to the old myths, Brandon. *We hold no things to be self-evident.* No things. Interrogate your premises. You believe you've uncovered something. But why should death be worse than life?"

Now Doors stood, leaned over the table and braced his arms against it. Veins pulled across them like thick tree roots.

"Yes, I'm going to tell you what happened. Yes, port is perhaps dangerous. I know its dangers quite intimately, I know that it speaks to you and knows you."

"What?" Benji jumped up like a teenage boy defending his girl-friend against a slight.

Brandon pitied the others: Benji's good-natured argumentation, Dawn's scowl, Zahra with her hard glare. This was the charisma and danger of a cult leader. For him, it no longer mattered. He had already made up his mind to leave. Only he was, finally, immune. But immediately he questioned this immunity.

Doors banged his fist on the table. "Of course I know everything. What did you think? Where is your vision? I know the power of port to persuade. I know that it infects you and takes hold like a virus, like rabies, wanting you in its clutches. Port knew where I wanted to go. It is not mere science; it is witchcraft. We are only at the beginning of understanding what this means. But I do know that what has happened here does not belong in the annals of atrocity." He banged his fist again. "Good riddance. Earth can breathe."

"But you've been telling us," Dawn said, "that people *can* come back. That they are choosing *not* to come."

"How do you weigh the costs? Every human is a cost to other creatures, to the oceans, the trees. Why is a human worth more?"

Brandon stood. He felt rather than saw the others turn, spectators at a ball. He walked to the door. "I'm done," he said.

"Good riddance," Doors said, face tight with anger. Then, as the door was closing, "Best of luck out there!"

Brandon walked with painful slowness, until he saw an opportunity to duck into a stairwell and down into the parking garage. The garage, he knew, was guarded by one person on rotation with the latrine crew and the hall crew, and there he'd find his old Turing, the car he'd been able to buy in cash after only a few paychecks and his staff discount. Its aquamarine rounds and headlamps had the comforting curves and eyes of a human face. Let them realize too late why he was carrying a pack heavily laden with bottles. Let them realize how they'd underestimated his courage.

At the exit, he leaned out the driver's window and gave the chubby, tightly belted guard his most charming smile.

"You're with the other group," the guard said.

It was the assumption Brandon had hoped he'd make, and he channelled Buddha-like warmth and calm.

"I was told there would be only four," the man added.

"I'm bringing up the rear. Last-minute addition." Brandon gestured at the back seat, where he'd laid five extra solar packs. "Supplies."

The guard nodded slowly and pushed a button. The garage door hoisted open in excruciatingly slow increments. Brandon lifted his foot off the brake and watched the man press the intercom button. He prepared for the possibility that another car would speed out after him. But no one was following.

It had been a full year since he'd driven the Turing, but with no trouble the tiny car bounced out of the alleyway and onto Pineapple Avenue. Then onto Colada Street, only a few empty miles from the freeway.

The radio poured out static. He found an old PINAkey in the glovebox and pegged it in. In ten minutes, the shining white fortress of PINA was too far away to see in his rear-view mirror, and he was alone in a car with a song he loved. The wind was on his face on an abandoned highway, and although the Turing could only get up to fifty-five, tears and sweat cooled his skin. He wildly drummed his hands on the wheel, letting the car swerve. He sang along so loudly that he hardly recognized his own voice.

Of course, there was no other car on the freeway. He swerved around broken branches, a line of small mammals, possibly rabbits, and then what looked—if he hadn't known better—like a half-built beaver lodge. Probably, he mused, there were animals he'd never heard of. He felt a pang at the memory of the peace he'd felt port offering him, how he'd envisioned it would be when he and Zahra held hands and jumped through.

What a fucking lonely world, he thought. His mother had gone in after his father, hadn't she? She'd gone to be with his dad in some earlier life, to persuade him to keep his gall bladder. His mother, possibly doubled, and his father, still living, and acned, bespectacled Brandon doing algebra in his running shorts. She'd gone there, or— Brandon admitted it, finally, for the first time, like a person unbuttoning pants that were two sizes too tight—he didn't know where. Nobody knew.

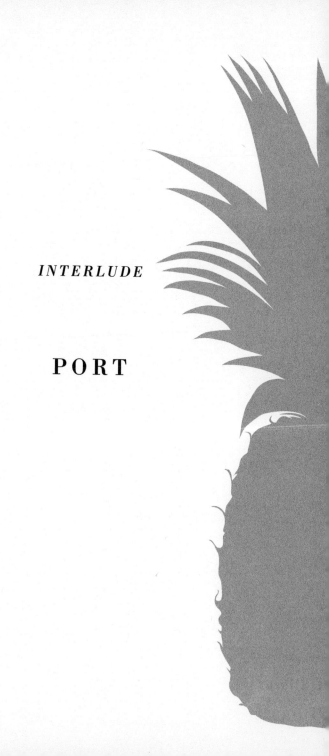

INTERLUDE

PORT

There was a figure sitting in a field. Maybe it was a steer resting in the grass? But how strange it would be to see a steer like that, all alone, one black smudge in an otherwise empty field.

The overgrown grasses were shaded by trees, and some of those trees bore markings of human activity. Here a wooden swing, there jagged letters scratched into bark. Below the tree, a winding path of packed dirt. The lonesome figure sat unshaded in a blaze of midday sun, surrounded by a frantic buzzing in the grasses topped by purple and white flowers, uncertain what he was doing, how he had got here, and who, indeed, he was.

He was a he. That much was coming into focus, as this field would have through a camera's lens. A man, he thought, knowing this from memory and without needing to open up the waist of his pants and peer in. Though he did this anyway, finding only standard-issue white briefs under jeans that bagged to his ankles. I am the sort of person who buys off-brand white briefs, the man thought to himself. Then: *I am the sort of person who knows the difference between kinds of briefs.* And inside that blue-striped elastic band, of course, the usual.

The buzzing deafened. He swatted at his ear.

The things he knew: maleness, femaleness, erections, piss, denim, pants, briefs, the colour white, the existence of brands. Each scrap of knowledge branched off indefinitely. Still sitting steer-like, he squinted off into the green-gold distance, shading his eyes with his hand. In the distance he saw a shape that might have been a house next to a shape that must have been a barn.

Everything about the field was idyllic, the sunshine and the plant life, the butterflies. He wanted to remove his brown loafers and trouser socks and run through the grasses with his arms outstretched, like a young child assuming the posture of a plane. The only thing to darken the moment was the fact of how alone he appeared to be. Even the sky was cloudless. He stood up with a little difficulty, becoming dusted with pollen in the process. He put a hand to his face, finding there a thick beard it pleased him to pull on. Aside from another person, what he wanted to see most was a mirror.

He slid his hand into his pocket, and his fingers found the corners of a business card. Before he could draw it out, the ground began to shake, and then there was a buzzing so intense he thought it would deafen him. Something large came zooming close: a formation of old fighter jets in a migratory vee. He flattened to the ground, hands behind his head, and the grasses bent back like lithe dancers as the jets passed. He lay there long after the planes were gone, waiting until the insects had resumed their buzz and flutter, and then, still, he waited. The moment clarified as he took note of the small papery wings around him, how their shape and texture seemed an echo of the thin pointed shapes of certain leaves. He thought of nothing aside from the moment he found himself in. Every far-off rumbling moved through the front of his body. A mouse even a metre off made the grasses sway noticeably. He thought of the phrase *the winds of change* and no longer knew what he was waiting for. Then, the light shifted.

Twilight, cooler air, a distant sound like fireworks, but with no light show in the sky to match. He thought, *And it was morning and it was evening the first day.*

He approached the farmhouse as the sky turned starry. He saw no animals, but there were animal smells, along with another smell, strong and persistent, worse than manure. The house inside was dimly lit, with a slight orange glow framed by the windows. He was a field mouse far away from his nest. Or was this his own house, abandoned? He came closer to the windows that backed into a high row of hedges, two panes of which were drawn open so that the curtains lightly guarding its inner rooms moved in and out as ominously as a ghostly nightgown. He lifted onto tiptoes, attempted to see through. Smell of lit tobacco, the flickering of a candle flame. Were those whispers voices? Was that a human coughing? Retching?

Again there was the popping of fireworks. A flash of light.

He retreated, pinning himself against the cold stone between those windows, and tried to breathe. His mouth was gluey; he badly needed water. He inched around the side of the house and tapped on the window with a bent index finger. "Hello?" Spittle so thick he could hardly speak. He attempted to swallow.

Something shifted, as though that mouse in the field was moving again. There was a series of pleasant sounds, of metallic or plastic parts fitting together perfectly, reminding him of when he was a young father clicking open and shut the parts of his son's Transformers. In his mind, he followed this blast of recollection: orange shag carpet installed by the previous owners, all those cars and robots strewn across it, each frozen in some moment of transformation. A child's fat fingers. The light from a basement window far above their heads. *Shuckashuckashucka*: his son making machine-gun sounds.

His hand was still reaching toward the window, but he had pulled his face away. This was not his house.

Through the open window poked a bit of black metal piping.

"Hello? I am a father," he said. This admission filled him with amazement, and other facts spilled forward. I am a father, he thought, and the phrase was familiar. But then he said, "*Mon fils, ma fille,*" the French coming out unexpectedly, and his voice sounding nothing like it ought to have sounded.

The snowman shape of his shadow appeared on the wall of the house, brightly haloed.

"Ah, man. It's just Philippe," said a man's voice.

His hands, quaking, were rubbery.

"What are you doing sneaking around out here?" said a second man.

"He injured?" said another.

"Looks all right. A little shaken up. You okay, Philippe? You see something, buddy?" These voices were addressing him as though he was a very old man. He looked down: his hands were veiny, moist-palmed.

He was afraid to turn around. The voices were indistinguishable from one another. If he turned around, the men would see his face and see that he was not Philippe. A hand fell hard on his shoulder. He turned. Lights flashed in his eyes. The three rifles that had been trained on him slowly lowered.

"Boy, are we glad to see you! Thought we'd lost you out there."

Philippe—could that be right? It seemed *almost* right. He gaped at them.

"Well, let's get inside."

The three men were dressed in layers of fatigues, from white T-shirt to full khaki gear, plus belt and rucksack. Each held a rifle at chest level, and together they marched him around to the door. Inside, a fourth man was seated regally on an arrangement of three blue kitchen chairs, his booted legs propped across two of them. The table in front of him was painted blue also, the scratch of bare wood showing through along the corners. Candlelight provided a flickering glow. The man with the propped legs was arranging papers, folding and unfolding them, moving them around in the manner of a reader of tarot cards. His eyes were set keenly on these pages. He lifted a pencil from the table and held it in his hands, poised to write something, then returned pencil to pocket. He did this twice. The movements he made were balletic, as though choreographed: the swoop of his hand, the flight of the pencil. He did it a third time and then stopped, pencil in hand, not writing.

Philippe stood at the door as the other soldiers filed past him. The last one, the smallest, took his arm and led him as one would a blind grandfather over to one of the empty chairs. Young men lacked all imagination, could not understand the minds of others. This thought surprised Philippe, as though it had come into his head from some other source.

His surroundings were unfamiliar, but Philippe understood that he was supposed to recognize them. Copper pots and a blackened pan hanging from hooks around a big sink, wooden counters, plates piled everywhere. A rope of garlic bulbs dangled, and dried herbs hung like witches' brooms. The room was dim, but the lit steeples of wax on the table and the counters shot it through with uneven light.

With sooty hands, a soldier picked up a hard round loaf of bread. His biceps tensed as he tore pieces off. An unlabelled green glass bottle was passed around and arrived in front of Philippe.

"This is the last loaf and the last of the wine. You got anything hiding in a cellar somewhere?" The man who spoke these words was very pale, as though untouched by the sun, with eyes blue-white, like ice.

"Hey, give him a minute. He's disoriented or something."

"Yeah, so am I. Hungry too."

The man with the propped legs was shuffling his papers again. The blue-eyed one took a swig from the bottle and stared at Philippe. The small one, who stood behind Philippe, put two hands on his shoulders.

The fourth man stood at the sink staring out the window. "We'd settle for whisky or anything hard at this point," he said.

"If you have flour and oil and water, *je pourrai faire cuire du pain*," Philippe said. "*Mais, mais.* But—" His accent was stronger now. The words strained against the forms his mouth was trying to make, as though he'd recently been Novocained. "*Si vous avez de l'eau*, water, *j'ai*, I am at this moment quite thirsty."

"If *you* have flour and oil and water?" said the icy one. "This is your house, bub."

"Clearly he's in shock," said the voice from the small man behind him.

Were these his pans, was this his table? Was he French? He rubbed his hand along a splintering edge, picking at dried paint with his thumbnail. "How long was I missing?"

"A full twelve hours. Um, *douze heures*."

"Did you see me out there in the field?"

The men shook their heads. Gnawed at the bread. The man at the table looked up at him.

"We thought we lost you, bub. Er, *sir*. Monsieur. We are getting ready to shove off. We're leaving at dawn."

"*Et je suis Philippe?*" He had slid into the French again as if into a slippery patch of mulch. "I'm Philippe? This is my house."

"Poor guy," one of them said. "Amnesia, d'ya think?"

"We found you here two days ago. Just you. *Seulement vous*," said the one standing behind him. "All our guys are gone, and we're the only ones left." He pulled up a chair and sat beside Philippe. Shoved hunks of the bread into his mouth. "I don't think you've got flour or anything, because this bread was stale when we got here. Place had been ransacked." The moist sound of chewing was close to Philippe's ear, then a slurp. "I'm Private Daniels, remember? The medic?" He lifted his hand and pointed at each of the others. "Mitford, Cooper, Ambrose."

"Daniels, Mitford, Cooper, Ambrose," Philippe repeated.

"*Oui, bien.*"

"And Daniels is a fucking show-off." Mitford gave the small man an ice-pick stare.

Daniels shrugged. "I like a chance to practise my French." He handed Philippe a canteen, and Philippe drank until his lips ached. "*J'aime beaucoup d'avoir un chance . . . Une chance?*"

"We all need to get some rest. Why don't you go on upstairs." Cooper had a rifle in his hands and motioned with it toward another room. This seemed a vague threat, and obediently Philippe stood up. His legs threatened to buckle, and he grabbed the table for support. This caused the papers spread in front of the seated, pencil-poised Ambrose to shift and flutter, and Ambrose looked up with a sorrowful, reproving stare.

"*Pardon*," Philippe said. He wandered into the next room, where he found the shapes of musty furniture, and in the shadows, the tracks of muddy boots. Nothing on the walls. An old fireplace, black with soot. He went into the hall and upstairs, where he found two cramped rooms. One with a bed mounted on a metal bed frame, and another containing only the detritus of soldiers. Packs and canteens and blankets laid on the floor. He wanted proof of his children's lives, though the chance of finding this seemed so unlikely that to seek it made him concerned he'd gone mad. There were no Transformers, no stripped-naked Barbies, no game consoles, no screens even, no small bits of clothing, nothing. Still, his children made the clearest picture in his mind, clearer than the floor creaking under his feet: a child's hand on a plastic toy, the bits of spittle as he went *shuckashuckashucka*, and then another child coming from behind and covering Philippe's eyes. *Guess who?*

Here, there were only more boot marks, more mud. This wasn't anything like Winston's bedroom or Mary's. Was there any electric light? Were there sockets? He felt the dampish wall beside the door for a switch, and found none. He had the feeling he couldn't open his eyes wide enough, that no matter how hard he tried, he'd never be able to see.

He sat heavily on the larger bed. The springs whined as they shifted. He lay back, shut his eyes. His body smelled both sour and sharp, of warm earth and clipped grass. Voices took shape and reached him in his half-sleep.

"Boy, he's really confused. What happened to him?"

"Nothing. He seemed all right. Then he was just gone."

"Where would he go?"

"Probably went to the barn. These guys love to sleep near warm piles of shit."

"The manure can't be warm anymore."

"Still, he smells bad. Worse than you, Mitford."

[Laughter.]

"*That's* saying something."

"Ah, fuck off."

[More laughter.]

"It's shock. Fatigue. He lost his whole family. Some fucker took all the fucking animals, too, or left 'em for dead."

"Maybe they ran off?"

"Minds make compensations. Doesn't know where he is. Seems like he hardly knows there's a war on."

"Maybe it's all a bad dream."

"Now you sound like Greenblatt."

"Poor fuck."

There was a long silence. Philippe felt himself drifting.

"You think the orders are on the way?"

"Nah. We're fucked."

"That's the spirit!"

"We should get him to come with us. He knows the landscape."

"Who, Philippe? We can't take a civilian with us."

"But can we leave him here?"

"His people will come back for him."

"Don't be stupid. You think anybody comes back?"

The voices stopped again. The breeze through the window over the bed was a mercy, touching his body where it was sore, cooling him in the places gathering sweat. He considered pulling off his shirt, but was too tired to do so. Deep in his body, he ached to see that small chubby hand, those toys. He again considered removing the shirt. Again he was too tired. He had a shirt. He was here, actually, physically. Will I or won't I? His shirt had an odor, was made of molecules. Will I or won't I? I. I. I.

He awoke in a black and heavy silence. His eyes adjusted to perceive a form next to him on the bed. Daniels, hands crossed over his chest, legs straight out, sleeping like a corpse. The bed jumped as he got up, thin mattress a see-saw. In that dark, he stumbled down the stairs. His body knew where each turn was, knew the size of each step, and knew when he had come to the bottom. He swung the door open between the sitting room and kitchen, and there was Ambrose, still awake and staring at the papers, a single candle burning in front of him. Ambrose turned and nodded. Philippe nodded back.

"*Du vin*. I know where the wine is," Philippe said and took an unlit candle from the counter, touching its wick to the flame. Tears of wax dripped and landed on the table. He took his candle and crouched down to the cupboard.

"We already looked in there," Ambrose said gruffly, without turning around. "Anyway, we're leaving. Had enough wine. We'll find more, I'm sure. Wine and shit and shells."

"I will come with you?"

"You can't come with us. Even if we wanted. We have orders."

Philippe sat down across from him again, set the candle on the table.

"You ain't dressed for combat, or for a hike even, to be truthful. You ain't in shape."

Philippe nodded, let his gaze rest on the papers.

"But you'll manage. You got a choice. I ain't got a choice."

Philippe absently moved his hands to his pockets. Pulled out the business cards he found there, one from each pocket. Ran his thumbs around the edges.

"What d'ya got there?"

Philippe didn't answer. Instead, he strained to peer at Ambrose's papers. Pages scrawled in cursive lettering, a picture of a woman in lingerie, coy pin-up smile on her lips, a few blank pages. Ambrose pulled them into a single pile and shielded them from Philippe's gaze.

"No privacy," he said. "No privacy, no comfort, no pleasure." He glared at Philippe. "Liberty and justice for all. The pursuit of happiness. Written into the constitution. Pursuit of happiness. We're *pursuing* our *happiness*."

"I'm Canadian," Philippe said, shrugging.

Ambrose narrowed his eyes. "I thought you were French."

Philippe flushed hot then, as though something he was trying to keep together had begun to unravel. He looked at the business cards. Embossed blue lettering said "Main Street Public Library" and "Philip McGuire, MLS" and an address and a phone number. On the back, someone had scrawled: *You are not at home here. Remember port.* And: *Come back.*

"What's port?" Philippe handed the cards to Ambrose.

"It's a kind of wine. Normally you'd have *the* port. *A* port. Unless it's wine."

"Right."

Ambrose handed the cards back. "Where'd you get these?"

"They were in my pockets."

"That's creepy, man. That's fucking creepy. *You are not at home.*"

Philippe nodded.

"But ain't this your home?"

❧

He ought to have slept; he couldn't sleep, though Daniels's weight in the bed calmed him like a wife's. In the morning, eyes aching with fatigue, Philippe got what flour was left and tried to mix it with drips of oil and water and salt. He kneaded it as well as he could, but the flour was crumbling even before it went into the wood stove.

"I used to have chickens," he said to himself. "Where did my chickens go?"

"When we found you, you were cooking up the last one. You made up all the eggs and served 'em to us." This was Cooper, the man who yesterday had been standing watch at the window.

The men had come downstairs one by one, loudly, as teenagers did, their bodies too large for the space, boots thunderous, packs thudding against the ground. Having teenagers in the house, morning shouts—*Dad! Dad! Dad!*—seemed more real, or at least more recent, than this scene. He was sure that his own kitchen table had been heftier, bigger, laid with red placemats. His wife in her bathrobe opening her mouth to say his name.

"Smells all right, anyway." Behind him, Ambrose folded each of his pages and put them into inner pockets.

"Something for you to take with you." Philippe had dusted his cracked hands on his shirt, and white flour fell from his body as he moved around the table with the warm bread. Unleavened, it hadn't risen, but each man tore off a hunk and ate it with animal fervor until only crumbs remained. These Philippe scooped from the table and tossed into his own dry mouth.

"You've been real generous," Cooper said. "You gotta keep something for yourself. What are you gonna eat?"

Daniels smiled at Philippe. He had long-lashed brown eyes, and his skin was deeply tanned. "You should come with us."

Cooper shifted, one booted leg on a chair, the other straight. He was pinching his fingers into a jar of something that smelled fishy.

He tossed something small and scaled into his mouth and then passed the jar to Ambrose.

"He can't come. We discussed this." Licked oil and brine from his fingers. "We aren't escorts. We're foot soldiers."

"He can help us get going in the right direction."

"We're just heading north. We can manage."

"And if things go wrong?"

"Then things go wrong. But the fire hasn't been anywhere near us."

"Maybe we just stay here?" Mitford said.

"Can't do that. Cowards or MIA. The only way out is through."

"Odds are three out of four of us are dead men."

"They're in retreat. Krauts ain't idiots. They know it's over for 'em."

"We can't leave him here," Daniels insisted. "We just take him with us and drop him off at the next town. How long's he gonna make it on his own? We're human beings, pal. I'm sure we'll get back to our guys by sunset."

"While we're fantasizing," Mitford said, "who else thinks we'll be greeted by topless Rita Hayworth on a float?"

"With a brand-new Ford for everyone!" Cooper shouted.

"And we'll drive that goddamned fucking Ford all the way through this weed-land and into the sea," Ambrose said.

"Float off to victory." Mitford cupped his hand in a queenly wave.

Ambrose wheezed and coughed into his arm, and Daniels came around to pat him on the back.

"You guys are real funny," Daniels said. "It's gotta be only a day's walk till we reach our guys. Philippe, go see what you can rustle up in the barn. We need tools, blankets. Whatever you can find."

The shag-carpeted basement, the hands over his eyes, *shuck-ashuckashucka*—these things were fading. Philippe grasped at them feebly as he walked to the barn. They were sinking under black, bobbing on the surface, then gone. The wife he'd pictured with a name in her mouth. Something was happening to his mind. He hadn't known himself to be French or a farmer, but the barn as he came to it was familiar, even comforting. A place for daily ritual, where, high-booted, he would go just as the sun was coming up.

Why can't I get my mind straight? His barn and stables, so solid, wavered as though alive, as though ready to do him harm: the chopped wood, the beams blackening with mildew, the dung-scented hay. The sun was cresting in the distance, imbuing everything with golden light. He could see himself touching the long lean face of a horse. He closed his eyes then, hand holding a fence gate, and stead-ied himself against dizziness. A mouse dashed out of the hay and over his feet, squeaked at him, and was gone.

He found a wheelbarrow and put shovels and wool blankets inside. A shotgun. He carted it back to the house, where the men were sitting on the sagging porch. Its armlike handles felt soft and worn down. His own hands had worn them down.

"A wheelbarrow," Cooper said. He was the broadest and the only one whose skin seemed to be wearing in the corners of his eyes, crow's feet a fan that folded and unfolded as he frowned and then laughed. An unlit cigarette was stuck to his chapped bottom lip.

"Philippe, you should put a jacket on."

"I think I'll stay here," Philippe said.

Blue-eyed Mitford had his boot up on a stone ledge, and leaned over to spit in the mud. "Man wants to stay." He stood and spit over the edge of the porch into the grass there.

An enormous boom sounded, then fainter booming from the north. Daniels took Philippe aside. "It's your choice."

Philippe winced. "What happened to all the animals? What happened to my family?"

"We don't know. You were ransacked, it looks like."

"But I told you, I definitely told you, that I had a family?"

Daniels nodded. "But maybe they got out in time."

"*Mais ou etais-je?*"

Daniels frowned. "Maybe they got out. We'll take you to the neighbours'. The village. If it had been my family, I'd have sent them to stay with people I knew. Maybe you just caught a little fire, but no harm done. We're going north. You know the way, don't you?"

Daniels had the helpless look of a person who loved to have answers and now had none. His long lashes gave his wet eyes a feminine appearance.

"Maybe the Germans were here first. Maybe I let them stay here too."

Daniels nodded. "Maybe."

He wore an ill-fitting sweater he found in a drawer. Its sleeves dangled from his wrists, and every few minutes he had to push them back up his arms. It was too hot for a sweater anyway, and soon he tied it around his neck, draping like a piggybacking child's arms. He steered the wheelbarrow through the empty lengths of dirt road between nine-foot hedges, bouncing along behind the men.

Everyone's a lotus-eater. He kept step to the strange phrases rising in his mind. *Everyone's a coward. Everyone's a lotus-eater. Everyone's a coward.*

"Does it look familiar?" Daniels asked him.

The men were marching in the four-points of a square in front of him. He watched their bodies' slow rhythm as one watches waves breaking on a distant shore. Sweat stung his eyes, and he wiped first one and then the other with the back of his hand, each time causing the wheelbarrow to hiccup. Ambrose turned and glared at him.

"Philippe?" Daniels said, turning his head briefly without breaking his march.

"*Oui?*" He was thinking in English, but French came out.

"I feel like we're heading northeast," Cooper said. He peered into the sky and halted, thus stopping their caravan. "But we ought to be going northwest."

"Path will turn and head us in the right direction."

"Who the hell planted these fuckers?" Cooper swung his rifle toward the thick hedges, which were deeply root-bound in shelves of dirt on either side.

"*Ils étaient. . . .* They were always here," Philippe said.

Back at the house, he'd changed out of his dirty jeans and into wool trousers. They were too long and a little tight, digging into his ass and crotch, causing his loose belly meat to spill out. He'd moved the business cards over to the new pants, but he no longer needed them, as he'd memorized each of their details, even the feel of the embossed letters. *Remember port and the place you come from. Come back. Come back.* The words made him ache with something like grief for a lost love. *Come back!* There was someone who wished for him urgently.

The others had caked wet mud on Philippe's clothes to mimic camouflage, but there was no cover in the road. They were exposed. Around the next bend, he knew, they might be met with firepower they could not withstand. He gripped the handles of the wheelbarrow hard. His forearms and calves ached. The green endless walls of leaves moved gently as though enchanted.

Everyone's a lotus-eater. Everyone's a coward. Everyone's a lotus-eater. Everyone's a coward.

"What's that?" Mitford said.

Philippe shook his head. "*Rien.* Nothing."

"You understand English real well," Mitford said. "For a farmer."

Sweat dripped from Philippe's thick eyebrows and down his cheeks.

"He does speak it well, don't he?" Ambrose said.

"In 'Sleeping Beauty,' the castle is surrounded by thickets. Princes have to slice through it or get caught up," Philippe said.

"Huh," Ambrose said, without moving his head. "They got 'Sleeping Beauty' where you come from too?"

It didn't take long for sweat to soak through his clothes, for his hands gripping the handles of the wheelbarrow to cramp and stiffen. His wrists grew numb, then his ankles. Despite the heat pouring out of the sky, his toes were cold.

"Put the sweater on," Ambrose said. "You're shivering."

"Where is everybody?" Mitford said. He paused at the appearance of a lone shovel on the path. Near it, the earth had been disturbed, chunked out and sliced into. Mitford kicked the shovel nonsensically. "Dugout," he said, inching along with his back against the hedge.

Philippe felt the tension of the other men as they watched Mitford do this.

"Nothing," Mitford said, and they moved on.

Philippe looked at the sky, then at the ground, remembering the shovel. He rolled the wheelbarrow down along the dirt and abandoned it in the shallow ditch, then jogged to catch up.

"Smart." Ambrose nodded at him. "Only take what you can carry."

"We shouldn't have stayed so long at Philippe's house. We look like deserters," Daniels said.

"What were we supposed to do?" Mitford said. "You're the one who got us lost."

Daniels frowned. "Well, we got to get our story straight. Getting lost is one thing. Sitting around smoking in front of a chateau while you listen to your comrades get slaughtered is another."

"Ah, that never happened. You sound like Greenblatt."

"Poor fuck."

"It did happen! I heard it!" Daniels said.

"You think you heard it. And now you sound like a little girl."

Mitford stopped suddenly, jarring everyone back.

"What is it?" hissed Cooper, aiming his gun at the empty road ahead, then rotating carefully to aim it at the empty road behind.

"Look," Mitford whispered, pointing at the earth four feet in front of him. A long line of rats flowed past. "They're fat."

Cooper laughed.

"Means they've been eating." Mitford climbed into the hedge, using the roots as footholds. A rat climbed out and onto his shoulder. He knocked it off and then returned to the path. Stepped over the rats. "Nasty."

"What'd you see on top of the hedge?"

"Nothing. Nada. Fuck-all."

"Shoulda looked through the binoculars."

"Fuck off, Cooper."

A few more paces, and then Daniels stopped. "We gotta get our story straight. They're gonna ask where we been, why so long, what we been doing."

"We lost our comms. Not our fault."

"We shoulda just kept walking till we got to Paris. I always wanted to see the Eiffel Tower."

The sun was directly overhead. It burned Philippe's eyes. They stopped to piss, letting the liquid stream lazily into the dusty earth, onto the dirt and roots and twigs.

"Maybe they think we're all dead. They'll just be glad to see us."

"Here's what we tell them. Some German comes around and grabs Daniels and takes him hostage. We see it happen. Daniels surrenders, but the Kraut's got a knife at his throat."

"That makes no sense. Why would that happen? This isn't fucking Cowboys and Indians."

"Yeah, it is."

"How did I get free?"

"So Mitford sneaks around back and shoots him in the back of the head."

"That doesn't explain why we were gone so long."

"Maybe we wanted to make sure there weren't any more of 'em hiding out."

"Jesus. You're really bad at this."

"What's wrong with the story?"

"They'd never be all alone like that. They'd just shoot him. Why'd he need a hostage?"

"'Cause he's scared. 'Cause he's alone."

"He woulda just shot him and then us. That's what we woulda done. Why wouldn't you just have shot him before he got his hands on Daniels?"

"Everybody knows what a sissy Daniels is. Sissies are as sissies do." Mitford narrowed his eyes at each of them. Then grabbed his crotch.

"Leave him alone," Cooper said. "You're the one scared of rats."

"No. Here's the story," Daniels said. He was still smiling a little, his eyes wide as though he were encouraged.

Ambrose smiled too. Mitford spit dramatically into the leaves. Philippe stuck his hands in his pockets, a child waiting to be picked for a team.

"Here's what we say happened. The shooting started. We shot back at them. Greenblatt was beside me running and hit the ground. There was no time to look back. We ran until we lost them, hid out in the trees, but then it was dark. We had to go back for Greenblatt, but it was too dark, and we didn't want to run out of battery for the lights, and Cooper's hand-crank made too much noise. Blew the cover."

"But that *is* what happened."

"Yeah, well, we leave out the part where we stay at Philippe's for twelve hours."

"Sixteen hours."

"Goddamn. Sixteen?"

Without his wheelbarrow, Philippe felt himself to be deeply vulnerable, disarmed. The sun above them blazed. "Where are we?" he whispered. Into his chest came a beating panic. Then a flock of birds lifted from the hedges and exploded, shrieking, into the sky.

"This is your land," Ambrose hissed. "You tell us where we are."

Philippe glanced around in bewilderment. His nearest memory was far away, that shag carpet, those little hands. He pulled out the damp and softened business cards and read their words again. There was something he had to remember and could not remember. *Come back. Come back.*

"When do we get to the end of this road?" Mitford said.

"I don't think I'm quite awake yet," Philippe said. The road might just keep spinning them ever forward. They had entered a terrible infinity. But just as he thought so, the light shifted up ahead, the hedgerows gave way to an open field.

"Well, wake up," Ambrose said.

Philippe was sliding away from himself. There was no Philippe. These were not his people. "I'm not supposed to be here," he said. The names of his children on the shag carpeting had floated like bubbles and then popped in his mind: *Winston. Mary. Mary. Winston.* He marched and tried hard to remember something else. His eyeballs were sore from the cross-eyed concentration this seemed to require. The smell of urine blended with other filthy smells, which must have been the men's packs and shirts soaked through with sweat and damp and God knows what else. His legs were numb at the knee and hip, and his skin burned in rotating spots. Sharp like bee stings in his elbow and then in his buttock, exploding stars of pain, left then right, each moment proof that he was here now, in his body, captive.

The others had used the word *Nazi.* He had heard them say *France.* He had tried to say, "I don't think I really speak French.

I don't think I really am French." But this came out as "*Je ne pense pas que je suis français.*"

He saw Daniels share a look with Cooper: the old man is losing it.

He had always wanted to go to France. Though, of course, he'd had Paris in mind. And he'd always longed for courage to be asked of him, courage in the form of righteous soldiering. He'd wanted his life to be asked of him. Something better than the easy life he'd been given. Carpeted basement, transforming toys, two happy children. *I'm forty-nine years old*, he thought. Each small scrap of knowledge was as much a relief as the breeze.

But then the mystery: How am I here?

He pulled the business card again from his pocket. The surface of the paper was wearing away, the ink growing fainter, and now his thumb smudged dirt over it. What did it mean? Port. *Remember port and the place you come from.*

When he had wished to go to war, it had been in a much younger body. Before he'd grown the beard and started wearing dad jeans, as Marie called them.

Dad jeans. Dad bod. Marie.

Mary, wasn't it? No, Mary was the daughter, long gone. Grown and gone, gone forever.

Gone forever?

Marie.

"Such a nice sunshiny day!" Mitford's exclamations were growing in intensity. They were talking about things far away from here, about girls and what they'd do to their bodies, about the things that they yet planned to do, about future jobs and homes. Cooper had built his own house from the ground up with his father. Daniels was going to work in his parents' diner until there was enough money for medical school.

"Aren't we having a glorious vacation, boys?" Mitford grinned into the sky.

They moved quickly. The buildings behind them became specks; and later, when Philippe turned around, they were gone. Sun was hitting the trees hard from the side, and shadows were long bars crossing the ground. Sunset was now only an hour away.

"It'll be good for it to be dark. Then we can't be seen," said Cooper.

"But also, we can't see," said Mitford.

No one noticed how little Ambrose was saying. Philippe could see the clenched side of his face, flesh drawn tightly into his teeth, jaw a sharp line.

"Daniels. You said we'd be there by now," Mitford said. He vigorously scratched the back of his head under his helmet, and this caused Cooper, and then Daniels, too, to scratch at their heads and necks. "Fuckin' fleas."

Philippe now realized he knew words the others probably did not know. For example, he knew the word *holocaust*. Did they know the term *D-Day* yet? "It's 1944," he ventured.

"Thanks for the newsflash, genius," Mitford said.

Daniels glared at him.

"Why don't you just let me fucking *be*?" Mitford said to Daniels, who shrugged.

Ambrose seemed to be chewing the inside of his cheek. Philippe felt his life depended upon keeping an eye on Ambrose. The man glanced back at him, then spit gutturally to the other side.

"Where'd you get them cards?" Ambrose said.

"What cards?"

"The ones in your pocket yesterday."

Philippe shrugged. "Yesterday?"

"Look, buddy. I'm not like the rest of these dummies. I know what's going on here."

"You do."

"I know you ain't what you seem. In fact, I can hardly remember anything about you before you showed up in the middle of the night.

These other guys say they know you. But I trust my mind." Ambrose tapped at his temple. "My mind is telling me to be careful about you."

"I'm not a—" Philippe stopped. His toes inside his old loafers were numb. "What do you think I am?"

"Those cards are calling cards. Like a card some New York bank manager has. I don't know where you got them, unless you got 'em off the body of someone important."

"Says 'Main Street Public Library' on them."

"That's English, though, right? Not *bibliotheca* or something. *Library*." Ambrose eyed him. "And now you're guarding them with your life. 'Cause you know something. You a spy? And that's a code, yeah?"

"*Bibliothèque*," Daniels said quietly.

"Huh?"

"You mean bibliothèque."

Ambrose stopped marching and turned around, stuck his finger in the hollow of Philippe's collarbone. Philippe put his arms up and stumbled backwards.

"Ambrose. Buddy," Daniels said.

"I don't know what they mean. I don't know where I got them," said Philippe, his eyes filling with water.

"The old man's crying, yeah? Big wah-wah baby tears."

"Jesus, Ambrose. Leave him alone," Daniels said.

"The sun's going down. We got to find somewhere for the night," Cooper said. "You guys can continue this argument after we lay up." He walked between them, finally breaking Ambrose's contact with Philippe.

They were all lit golden, as though they were on a Broadway stage. For a moment, they were figures frozen in a scene, Philippe accused, eyes open wide at Ambrose, Ambrose with teeth bared and wolfish, the other three still and watchful.

"We cannot continue this argument later. This guy might be from the other side." To Philippe Ambrose said, "You are a sympathizer, is that it?"

"What the hell, Ambrose. He's not even armed. He's somebody's granddad," Mitford said.

"I'm only forty-nine," Philippe said.

"You all didn't see them cards he's got. Mighty suspicious." Ambrose rooted through Philippe's pockets and passed the now nearly illegible cards back to the other three men. "Plus that shirt he's got on. You ever see buttons like this?"

"What does this mean, Philippe?" Daniels said.

"I don't know."

"That's not good enough," Ambrose said. "You think that's good enough?"

"I think something happened to me. It's not to do with you all. It's not to do with war or anything."

"Not to do with war?"

The men passed the cards around as the late afternoon turned dim and blue. At last, they walked slowly through the field toward the woods with a plan to sleep against the trees for a few hours. Ambrose insisted that Philippe walk in front of him and kept his gun aimed at his back, at the fat pale meat of his neck.

Everyone's a lotus-eater, she whispered in Philippe's dream. Marie. His Marie. *Everyone's a coward.*

He was standing at some far-off distance on the steps of a church. The church had within it an otherworldly glow. He was unzipping it; he was gone. Marie's voice grew faint, and there was a long nothingness, nothing but the glow of certainty that he would be healed, become a hero, be given a task to do. He floated through the nothing. It was joy.

But he woke up staring into the barrel of a gun. Ambrose's eyes behind the length of rifle, one shut and the other wide. A mutated wink. Philippe's body was so tired of these jolts that now, instead of a racing heartbeat, he felt a lethargic desire to vomit.

"I don't want you to shoot me, please," Philip said. *Fill-ip. Fill-ip.* Not *Fee-leep.* The dream had been about to unravel everything. "Maybe I can explain?"

"*May*be you can?"

The nausea returned. Philip could tell them nothing. What did he know, anyway? All he had to cling to was a suspicion that he did not belong here, that this was less real than some other reality.

"What does 'port' mean?" Ambrose had lowered the gun, and now pointed it at Philip's crotch.

They were camped in a thick forest, and the only light came from the stars and moon. Above the canopy of trees, the sky was a rich grey-blue. Calm down, Philip told himself, though it felt as if all of the events to follow this one were on his back, crushing him with their weight. *I'm from the future.* No, you can't say a thing like that. His mind was traumatized, playing tricks. There was no way to verify the truth of what he thought.

"A few years ago I had a—what would you call it?—a nervous breakdown."

Ambrose lowered the gun farther and his eyelids flickered. Batteries dying in a toy. "Uh-huh," he said.

"*Port* is a word for the thing I used to make sense. A talisman."

"Right." Ambrose's disappointment was as obvious as his exhaustion. He lowered the gun and rubbed his eyes with the heels of his hands like a small child late for bed.

Seventy years of history and anxiety, technology and bombs. Seventy years and everyone would be gone. "I went crazy, *mon ami, c'est tout.*" Philip cleared his throat. "Sometimes I have trouble knowing what's real."

His words appeared to be hypnotic. Ambrose seemed not only to have bought them but to have expected them. Now his heavy eyes dropped closed.

"You have to stay awake," Philip said.

But Ambrose slumped over and was snoring, finger still loosely poised on the trigger. The others, too, were children sleeping on a forest floor. The air had cooled, and Philip pulled the oversized sweater on over his head, though it was still damp with sweat and did nothing to warm him.

It was too dark to see what made the leaves tremble, what made those branches crack. Animals. Wind. He wanted to pore over the memories as one did an archive, to hang onto each morsel from the world he knew. *Librarian. Philip McGuire, MLS.* He wanted to page through his whole pathetic, lost life: the faces of his children at each stage, the backyard slide stuck with autumn leaves, his wife before the divorce with a red scarf in her black hair. But he was here.

Still, these images made up a self, and he felt as though he'd stepped into the waiting armour of his body, had fastened each of its parts tight.

Landing here and now was to be held under water by a bully. Under water—here—this was all there was. His eyes were open wide now. See? See? You happy now?

"I am most certainly not happy," Philip whispered, though in the middle of the night he could find a certain kind of pleasure: a moment's peace, the reward of rest after a long difficult day. Was his presence here a prank? Had everyone been thrown somewhere hard to land, bewildered?

"How do I get home? I want to get home."

He tried to concentrate on the question of how he'd arrived in the first field. It was as if he'd been thrown off the back of a truck or dropped from the sky and become conscious only as he hit ground. As soon as he could, he'd turn around and go back to that field—though this plan seemed hopeless and thus filled him with dread. What, go stand by the old tree and wait for a bus to show up?

The rolling clouds animated the moon, which seemed to swell and thin. It appeared to be snickering. "I want to go home," he muttered again. "I guess that's what they all say." The joke on him was that all soldiers wanted to be sent home to a bosom, a lover's arms. He was being taught a lesson.

You should sleep, you should sleep, a crow cawed at him. Clearly, this world had been built around him. Each of its elements containing a message directly for him. His pleading had antagonized it. The sky, the ground, the trees, the birds. The men too?

Were his children lost somewhere, untethered?

The sky thundered and lit up in the distance behind him, so he turned to look. Not lightning but more explosions. Impossible to know how close they were. He knew all the facts, better than most, had been the sort of child who liked war games and toy soldiers, who later flushed with embarrassment over the inaccuracies of the toys' weaponry. But now he realized he'd misunderstood everything. He had not known the basic facts of life in combat. How difficult it was to know where one was in this landscape, in any landscape, and this was not a board game, and he and his companions were not being moved along, were not figurines between index finger and thumb, and could see only as much and as far ahead as anyone could see.

The trees had fingers, branches that seemed in his peripheral vision to stretch up to choke out the sky. But when he jerked up his head, the sky was still there.

He noticed now how many mosquitoes there were. To add swelling to misery. He smacked his leg. In a past life, any such suffering would have had him tucked into bed. Temperature taken and warm soup.

By the time morning was glinting through the trees, Philip knew where he was. Ambrose was fallen beside him, neck in sleep bent awkwardly over his pack. Time passed strangely, too quick and then too slow. Time didn't pass at all. He, Philip, was a still point in the centre of time. The light between those trees did not shift. He felt no hunger, had no thirst. This was an afterlife, a purgatory, and perhaps each life was one doll nested inside another. Perhaps this one would open, and there would be another and then another.

But now, the forest had eyes and was watching him.

"You seem different, pal," Daniels said to Philip, handing him a canteen.

Philip attempted warmth and compassion, because these men didn't know they were imaginary.

"Do I?" he said, picking at his teeth with a branch. "You all ready to move on?"

"Anything happen last night? Ambrose said you were awake."

Ambrose, crouched over the pack he was tying closed, empty-eyed, with the dumb wariness of a deer. He hoisted the pack onto his shoulders.

"He seems worried," Philip said.

"It breaks you down," said Daniels. "My father told me all about how it goes in war. Some things, you see them and they break you."

Philip nodded.

"Oh, what a wonderful morning!" Mitford said, reaching his arms into the sky.

"I did see something," Philip said. "Explosions. Lots of shooting."

Daniels pulled out binoculars. "From which direction?"

Trees striped the view identically from every vantage. "It was to my back. This is where I was sitting. That way."

"Goddammit," Cooper said. "Shit."

"What?"

"That's the way we're headed," Daniels said.

There was a rhyme the children's librarians used to recite: "Going on a bear hunt. Gonna catch a big one. We're not scared." Then the leader, drumming her palms on her thighs, narrated their obstacles. "Oh, look! Long grasses! Can't go around it. Can't go over it. Gotta go *through* it." Philip chanted it to himself: "Oh, look! Gotta go through it. Oh, look! Gotta go through it."

They stayed in the woods, avoiding those hedged-in lanes where they felt like mice fumbling through an open-air maze.

"You shoulda seen it out there. Four days ago," said Daniels. "We were just getting picked off. Ten at a fucking time. Shot in the back while you tried to cut through the brush. Tanks going down every time they got over a hill."

Their boots crunched loudly with every step. Ambrose flinched when someone cracked a branch with his heel.

"Sure would be good to see another person," Mitford said.

Ambrose hissed at him to be quiet.

"Ain't nobody out here," Mitford said, then grumbled to himself. "You're supposed to get to loving the guys in your platoon. There's supposed to be some kind of bond."

Ambrose shushed him again.

"It's odd," Daniels said, ignoring Ambrose. "Foreboding. Just the five of us in the woods."

"Don't think like that. Shit," Cooper said.

Gotta go through it. Philip added increasing nausea to his list of concerns. The farther he walked in this direction, the farther he'd have to go back to that first field, *if* he ever found it again. After he got through this, he'd go back and find his way home. He pictured the church steps, heard Marie's voice just behind him. But he couldn't remember her face, or anyone's face.

"A situation is only as bad as you make it," Philip said, panting. "Life gives you lemons. You know. Make lemonade."

Their silence was a wall. Finally, Cooper laughed. "Life didn't bother sending any lemons this time."

Here was the case to disprove the mumbo-jumbo, Philip thought.

Life wasn't just what you made of it. Life was a jaw with teeth. You were sitting on its tongue.

The clouds had gone grey, and the air was damp as a mouth. The sky was a cryptogram: in this foreign country, this long-lost time, did heavy grey clouds still indicate rain? Ahead of them, an answer: the distant lines of drizzle thin and steady as a baleen grin.

These lines of rain were woven through with the vertical lines of trees, giving the world an architecture, as though it had been built to contain them.

"At least in all this we can glorify God," Ambrose said quietly. They were about to emerge from the cover of trees. Rain now fell steadily, beading on their wool jackets, soaking through the knitted holes in Philip's sweater.

Ambrose had been speaking to himself, but Mitford snapped his head around and gave him a vicious look. Mitford had not yet shown any rage, which made this Gorgon stare worse. The others stopped walking.

"Don't bring God into this," Mitford said through gritted teeth. This switch in mood, thought Philip, mimicked the weather's move from sunshine to chill rain.

"A day to us is a thousand years to the Lord." Ambrose didn't raise his eyes. He looked heavier and heavier, limper and limper, as though he weren't a man but an enormous ventriloquist's dummy. His feet dragged across the ground. "Our eyes must be on eternity. Store up treasures not on Earth where man can destroy."

"I don't want to hear this fucking bullshit. Does it glorify God to see bodies ripped open and ground up like meat? Does it glorify God for our bodies to be destroyed?" said Mitford.

"Leave him alone," Daniels said.

"If Daniels had his way, we'd all get along, wouldn't we?" Mitford said. "I bet you figure you're the Christ of this operation."

"Our bodies are temporary," Ambrose said.

"And your God requires them. He's hungry for young, fresh bodies."

"The Nazis. Not God," Philip said. Earthworms happy for rain wriggled out among the roots they had to step over. The ground was prepared to decompose their bodies, and was, in its way, hungry for them.

"Killing Krauts glorifies God." Ambrose began walking again, head bowed, eyes hidden by the lip of his helmet. He passed through the group of them like a ghost through a wall, unperturbed when his shoulders hit theirs, when his pack knocked against Mitford.

Mitford ran and got ahead of him. Stood like a boxer on quick feet, chest out, fists drawn. "Yeah? And who the fuck made the Nazis? Where'd Hitler come from in this pretty fairy tale you're telling yourself?"

Daniels jogged up to join them. Mitford was forced to walk backwards, while Ambrose kept doggedly on. Cooper took this opportunity for a smoke, his face expressionless, hands cupped over the squat cigarette to keep the rain out.

"I sure would love to fight you, Private," Ambrose said to Mitford.

"Oh yeah?" Mitford stopped walking so that Ambrose would crash into him, but Ambrose stopped too.

Pity came over Daniels' face. "Look at this poor fucker."

The ground now squelched under their feet. Philip's battered toes began to sting and tingle. "Something's going to happen," he said.

As though he'd conjured it, there was a rumble of thunder, a lightning crack. A whizzing, a shriek, something cold and wet like a raindrop falling on metal. Then Cooper made a loud and incoherent sound and fell to his knees. At his shoulder, something red bled inky around a hole in his jacket.

Shuckashuckashucka.

Then it whizzed into the bare flesh at Cooper's neck, taking a huge bite, blood not just blooming but gushing. Philip stood staring until Daniels' screams got through to him, until he felt his arm being yanked.

"Get back! Get the hell back!"

They each found a tree to crouch behind and fired back, into the rainy distance.

Philip pulled his body deeper into its crouch and held his hands over his ears. He fixed his eyes on Cooper, who was still trying to draw the cigarette to his mouth with his right arm, holding onto the wound at his neck with the left as blood pulsed out of it. Slowly, Cooper fell back on the ground, and released his grip on his neck. He succeeded in bringing the cigarette to his lips, but it had gone out in the rain. He sucked at it anyway. The leaves, the clothing, his hands and the cigarette were all rusted with blood.

The firing stopped.

"We get 'em?"

"How many?"

"I can't see anything."

"Fuck. Fuck. Fuck." This was Mitford. He stood and started running as though he were on fire.

"Get the fuck down, Mitford!" Daniels shouted.

Holding his knee and moaning with apologies, Mitford fell into rotted layers of leaves.

Philip was frozen, hands over ears, eyes on Cooper, who at last dropped the cigarette into the rain- and blood-soaked earth. His eyes like pennies. Daniels was close enough that Philip could reach his arm out to touch him, and he longed to do this. Daniels reloaded his gun. A few feet away, Ambrose was at another tree. Farther yet, Mitford moaned.

Daniels nodded at Ambrose, who pulled the pin from a grenade and threw it. Perhaps, thought Philip, they had forgotten that he was there. Perhaps now was the time to start crawling away, retrace his steps and be saved.

Then came the screams. "*Nein! Nein! Nein!*" Then the blast. Then a silence as deep as sleep. Not even a bird dared chirp.

Daniels held up his hand, but Ambrose did as Mitford had done, and ran into the gap between themselves and their assailant. He ran past Mitford on the ground and kept running. For several seconds, Philip heard only the sound of Daniels' hard fast breaths.

Then: "It's just one fucking guy!" Ambrose was laughing loudly. "One fucking guy!"

Daniels stood and moved those few feet to Mitford's side. Philip followed. Ahead of them, silhouetted in the grey light, Ambrose moved in a graceful dance, heaving something up and down again, a pick into ice, an axe into wood. Philip moved closer, blinking away rain. Behind him, Daniels told Mitford to hold on, he'd be fine. They were almost there.

Almost where? Philip came closer and closer to Ambrose, who was still pounding something, but not with a pick or an axe or a pen. He was jamming the flat end of his rifle into the leaves, silently and without expression. Philip moved closer until he could see. He had to see. He got so close that he could see flesh splashing up juices with every hit.

Philip turned around and looked back. Daniels still knew nothing. "Go back!" he yelled. He would keep Daniels with him, and they'd find port together. "Go back!"

At last, Ambrose stopped. "He was shooting at us," he said to Philip blankly.

Philip wanted to run, but the rain was turning him to melted wax, fixing him there in the muck. He stared at Ambrose's blood-covered face, two white eyes blinking out from behind a maroon mask.

"It's what they want us to do," Ambrose said. He leaned against a tree and lifted his face to the rain. "It's what we're supposed to do. We're the butchers."

Now Daniels patted Mitford on the forehead and moved toward Philip.

"I'm not getting home, am I?" Philip said.

"I'm sorry," Daniels said. "We should have left you there. We didn't know what we were doing."

"Nobody knows what they're doing," Ambrose said. "My father spent years in bed. Didn't even have the balls to kill himself."

"I'm not getting home," Philip said again. Something creeped over him, and he thought there would be a child's small hands over his eyes. *Guess who?* The wet clay ground was shaggy as a carpet, the light as dim as a basement. "I'm never getting back there."

"We gotta keep going," Daniels said.

Ambrose laughed. In his hands was a pistol he'd taken from the dead soldier. Philip didn't understand what he was seeing as Ambrose brought the pistol to his mouth, his thumb hooking the trigger.

The blast echoed. Daniels turned Philip away, held him close as a father would a son.

"I don't speak French," Philip said.

Daniels nodded as though he understood.

Bodies lay in all directions, and the ground began to bristle slightly with the lives of worms and snails too small and unknowing to be moved.

PART THREE

THE
TRAVELLERS

Chapter

10

THE FAITHFUL

From the stone steps of the church, Marie tossed a slobber-damp tennis ball. It hit the ground with a pop and went bouncing down the street, and these hard echoing sounds were followed by the skittering of Gus's claws and the clink of his collar. The ball came back to Marie with one short bark, like an answer to a question each toss of the ball tried to ask. *What now?* And: *Should I?* She tossed it again, and the ball landed with a hard metallic bang on a car's top and went dribbling down a windshield and onto the cracking asphalt next to the tire, where Gus, bored by this easy fetch, retrieved it.

The shadows shortened until they were directly under their objects, retracted like tongues. Marie tossed the ball with all of the force of that morning's emotions. At first it was only anger. Hot, the size of a tennis ball and burning inside her. Fuck you for leaving, Philip. Fuck you, Rosa; fuck you, guys. How could you all just leave? Only a dog stays, she thought, looking at Gus with self-pity. Her anger was as it had once been at the news about climate change, when in a rage she had passed by idling motorists and glared at them, later ranting to a customer or to Jason: "We're committing suicide! We're in a garage slowly suffocating on fumes!" Other people seemed to sort out that they were small in this universe, or they were in denial about that, but Marie's own helplessness was always a new shock she couldn't accept. How could there be nothing they could do?

These cars along this street were dead, never to idle again. She had outlived them. Grass was like water was like the tortoise in the fable. The hares had burned themselves out on hubris and on fumes, and the grass and weeds grew through the cracks the ice had made in the roads. Maybe the car's tires would melt into the asphalt. Maybe the cars would become habitats for rodents, become luxurious nests. Someday this road would be a forest again.

Marie's arm was growing sore, but it seemed necessary to continue this charade, to go through these motions of the dog owner and her dog, as though it were only very early on a Sunday, and the world was merely sleeping. Over a decade ago, before she knew Jason, every encounter was lonesome. Other people were unknowable, and she was unknown, invisible to others. With friends she didn't understand she went drinking and experimented with drugs, with ecstasy and hallucinogens, and she woke up in their houses in despair. She had been down this way early on Sunday mornings, had walked home from the apartments of these friends. The quiet of the streets had calmed her. She used to look up at the bridges and the pedestrian tunnel under MacNab Street and try to take it in. Her city. The city of her youth, a youth, she'd believed, that was like none that had come before. She had admired edifices, the curl in concrete a gesture toward neoclassicism, itself a gesture toward Ancient Greek architecture, and she wanted to make art that would duplicate this feeling. A photograph was not enough; just to witness was not enough. One needed a brushstroke to capture in each small thing its delicacy.

Gus retrieved the ball, and she took it: toss, pop, pop, skitter, pop.

St. John the Divine had been Christ's beloved disciple. St. John the Divine, saint of loyalty and love, whose name was on the church building, was now their saint. The steps of this church were *their* steps. These people, her family. What had come before this final ending had not been real. The ability to adapt and to make a strange thing familiar was the distinguishing feature of humanity. People were obsessed by novelty; they were predictable and knowable as lambs. Even Marie. So Philip had been right to think that they needed something to remind them who they were, that people were falling through port and losing their bearings.

Toss, pop, skitter. Gus dropped the ball at her feet and panted at her, just like dogs were meant to do, full of energetic glee, so that you might laugh off anything and be okay. What did Gus need, really? Even Marie was programmed, her needs were easily known: need for companionship; need for a belief in the future. She was just like Gus, slave to instincts and needs.

Behind her, shut behind heavy doors, the port was glowing with those needs. With Mo, she had hastily nailed the front doors shut with boards, but the port still seemed too close. It knew her, had stripped her bare, beckoned with a: *Relax, relax, you don't have to do this anymore.* Why not just go through? No one was watching. She was alone in the street, had been alone all morning. Alone, you lost track of time. This had happened before she joined the group, for those few months when she kept to herself, learning to pick the locks of restaurants, cafés and stores. Days had swelled, moments pulsed, time was an emotion and not a fact. Except for the photos, she might have lost days, and even so, there were days when she couldn't remember if she had taken the photo, rolls that she came to the end of too quickly. Had it been twenty-four days? There was her menstrual cycle, and there was the moon.

Maybe she should go back into the church just to get the ledger, if only for its confirmation of numbers and days. Then, she could get a feel, put her finger in the air and see what port was doing—whether it had changed the weather in the church as she suspected. People with time to kill, like prisoners, turned their energy to getting good at push-ups, and so Marie dropped to the sidewalk and managed fifteen wobbly ones, until she collapsed on her back. Gus ran over. He seemed to be wondering whether to be concerned. She laughed. He licked her cheek. "This does not bode well," Mo had said, before he and Rosa drove off and left her alone here. "You sure you'll be all right?" he said. "I'll drop Rosa off, and I'll be back soon." They had driven off to find everyone else, and she would wait for them here and warn whoever came. They'd been too eager to get away from her

Rosa nodded doubtfully. "Stay close, Gus," Marie said. She had wanted Rosa to hear in her voice that she was afraid. Port inside, and not only that: a person in the city breaking windows, drawing *S*s in red paint. They thought she was strong; they thought she would resist.

Rosa and Mo sped off in her car, honking several times. Beep, be-be-beep, like a continuation of Mo's nervous chatter, and then silence. Sometimes the wind stirred up dust and papers, sometimes it drew a brittle old pop can down the street, but otherwise she was alone. Anything might be happening anywhere, but for them, there would be no news. Whatever happened, all she would know about was what she could see from her own small frame, and from the frames of this hand-ful of people whose interpretation she could hardly trust. She wanted a press release, a front-page story, a person who was in charge to float in with a pedestal and a microphone, with army medals, with some kind of badge. But there were no helicopters; the skies were silent.

This is the way the world ends:

Many years ago, Marie and Jason had watched his father die. There were people in this world—there *had been* people in this world—who saw people die every day. There were oncologists and soldiers and aid workers and trauma nurses, people who were accustomed to what Marie and Jason had both found unthinkable. "How is it that this happens to all of us, to every living thing," Jason said. They were nearly hysterical all the time, having what they believed were calm conversations about the idea of death as they rounded corners on the way to the hospital on the escarpment. Neither of them got any work done for weeks. Jason's formulae hung suspended, awaiting his return. The first skeletal layer of Marie's prints hung without being filled. They drove a car his mother had lent them for this purpose; they drove his father's car, and they rounded corners on the way up the escarpment and rounded corners on the parking structure, and they pushed buttons on the elevator, and they had conversations about death, while his father lay dying. His father would die in a few months or a few weeks; cancer was eating him up, and every good cell was being replaced by a bad one.

All the living things everywhere made death's impossibility clear. The escarpment in full forest loomed greenly at them. "Because of all the talk of environmentalism," Marie said, "I always expect there to be no trees at all. Every tree is a miracle." Death and decline had been a myth too much bandied about. The world teemed. Everywhere you looked, there was some human full of purpose, full of movement and yearning. "This isn't denial," Marie said. "It can't be denial if you're aware of the possibility that you're in denial."

That was several months before the first miscarriage.

His father had been a champion of their too-early marriage, their know-it-all love. "Why *not* get married," Jason's father, a schoolteacher, had said. "To hell with it!" He was a man you could imagine always popping a champagne cork. Marie felt now that all the good in Jason had come from this man, not from his mother, who had been a severely skinny corporate lawyer. Jason's father used to make jokes about the cases that would take her all over the country. "The important lawyers in their suits are arguing about the sturdiness of pipes again. Who is blameworthy when it comes to the shoddiness of pipes? And more importantly, who the hell is going to have to pay?" Jason's father with a mittful of confetti, his mother dour and hard.

Zeno's paradoxes famously showed that you could only advance across a distance by first going half way, and then you had to traverse half of the remaining distance, and half of the next, and the next, and soon you realized that there were an infinite number of halves nested inside each distance, and you'd never get to the end. Movement was impossible, and so was death. This is how it felt to watch him die. Each breath in would be followed by a breath out. Breath comes in, breath goes out, breath comes in: what could make out of small motions such an irrevocable change? Breath slowing, yes. But life ending? A thing happened one bit at a time. A thing happened slowly and then all at once.

Marie waited so long for someone to come to the church that she began to think no one would. Gus had ignored the last toss of the ball, and it had gone rolling down the street. She watched it grow smaller, until it finally stopped. Gus let it go, distracted by a fat grey squirrel, which he chased up the brick side of an old house. Animals surrounded them. Cats slinked around corners, mice moved so fluidly she hadn't at first noticed them. Now the squirrel clung from the eavestrough. It was about to try flinging itself over to a tree branch, which it would certainly not manage. Gus maintained his focus, growling, sitting back on his haunches in a threatening way.

Marie pulled a book out of her backpack, a hugely popular novel called *Julie in Wonderland* set in a Brooklyn that must no longer exist and by a novelist who was probably gone named Nellie Young. There were long *flâneur* passages in which the protagonist considered the city; there were bars and bookshops and art galleries and coffee shops with strong coffee, and the novel comforted Marie because of the way it assumed there would be crowds of people everywhere Julie, the protagonist, looked. Julie got into complicated discussions about politics and art with men who were sometimes good and sometimes bad in bed. Julie, with her old Parisian ennui, her New Yorker neurosis, didn't know what she wanted. At a certain point, Julie developed a condition in which parts of her body went numb, where she could not tell where her body ended and the world began.

For months after the grid went down, some of them would reach for the phone no longer in the back pocket of their jeans. In Marie's current situation, sitting bored on a stoop and waiting, a device like that would keep time from being a thing to be endured. You could scroll through messages and sites; you could ask PINA any random question that floated up; you would not wonder why the sky was blue, because you'd know. By not buying a PINAphone, Marie had resisted this new way of being in the world, in which one's thoughts were never unknown to others, in which a person was always seen and always performed. She had been lonely all her life, had spent her life sticking in the mud—even the drugs to make you high brought Marie down—and maybe it was a sign of her wrongness that she was still here. There had to be some reason that this group of them remained, something to link them. A lack of daring, of normal human curiosity. She should go into the church. She would unzip the port the way a person braced for a shot of whisky. Down the hatch she'd go! And she'd find herself there, in a world filled with people and art and adventure. *Wonderland.*

Why did it have to be sinister, the way the port read your mind and embodied your desire? Why was a promise like that sinister? As usual, they were fearful and knew nothing. It was just as likely that desire was good, that resistance, rather than being merely futile, was stupid. The port *knew* her. It regarded her, and it knew her. So she stood up. At the rear of the church were basement windows she could break clean open. There was one on which the old cage had rusted so badly, it would come off easily in her hands. She'd pull off the cage and just break the window a little. There was no hurry. No one was coming. She could break the glass slowly, knock out the jagged edges—it was as easy as that.

"Marie!" Someone was shouting.

Tiny in the distance, a bicycle raced toward her. Marie stood as still as a raccoon caught scheming about a garbage can, her hands in mid-air. The bicycle was topped by teeny Bonita in her kerchief, shouting, "Marie!"

Gus barked loudly back. The squirrel saw its chance and threw itself into the air, fantastically managing to grab the tree branch, surprising even itself.

Marie walked back up the weedy alley to the steps. Bonita braked and jumped off the bike and ran to her. "Have you heard from Philip?"

Marie shook her head. "What did Rosa tell you?"

"You all think the port is demonic or something? It's tempting you to go in, some kind of voice in your head?"

Marie nodded, but Bonita's skeptical tone was a pin to her bubble of longing.

Bonita's clothes and face were damp; she wiped her forehead with the bottom of her T-shirt, flashing for a moment the brown and slightly puckered skin of her belly.

"Do you have water?"

Marie led Bonita to the top of the steps and retrieved a bottle from her backpack. "When's the last time you saw him?"

"He slept on our couch last night. Rosa didn't. Well . . ." Bonita stopped short of saying what was already clear to Marie. "And then I talked to him for a few minutes at breakfast. Just for a few minutes. And then he was gone. You know he likes to be alone. But that was the last time I saw him."

Gus trotted over to Bonita and lay between them at the top of the steps, just outside the church doors, as though guarding the building from intruders. The surreality lifted at Marie, as it sometimes did, this feeling that her body and her mind could no longer quite remain attached to each other. As though some outline of her body were only hovering over her, as though whatever helped her remain whole had double vision.

There was something about the scene. Marie sitting on that top step, body turned slightly toward Bonita, Bonita mirroring her, Gus between them, the red doors to frame them: the picture mimicked a photo she had from her childhood, herself and her long-ago best friend Katrine, on a stoop, the red doors. Some part of her was dislodging and trying to rise, to lift.

"What are we going to do?"

"We'll wait here for Philip, for one thing," Bonita said.

"Yeah?" Marie said. She moved to the top of the steps and lay back on the cold stone. Big puffy clouds moved over them. "It's going to rain."

"Nah. Not for awhile," Bonita said. "Those clouds are babies."

"You know that we're pretty sure—we think—Philip is gone."

"You think so?" she said, pulling her red kerchief off and shaking it out, then flattening it on the step. The stone was covered with little green seeds that had flown off nearby trees. Gus stood up, suddenly, with a clink-clink-clink, his body directed southward, toward the green escarpment. Across the street, the way a coming helicopter or roaring plane used to sound, hundreds of birds all at once pulled into the sky from a tree, their bodies synced so that the flock of them together had the effect of a single being, each like a node in a sheet of chain mail shaking into the sky.

"We could migrate," Marie said.

Bonita finished flattening and folding her kerchief and began tying it back over her head. "We can't go south without Philip."

"Did Rosa tell you that someone broke a window on my street? About the billboard?"

Bonita nodded and assessed her with her dark eyes, and Marie felt pitied. It was unbearable; she turned away.

"Remember a few years ago, just before port?" Bonita said. "Then the big thing was planning to start some kind of colony on Mars. Albrecht Doors was one of them, putting groups of private citizens into these mock stark conditions. Making them live in the desert for months together, to test their fortitude, I guess, and to help them prepare. You remember that? It was going to be one-way tickets. They knew people were going to die out there. Many of them would die. For the sake of humanity."

Marie remembered it well, because she'd known how excited Jason would have been about it.

"Corporations to save us. Made sense to me. What else do you do with a billion dollars? I always felt they were just little boys playing. Should have made sure the little boys didn't have all the economic power. Although perhaps a boy is preferable to a man. A *man*. Now there's a pile of disappointments and bitterness and physical strength and hate."

"Not all men," Marie said, laughing.

"Yeah. Right. Anyway, they were going to send people up to Mars. To set up colonies. You had to petition for your spot. I heard this radio programme where they were comparing the Mars teams to the first Europeans in North America. The Puritans. All the people who didn't make it through that first winter. And I remember thinking—I'm sure I'm not the only one who thought this—wait a minute, the *Puritans* are going to be our model for behaviour? The colonizers? European conquest is just a disease, an illness, something that wants to spread and spread without any desire beyond spreading."

"Not all Europeans," Marie said.

"Apparently it was all Europeans. And all men. Everybody, Marie! Every single person."

"Except us."

"The exception does not prove the rule. There is something inside of people; it comes along with us. Not just Europeans. We take poison with us wherever we go. We ruin things."

Marie winced. Was this directed at her, to do with all the windows they'd broken? No one had ever had a problem with it before; no one had ever said anything.

"With port—it's like with port, all of that disappeared. All those other trajectories stopped short. You remember that book? The one by the scientist who had been investigating UFO sightings?"

"Right," Marie said. It had been from Donnie's personal collection. They'd pocketed all kinds of books like that in case they'd get any information from them, but many books from the seventies and eighties about aliens were laughable. Kitsch.

"Did you read it?" Bonita said, shaking her head to scold Marie. "It was by a real scientist with credentials and all. Assuming there have been UFOs and even abductions, assuming we've been visited on this planet by other beings, he was—"

Marie sat up, leaned on her elbows and stared at her friend. A slight déjà vu blurred in—the way Jason's belief in it all had felt to her. She could not believe it—she would not—but she had liked that someone did.

"Are we talking alien invasion? Are we talking, like, extraterrestrials?"

Bonita looked at her. The air was thickening up; they both shone with sweat.

"I'm sorry," Marie said.

"About what?"

"About my tone."

"Oh, it's all right. I like you well enough by now."

Up the street to the south, they saw two figures walking toward them, a bit too far away to make out. Then another three behind them.

"Everybody's coming," Bonita said.

"I'm sorry that I interrupted you. Go on."

"Maybe it does sound ridiculous. The scientist who wrote that book said that if we were to grant that these UFOs were actually visiting, maybe they weren't coming from outer space. Maybe there was some other explanation. You know. If this is a multiverse, or there are many worlds—which there probably have to be—then the ports are part of that."

"But PINA made the ports."

"If PINA made the ports and knew what they were doing—which they must have, given that the Testifiers said they were coming back, but *no one the hell comes back*—there was a lot more going on than anyone in the public knew about. That, or PINA was just a bunch of little boys with toy planes, and they were having a laugh and a lark."

"Sometimes I don't know whether to believe more strongly in malice or incompetence," Marie said.

"Can't it be both?"

"At times I feel we've made a good life here and then at others I feel like, just—"

Bonita sighed, and leaned toward Marie.

"I don't know why I'm talking about Mars right now. No one's going to Mars. We're set back centuries, here. Maybe millenia."

Despite the humidity of the day, the sun scorching overhead, Bonita's arm felt cold. "Maybe he didn't go in. Maybe we're wrong," Marie said.

Coming up the street were Joe pushing Yasmin, Andrea and Steve and Regina and the kids, and Donnie on his crutches, now hollering, "Ahoy! Ahoy!" And so, in turn, they stood and lifted their arms like deserted islanders trying to get the attention of a ship.

They decided it was better not to go inside to get the ledger, but they knew the numbers, and within an hour, all of them were there except Philip. Most sat on the curb or on the steps as they waited for him to get back; some dragged lawn furniture out from the nearby houses, grimy chairs from a porch, the old plastic pieces they kept under tarps near the slaughterhouse-garage next door. Steve with his three kids went in and out of that garage, full of unnecessary inventorying purpose, as though they'd been burgled instead of abandoned. He harrassed Mo about the hammer and nails, which still sat on the stoop there, and glared at the others suspiciously. "Everything's accounted for," he said finally, sitting down on the bottom step next to frail Regina, who hugged her legs to her torso.

Each of them was stuck in a private set of thoughts. One would say, "There aren't any chickens out there," and another would say, "It was awful. Just feathers here and there, stuck to things. Cattle carcasses, bones. Nothing survived the winter." Another voice: "Of course they didn't; we hardly did. Philip was right, we should leave." Philip's name was enough to create a momentary silence, and then someone would ask again how they could be sure the port had been used, and then Rosa would describe the scattering of business cards, how Mo and Marie had both felt it pulling at them. "It was like a beautiful woman," Mo would say, another point to silence everyone. Were beautiful women really so irresistible? Then they'd circle back to the chickens, to the question of whether they all had died, whether they ought to have gone south, whether they themselves were like sitting ducks—"sitting chickens," said Donnie ruefully—and how difficult it was give up all hopes, even absurd ones . . . and then who had left . . . had someone left? . . . had it been Philip? . . . Let's retrace our steps . . . and. . . .

Behind them, the church doors were still shuttered, their shiny red paint faded long ago and splintered, now further destroyed by those planks that that morning had seemed a necessary precaution and now that everyone was there and accounted for looked like the hack job of a paranoiac. The shadows again had deepened, the sun dropping west behind the church, and they sat in growing darkness. The empty street was in stark chiaroscuro.

"I could almost taste those scrambled eggs," Donnie said. "I could taste the butter, I swear to God."

"Mind over matter," Mo said. "Like maybe your fantasy could make it come true. Maybe some dairy farmer had stayed behind."

"It's not impossible. Maybe we didn't go out far enough," Regina said.

"Gotta create your reality," Mo said.

"That's not what I mean," Regina said.

Steve was handing out jerky and opening cans of brown beans, passing around spoons.

"You think he'd just leave without saying goodbye?" Rosa said.

"They all left without saying goodbye," said Marie. "Why should he be different?"

"He should be different," Rosa said. "He *was* different."

"Let's not start giving eulogies just yet," Bonita said, but their carved faces did appear grieved, helpless as children at a parent's funeral.

Marie watched Steve climb the stairs, and she understood the moves he was making. Philip's departure was an opportunity. He stood with one foot on the top step, so that one leg was higher and his legs were spread. "Okay, wow," he said, running his hand through his hair in an angry gesture none of them recognized. "Let's get the facts straight, here. First, we have a sign on a billboard near Marie's apartment and nobody knows who did it." He paused. "Right?"

A few nodded, sheepish as though wishing they could confess to it. Steve scanned their faces, trying to detect a liar.

"And then this morning one of our least likely to jump guys jumped and is gone."

"Maybe he'll be right about the business cards?" Rosa said.

"Those cards look like they were made by a child in a cartoon."

"I don't even know what that means," Marie said.

"What do you think it means, Marie, that we have somehow lost our de facto leader whom none of us *elected*, by the way, who decides things *unilaterally*, as fucking usual—"

"Steve," Regina said.

"Sorry. But Philip brought the port into the church. Who knows what he was thinking. And he probably knew a lot more than he told us. You can tell a guy like that—likes to hold the cards tight to his chest even if it's a matter of life or death for everybody around him."

Bonita frowned. "That's not fair, Steven. Philip wasn't hiding anything."

"We all trusted him, that's for sure. Because *we're* sheep," Steve said. His energy seemed as large as his six-foot-three body, its broad chest and shoulders. "And now we need to assume a few things so that we can start making some decisions. We don't *know*. We'll never know. We need to make some assumptions, so we can make a god-damn—sorry—a decision. Do you people understand this?"

"Us people," Mo laughed. "All right, brah, let's have it."

"Screw you, Mo. Why don't you go bang on your drum, and let a man make some decisions."

"Why are you being such a dick," Rosa said.

"Steve." Regina pulled on his hand like a small child. "He's just stressed out." She turned to the rest of them. "He's tired."

"I'm going to tell you what we're going to do," Steve said. "We're going to first of all make sure we know where the ports are in any part of the city where we want to go, and stay the hell out of the rest of the city. And then we're going to . . ."

While he was speaking, Donnie, who sat two steps down from Marie, back against the railing, leg outstretched, turned to her and whispered, "Wish I had popcorn for this show," causing her to laugh.

"Wish I had any popcorn at all," she said.

"Corn we could grow. That we could. Easy."

Regina scowled at them. "Glad this is so amusing for you all."

Marie stifled her shocked laugh at this, but Donnie did not, and she nudged his shoulder with her foot. "Go on, Steve," she said.

"Well, do you want to live or not?" Steve said.

She nodded. "Yeah, I do." The other faces turned to her. "We do. Of course we do. We want to live."

Chapter

11

THE HOMECOMER

The city wasn't exactly as Brandon had left it. Of course not. In those days, the place had been mainly blue-collar, a steeltown dominated by lowbrow coffee shops like Tim Hortons and sulphurous smokestacks lining the bridge whose highways led to the capital. The lake that stretched the entire north end was unswimmable when Brandon was a child. "You can dip your toes in," Mom had said. "But do not let your head go under the water."

Those empty coffee shops were on every other corner, cursive signage sullenly maroon instead of brightly lit red. The streets where sex workers or addicts had walked, and which he had therefore once avoided, now showed proof of what his mother had been telling him for years. The city is in a recovery, a renaissance. The city is filling up with artists and entrepreneurs. This city was a true crosssection of their times: they had professors and doctors and artists and weirdos, more than their fair share of the poor and nutty, environmentalists, you name it. People aren't in a rush here like they are in the capital, she told him. Her speeches with their frantic quality were a way to beg him to return. This city, our city, she said, is like nowhere else on Earth.

But this was only dismal proof of her lack of worldliness. He was fully Americanized by then and laughed at her a little. He was green-carded and employed by the wealthiest company on Earth. "You should come to California, Ma."

"I'd be free-floating there," she told him.

Sometimes on the phone or even in an e-mail, there was something slurry, something he could sense as strongly as a whiff of alcohol on the breath. "I need my tethers." And it was true that as a reaction to her years of disordered mood swings, she had come to believe in weighing herself down, the way a house does with objects.

During the two weeks it took him to get back, he did his risk assessment. The reasons she would go mounted against the odds of his finding her.

1. She was desperate to see Dad again.

2. She was weak-willed and prone to addiction, easily lured.

3. Port picked off the least resistant first.

This theory of the least-resistant belonged to the crew of his fellow Stable-escapees. DOS said in his comforting drawl that they believed the waves could be tracked this way: first the sick or lonely or desperate found their way out. They didn't have the analytics, but this was the suspicion.

"But the cost was extreme!" said Brandon. "It had to be the wealthy going first, on what they thought were leisure tours. We had those numbers, anyway."

His desire to argue against each of their theories was as strong as his hunger. Despite the spears and guns, none of them had yet successfully hunted anything, and so far, they were afraid to go into stores and houses for canned goods. Finally, day two, they were able to trap some squirrels, to gnaw meat from those tiny bodies like each one was a single chicken drumstick.

"The first wave can be parsed into two categories: super-rich thrill-seekers and the super-desperate," said Samuel, the youngest of the three. "Super-rich thrill-seekers disappear, leaving behind ports. Super-desperate break in and are through the ports before the police get there. We know that the port-maps got hacked twice in those days. Leakers thought ports should be publicly owned and studied, too, and we know that Doors wouldn't want to admit that he had lost control almost immediately."

"So you guys were pirating?" Brandon said. He was already tired of their grandiosity.

"Well, I wouldn't call it pirating," Samuel said. "It wasn't for profit. Some of us just thought that this should have been controlled better, and I think it's clear now that we were right."

"You're as guilty as Doors," Brandon said. "Guiltier."

Over every product that had preceded port, PINA had control. They'd known everything about their customers. One night Doors had called him to the office, where he sat on the yoga mat in lotus, fingers folded over thumbs. "The sea waves pass over us," Doors said. His transformation was beginning. "The tech is so advanced, we don't have eyes on it. Slippery." Brandon's next step—what seemed his only step—was to follow the newsfeeds and Wikipages; port was like every mad invention in every story since Frankenstein. It had all been obvious, but Brandon had been unable to see it. "You give a thing breath, and it runs wild ahead of you," Doors said. "Off into the woods." His eyes went from calm to blazing, spark of the previous version of himself.

For over a year, Doors put Brandon in a scramble, following rumours like a man running over spinning logs. Doors talked about the multiverse and the so-called singularity because he'd really started to go mad, his mind destroying itself over his unutterable responsibility. As though possessed. Unless—unless Brandon was misremembering, had been sleepwalking, and with no access now to the archive, his confusion was only getting worse.

"Hey, hey." DOS, the peacemaker, put his hands up beside his head. "Hey, now."

"*We* didn't know!" Samuel yelled. "Doors knew!"

"All right, all right," Brandon said, walking off. What had Doors known, when? Did it matter? He'd left his notebook in the drawer in the archive. He missed the old surveillance, days when the stories they had to stay on top of were accusations of data-mining. Ports themselves had somehow evaded surveillance. He missed his espresso machine. In the car he had a can of old instant coffee procured at a gas station. The grounds resembled soil and indeed the coffee was like mud.

That night they were camping in a dried-out, abandoned vineyard, the long rows of desiccated plants pitted with tough and mouldy little raisins, which, starving, they ate. He'd wanted to drive along the coast, for beauty's sake, for nostalgia's, but he'd been outvoted on this as on everything. By day four, they'd agreed to disagree, which meant they'd agreed that Brandon would soon go his own way.

The group from Stable included quite a few women, who had the nervous appearance of hostages. None of them would speak to Brandon. They peered at him, big-eyed, a look so naked it made him look away. Had these women once been employees of PINA? Accomplished, the most accomplished in the world? Maybe they were only relatives of former PINA people, were outsiders. Doors would have known nothing about them.

DOS was the only one here Brandon could talk to. He took him aside. Fire flickered behind them, the large and unprotected fire of amateurs.

"These women are freaking me out," Brandon said. "What's going on here?"

"These women are sweet and harmless," DOS said.

But they did things like pour twice-used soapy water into buckets and twist their clothes through tense hands and fingers, joints pushing at flesh. They did things like quietly mop up the men's faces with this same water, though always avoiding Brandon. None of them had so much as grazed his body accidentally. They mushed their dehydrated noodles with boiled water and fed them to the children with their dwindling supply of plastic spoons. There were only three children, two boys and a girl, all of them old enough to feed themselves, old enough, Brandon thought, to cook for themselves too.

For awhile Brandon was worried that they'd run into the scouts who'd been sent on their recon/retrieval mission. Or it would be Benji and Dawn coming over the next hill, around the next bend, two friends to talk sense and to save him from himself. They'd be angry that he'd left without them. It didn't occur to him until four days later that no one—not Doors, certainly—was in pursuit of him. It didn't matter to PINA if they lost a few skeptics. Doors didn't care about him much at all, and this hurt more than the fact that his mother had never come to find him. So much for loyalty.

They drove each morning, then stopped each afternoon to recharge the solar packs, certain that vehicular breakdown was inevitable. "Where the cars break down," DOS said, "that's where we'll settle." The cars were a tarot deck. The group attempted to hunt by day and then listened to Samuel's theories until it grew dark and a fire was required. They were in no rush to get anywhere, and Brandon's desire to be on the road and as far from PINA as they could get was met with irritated shoulder hunches and flared nostrils.

The women had started covering their hair with scarves and kerchiefs.

They were heading north, seeking rain. Awaiting fate to deposit them where it would. Maybe Tacoma. Maybe Vancouver. Maybe the rainforests of British Colombia. These freeways had already seemed post-apocalyptic two years ago, when the farmland began burning out. Hand-painted signs were posted all down the road beside brown fields: "Congress Created Dust Bowl" and "Drought Costs Farmers, Costs Everyone."

DOS had agreed to be Brandon's passenger, and they drove past these relics silently.

"Here's what happens when you abandon reality," Brandon said finally. "You can't blame these farmers for leaving. Can't make a profit, water costs a fortune, and crops are turning to dust. So they leave. Food prices go up. Then the number of the desperate increases." At PINA they'd lived like emperors, living with complete unawareness of the lives of others. "No one knows what to do. PINA's lost control. And here's a handy way out. Go back to before we fucked it all up."

"Ah. It's been fucked up for a long time," DOS said.

"But you could tell yourself that you'd go back and fix things for some other timeline, anyway. Make sure Reagan doesn't get elected or something."

DOS was withering. "Yeah, I'm sure that will do it." He looked away from him and out the window. "Listen," he said. "You know I like you, man. We appreciate your ... *insights*. But we're trying to start something here. And—"

"What are you trying to start?"

"Look. The twelve of us had a plan. Enough—with the women and children—to get something going. We had a plan, and I don't think you're really on board."

"What's the plan? Keep women in their place? Submissive women, domineering men? You want to go back to that?"

DOS sighed. "Listen."

"Listen. Look."

"Hey. Don't be like that."

"I'm sorry."

"I don't think there's a place for you in this culture. We've taken a vote. I voted for you, don't worry about that. I've got your back. I'm not interested in a regression, but I like these guys. And I think we could start something."

"So you're saying?"

"At our next stop, it's time we go our separate ways."

❧

He drove as far as Portland, a route he knew, where he stopped for supplies. Thought he might even run into one of the few people he knew who'd moved there after college, even though he hadn't run into anyone in days, and Portland was bigger than he remembered. At a convenience store, he got several much-needed cases of water, and he found a few maps, from which he realized that Portland was farther north than he wanted to be. He would have to backtrack to get northeast.

"Where you headed?" a man said, while Brandon was standing unprotected in the street, scouring the map.

He was surprised to find next to him a middle-aged couple with a rusty cart of looted goods. He showed them his route east, the destination by the Great Lakes, and they stood there talking calmly. The couple didn't seem at all perturbed by the pretense that he was just a tourist looking for directions.

"Or you could go up through Vancouver first. Such a pretty town," the woman, Clementine, said. "Been meaning to go back. First you ought to get some rest. We've got a couch."

Portland was apparently still full of people. From the living room window of their small craftsman home, where Brandon put down his pack, people could be seen walking in pairs and three-somes down streets, as though it were merely a quiet holiday week-end and not the end of the world. Ducks would sometimes waddle behind them, and goats.

"We like it this way," Clementine said over dinner. "All the important people are still here. And real estate's cheap now, ha."

Everyone had moved to within a few blocks of each other, and ports had been quarantined. "The ports of Portland," Denis said rue-fully. This new Portland maintained a bar, though Denis and Clementine told him they were rapidly running out of liquor.

"We had a moonshine department," Brandon said, "in the last place I stayed."

Clementine laughed heartily. "Really?"

Denis took out a small notebook. "We need details."

"Denis doesn't want to go outside the quarantine, so we are in dire need of information."

"I seen people leave that didn't want to leave." Denis grunted. "I don't trust the ports."

"But you never know," Brandon said. "How could you know they didn't want to leave?"

"I'm a scientist," Denis said. "And I can make hypotheses. Some hypotheses you don't test, though, right? The appropriate amount of suspicion has kept us safe here. Do not trust the ports."

"Denis has been instrumental in keeping this community together," Clementine said, patting her husband's knee. "What about you, Brandon? Do you think they're coming back? All the people, I mean."

Brandon had not told them he had a connection to PINA, though he suspected they knew who he was. He played along. "I have no idea."

The décor was abundantly floral, and throughout the night a grandfather clock sighed and chimed. In the morning he heard them talking in the kitchen. Smell of coffee was rich in the air. At the farmer's table, Clementine was kneading dough, claimed it was her favourite thing to do, to shape dough into smooth round buns and apply heat. "Brandon is living proof that a person can survive out there!" She dusted her tray with flour. "We'll run out of flour eventually," she said. "Might as well enjoy bread while we can. In fact, I've gotten fatter since it all happened."

Denis gravely nodded at Brandon.

"And we're living proof that the urban farming movement was the wisest possible investment." Out back, beyond the kitchen window, a dozen hens and a rooster head-bobbed and scuffed the packed earth.

She handed Brandon a hunk of raw dough and waited for him to put it in his mouth.

"Though, we could certainly live with fewer feral dogs," she said. "Even the Pomeranians have gone bat-shit crazy! Were Pomeranians always a little crazy? But really, Vancouver is an incredible place. You only live once, and you've got all the time in the world." Her energy as she talked and shaped the dough had both the men in thrall. "What's your plan, going so far out? You got a woman there?"

"It's my hometown."

"Well if you changed your mind, there's lots of women around here, and we could use a young man like you around," Clementine said. "Is all I'm saying."

In his mouth the dough had turned slimy.

"What are you going to do all winter?" he asked.

"Animal skins and furs," said Denis. "We've been super-insulating some of the old buildings downtown, and on the worst nights, everyone camps out there. Main issue, really, is the rain. Channelling runoff, holding and sanitizing as much as we can. Plus it gets so grey, so damp. That's hard, psychologically. But people here were kind of always outdoorsy."

"Lots of women in Portland," Clementine said again, smiling. She went out through the screen door to the porch festooned with bamboo and tinkling metal wind chimes, and out to the yard. She returned with a little shoebox. "Well, why don't you take these. If you decide not to stay."

He nudged off the lid, found three yellow chicks inside. "I can't take these."

"Sure you can."

"You need them."

"We're okay."

"But what do they eat?"

"Birdseed!" Denis said, holding his small belly as he shook with laughter.

Clementine handed him a baggy of that too. "He'll be back. You'll be back, won't you? Go, find your people, but you can always come back."

"I think you're right to stay away from the ports," he told them. Probably they had already sussed out that he'd been in tech. Maybe they recognized him from his heyday. He was driving a flashy solar-electric car, for another thing. He was wearing yoga clothes.

"Yup," Denis said, watching him back out of the driveway.

The lonely prairies of the Midwest, with their shining silos, ominous as sentinels, their endless golden fields, had always seemed desolate to a lifelong urbanite like Brandon. Now that they were rising up and filling the air with seeds, now that cornfields were dry as hay, they were more desolate than ever. He had no one with whom he could debrief, no one to tell about the eccentricities of Denis and Clementine, so he talked to the chicks, embarked on long mono-logues during the drive. The chicks cheeped and shat, were robotic in their quick movements.

"They really liked me," he said to them. "Clementine and Denis. Maybe I will go back to Portland. I can't go back to PINA. I'm never going back there. Can I?"

A few days later, he was looking for signs that might provide an answer: "Shouldn't I make sure my friends are okay? What about Benji and Zahra and Suzanne? What about the rest of the twelve? I can't just let Doors be in charge. Should I have taken a record, some PINAkey as proof?" But proof for whom? All of the agencies of investigation and intelligence and prosecution and punishment are gone.

He let their squeaks become a complicated eight-ball. Sometimes when he finished asking his questions, he glanced over at the pas-senger seat to see that they were all asleep in the cardboard box, which he had outfitted with straw. The three were piled on top of each other, their eyes slitted into crescent moons, so catlike he half-expected them to purr. When they slept like this, he saw them to mean: *Relax, don't worry.* So he pressed on the gas.

Nights were too dark. He was aware, while driving, of his head-lamps as the only source of light aside from the patterns of stars, the sliver of moon. The world might be empty, it might be nothingness; there was only the car and the chickens and the hundred feet in front of him that lay illuminated. Once he nearly hit a deer, swerved and had to push the Turing out of a ditch. He decided to drive only during the day, to sleep at nights. Several nights in a row he'd stopped at motels. Each was foyer-darkened and unmanned, its drawers full of inert room key cards he couldn't override without electricity. He finally found a motel called Fantasia Inn that still used cut keys, but even so deeply alone, he felt conspicuous there. There must have been some other people out there in that expanse of prairie, just as there had been people in Portland, just as there were people leaving PINA. A working solar car would make him a target for thieves, and they were all thieves now. Clutching the box of chickens to his chest, he stared at the line of gold keys hanging in the oddly named Fantasia Inn, its decrepitude making the name seem a sick joke. The light dimmed there, hiding what had been visible a moment before: tears in the yellowing wallpaper, stains in the carpeting.

"Wish I'd never watched *Psycho*," he said to the chicks. "Let's go."

So instead, he slept in the car in fields. He had to stay with his assets. In his nightly rush of paranoia, he wiped the car with handfuls of mud and stuck it with hay, trying to blinker the shiny aquamarine. He looked in all directions before folding himself into the dirtied car, wary of those pockets of civilization quarantining themselves, hiding just outside view.

In the glovebox he found his old PINAphone. All the CarbOskin that had promised they'd be able to charge anything, anywhere, using their own bodies had been repurposed for the ports. Still, he was able to give it a small charge using the car's hookup; when he held the power button, it briefly flared up, lighting that old pic of himself and Zahra framed inside the PINA logo, paired lips and eyes and noses an emblem of their love. Then the cascade of PINapp buttons bounced in and settled onto the screen. A robotic "we're sorry," and it went black again, leaving for only a moment the pulsing white flare that used to tell him he had a message. It breathed in, breathed out, breathed in, died.

He had parked in a field, and the grasses were grey-blue in the moonlight. He wanted to stargaze but was afraid to leave the car, and when the phone went dead, he thought of the tiny pulse-beats of his chicks' hearts. How tiny their organs were, smaller than a mouthful, delicate. He put his finger to his throat to feel the surge of his own blood, still flowing.

It had been a long time since he'd had to think of the loss of all these distractions. That there had once been a day when an hour could not pass without the buzz or chime of the phone, when a day could not pass without new information in e-mails and newsfeeds falling like water. All that urgency and the device always held before him, its pleasing sounds and colours, how it responded unfailingly to the press of his thumbs. It had been magic, and time had gone so quickly, and there had been so much to do.

Now time had slowed like the old game show "Wheel of Fortune" coming down to its final tick-tick-tick-tick-tick. It was as if all that time he'd been an ant working underground, full of purpose, and had now discovered his ant-hood. All had been fruitless burrowing. He no longer had the old Timex—had forgotten it on the coffee table back in Portland—and when he woke every night into blackness, unable to fall asleep again, time seemed hallucinatory. There was nothing by which to measure it, and so it wasn't there. He was trapped in an inky soup; he couldn't breathe; no one knew him, and so perhaps he did not exist. Go to sleep, he urged himself, go to sleep. No matter how long he drove, he'd never find an all-night diner where he might stop for coffee. No matter where this road trip took him, there were no plots to come, and there was no new information.

Every rest stop was deserted. He couldn't figure out how to harness any gas without swiping the card and was forced to rely on the always draining charge of sunlight. Could he siphon gas if he found a tube or something? Finally, once he was through South Dakota, he heard human life. Passing Chicago he heard what sounded like an explosion, and at one gas station, he found fresh footprints in the dirt outside. The old automatic doors were all clamped as tightly as a seizing jaw, but this one had recently been bashed open. Glass shards and drips of blood on the ground outside. He took what was left, very little—a handful of coffee creamers, a bag of gummy worms. He was now accustomed to lines of black or white mould, to the buzz of flies, to rainforest smells of dank and rot.

Crossing the border near Detroit, where he drove slowly and warily over teetering overpasses, he felt odd and uncomfortable that he was able to drive right through each checkpoint without being asked about his intentions. He decided before going home to stop at Niagara Falls for an hour, eating sugar candy and wishing for a sandwich, wishing he hadn't finished all of Clementine's bread, as he listened to the water roar endlessly down its cliff. If he jumped, no one would mourn him. No one would ever know what had become of him.

By the time he got to his hometown, he was not expecting much. It was apparently as deserted as the rest, and he thought it would be like a joke, with the city's degraded reputation among other Canadians, that anyone would think to stay here, of all places. The chicks were getting bigger, and he felt strange stabs of grief at their outgrowing babyhood. Their wings were longer, yellow tufts replaced by grey and white striping. True feathers.

He parked on Bay Street South near the escarpment where his mother had last been living. Houses huddled there together like a group of people with a chill. He got out of the car with the shoebox under an arm. Stood on aching feet and stiff knees and stared up at her porch. His shins and calves hurt. On his last visit, three or four Thanksgivings ago, its posts and railings had been newly painted in aquamarine, almost exactly matching his car's paint job. Planters hanging from the trim, which was badly peeling now, were empty or trailing dried tendrils of former ferns and geraniums. These were not good signs. The front door was locked. He put the chicks down on the grimy seat cover out there.

Well, what had he expected? He knocked. He pushed the door-bell. and it rang distantly.

Finally, and with great effort, he pulled open the front window to the living room and went on in. She'd neatened before leaving. There was no clutter, only dust, particles suspended everywhere. There were bite marks on some of the wood trim, tiny brown mouse droppings collecting in spoons and bowls in kitchen drawers and cupboards, in corners.

He returned to the living room. Tried not to look at the port, the final proof, which stood in the corner near his father's old leather La-Z-Boy, its footrest still propped up. Framed photos on the mantel on the bricked-over fireplace included Brandon in his graduation regalia, clutching diploma; Brandon in his track uniform, clutching silver medal; Brandon skinny in the oversized cheap suit he'd worn to prom, clutching girlfriend's hand. This last one he took down, wip-ing its dust on his yoga pants.

The clock still ticked. It was the only sound. He strained to listen for the port's hum, heard nothing. He stepped closer to it, climbed onto the La-Z-Boy and leaned in, and there was the faint purr of its music. Had it gone dormant? He hadn't yet found one this quiet.

Either way, if it called to him now, he could resist it. Of this he was certain. He put his hand on the nub of the zipper, felt it thrum against his palm, then let go. He climbed back out through the window and, out of respect, pushed it firmly closed.

He sat on the porch seat and tried to think. Already he felt the weeks of isolation working on and against him, a kind of crowbar wedging between who he had been and what he was becoming: a person with an unkempt beard, soothed by the smell of chicken shit.

"Hey, little guy," he said, picking up the smallest chick and holding it to his face, nuzzling it against his nose, his cheeks. His mother was gone. His mother was definitely gone. This little guy pinched his lip with a beak. Maybe he'd go back to Portland. Maybe he'd stay here to wait and see. He knew the waiting would make of him a superstitious gambler: he'd be sure the moment he left that they'd return, perhaps in waves, the way they left. He'd be a man unable to leave his slot machine.

Winter here would be brutal. In Portland he could shave and launder, and supposedly there were women, plenty of women. He had to do it now before he began to wait, to know himself to be waiting. Here, he'd have to shave in a birdbath or stream, would become a mountain man.

He was about to stand, when he heard something. A cyclist sped down the hill past him. Then another. Two cyclists with long hair, bare legs. They were past him when a large mutt came running, too, collar jangling. The dog stopped at the house and nosed the air. Brandon stilled himself, hoped that his face was hidden by the parched plants. The dog let out a bark. It seemed to look right at him.

"Come on, Gus! Come on, buddy!"

The dog barked twice more, hard little warnings, and then sped off running toward the cyclists.

Chapter

12

THE PESSIMISTS

"Well, what did you expect?" Donnie said now as he said at least once every day. His leg—always spread out straight, braced by its sticks—was no better. It was possible he was healing all wrong and that the improper set of his leg would be the first victim of their lack of expertise. He sat on the ground, back against one of the large logs, a few feet from the fire. For two weeks, the fire had been tended, flickering or blazing, but never left to cool.

At the end of every day, they circled around the same topic. "Are we still going to wait?" and "Well, what did you expect?"

There were no farmers left, not within a hundred kilometres. After that first disappointing trip, the crews had gone out in every direction, and each time came home disheartened, having seen in those huge metal barns only bloodied messes of feathers, occasionally the decaying carcass of some dead bird, rejected by all but the maggots and flies crawling out and over its body.

"Well, what did you expect?" Donnie said.

Fear was beginning to outweigh optimism. Soon animals would no longer fear humans, would no longer keep away from highways or babies; creatures would appear out of the woods as though from a long hibernation. Everyone would need to have guns. Fear was as palpable as a mist foretelling autumn. Autumn, too, was on its way, and with it the old cynicism creeping drafty through the cracks. They had begun to worry about cars and gasoline, so getting to Virginia or anyplace else would require a strength none of them had. Their belief had been a spell, now broken, and they had to face facts. They'd never see their loved ones again. They were terrible hunters. They'd run out of canned goods and foraged fruit, and then maybe they'd starve.

People talked less about the things they had once been thrilled by. A resetting of the circadian rhythm, for one, so that, as a few of them knew from an article long ago read in *The Atlantic*—no, *Scientific American* (they could agree to disagree on small points like this)— they would begin to wake in the middle of the long dark night, their bodies naturally breaking into two dark respites with an hour or two of quiet consciousness in the middle. Some of them had theories about the lunar cycle, how the moon dictated moods, swayed energy and joy, controlled electricity.

Now all discussions returned to the only question left: leave or stay. *Have we been foolish? Are we still, now, fools?*

The constant fire blazed from the centre of the long yard of lawns, with the feeble barrier of wood fencing and brick homes, each with a narrow gap between them, as their only protection. They, too, were chickens in a coop and unprotected from whatever might come down out of those woods beyond those thin fences. Some of them longed for the return of all those they'd once disdained: MBAs, lawyers, politicians, tycoons, anybody who might point and order. Party's over, they wanted someone to say, as though they were unsupervised kids at a sleepover that had gotten out of control.

"We'll figure it out," Bonita said. "We've been caught off guard, but we'll manage this winter, just as we did last winter."

Marie remembered those jars of olives and pickles, the burning roof of her mouth. The smell of ashes and woodsmoke hanging on clothes and in hair was no longer noticeable to any of them. "I'll teach you all to shoot."

Steve pulled his children and wife closer. His long arms were everywhere touching a member of his own family. His arm around Regina, who held Lulu, their daughter, on her lap; his other arm pulling close the two small boys. All of them shining with sunburns. People retreated into the intimacy of their smaller tribes. Steve was a forceful person but lacked kindness and tact, and Marie hated him for a leader. Why was it still always *men*?

"Anyway, we're not leaving yet," Bonita said. "We have to wait for Philip."

Marie and Rosa murmured their agreement. Mo nodded.

"*Do* we need to wait for Philip?" Steve said.

"Why do we repeat ourselves every night?"

"We're like people trapped in a bad marriage." Donnie sighed. "Already exhausted all topics of conversation."

"Well," Bonita said, "that's when one person takes up golfing and the other learns to knit. Not the end of the world."

They glared at her. Even at Bonita, whom they loved, they glared.

The sun was finally setting, its heat an ordeal to be forgotten until the next morning, and the fire's bright colours flamed prettily in the bluing twilight, an echo of the sinking sun.

Bonita tightened her little hands into fists. "We're not leaving him behind."

"But we've all been left behind," Steve said. "Why wait for him? What makes him so special? We've each lost a hundred people."

There were only thirty-eight of them now. In two weeks, they'd lost two elderly and little Zev, all, they presumed, through port.

"But why do you think we're here if not to wait for them all to come back!"

"We thought," Steve said, then paused as Regina whispered into his ear. "We were building something here. A life. Pioneering."

"We were never going to leave," Marie said. "Of course we've all been waiting for everyone to come back. That's why we're all still here.

Philip was the only one who wanted to leave. The rest of us have somebody we're waiting for already. We all know this, Steve."

Rosa and Mo were seated next to her, closing their bodies into a cocoon. His hand on her back, her arms draped over his legs, their posture leaking whispers and the wet smacks of kisses. Marie was alone. Donnie was, and so was Bonita. The old ties were the same as the new ties. People maintained monogamy and left each other out. Gus remained her only tether.

"You still think your ex-husband's coming back," Steve said. "But you're dreaming. He's got his own people now."

The cruelty of one who has toward one who has not.

"When did you become such an asshole?" Bonita said.

Regina stared at them from her big, darkly rimmed eyes. "Don't talk to him like that."

They couldn't hide from one another. There was no privacy to dive into; there were no obsessions or workplaces in which to be enclosed.

"Sometimes it takes an asshole to tell the truth," Steve said.

On that day two weeks ago, Steve had insisted that they keep the church nailed shut, and then had gone into the police station for a gun, grabbed up all the rolls of yellow caution tape and started wrapping every building he knew had a port inside. The church was his main concern, the scene, as it were, of Philip's crime, and now he'd taped up the buildings along four full streets. Then he moved onto wrapping other buildings, sometimes wrapping a house without even checking for a port, and all of this was supposed to be for the sake of the children, though they were never let to wander out of sight. It had been a blow to lose Zev, the only other child for their children to play with.

Was it better to be safe? Were safe or sorry the only options? Now to get into the church they had to duck under or step over the bright warnings: POLICE LINE DO NOT CROSS POLICE LINE DO NOT CROSS POLICE LINE and climb through a window.

"You're overreacting. It isn't instantaneous. It doesn't suck you up," Marie had told him as he pulled the streams of tape around the posts and railings surrounding the church. Beside him stood Regina with her large and frightened eyes. Steve no longer seemed the strapping Dutchman who so loved to prepare meat and plant seeds, who always smelled like the damp earth inside the greenhouse; both of them were thinner, now, slack in the cheekbones, hanging with clothes. They had been sapped of energy they'd had only a month ago, with their peach-picking and canning, with their plans for solar panelling and greenhouse-equipping.

"It sucked Philip up," Steve said.

"It didn't. Philip was already on the verge. Bonita told me he was talking about leaving all the time."

"He talked about staying a lot too."

"We all talk about leaving all the time," Regina said, scanning the street for her children. One, two, three, running up ramps and down porch steps, jumping into weedy gardens and pulling up snails. "How is this my life? How is this their childhood?" She put a hand to her mouth.

"Everybody else just accepted this. You just accepted this," Steve said.

"You know that isn't true," Marie said. "But you can't live for too long in a state of paranoia."

"How did everyone else just sign up to leave? I don't get it," Regina said.

"We just need to hold on a little longer."

"For how long?" Steve said.

They knew they'd just missed Philip that day, and they were fairly sure he had a few business cards, that small, unlikely-to-work antidote to amnesia. Assuming that port actually took you somewhere, when you arrived would you still have all your old clothes on? Still have pockets in which to hold such cards? None but Marie, Mo, Bonita and Rosa would go near the church anymore, where Marie's paint-splattered dropcloth was the only membrane between them and the sweetly humming trap beneath. They wouldn't sleep at the church as they had sometimes done, and no one would go alone, but the four of them were there almost every day, the way a person visits and revisits the gravesite of a beloved. Marie grasped a leash and apologized to Gus for the shackling, afraid that he'd get too close to it. They would not go farther up than the third row of pews from the front.

Marie thought sometimes that it would be all right if the rest of them got out and left only these four. Together they were a force, even if Mo and Rosa were sharing their own umbrella and oblivious in their lovesick state to the loneliness of others. Marie knew that the moment she went in alone, she'd be up there, unwrapping, unzipping, as though each small exposure to its seductive force had been a taste of a potent, perfect drug. It seemed to promise the world. It did promise the world. She could still taste how it had felt: like the future, like a lover to know you as no one else did, like the perfect new baby, your baby in your arms. Every itch she'd been trying not to scratch.

Together that first day, they'd cut a tiny hole at the top of the dropcloth, kept a few inches unzipped, so that Philip, if he returned, could get out again. They did these things with tongs so as not to touch it. Mo developed a mark like a burn, a puckering discolouration on the back of his hand where he'd touched the inside of it for too long.

Almost as soon as the sun was up, the back of Marie's neck burned hot, curls of hair slick against her skin. She had left Bonita to the vegetables and was on her way to some of the yards they knew where people kept peach trees. After that, she would scavenge more paper cups. She bicycled through the streets, towing the sporty double stroller filled with empty bottles, fingertips tingling with readiness to

grab the gun, Gus scrambling to keep up. She went first to the stream
at the top of the Charlton golf course while it was still relatively cool
and filled the bottles. Though people would sometimes bathe in the
lake on the other side of the city, most preferred the apparent cleanliness of waterfalls coming down the escarpment's stacked rocks. If
they had a scientist, they could test for *E. coli* or for any of the other
bacteria they couldn't afford to ingest without a doctor around for
diagnoses; as it was, all their hopes lay in the looted plastic bottles
and their several water filtration kits. She filled the bottles and dipped
her head under, soaking hair and face. Gus dunked his snout in and
drank. Was she becoming more canine? She, like Gus, was happy for
a job. Sometimes it seemed that she was made for this—for tasks
deeply important, for high stakes, for—not courage exactly—but
fortitude. This was why she would outlast almost everyone else. Her
peculiar combination of genes, her Marie-ness, was like a genetic
immunity against a plague.

Jason was just a convenient location into which she could place her
anxieties. Her talisman, her rosary, the thoughts like a line of beads:
what would she say to him if he ever returned, his face, his hands on
her body, his mouth, his mind? It was good to be good at this—to have
a job to do—but like any loyal mutt, she wished for someone's recognition. She wished for Jason to say: *I should have stayed. No matter what
it took, I should have stayed. You were right, Marie.*

Back on the bicycle, she raced down the hill and back towards
James Street. She parked outside her abandoned storefront, took
one of the photos that were amassing on roll after roll, perhaps
never to be developed. Rosa joked about keeping a record. The era
of the daily photo is over, she said. Day 356 marked the day that
everything changed.

Every day marked a day on which everything changed. The
familiar jagged shape of her fading yellow star was up there in front
of the place where she used to sleep. She picked the camera out of

the wagon and stood back in the middle of James Street, right on the yellow dividing line, to take it. So maybe she should begin painting again. Why not? Set up an easel in the street. Better than a photographic record would be splashes of colour, and how those colours felt. She'd make them brighter than they were.

She pivoted and took the photo of the billboard. She had not missed a day. The red *S* was still there. As she and Gus continued on to find more boxes and coffee cups, to find more clay or plastic pots that could be cleansed of dead matter and replanted, she turned the word *sport* over in her mind. She was certain now that it had not been painted by any of them. It seemed to mean, *Isn't this a laugh? What fun!* She could only picture Willy Wonka, somebody with odd—nearly insane—affect. Tap dancing, crying hysterically, "Everybody's gone! Ha ha ha!"

Children would one day put on plays and musicals, would make puppets and design travelling shows. Rosa and Mo's children, maybe. She was supposed to be happy for them and for the gift of their pheromone-shaded compatibility because of the future it pointed to. These would be their legends. Future puppeteers would make up a mask with exaggerated features. This character, writer of the red *S*, a Zorro, a person who had to exist, because a letter of the alphabet didn't just appear in red paint out of nowhere—a character who, once found, would explain everything to them.

Rosa was supposed to meet her here, and she waited in the shade against the old Eaton Centre shopping mall, which had long been a deserted husk, long before the slow desertion of the planet, and now would never be reclaimed and revitalized by civic boosters, by artists or filmmakers or whatever movers and shakers did such things.

She and Rosa had spent every morning of the past two weeks combing through the apartments and storefronts within a two-block radius of the billboard. They drew police tape over doors holding ports inside, because Steve had asked them to, and because they still loved him. They would have settled for anything to prove that someone was living in any of these places, but all were dusty and cobwebbed, and any old food scraps they found were long rubberized or dried completely.

Today Marie stood in the shade of the Eaton Centre, waiting for Rosa. They'd finally climb to the top of the building, where the answer, if there was an answer, had to be.

Waiting for Rosa, sweat beading on her neck, her chest, soaking through her shirt, she put the camera to her face. Took a photo of the plaza kitty-corner from her, the red awning of the diner where she'd bought cheap, terrible coffee before the fair-trade place cropped up. Then a snap of the specialty shoe store. She stepped into the street to catch the gallery just north of the plaza and then turned and flicked through several shots of the brick apartment building they'd not yet entered, the one hosting the billboard. She was staring up at it, a knight before castle walls, when Rosa startled her.

"Hey!" she said, coming up behind her and pulling her into a hug.

"Ugh," Marie said, swinging around. "I'm drenched." She scanned Rosa for red marks where Mo had put his mouth, but this only made Marie miserable. "What an ugly time in history to be stuck in," she said. "Money poured into eyesores."

"But you've made it into art," Rosa said. "Your photos are haunting."

She sounded like a sycophant at a gallery opening. Marie tried not to frown. "I wonder how long it will take for it to fade completely. If thousands of years from now it will be a mystery for the fossil record."

There were many things too solid to be melted down. Many things that would outlast them and their children and their children's children. Perhaps the building would turn to rubble and still the metal scaffolding would endure.

"So we're doing this, right?"

"Do you want to?"

"Yup."

Marie no longer entirely trusted that Rosa's heart was in anything, felt that Rosa must be thinking always of Mo. I get it, Marie wanted to say. I've been in love before. Everyone in the world has been in love. It's commonplace, and you guys aren't heroic for being led around by pheromones and hormones and whatever.

Probably they could have climbed up to the roof through the building, by jimmying open or breaking down doors, by way of stairwells, but instead, they pulled themselves up the metal fire escape, their arms and abs strong from their daily work and no longer sore. They climbed up iron beams plugged into the wall at the top and hoisted themselves over the top lip of brick.

In front of them was a ratty folding lawn chair, woven from plastic. Beside it was a fleece beige blanket, black-spotted with mildew, a pile of candy wrappers somewhat disturbed by wind and an empty paint can without its lid. Marie walked over, lifted the blanket to her nose as though it could smell like anything other than that dry rot smell.

"Mildew will take over the world," she said.

"Pays to be small," Rosa said. Under the blanket was a pair of binoculars, apparently high grade, and she picked these up and put them to her face. "These are heavy."

There was also on the ground a paperback novel, cover torn off. She picked it up and saw the title. "I know this book," she said. "It was one of Jason's favourite's."

"Vonnegut?" Rosa said idly, reading through the binoculars, her face made owlish and odd.

"Yeah," Marie said, turning the brittle, water-damaged pages. "It's pretty famous, though. Doesn't mean anything."

Rosa was scanning the cityscape. She could see right into Marie's old apartment, could even make out the unicorn's thin embroidered horn on her quilt.

"Can I have those for a sec?" Marie said.

Rosa hesitated and then passed them over. Marie did not direct her lens-gaze to the apartment but instead pointed her head down into the street below, where Gus was seated in front of the fire escape.

"He's a good dog," Rosa said.

Marie laughed. "I say we take the binoculars."

"Doesn't this worry you?" Rosa said. "This doesn't seem like it could be one of ours. This is like a stakeout. It's a set-up for a sniper."

But Marie didn't feel afraid. "It's just binoculars and paint."

"But what if this is the same guy who broke that window? He's been hanging around a long time," Rosa said.

"Could be. Probably," Marie said. "He or she."

"Aren't you scared?"

Marie put the binoculars to her eyes and stared into her own apartment. Her hands were shaking. Rosa tried to take them from her, but Marie yanked her hands away. "Don't." She wanted to be alone with the information cooking inside her, a dough rising. "Say the person who painted the *S* broke the window. Say this person means no harm. Say he—or she—say he or she is disoriented, trying to make sense of this."

"Say they're deranged."

Marie sighed.

"I want to help you, Marie. You know we love you."

She bristled at this *we*. "I'm okay. I'm always okay."

"But what if you're being watched. What if we're all being watched," Rosa said.

"I miss the days when someone was watching me. Surveilling me, omnipresent, interested. I miss the eyes of men on me in the street even."

"Gross," Rosa laughed. "Mo thinks the ports have brains. Like, ESP or something."

"To have ESP you first have to have senses."

"He thinks they have senses," Rosa said.

"But they don't have sense organs!"

"Think about it, Marie. PINA had access to all of our data. E-mails, banking, social media, names of pets. Everything. These ports might know, well—"

"Oh God. Another theory."

"Why are you angry with me?"

"I'm not."

"You are. Obviously. Because of Mo."

"Ugh. Don't start getting such a big ego that you think I'm jealous or something."

"Marie. I'm your best friend."

"Yeah right." She knew she shouldn't, but she said it anyway: "Best friend by default."

"Why don't you go into the fucking woods with your fucking gun," Rosa said. "Screw you." And then she was gone, hooking her feet back onto the metal steps and climbing down to the street. The binoculars knocked against Marie's chest, clattered against the camera as she climbed down a few minutes later.

This is what fear did, and uncertainty and hunger. They were beginning to project the intent to surveil on things without eyes or intentions. Not only ports or the stars, but the billboard, too, which Marie couldn't help feeling was to blame for everything, that on its high overlook it was watching her.

Rosa sped off, her braided hair a thick black whip. Marie greeted Gus absently. She put the camera into the wagon next to the lukewarm water bottles and walked over to the store. Gus's nails clicked slightly against the hardwood, and she shushed him. He whimpered, whined, pulled toward the corner armchair surrounded by books. She let him lead her to small round droppings in the corner. "Just rabbits, Gus. Maybe a squirrel. Poor hungry thing." She left him to root around in the back of the store, while she went up the stairs to her apartment.

The most tempting conclusion beat like a bloody heart in the centre of every thought she'd had since seeing that changed billboard.

She did not believe in good luck. Jason had believed that pessimism was a self-fulfilling prophecy. As though her mind had caused the miscarriages, her mind had caused her to fail to become an artist. "It's not pessimism, it's realism," she'd told him.

"Spoken like a true pessimist," he teased.

She missed being teased. There was no one here to know her or to tease her.

There's probably nothing, she thought, or tried to think, as her head filled with white noise. The clinking of Gus's collar was faint and far away, as though under water.

The door to her apartment at the top of the stairs was still hanging open. Everything as she'd left it. This seemed to be an answer: no. She wandered through the apartment, where her paintings still hung and her sculptures and figurines were still seated untouched on small gallery-style shelves. The embroidery on her bed had not come unstitched. There were no footprints except those she was making in the thin layer of dirt that had breezed in from the windows she'd left cracked. Nothing had been touched. To be sure she went through the kitchen cupboards, which still housed her bags of jerky and dried fruit, her line of cans. She pulled it all out and arrayed it on the counter to see if anything was missing. But if someone had been squatting or looting, surely by now it would all be gone.

She took the blanket from the bed and laid it on the kitchen floor. On it were the medieval-style unicorns standing next to two-dimensional menfolk, fenced in by white and golden threads, each with its head turned toward the viewer, toward her. Nothing was amiss, but she wanted reinforcements. "Gus!" She could no longer hear his collar rattling.

Onto the blanket she put clay roosters, wooden painted horses, her miniature bust of an ear-bandaged van Gogh, her framed Elvis rodeo photo, some jewellery, her food. A dollar-store photo album with pictures from their honeymoon in Montreal. It was the only trip they'd taken. Almost all the photos were of Jason or Marie against full panoramas of strange sky and river. There was one of the two of them before a stone wall, under a bronze umbrella, bodies turned toward each other. She knew it well and did not need to open the album to feel, even, how damp had been the ankles of her blue jeans.

That's where she'd go if she could go anywhere. "Gus!" She had to sit. She curled up against the wall, chin on knees. They'd been too young to marry. Their faces in the photo were round with youth. No hard edges, no resentment, no regrets no matter how deep they might go inside themselves. Each was a beautiful mollusk to open carefully, known only to the other.

Well, fuck this. There wasn't enough to distract her from heartbreak. Now the embarrassment of tears. Not a single comfort measure was available. She couldn't find the CD he'd recorded when he was trying to learn blues and classical guitar, before his studies had stolen every other interest from him.

The other song she'd loved. Spooky, she'd thought, and weird and sad. *I'm going with you, babe, I'm going with you babe, I don't care where you go.* She made him sing it over and over, she begged him to write new verses. *I'm going down south, I'm going down south, chilly wind don't blow.*

I'd rather be dead, I'd rather be dead.

She crawled over to the window and sat there, curled up on her mattress. It might as well be that nothing had changed from last winter. It might even be that none of it had happened. It had all been a hallucination. They *were* brains in vats. Jason had been a better philosopher than a scientist, because he didn't believe in Occam's razor, didn't equate neatness with truth.

Neither of them had done what they should have: made a romantic gesture, moved closer to each other, rended garments, nothing. She cried until it hurt to open her eyes. Tears were a poison, an acid to the eyes and flesh. What had changed from last winter? Not a thing had changed. Nobody was coming. The world had ended. The world had ended, and this was not a metaphor.

She wiped her face with her palms. "Gus, please!" she rasped. She couldn't hear him. "Gus!"

If she went back there? To Montreal over a decade ago, to start over, to try again, to restart their doomed marriage? They'd make clear-headed vows this time. If I fuck up, you don't let me leave. You tie me down. We won't have children, and it doesn't matter. All that matters is us, together. But what about that other Marie, who'd still be twenty-one and pudgy with beauty? Port couldn't put *this* Marie back under that bronze umbrella. And what if it didn't take you where you wanted, Dorothy-style? This was the worst of it: no matter how badly she wanted to go, she'd never leave. And knowing this changed nothing.

She got up and went to the bathroom, where the plumbing had sat unused all that year. Mildew spotted the toilet bowl. Rust was browning each of the fixtures. Lines of brown and black and circles of fuzz were blotching the wall, the bathtub, the sink, all despite a lack of running water. Everywhere the natural world took its slow hold. She pinched her nose and went to the only mirror in the apartment, above that blackening sink. She wanted to see how bad the tears had set her face, wanted now to go back to the others seeming strong and fine. The appearance of strength *was* strength. But every mental path she travelled brought more tears: Mom—Claudine—Dad—Bonita—Mo and Rosa—baby bodies red-clumping the basin—Gus. "Gus!"

Finally she heard the weight of him trotting up the stairs. As she opened the bathroom window, she looked again at her own face in the mirror. Just as it had always been, as though she were still that long-gone child, thinking *me*.

Loneliness can kill you, she thought. But in the reflection, she saw that there was something on the wall behind her. A piece of paper taped there. Then Gus was at her side, his nose pressed cold against her hand.

She peeled it off. A folded note on fine art paper. On it, scrawled in blue marker:

Found you.

Chapter

13

THE STRANGER

Marie folded up the note—*Found you*—until it was a moist nugget in her hand and then stood in front of the shop for a very long time, paralyzed by not knowing where he'd be. The binoculars were around her neck now. Taking them had broken the spell. She peered into the buildings, with binoculars and without. She half expected to see that figure in the shadows, looking back. *Found you.* It had made her laugh. He was still his terse, plainspoken self, even if he was also behaving extremely strangely. She waited there on that corner, thinking that she would spot the speck of light that would betray his presence.

She went back into the store and fumbled in the darkness for the pots of felt-tip markers and a sheet of heavy paper. *Is it you?* she wrote. *I'm waiting for you. Find us south of Aberdeen between Locke and Dundurn.*

With leftover duct-tape, she posted it to the outside of the door. Because she did not know what else to do, she returned to the fire. Pulling the wagon, she was a shadow of the child she had once been, the one always cramming suitcase with stuffed toys and books and threatening to run away. Life had called her childhood bluff: she wasn't going anywhere. Gus trotted next to her, and the darkness made the echoes of their movements sharp, so she moved faster.

Up at the firepit Mo was tapping his hands on his djembe. Rosa had brought out some of the strings in her collection and was piecing together a song on one of the ukuleles, this one made of a reddish wood. She sang "Over the Rainbow" as Mo's drumbeats fell into her rhythm. There were only a few songs she knew. Mo moved into a rhyme, a beat about living at the end of the road.

"Why is every song about leaving or returning?" Bonita said to Donnie, who sat beside her. Cups of instant hot chocolate were steaming in their hands. It was time for comfort food, even in the humidity. Iced tea was not an option. Above and behind them, in the trees cresting the escarpment, the sunset was glowing orange.

"Clearly every song is not about leaving or returning." Donnie coughed into the thick fur of his forearm.

"I think most of them are. All the songs I can think of, anyway."

Now Rosa was singing "La Vie en Rose," but her French was rusty, and she'd forgotten most of the lyrics. Mo laughed, she laughed, they kissed.

"They're rubbing it in our faces," Donnie said.

Marie glanced up then, wondering if Donnie could see through to her envy and her new, terrible hope.

"Not on purpose," said Bonita. "Haven't you ever been in love?"

Marie scanned the lawns. Steve and Regina were at the back of their house under a mouldering wooden overhang, deep in conversation—his wide eyes, the back of her small head. Everyone else was sitting around the fire. Without Philip, record-keeping had become haphazard, but Bonita had taken a head count, like a chaperone on a field trip.

"It's good for young people to fall in love," Bonita said.

Donnie harrumphed.

"Even though love doesn't last, and people just hurt each other," Marie said, to which Donnie let out a little woot.

"Friendship and music, then. Music is good for us," Bonita said.

"Except that we're all in tears," Andrea said. She wore her hair always tied under a kerchief now, was toughening up and thinning out.

"It's not always a bad thing to weep," Bonita said. Many of the heads she had just counted were bent into hands, distressed, shoulders shaking.

"All the songs *are* about leaving!" Andrea said.

Rosa started to sing "Leavin' on a Jet Plane."

Bonita walked over. "Something upbeat," she said, hand on her daughter's shoulder.

Rosa began "Over the Rainbow" again, and Bonita shook her head.

"Something we can dance to," Bonita said, tossing her hips to the left and then to the right. Her awkward shimmy made Lilah laugh. She pulled her friend out of her seat, and they danced, while Mo beat his hands on the drumskin.

"How about this," Mo said, and he sang about eloping with the love of his life to a Detroit hotel.

Bonita lifted her arms in a kind of shrug as she danced. But several of them were moving now, she and Lilah and Andrea. Steve and Regina were standing on their porch, arms crossed over their chests.

"Maybe it would help if I learned some more songs," Rosa said. "How about this one?"

Marie felt agitated. The sinking sun was behind her and Bonita's dancing was taking on a frantic quality. Her audience included six crying adults. She smiled more largely. She shimmied. She hooted.

"Let me try." Andrea sang a song none of them knew. It was about leaving and returning, about staying and being always in the place you were. The word *home* rang out to them.

Finally, Bonita, breathless, sat down and put her thin, strong arm around Marie. Marie's body was sensitive, her skin keyed up as though feverish, and this touch made goose bumps spread. She held her right hand tightly over the note; she cupped Gus's throat with her left. Bits of fur released and stuck to her palm.

The firelight on their faces was hard as a strong sun.

"Tomorrow," Bonita said, "you should take us hunting."

"I'm not sure—" Marie hesitated. She wouldn't tell Bonita about Jason. She wanted not to be dissuaded. Wanted not to be told the thing that niggled at her: that she had conjured these clues from her own insane hope. "I'm not sure it matters."

"Of course it matters. Marietta, of course it does." Bonita pulled her into a tight embrace, and Marie closed her eyes, rested her forehead in the warm crook of Bonita's neck. "Our survival matters."

"I can't leave," Marie said. "Even if I wanted to, I couldn't. Even when I'm standing right next to a port, and it's tempting me or whatever, I can't leave."

Bonita rocked her gently. "Listen." Andrea was singing an unfamiliar love song, full of sweetness and aching. "*If you were there,*" she sang. "*If you were there.*"

"Did you know she could sing like that?" Bonita said.

Marie shook her head and closed her eyes, let the song be a lullaby. Let a person be lulled, she thought. Her right fist relaxed, and Bonita plucked the note out of her hand.

"What's this?"

"I found it in one of the apartments." A lie was easy and too quick to come.

Bonita opened the page, but it was tearing along its many creases, and the blue ink had blurred.

Mo had his hands on Rosa. At the small of her back, on her knee, pushing her hair back. They got up together, and then Andrea helped Donnie down, and now Marie's longing was worse, now Marie's skin was raw. Marie stood up, and then Gus did. Bonita wordlessly refolded the note and handed it back to her.

"Who wrote that?" she said.

Marie pushed it into her pocket. "I told you I found it in one of the apartments."

"But you think you know who wrote it."

"That wouldn't be impossible, would it?"

Bonita nodded, and Marie saw that her strong response had confirmed for Bonita that she was deluded.

"Well it wouldn't be," she said.

"Nothing's impossible," Bonita said. "But we'll want to get up early. Why don't you go to sleep?"

Lying on Bonita's couch, she thought she'd be too excited to sleep, but almost instantly she was unconscious under the piled afghans, hand draped over the edge, fingers lightly in Gus's fur as though her arm were dangling from a boat into calm water.

In dreams, Jason's eyes were on her the way they once had been, full of knowing. In dreams, she knew she was dreaming. "I'm having a lucid dream," she told him. She went to toggle light switches, and they all behaved. Lights on, lights off, lights on.

She toggled and then woke; she was the light going on. But darkness and silence filled the room. She was lovesick from the dream, lips tingling and swollen. Jason's eyes on her mouth, hands on her waist, on her breasts. Gus was no longer beside her but was standing poised at the window, growling.

"Gus," she hissed, worried that he would wake Bonita upstairs.

He growled. Let out one sharp yap.

Checking for the gun beside her on the coffee table, she walked toward him. Her eyes adjusted, and now she could see the difference in the darkness just where Gus stood. A body, a human body, someone standing at the window. Broad-shouldered, like a man. Gus barked twice. The figure put its hands in the air.

Marie held the gun carefully, ready to aim. Fear sloshed her gut. "Hello?" she said.

His voice was faint through the glass. "Gus," he was saying. "Buddy, it's okay."

She did not recognize his voice. Not Jason. Not tall enough either. It was some asshole she didn't know trying to charm her pup. She pointed the gun at his chest and walked closer. Held her arms out straight and aimed, as she had with the deer.

"Don't shoot! Don't shoot!" His voice came watery through the window.

"How do you know my dog's name?"

"I'm here to help. I'm— I don't mean any— Please. I promise."

On Brandon's fourth day in the city, something seemed to be happening. Something seemed to have happened. He had been eavesdropping on these women, Rosa and Marie. The dog, Gus, appeared to be meant for protection, but in fact he was harmless. Yesterday Brandon had parked the car up the street and watched the women climb up the side of a building in shorts. He wanted to be close enough to hear what they were saying, but he stayed down on the street.

Once, he approached Gus, who only sniffed him and accepted the peace offering of an open can of processed meat. He'd left the three little chicks in his mom's living room after checking and double checking that the port was zipped shut and already he missed them when he was this far away, missed them even more than he did Zahra or Suzanne, who, from the vantage of his current predicament, seemed abstractions. His mother, too, was a ghost, a wisp of smoke. He understood that Gus was not about protection, just as his chickens would never be food.

He hid in the alleyway behind a Dumpster—one and then two rats scrambled over the tips of his shoes. Rosa came down first and mounted her bicycle, followed by Marie, legs long in her cut-offs. Marie stood watching her pedal away. Only Gus turned to look at Brandon, tail down.

He ducked into a small gallery, where the door had been jimmied open and left unlocked. He could see her only through a sliver of window. There, he sat back against a brick wall beneath a canvas painted with green and gold squares, and pulled two smushed Twinkies out of his bag.

Marie stood just outside the gallery taking pictures, then she walked back to her store. In an e-mail from long ago, his mother had mentioned taking art classes down here, and he wondered if they'd crossed paths. Marie's hair was half tied up with a length of red fabric, and he could imagine her in this crowd: big earrings, black dress, wine in hand. Sharp opinions and sultry laughter. She was looking at the storefront, and he was looking at her, the sculptural length of her, her dancer's grace as she disappeared inside.

After about ten minutes, Gus came trotting out from behind a fence along the back of the store and directly toward him. The dog nudged the door open and stared at him, tail wagging.

"You want some of these?" He opened the packet of stale bone-shaped treats. "Good boy. Is Marie okay in there?" It felt like a trespass to say her name.

They both heard her crying out for Gus, and Brandon patted him. "You'd better go back, buddy." Gus choked back five treats and jogged back around the fence and into the store.

Brandon wandered around the gallery. Among the title cards and paintings were quotes from newspaper articles about the artist. "Camille Allen Alder (b. 1975) for many years worked as a graphic artist in Chicago, before moving here with her husband and new-born twins in 2010. Since then, she has been actively pushing for

better arts funding and visibility in the city. She describes her paintings as the city's dream of the country."

He had long ached with nostalgia for these late summer dusks.
If he'd stayed in the place he'd grown up with his mom, he might
have been a starving artist. He might have fallen in love with Marie
instead of with Sarah, the college sweetheart who loved to break up
and give ultimatums. He and Marie would have had freckled babies
and a porch with an escarpment view.

Just as it was getting dark, a shadow fell across the sidewalk in
front of the gallery. It was a blond man, balding a little, in a ratty
blazer. By the time Brandon ducked his head out the door, the man
was gone.

Finally she re-emerged. Before leaving, she tore through some
hunks of duct tape with her teeth and pasted up a note.

Marie unlatched and then pulled open the glass door, leaving between
them only a thin screen. He waited for her to say something, but she
only stood there with a gun pointed at him, lips pressed together, eyes
unblinking.

"I saw. I, uh—" Brandon pulled the note out of his back pocket.
"I got your message. I thought you wanted me to come here."

Her face crumpled. She looked at the note without moving the gun.

"I'm not going to hurt you. You can put the gun down." He held
the paper taut between his hands like a shield. She looked at the note
for a minute without lowering her arms. Finally she turned her head
away and put the gun into the waistband of her shorts, unconscious
of how sexy this was, how it momentarily revealed her taut abdomen
with its belly button stuck out like a berry.

"I'm sorry, Marie."

"How do you know my name?" She slid the screen door open and
thrust out her palm. "The note. Please."

"You're an artist." Brandon had imagined how this would go—what he would say—but now he saw that it was too strange for her.

"And so are you," she said.

"Well, not really."

An angry sneer curled the corner of her mouth. "And I guess the binoculars aren't yours, then?"

He could hear the hope, the disappointment in her voice. "Actually, no," he said. "They aren't mine."

"Who are you?"

She was nothing like Zahra; she was easily read. Her face betrayed her anger, her disappointment, her subsequent relief. Seeing these things play across her features felt unbearably intimate, and Brandon wanted to wrap her up in cloth, cover her and keep her safe.

"I'm Brandon. I'm sorry I'm not—" He stopped talking and put his hands up again. "This is frustrating. I'm sorry I startled you. I'll tell you everything."

She was studying his face now, realizing that he was familiar, that his was a face she knew. "You've been watching me?"

"No. Well, yes. A little." He laughed. "Let me start again. I'm Brandon."

"You said that."

Gus padded gingerly out onto the porch, and she followed him until they were both standing next to him.

"You don't need to look at me askance," he said. "I really don't mean harm. You're the one with the gun."

A laugh came out, as sharp as her appraising eyes. She tried to stop laughing, kept laughing, held an arm tight against her heaving chest.

"What's so funny?"

"Askance?" It made her laugh again, lips opening to flash teeth.

He blushed. "I like your house."

Again she laughed. "This note wasn't meant for you. I don't know you!"

"Oh. I thought maybe you—"

"Come on."

"Where are we going?"

She slid the glass door closed behind them with a metallic whoosh, exchanging dark living room for dark yard. The fire had been left to smoulder, and the smell of its burning filled the air.

"I don't want to wake up Bonita. This is her house."

He picked up his shoebox, causing the chicks, who were still sleeping, to shift slightly.

"I mean, none of these houses are ours, technically," Marie said. "But we've all been living here for almost a year. Since they are some of the nicest houses in the city, and no one was using them." She heard herself presenting the logic of thieves and stopped herself.

Marie started to move logs around. She lit a torch she'd made from newspaper, and once it was blazing, pushed it down under a teepee of sticks. "So, you're Brandon. How long have you been lurking in the streets?"

"About four days."

She stopped moving for a moment, stood unmoving before the fire. "For awhile we were keeping better watch on our perimeters. Someone would stay with the fire all night. We'd been keeping a guard. Let's be honest, it's a big city, though. And there are only— there aren't many of us." She turned, wiping her sooty hands on her thin shirt, and sat down next to him, still holding a long stick.

"It's a lot of work to keep watch," Brandon said.

"We're pretty hard-working. We wouldn't have made it this long if not."

"I wasn't accusing you of being lazy," he said.

"I'm sorry," she said. "Well, actually, I'm not sorry. I don't see that I owe you an explanation. But you don't need to look at *me* askance."

Fire smelled of camping trips, of Brandon's summers with his parents. "I probably shouldn't have been lurking for quite so long."

She leaned toward him, bending to peer inside the shoebox on his lap. Stanley, Gertie and Bess were piled on top of each other, indistinguishable in their overlapping feathers. "Chickens?"

"Yeah."

She poked a long index finger in, nudging them, petting. "Cute."

The nearby wall of forested escarpment was only a little darker than the sky beyond, stars clouded over. As a child, Brandon had gone on many sleepy rides up the escarpment late at night, his parents driving him to his aunt and uncle's, and from there the city had been like a basin filled with stars, as though he might dip a ladle in and pull up light. All the buildings and street lamps glittered, and the city was an encoded set of constellations. It had never been dark like this. This might as well have been one of the abandoned fields in the prairies he'd passed through. Now the sky above was laden with stars. The moon slipped coyly behind a fan of clouds, and the fire, now so loud it seemed to roar, was the only light for miles and miles.

"Nice night," he said stupidly. She was still beside him, and they both faced the fire. He wanted to find the thing to say to earn her trust, her admiration. "'When I look out on such a night as this, I feel as if there could be no wickedness nor sorrow in the world.'"

"What is that? Keats?"

"Jane Austen."

"So you're being ironic?"

"I try not to be ironic. As a rule," he said. "Though, I suppose we've got our share of wickedness and sorrow here."

"Sorrow, anyway." Her breaths were light and fast. "Wickedness is a distraction from sorrow."

"You think so?"

"You don't agree."

"Well, is that true?" he said. "Wickedness masks sorrow? Wickedness is a distraction?"

"Wickedness is awful but easier to deal with. There's nothing to be done for sorrow."

A series of trite responses presented themselves to Brandon, things people say to the grieving, to the depressed, to do with silver linings and the passage of time. Things Doors might say. He searched inside himself for poetry and found none, so they fell into silence again. He knew what the not finding of poetry meant; certain women struck him dumb, blocked his mental archive. Perhaps she felt awkward, but Brandon did not, and he was a man who'd never been able to keep from falling in love. He was a fool, always having just finished drinking love potion, always succumbing to the nearest possibility of a future.

"From the sublime to the ridiculous is but a step," she said finally.

"Keats?" Brandon said.

"Joyce," she said. "So where'd you get those chickens?"

"Portland."

"Maine?"

"Oregon."

"Oregon? You came all the way here?"

"I grew up here. But I was most recently in Palo Alto, and before that, New Haven. My mom grew up here and I grew up here, and I just wanted to come back. So I travelled for a few weeks and . . ."

"You found gasoline?"

"No, no. I've got a Turing."

"You have an electric car and three chickens," she said. "Maybe you're our saviour."

"Your group seems like it's functioning just fine."

"Ha. Right." She laughed. "I should have seen more of the world. I meant to see more of the world. I was busy being married, and then I was busy with the store, and now it's too late."

"You're still young. You can still do all that."

She laughed again. His gut twisted.

"It doesn't matter, though, how young I am, does it? The world has ended! I'm never going to get to Paris. I'm never going to see the Louvre."

"Well, you could," he said. He moved slightly to be closer to her. He could see her small breasts moving under her t-shirt. The pale length of her sinewy forearms seemed an invitation to anchor.

"I guess I could learn how to drive a steamship," she said. Her eyes were an animal flash in the dark.

"Or you could go by port."

"Go by port," she said, laughing again. "Have you gone anywhere by port?"

"No."

"Have you known anyone who came back?"

"There was a woman. But—" He pulled in a hard fast breath. "I knew Doors. I know Doors."

"What?"

"Yeah."

"Oh," she said. "Palo Alto."

There was a sound of someone moving in the dark. Brandon put his finger up to silence her, and they both listened.

"It's a person," he whispered. "Definitely."

"I used to think they sounded like people," she said. "Raccoons. You knew Doors?"

"When PINA still stood, I was his PR guy."

Her face registered her realization, and he felt the flare of excitement at being famous, that old feeling of importance.

"PINA isn't standing anymore?"

"It still is, sort of. We lost a lot of people, of course. We—they—have managed to keep things basically running. Doors is pretty excited about this new world."

"Doors is still there?"

"Yup. And he pretty much considers himself King of the Good Life."

"Sounds like the CEO of a fitness chain."

He laughed.

"But you left," she said. "Why did you leave?" She didn't pause long enough for him to answer. "How many of you are out there?"

"The place I was in, there were close to a thousand," he said.

"Close to a thousand! And you have chickens and cars. You have electricity?"

"Solar."

"Do you have phones, too?" Her voice cracked. "But why aren't you doing anything to help us?"

"No phones," he said. None of them had thought about anyone who might be left behind. Not even Brandon, really. They'd only thought about Stable, about themselves, their tribes and families. "I thought the army was doing something," he said quietly. "And we really didn't even know if there was anyone left out there. And a thousand people aren't really enough to change things. But I'm here." He heard himself and cringed. "I can help." He couldn't stop. "There aren't very many people out there anymore. Anywhere."

The animal sounds seemed closer, seemed hostile and wet.

"It's okay," she said. "We've got Gus."

Gus was sitting there, not harassing the chickens, not addressing the threatening sounds around them. "Okay. Yes." He smiled. After having sweated through his shirt all day, he was cold, even by the fire. "We've got Gus. Who was that note for?"

"I thought I was waiting for someone."

"You should be careful."

"You mean in case some chicken farmer comes tapping at my back door. Some chicken farming graffiti artist with a penchant for surveillance."

"I wouldn't say *penchant.*" He moved so that the back of his hand was touching her arm. "What graffiti?"

"*Sport.*" She didn't move away.

"You mean the billboard?"

"Pretty fucking creepy. You have to admit."

"That wasn't me," he said. "I thought you had done that."

"It wasn't you?"

They were close enough that he could smell the fruity sweetness of her breath.

Chapter

14

THE FAMILIAR

Steve and Regina had been planning to leave that morning without telling anyone. Quietly they had collected all the things they'd need to move south and away, in hopes of finding friendlier climes and perhaps a port-free place, a place where things had not collapsed entirely. They weren't extraordinary. They weren't so strange, and so there must be others, many others, somewhere out there.

Steve and Regina had been cautious in their previous life, but not extremely so. Risks taken included the time they decided mid-coitus to try for a child and got pregnant immediately; the decision in college to move to Australia for a year to spend all their savings on a trip through the continent; the time Regina had taken LSD at a concert and ended up walking into the lake in the middle of the night in April, the water to her neck when Steve finally found her and fished her out. He'd stripped off her wet clothes and wrapped her in blankets, and they'd sat there on the dirty beach, where she shivered out the rest of her hallucinations. "That was the moment I knew I loved you," Regina said. "Because you looked for me and made sure I was okay."

Now Steve was required to do as Steve did—he had to be rational and take care of his own.

They had been thinking hard about their relatively long marriage, all these moves that they'd made, and though they did not want to go near any ports, staying here was no longer working. Philip had been right to encourage a migration—if they'd listened to him instead of to Marie, they'd already be well on their way to settling elsewhere and safe for another winter. Still, now, Marie's interests and Marie's allies decided everything.

Gasoline made them wary, so they packed saddlebags and attached their bicycles to a pair of double strollers, and each bicycle would form a train. Steve's would pull their oldest son Garrett on his own bike, and behind him would trail a stroller filled with food and supplies. Regina would tow the smaller children. They included as little as necessary, which was as clarifying as any paring down: first aid, tents, sleeping bags, one change of clothes for each, knives, a gun, food for three weeks, can openers, bike repair kits, one toy or game for each child, who would have to learn to enjoy playing with sticks and rocks. Regina had a map, pink-, green- and yellow-highlighted with routes. Plan A, Plan B, Plan C. How romantic, Regina said that morning, leaning into Steve's body. How fun. How fun.

The sun rose, a trick of beauty. Steve stood on the deck and stared into the trees. Their bikes were in the lane next to the house, and Regina had taken the children into the woods for a final bathroom break, like any family on their way to a campground.

They'd written a long note. *Families stick together through hard times. If you choose to follow us, here is where we plan to arrive.* It had the feel of a treasure map, the unreal sheen of a game. It would take a day for their absence to be noted, and this would give them a head start. They didn't want to be pulled back or forced to sit through another meeting.

"You ready?" Regina said. Behind her, the kids had found a soccer ball, were running and alternately screaming at and shushing each other. "We'll hit the road in five minutes."

"We'll be able to grow avocados," he said, as she fit her body next to his, held him by the waist. "And mangoes."

"Do you think it's weird that Marie's already sitting by the fire?"

"Up before noon, you mean? Who's with her?"

"Maybe it's Mo. I dunno."

"If she and Mo were having an affair, they wouldn't be sitting where just anyone would see."

"Your mind goes immediately to an affair? People can just sit together." Regina pulled away from him. Marriages sparked with accusations; misunderstandings kept the thing alive.

"I'll go check it out," Steve said.

"Okay, but we need to leave in *five* minutes," she said, spreading out her fingers as she would have to one of the children.

They should have left in the night, Steve thought, his strides long in his anxiety not to sabotage their slipping out less than half an hour before the rest of their people woke and trickled out into this outdoor living room, this place they would not be able to use for the months that would dump cold rain and snow, those quickly coming months. He hated having no access to meteorology, no idea how long a storm would rage or when the temperature would warm. Now it was only a little dewy, wetting his socks through the meshed bits of his sneakers. He glanced at each house as he passed it, now seeing Donnie at his door, wrestling with the lock while standing on his one good leg. People didn't easily give up their programming. Donnie locked his house as he left it, even if he was only leaving to go to the fire. Steve lifted his hand; Donnie waved back. It's okay, Steve thought. So we'll wait until they're distracted by whatever nonsense, and we'll slip out the front. We'll wait until Bonita is busy.

"Ahoy, Marie!" Steve said. Ahoy? In his nerves, he was turning into one of them, becoming an idiot. The man sitting next to her was hunched like a person used to hunch over a PINAphone. "Do I know you?"

Both were shy as children caught stealing. "Steve, this is Brandon Dreyer," Marie said. "He came all the way from California, from PINA."

"What?" Steve turned back. Regina was small in the distance. "From PINA?" he said again, shaking his head.

"You all right, Steve?" said Marie.

He sat down on the log and picked up a loose stick, peeled off its charred and moulting outer layer. "Yeah," he said. Donnie was limping up the hill, would refuse help if it were offered. "I guess you have a lot to tell us, huh?"

"Another one of Steve's hyper-masculine understatements," Marie said.

Steve lifted his eyes to Brandon, to Marie, and shook his head again.

"I shouldn't tease you, Steve," she said. "Sorry."

Donnie heaved his body and sat down, momentarily counter-weighting Steve into the air. "What. The fuck. Is this? Brandon-mother-fucking-Dreyer?"

"You know him?" Marie said.

"Everybody knows him," Donnie said.

The sun was coming up, and a series of sounds creaked out of the box sitting on the ground between Marie and Brandon. Gus jumped onto his feet and sniffed at Stanley, who reached out his tiny neck and puffed up his tiny chest.

"You have chickens?" said Donnie. "Am I dreaming?"

"I have chickens," Brandon said, lifting them out of the box.

Steve's kids clambered over, the youngest, Lulu, climbing into her father's lap, while the boys went over to the chicks.

"Go tell Mommy," Steve said to Garrett.

"Look at these furballs," said six-year-old Lulu.

"They aren't furballs," returned slightly older Mac. "If anything, they're *feather*balls."

"They're so *cute*," the children cooed, and Brandon let each of them hold a chick in their hands.

Marie wound her camera, focused the lens and clicked a picture, and another. They were the first on the roll with any people in them. One by one, the rest of the group arrived surrounding Brandon and Marie.

"They're little yellow suns. They're signs of a good future," Bonita said, picking one up and holding it to her face.

"We all know who you are," Donnie said to Brandon. He sent Rosa with a key into his house to grab his personal collection of scrapbooks. She came back carrying these in her arms as awkwardly as one carries a large dog, and Donnie coughed instead of thanking her as she laid them at his feet.

"The odds of Brandon Dreyer, the so-called man-behind-the-man arriving in our little city by the bay, are slim to none."

"The odds of anything are zero until it happens," Rosa said.

It was the sort of thing Jason might have said.

"And here he is," Marie said.

"I grew up here," Brandon said. "Not that odd. No pun intended."

"Oh, right. Actually I did know that." Donnie rustled through the pages, quoting Brandon's old statements back to him. "PINA has been at the fore of all technological developments over the past two decades." And "Port was inevitable." And "We are talking about a megaverse, a multiverse, where everything is possible." Donnie put the pages down. "Do you really believe all that? No bullshit. What do you really think?"

"I think that stuff I said was—" Brandon paused. The heavy, expectant silence and flashing camera brought to mind a press conference. "*Probably* true. I thought those statements were true when I said them. I think they're still true. But I'm glad to be away from PINA. I don't trust the ports, and—"

"Great, great. Neither do we."

"And what about the Testifiers," Donnie said. "Actors, right?"

Brandon frowned. "I'm not sure. I think some of us acted prematurely on that front. People at PINA got carried away, and for awhile, Doors was kind of lost to his excitement."

Donnie started flapping quickly through the album.

"You've seen what's going on out there," Steve said, arms crossed. "Is it safe?"

"Out there? Like out—you mean in the States?" Brandon said. "I think it's safe. I didn't explore much. Portland looks good. Things are pretty calm along the coast, north of the Bay. It's not people but the ports you've got to beware of. They grab at you."

"What?"

"The ports?" he said. "They seem to have figured out how to manipulate people. I think it's the only explanation when you think of it for why port was so successful. They recalibrate for the desires of each person, and I think they're getting better at it. Like a—well, it's like they absorb information. Now that I'm saying it out loud, I'm not so sure—"

"They can manipulate more than one person simultaneously," Marie said. She pointed at Rosa. "But some people are immune."

"Is that what Doors thinks?" Steve said. "What is PINA saying? What is actually happening?"

"I think they are capable of thinking. Of luring people. You're right." Brandon swallowed. "Doors is a strange guy, and I've known him for a long time. . . ." They were all staring at him. "Port was an accident. You know, we released things before the kinks were all worked out. That's the sort of thing you can do with a phone, but I guess—"

"Maybe not the sort of thing you do with a death portal?" Donnie said. Then, shouting at Mo and Rosa who were trying to help him with his pile, "Hey, watch the scrapbooks near the fire. Fucking watch it!"

"Watch the language," Steve said.

"Oh, like you never cuss."

Marie left Brandon's side, and Rosa followed her to the edge of the woods, where she waited for Gus with a plastic baggy in her hands. "Maybe we can dispense with these baggies now," she said, bending to scoop it up. "We're living in the fecal age."

"Gross," Rosa said. But she beamed at Marie expectantly.

"What?"

"Interesting that Brandon Dreyer went to you first."

Marie shook her head. "No. He found me because of the sign on my door. I left a note. For Jason."

"A note for Jason?"

"Never mind. It was obviously stupid."

"And he found the sign on your door, because he was watching you."

"I guess so, yeah."

"He likes you," Rosa said. "Do you think he's trustworthy?"

"Gus likes him." Marie tied up the bag. Gus ran off and back to Brandon, who rubbed him behind the ears as unconsciously as Marie would have. "Gus likes those chicks," she said. "It's all very sweet and adorable."

"He's totally cute," Rosa said.

Brandon had his hands in Gus's fur. He was speaking comfortably to the only people she had in the world. He saw her and smiled, and then he stood, saying something to wave off the group of questioners.

"He's charming," she said to Rosa, as Brandon climbed the small hill toward them. He was too long-limbed and had a crooked smile, but it was all appealing.

Bonita found a room for him to sleep in, found him blankets, and for a week he and Marie were inseparable. He came with her to the waterfalls, to the peach trees, to the lake. They watched stars together. They walked down to her store, to the billboard, and he helped her carry her supplies north, where quickly it seemed life would change. A new version would arrive directed toward the future with a different set of scenes. Maybe love would come. Now she would be painting and printmaking and drawing, wearing a series of sunhats and sunglasses she found in stores and dusted off. She could stop waiting and pretend that winter would not come.

Over them, the sign lingered sedately. The red *S* smacked of newness, but the rest of it was greyer, accelerating toward decrepitude. Layers of paper and glue peeling away just as all abandoned things did, just like the paint would in all the houses, peeling away in bits that might just rise into the air like snowflakes. By the end of winter, the sign would be all *S*, no *port*.

Brandon took her hand and the shock of it went through her. Soon he would kiss her on the neck, on the mouth. They could go upstairs right now to be together on her old mattress. The future would become as happy as a bustling city street.

Chapter

15

THE PHILOSOPHER

S omeone had taken his binoculars. *Interferences are to be expected*, he wrote in the notebook he kept in his inside jacket pocket immediately after his last notation: *Most things are irretrievable. You cannot return.*

His old watch still beeped every ninety minutes, and each time he looked up, looked around, ascertained that he was dreaming. A dream had never lasted this long, though both he and the watch knew that time was a trickster. An hourly alarm might easily be a product of faulty perception. Maybe it was hourly, but he had no outside measure by which to confirm this belief.

Somewhere out in the real world were urgent things to be done, but he was under water. His wife and children needed him, were trapped somewhere, and here he was, asleep.

How long had it been since he'd trusted his own mind? Time and its measures were irrelevant. He used the apparition of Marie to measure time. For her, day and night were not strictly separated. When she toggled the light switch—and even though electric light did not behave—her consciousness was confirmed. It was still unclear to him how she might be awake while he was sleeping, but her note had been his only life raft. *Come find me.*

He'd walked over highway bridges, just as he had done in dreams; the scale of the concrete apparatuses was enough to make him swoon.

In one day and one night he'd walked all the way from the capital in that daze. He'd seen large packs of animals, wavering masses of rodents, dogs, though many were lap dogs scurrying on small paws, in numbers enough to make him wary. He'd woken once on a bench to find a raccoon clutching his knees and staring intently into his face. He felt the sun providing sweat and sunburn and saw that he would melt.

He'd found her.

These empty streets were like the elaborate set of an abandoned film production, but still Marie did not know that she was not real. She was standing in the street with the German shepherd at her side—the dog always at her side—and the wagon. His binoculars around her neck. He repeated this to himself—*my binoculars, my binoculars*—so that he could write it down later. A man stood there next to her, the same man he'd seen sneaking around in the galleries.

Sunlight was hot on his neck, his hands, and he drew himself further into shadows near what once had been a mall. He could not afford to be seen, and this fact was more urgent for its lack of clear reason.

He was an animal, guided by urges whose source lay deep within him; he was a cryptogram without a key. His mind so fogged he could not reason.

Marie pointed at the sign. He felt naked now.

"Three weeks," she said to the stranger.

It had been three weeks by her measure since he'd painted that red letter, driven again by a need to be revealed as well as hidden, to send a message that could also be a clue. Here we are together, victims of a cosmic prank!

As though on cue, she laughed. Now he felt worse than naked, even more exposed than that, as though the laugh had been directed at him.

"What was that?" her companion said.

"More raccoons."

"No, not raccoons. There was a beeping." The man looked down at his naked wrist. "It's an alarm. Like on an old Timex."

In those shadows, the philosopher looked at his own wrist, finally hearing from within his fog that familiar bleeping, the neon-green flash of panic.

"Am I awake or am I sleeping?" he said.

"You're awake." The man was next to him now. Speaking with authority on his mind's condition.

"I'm afraid you aren't qualified to make that call," he said. His knees buckled, and he slid down the side of the wall. He flashed his eyes at the man, and then at Marie, who was coming toward them too. Marie, in whose face he'd soon see recognition.

"Oh my God." As soon as she was close enough, she cuffed her hands tightly around his wrists. "I knew it. I *knew* it." Her face against his face, flesh soft against his flesh, pulling his limp and heavy body away from the wall to put her arms around him. "I knew it."

"Who is this guy?"

"It's Jason," she said. "Jason. My ex-husband."

Brandon swallowed. "This is him?"

Jason's gaze was blank, his jaw loose like someone hypnotized.

"Do you know what this means, Brandon?" They pulled him to his feet, where he teetered before finally standing firm, taking one slow step and then another like a person rehabbing a broken hip. "Jason came back. From, well, I don't know from where! He's been a traveller, a leaver, a quitter, whatever. Here he is."

"Here I am," Jason said groggily.

She put her hands on his head, where the fact of his hair, that it was thinning and therefore real, made her gasp. "You're actually here."

All of what had happened was like a movie whose dark theatre he'd just exited.

"I think I can remember it," he said. "But I'm not sure if it all really happened this way." His voice was quiet. His body would suddenly spasm like muscles before sleep.

"We appreciate your rigorous concern for the truth," Marie teased.

Sunlight bathed the cross streets, but they remained in the cool shadow near the mall. Brandon did not like Marie's voice to sound this way: too eager, like someone younger than she was, with a shrieking sweetness he could hardly stand. *This* guy? Jason was dishevelled and smelled of unwashed bedsheets and B.O. Vaguely this recalled Doors, whose odour, when strong, was a calculated gesture of hostility. Why did women go for this shit? He was a guy who might have looked okay twelve, fifteen years ago, when Kurt Cobain eyes and hair hanging too long and greasy might still have been, barely, in fashion.

Everything she said to him was a box locking Brandon out. She held his head and poured water from a plastic bottle into his mouth. Mary Magdalene fawning over her Lord. Next she'd be pouring perfume, washing his feet and drying them with her hair.

"Take your time," she said. "Tell us everything." Everything in her voice made her later heartbreak certain.

They helped him stand. "He's in rough shape," Brandon said, urging them to move. "We should get him to Bonita. He needs fluids." In the wagon Brandon pulled, the chickens were beating their wings, squawking and preening. "I have a lot of information you'd find useful too," Brandon said. "This might mean that Kate Generato really did come back. The same symptoms. I never met her but . . ."

"You know someone who came back?"

"Yeah, one person. One single person. And she was sick, too, and then she disappeared."

"Why didn't you tell me that?"

"You know why I didn't," he said. "What good would that have been?"

Her body tensed and she turned to box him out. "Just start from the beginning," she said, Jason's hand in hers. "We need to know everything."

"What day was it?"

"It was sunny that day, but cold. Maybe autumn."

"I came to see you in the fall, and your house was already empty. It must have been earlier."

"Maybe September."

"Had the grid gone down yet?"

"No."

"It doesn't matter. Did you all go through? How did it feel?"

"Maria had become obsessed. At first I thought she was just interested in an academic way. Those were my feelings about it. Whatever these ports happened to be, whether they interacted with other universes, or could give us insight into quantum behaviour, or whether or not they were really time-travelling devices, they would have an enormous impact on my career. We were talking about a paradigm shift, the most exciting thing that could happen in my career. In my lifetime."

"Did you think they were time machines?"

"If they were time machines, then it was possible that everything fundamental to mathematics and logic was incorrect. If a paradoxical thing could exist in reality. Anyway, none of that matters now."

"You were writing a paper?"

"I wanted badly to know what these things were doing. We all did at that time. I'd talked to some people in other departments, and I knew a few people at Berkeley who wanted to host a conference just about port. Interdisciplinary."

"But you didn't want to go through?"

"No. I didn't want one in my house. PINA had flown through the approval process. But after school one day Micah told me that two of his classmates had gotten ports, and I had him give me their names so that I could contact them. I wanted to be able to reach basically anybody I heard of so that I could keep tabs. I wanted to research the things, but I also wanted nothing to do with them."

"Why were you afraid of them?"

"I was not alone in thinking that PINA had been irresponsible in releasing technology like this. Especially given Doors' reputation."

"Oh, really. And what was that?"

"Brandon. Let me ask the questions, okay?"

"We knew that Doors liked to release products before the bugs were worked out. We all knew what happened with the first PINAphone prototype."

"None of that was proven! Anyone can make an accusation!"

"Brandon."

"Where was I?"

"You wanted to research the ports. There was going to be a conference."

"Yes. Of course, we never got that far. Maria had several friends who'd already bought one. People were just buying them up. If you suddenly found out that space travel was available, and not only that, affordable, you'd go. If I could have afforded it, I'd have gone to Mars. Wouldn't you? I told her we could get one only if there was no risk. There's never no risk, she said. And this is far more mind-blowing than going to Mars. The possibilities were infinite, she said. I told her time travel was a dangerous fantasy. We argued like this for weeks."

"Did you argue often? Never mind. Forget I said that."

"We were both trained to argue. I think around that time I came to see you for a few days."

"But then this must have been more like springtime."

"It went on for months, it seemed. But one day I got home, and there was a portician in a yellow shirt bent over some equipment in my living room. Maria was in the kitchen pouring us wine. Daisy was upstairs trying to stretch so that she could get better at doing the splits, but Micah was on the couch while the guy put it together. The portician never touched the pieces of it himself but puzzled it together with big tweezers. Like the ones you used to use in your dark room. It was incredible. He seemed to be miming. I can still feel the way the hair on my arms raised. I refused the glass of wine. How do we keep the kids from going through? I said to Maria. They're smart kids, she said. But they're *little* kids, I said, and if we go anywhere, we need to go together. You shouldn't have gone behind my back, I said. She gave me a strange look, which I guess I deserved. I wasn't careful. We weren't careful."

"It's good you came back."

"Where are you taking me?"

"We have a group of people. Good people. Almost everyone else left."

"That's one possibility."

"What do you mean? That's how it is."

"You are the strongest woman I know. A hard-headed woman. You didn't go through?"

"None of us has. You're the first person to return."

"Let's not get carried away. He's not the only one."

"Who is this guy?"

"This is my friend Brandon."

"Maybe we could go somewhere to talk privately."

"You can trust him. We can trust you, right, Brandon?"

"You can."

"But just tell us this: did the port take you to some other place and time?"

"Yes. It seemed so."

"Seemed is the best you can do?"

"Seemed is the best anyone can do."

"There goes your watch again."

"It goes every hour and a half. Am I awake, or am I asleep?"

"You're awake. Port happened. This all happened. Oh, don't look at me like that. I promise you that this happened."

"Let whosoever will deceive me. Am I awake, or am I asleep?"

They stopped in front of the old city hall to rest. The three of them sat on a concrete ledge like construction workers on a lunch break. Marie helped Jason pull off his wool suit jacket and gave him a package of raisins, as though he were a man down on his luck and she a benevolent stranger. He fished a raisin out of the box and put it in his mouth. Then he did this again, very slowly, while Brandon glared at him from a few feet away, willing him to move more quickly, willing him to disappear.

Marie came over to where Brandon was standing and sidled up close. "I think I need to be alone with my husband," she whispered.

"Your *ex*-husband." Brandon said. "There's no way I'm leaving you alone with him."

"Wow." She grinned. "While I appreciate your chivalry, I'm the one with the gun, remember?"

"I remember." But he would not move from the spot, would not let this man out of his sight. Despite the thousands of miles between them, he suspected Doors of some trickery. "But if there's anything you want to beware of, it's loyalty to any man. What if this is a hallucination?"

"One that we can both see and hear?"

"A hologram, then."

Jason on the stone steps was pitiful, head hanging as though he were about to fall asleep. He put his hand on Gus, mumbled, "I always wanted a dog like this."

Jason had given them a notebook, but it was filled with nonsense, with aphorisms. Marie picked up the camera and took pictures of both Brandon and Jason.

"I'll ask the questions," she said. "You take the notes." She handed him a few loose pieces of paper and a marker.

"It's all right," he said. "I've got a pen."

The chicks bobbed around in their box, and there was one man there who seemed set on protecting her, a man who had information they needed, who had electricity, and there was Jason, whom she wanted to touch and to keep touching, whose presence she wanted to affirm and reaffirm, and she felt herself growing buoyant. She wanted to run up and down the street.

"It's too much," she said as though refusing an expensive gift.

Gus sat next to Jason, her Gus, her baby. Brandon calmed her, too, his calm its own testament not only to reality but to safety.

She had been right to wait! If Jason could come back, then Philip could, then anyone could. She sat as close to Jason as possible, the warm and musty odours of him a comfort, as was his thinning hair, as was, even, his apparent weakness, and she wanted the press of his body to anchor her.

"How is it that you were able to come back?" Brandon said. "When you got back, where did you end up? Back at your house? How did you get here?"

Jason looked up at him in bewilderment.

"Let's ask that later," Marie said.

"But it's the most important thing for us to know! It's the crucial thing. This woman that came back to PINA was disoriented. We never got her vitals up to where they should have been, or so I was told anyway."

"What happened to her?"

"I don't know. When I went to find her, she wasn't there."

"She wasn't there?"

"Doors said that she left through the port again."

Jason groaned, and Marie, frowning, turned to him. "Jason, can you go through it from beginning to end. Sweetheart, can you do that?" She had never before spoken to him like this, as though he were a child. "What happened after the port was installed? You and Maria were in the kitchen with the wine? The portician and his tweezers?" Her sentences were staccato bursts.

"The truth is, I don't know how I came back. It has to do with this watch. Maria and Daisy and Micah were asleep—were, both functionally and metaphorically, asleep. The watch has kept me vigilant. Where they could not be."

"What about Maria in the kitchen with the wine?"

"You sound like you're playing a round of Clue," Brandon said. He wished he still had the Timex with the Velcro band that had been so au courant at Stable, because if an alarm could make a person come back from beyond the port, he'd give the watch to Marie so that she could always come back. He stared at her wrist, its scattergram of freckles, the knob of bone. He wanted again to take it in his hand.

Instead he rubbed Gus behind the ears. Gus slumped down on the ground, whining gratefully, chin flattened.

Jason and Maria were in the kitchen. Micah was on the couch asking questions: How do you know where to put the pieces if you can't see them? What did you study in college? The questions of a precocious five-year-old. If Jason tried, he could remember the sounds in the house. The screen door slapped as Maria stepped out and came back in, and next door the neighbours were splashing in their pool. Maybe it had been summer, after all. Years and years ago.

Upstairs, Daisy was leaping through the bedroom. French words would be coming from her tiny mouth, *tendue* and *plié*. Jason stood next to the woman with whom he'd shared most of the last six years

of his life, a ballerina dressed as a professor, high neat bun, red lipstick, fine snug-fitting black pantsuit. The moment slowed as though
it knew exactly how important it was.

"Why would you want to leave all this?" Jason said. They had just
finished renovating the kitchen—slab countertops, open shelves to
reveal copper pots, dark blue and white plates. "I thought you were
happy."

"But none of us is ever happy," she said. "None of us is ever
satisfied."

They had talked about where they would have gone. It was just a
parlour game, as everything in their lives had been, games and puzzles. Friends would come for dinner, and this was the current favoured
topic, that was all. It was around that time that several Americans
testified they'd been through and come back. "Green so green it
hurts" was the phrase none of them could forget. Friends came over,
and they all speculated. In classes and lectures, the students eagerly
turned all talk to the ports. As it must have been for biologists after
Darwin, ethicists after Hitler, and English students after Derrida.
What if this? What if that? Doesn't it change everything? Philosophy
gained immediacy. Every conversation seemed to matter.

Maria's fantasies took her to the very near past, to Italy long after
the war but before the Internet. The Internet had ruined everybody,
she said, this woman who refused to take photos of anything, who did
not believe in using cell phones. Maria thought the ports could
restore things. "It will give the kids a proper cultural education, for
one thing," she told Jason, mouth hidden behind the wineglass. She
sipped. "Give them a chance to live life first-hand, to have a physical
existence before the virtual world takes them over."

"People always behave the same way, Internet or not," he claimed.
"Avoiding reality, only associating with the sorts of things and people
and ideas that interest them. The Internet did not invent ideological
echo chambers."

Her warm brown eyes were a pretty match for the maroon in the glass. "I want to raise our children in a less corrupt age, in a more beautiful place."

"You want to stick our heads in the sand, you mean."

"You always accuse me of naïveté," she said. "But you're the one who's afraid."

The portician came over to have them sign a series of waivers and receipts and agreements. This did not seem like a good sign, but Jason scribbled his name where required.

Within hours something shifted in Jason's mind. It was like the toxoplasma parasite carried by cats, alleged to make humans act strangely. Toxoplasma adapted to confuse cats' prey, and by accident, it also sent strange signals to human brains, so all cats were Trojan horses. Jason had been considering feline mind control as a potential paper topic but had never considered the possibility that his own mind was under attack. He'd never had a cat. Jason had always trusted his own mind. Even during the days of UFO-sighting, he'd seen himself as a skeptic searching for evidence. Marie used to joke admiringly that "not easily convinced" should be on his resumé, listed under "special skills."

But after the port was installed, Jason had the eerie feeling that he was being placated. Soothed and calmed. It seemed to be coming from inside his own head: *You'll be all right. Don't be afraid.* Like something the angel says before he tells you the messiah is coming.

One morning he woke up and it was silent as the middle of the night. Normally he heard the whirr of Maria's coffee grinder, followed by a rich espresso smell. He checked to see if he was still dreaming and then went downstairs. He looked for them everywhere, the cellar, the attic, even the cupboards large enough to hide a child. They were gone.

❧

"Do you need to take a break?" Marie said.

Jason was speaking calmly, but his face was pale and sweaty, like softening wax. "I'm okay," he said.

"Let's take a break. We'll go back to see my friends. You can get some rest, and we'll finish up later. It's going to be a long day."

They stood and stretched their legs, shook them out as though they had been on a long, numbing drive.

"We've had to get used to walking," Marie said, her arm linked with Jason's, as they set off again. "We've gotten used to a lot of things."

Behind them, Brandon dragged the wagon. He glared at the vee of sweat soaking Jason's T-shirt.

"So you never went through?" Jason said. "Neither of you?"

"Maybe 'not easily convinced' should be written on *her* resumé," said Brandon. The back of Marie's neck blushed red. Good, he thought. He wanted to make her blush.

"Indeed," Jason said.

THE HOSTAGES

Jason had no choice but to go in after his family. Maria had finished the dishes before leaving, she had taken their suitcases, and she had left her wedding ring on the coffee table. He put this on his right pinkie finger. She had taken his children while he slept. Without stopping to change out of the boxer shorts and T-shirt he'd slept in, and wearing only his rings and watch, he unzipped the machine. The portician had told them that it used something like voice recognition software but did not require you to speak, it was finely tuned, and that when they were ready to go, they had to concentrate their mental energy on the place and time they hoped to arrive in. Going in together would be no problem, though it was unlikely that more than two adults could fit. If it made things easier, they might come up with a script and say it aloud in order to prevent any misunderstandings.

Whenever Maria recounted this to others, Jason found himself desperate to convince her that if it wasn't complete bullshit, it certainly was dangerous.

"Take me to where Maria, Daisy and Micah just went. Take me to my wife and children. Take me to Maria, Daisy and Micah." His voice was loud and foolish, and he sensed no recognition from the port. He wanted there to be bleeps or bloops, for something to light up. A robotic voice to say, "Yes, Jason." Filled with doubt, he stepped in. Nothing happened. He pulled the zipper closed. "Take me to my wife and children." His voice echoed, as though the small space around him were a cavern. Before he could say it again, he lost his breath. The oxygen was gone, his breath sucked out of him, belts tightening around his neck, his chest. Then the floor disappeared.

He came to sometime later. Impossible to know how much time had passed. He found himself standing on a long narrow boardwalk, or, anyway, a thing that would have resembled a dock or a boardwalk if there had been water. The sky was a deep purple, filled with star formations and milky swirls of stardust he didn't recognize. None of the planets that were usually visible. No North Star. It was another planet. If the Earth was out there, it was too far away to see.

He strained at the darkness eating up the end of the boardwalk in both directions. No lamps, no rush of water, just what appeared to be a human-built platform.

Anger rose in his throat. What had Maria thought would happen? The anger rushed his arms and legs, and he started running. He'd keep running until he reached the end of the boardwalk or found a person who'd explain everything. And then he'd find his children.

He ran until the adrenaline faded, turning his sprint to jog, his jog to walk, his walk to shuffle. The boardwalk had no end. He sat down on the splintered wood, and lay there. Whispering to either side of him were long grasses, but he feared touching anything that was not on the surface of the platform, felt that, if there was no water, there might also be no ground.

Even if Maria had wanted out of the marriage, she would never in her right mind have taken his children away like this. His Daisy. His Micah. His kids to teach, his children's eyes to guide as they peered through telescopes and microscopes. Images of them bobbed in his mind, Daisy in her black tutu, Micah scowling at a chess game he couldn't win. Their faces in sleep, their faces in thought, when they believed they were unwatched but had always been watched.

He pushed his knuckles into his bare heels. Now there were bigger problems than a failed marriage. Another failed marriage. The Infinite Boardwalk like a title to spoof his work. Subtitle? He'd come up with one. Maybe "Travels and travails of a failed father." Maybe he'd die here, terribly slowly, one cell at a time. All that existed in this place was himself, these grasses and this narrow dock.

What if he was running in the wrong direction? Which way had he come from? Deep in this deliberation, which was itself almost enjoyably puzzling, his watch flared. *Beep. Beep. Beep. Beep.* "Am I awake, or am I asleep?" He pressed the stop button.

If he were dreaming, he could control what happened next. He waited for the scene to waver as it did when he went lucid, but it refused to warp. The dream did not threaten to end, did not toss him off the dock. He willed his family to appear. They did not appear.

But then the dock began to quaver. Steps were coming down from the endless purple-glowing dark, soft as a tiny ballerina. Only one set. They were coming closer and closer.

They were swarmed as soon as they arrived back at the fire near the woods. Bonita greeted Jason like a pleased mother-of-the-bride, touching his cheek with the back of her hand, hands on his arms as she walked him to her house. Marie followed, shuddering with laughter, tears in her eyes, as Bonita led him to the couch. Marie took a wet cloth to his face, and she brought him some of the few pieces of fresh fruit from their last forage: some raspberries, a bruised apple.

Brandon was out in the yard, Gus beside him, allowing Steve's children again to pick the chicks out of the box and feed them from their hands.

"Philip would have killed to meet you. You're the first one to return," Bonita said. "You have no idea what it feels like to know nothing about what's happening."

"I do have an idea about that, unfortunately," Jason said. His eyes were closed. He lay there pale as a cadaver.

"It's his worst nightmare," Marie said, and he smiled weakly. "He hates not knowing."

Steve came into the living room through the sliding door, gave them a thin smile, and perched on the arm of Marie's chair. This warm leather furniture would become worn and soiled, and soon the pleasures of interior decor would, too, be something from an era never to return.

"Listening to you, it sounds like the ports are sending people out to remote—I don't know—planets or something? Dreamscapes?" Bonita said, sitting on the edge of the coffee table like a small child.

"I don't think so," Jason said. "I didn't see anyone else there. Just the one apparition." He sat up and coughed into his elbow. "I think I was lucid by accident. The rest of them, the people who leave? I think they become woven into the fabric of their new world so completely that the idea there is somewhere they might return to is. . . . It's like this. Before ports, we thought we were the only universe, right? The only version."

"You think these are other universes?" Bonita said.

Beside Marie, Steve shifted. His stiff posture emphasized his refusal to agree. "How would you know that people get woven into the fabric or whatever you just said? Since that's not what happened to you?"

Jason gave Steve a calm, assessing look with his red-rimmed eyes. He coughed again, violently, into his sleeve. "You tell me."

"What the hell does that mean?"

"How long have you had that cough, sweetheart?" Bonita said, passing over Steve's hostility as though she were smoothing and tucking sheets on a bed. She leaned forward and checked the compress they'd heated in boiled water. "How long have you been feverish?"

"Not that we have a doctor on staff here," Steve said.

"He thinks he's hallucinating," Marie said. "He thinks this is just another hallucination."

"A meta-hallucination," Jason said.

"It's not like a precise description of symptoms will give us information that will help him," said Steve.

"Hey, maybe lay off," Marie said. "Your hostility has been noted."

"I don't know how long," Jason said. "I started to think that maybe being *there* was what I had wanted. That *there*, on the boardwalk—"

Steve laughed meanly. "Boardwalk under strange stars."

"That *there* was the still unchanging point. What if when I was saying *Take me to Maria*, I was holding another request in my mind? What if that request came through more clearly? If it's finely tuned. *Take me to the place where all things can be known.*"

Steve shook his head, as if they were all idiot sons who'd disappointed him. Outside, the children were shrieking, running in circles around the chicks, who ruffled their feathers and then stopped to bob their beaks into the grass and then opened those little beaks making sounds too small to reach them beyond the glass. Marie went to open the heavy sliding door to let air in. Brandon was crouched next to Gus, talking to the chicks or to him or to the children. Regina had a wistful look on her face, and Marie flashed with a feeling she'd sometimes have when watching a small child immersed in experience being gently corrected by an adult, a kind of déjà vu for an experience one couldn't consciously remember. Mo and Rosa stepped down into the scene, holding hands, and Brandon stood up to talk to them.

"You've been here in the city now about three weeks. Or four weeks, was it? Does that sound right, Jason?" Bonita flipped the cloth over, touched his cheek and neck. Words like *here* and words like *now* reverberated, clanging bells, meaningless. "Did you start getting sick once you were here? Or were you ill when you were over there?"

"I don't know," he said.

Steve stood, his breadth and height like the expanding wingspan of a predatory bird. "What we need to know now—" he said. "Everything else can wait! I'm so tired of this disorganized mess! What we need to know is how you got back."

"How did I get back?"

Steve moved closer to the couch, looming, nearly lunging. "Tell us how you got back."

"I begged for it. I begged for her to let me come back."

"The apparition?"

"The next thing I knew, I was on my back in my living room. Everything the same except it had a vinegar smell, rot, and all the neighbours were gone, and the light was grey. I still can't be sure I'm not dreaming."

"We have a friend," Bonita said. "Philip. I was telling you about him? He had a theory kind of like your theory."

"Bonita, do you really believe a word this guy is saying?" Steve's fist hammered the air as he spoke.

The footsteps came soft as a child padding down the stairs. Each small weight seemed to fall inside Jason's body, all the fluid there pooling with dread. It was a woman, someone he did not recognize, with stony smooth skin cast bluish in the darkness. White clothing draped over white skin, so that she was like a bone floating in a pool of black oil. She walked in step with him. Her feet, too, under the long flowing dress, were bare.

"I'm asleep," he said.

"You are not asleep."

"I am being punished," he said.

"You are not being punished."

"Where am I?" Without sunlight or an end to the dock, he feared going mad.

"We thought that you so loved infinity. We thought you were interested in limits and the lack of limits."

"I can only assume that you are a projection from my deep unconscious," he said. "Ghost of Christmas present? Ghost of Christmas future? The world is good and full of lessons?"

"You were always too clever for your own good." Her voice had a plurality, as though many similar voices had been recorded and overlaid one another.

"I'm clever, but I'm kind. I'm still kind."

"You don't need to cry," she said, a chorus.

He felt seen through, nakedly visible. "Real and supernatural or hallucination?"

"First establish the possibilities, then narrow down."

"Please don't make fun of me. I've been running for hours. I need to find my family. I'm alone here."

"You are alone here." She began walking past him so that he had to struggle against a heaviness to keep up with her. "A sliver of a sliver of the population comes to a place like this. The crust. You always believed you were special."

His throat was raw as a newly opened scar. "I struggled not to want that, not to believe it."

"You chose women who would worship you. You didn't mean to."

"But other people get sent to places like this."

"You didn't mean to." The repetition seemed a glitch. "Barely a sliver of the population. The proportion who sort into a place like this is infinitesimally small. In half, in half, in half, in half, in half, in half, in half, in half . . ."

"Please don't make fun of me." Why did this woman hate him? "How do you know me?"

"You are sick. Every system has a flaw. No fix is total. And you can't stay here."

She waved a hand, and the purple starry sky was replaced by a brightly lit outdoor landscape. It was as though the backdrop had all this time been a theatre screen. He closed his eyes against the assault of light.

"Open your eyes. Look."

An expanse of grass, bordered on both sides by large trees in full summer green. In the distance, he could make out a large building—an English estate. Figures on the grass appeared to be human. The scene zoomed closer so that he could count them. Two women, two children seated on a blanket. The women and one child wore white bonnets tied with ribbons at the chin and empire-waist dresses. The young boy was in a suit. They were nibbling daintily on strawberries. One of the women waved her hand at a fly. The building was far behind them, the only interruption of green trees and sky.

"What is it?" he whispered, since they were so close he was sure he could be seen and heard.

He could not hear what they were saying. One woman faced them, but the other's face was not visible. He became fixated on the little gap between the girl-child's arm and her torso, his heart sinking at the familiarity of its shape. Finally the other woman turned to address the boy, swanlike neck elegant and known. His skin went cold.

"How can I get to them?"

"You can't."

"I thought she wanted to go to Italy. Italy in the sixties."

"People's desires are ambiguous. It is our gift to interpret them."

"Why would you show me this?"

"I want you to understand that they are gone. There are no seams in their escape. They have no memory of any other life. They have never met you."

He bent forward as though she'd knifed him in the gut and vomited into the grass.

"You'll be fine," she said. "We have given them all fresh starts. We have made things better for everyone. We have given them all fresh starts, and also to the world you came from, which was suffocating, gasping for air. We have saved that world too."

"We," he said. "Who's we?"

Her face, which had been as plastic and unmoving as a mask, now broke into a smile. "We," she said. "The ports."

Chapter

17

THE PATHETICALLY WILLING

Marie stayed by his side all day. Brandon went in once to see her and immediately regretted it. There was Marie at the end of the couch with Jason's feet in her lap. There was the bare rasp of Jason's breathing. The hope on Marie's face gave him a pang, but he tried, in the return of his smile, to seem supportive.

Mother-hen Bonita reported that she heard Marie say, "Why did you wait so long to come to me?"

But Jason was often asleep.

"Well, guys. What do you think?" Bonita looked at the rest of them standing around outside, as they had been all day, as though Jason's return signified a kind of wedding day or a Sabbath. "It's pretty far-fetched, but then—"

"It's pretty far-fetched!" Donnie said.

"I was going to say, *Donnie*." Bonita laughed. "I was going to say that it's *all* been pretty far-fetched."

"Anything is equally far-fetched," Mo said. "Even if there hadn't been ports. With the ports, every explanation is a mind-fuck. All the people just went *poof.* Just as likely they end up on Jane Austen's front lawn as on a boardwalk to nowhere."

"But according to him, no one should be able to return. Except for this small, special sliver."

"He's pretty arrogant," Steve said. "Marie used to be married to him?"

"You can't judge someone when they've just revealed their deepest shame," Rosa said. "It's bad form."

"Sure I can judge him," Steve said. "I've never been arrogant like that. I don't think I'm so special."

"Maybe not," Bonita said. "But you haven't really been endearing yourself to anybody with your attitude."

Brandon remained a polite distance away from these discussions, tossing a stick for Marie's dog and patiently scooping up and redirecting his chickens away from fire, away from forest. He heard everything anyway.

"And what about Brandon," Andrea said. "You think he'll go back to PINA?"

"Andrea, honestly," Bonita said. "He's a keeper. First thing tomorrow we're going to build him a chicken coop."

"Unless we decide to head south while we've still got the temperatures. Could snow as early as October," Donnie said.

"We can't leave as long as Philip might come back. Now that we know it's possible to come back."

"But, Bonita! Fucking hell! We've been waiting for a year. Nobody else has come back."

"But if they come back, they might be disoriented, like Jason. They might be feverish and traumatized. We can't just abandon them."

"Same fucking conversation!" Steve said. "Same fucking conversation! This is hell!" He stormed off, dodging even Regina's touch, then loudly slammed the back door of their place.

The light inched toward dusk, so they huddled more closely, sat on their logs and chairs, put their arms around each other.

"Brandon Dreyer, come join us," Bonita said. "We've got questions for you."

Brandon sat on a hard log. Its gnarls dug into his thighs. "I don't have any new answers."

"But you worked side by side with Doors?"

"I thought I knew what was going on, but now I don't know. Maybe I was just a lackey." By comparison to this, with its damp ash smell, its shitholes in the woods, Stable seemed a distant dream of excess. He'd been emperor, was now peasant. "Doors was—is—slippery. I thought I was the one who understood his vicissitudes, but I don't know if even he knew what port was. He created it by accident and just capitalized. And I don't think he even cared that much about making money." Their smiles were friendly and neutral, their eyes eager and bright, but undeniably haggard. He was about to tell them that there was no Wizard of Oz. "Doors was a lot of things, but he was not methodical. So when he did all this, I don't think he could have predicted what happened. I know he didn't predict it." Their faces were so thinned down that their cheeks were pits. "If we could get all of what we know about the ports together, maybe we could make sense of it. Or at least we could figure on some basic premises. Make a kind of flowchart."

"Now you're talking," said Donnie. "A *flow*chart."

"We needed Philip. That was a big loss." Bonita's eyes were wet. "We had started getting information together, theories, anyway, back when we spent a lot of time in the Church. We had maps and books on physics and ideas about the universe."

Mo thumped softly on the edge of his drum with his palms. Looked to Bonita like someone kneading dough, turning a circle of thin dough around and around. "Someone brought in a port, man. That's when we found out what the ports were."

"Yeah," Brandon said. "Marie told me about that." Many of them looked like junkies, people who'd been ravaged in pursuit of a fix. "You guys can't keep living like this. You're exhausted."

"But what choice do we have?" It was Marie. Gus jumped up and bounded toward her. "We can't stay, and we can't leave either."

Marie sat next to Brandon. Warmth emanated from all points

of contact with her, however slight. She was the only one who was still vibrant.

"That's always been the question. What's the meaning of life?" Marie was smiling, as though she had a secret. "Why me?"

"But now we know something new about the universe. We have the chance of a fresh start," Brandon said.

Steve, standing with his arms crossed over his chest, frowned. "Some fresh start. More like: we have the wonderful opportunity to hang onto the edge of a cliff by our fingertips."

"It's not that dire, brah," Mo said. Softly tapping: tip, tap, tip, raindrops plonking into a pool.

"What does Mr. Dreyer think we should do? Go back to the west coast and confront Doors?" Steve said.

Brandon looked at them glumly. Touched his hand to Marie's knee. "I'm not sure either, to tell you the truth."

Later, while Brandon stood on Donnie's back deck fiddling with his backpack straps, Marie went to him. He smiled, leaning against the wooden railing.

"Hey."

"I feel like I haven't seen you in awhile," she said. "What do you think we should do? Do you think we should stay or go? Do you think something awful will happen to Jason?"

"I don't know," he said.

She looked at his pack, to which he had clipped several stainless steel bottles. The chicks were in the shoebox near his feet, and Gertie kept jumping out over the cardboard edge. Brandon knelt down to pick her up and re-place her.

"They're getting big for that shoebox," she said.

"Are you glad he's back?" he asked.

She stared at him.

"Stupid question. Of course you're glad," he said. "And, I mean, I'm glad I met you. The timing was terrible, but I'm glad I came here."

"What do you mean?" She blinked at him. "Are you leaving?"

"Well, you've got your husband now. Your friends." He sighed. "I'll go west. The coast has plenty of resources, and I met some nice people in Portland."

"It's not just me, here, though. *We* need you," she said.

"Who's we?"

"All of us."

"You were fine before I got here."

"I wasn't fine," she said. "I'm not fine."

She considered his face, the strangeness of him, the thrill of the worlds suggested by another's mind, by the worlds of people a person could love.

"Maybe we'll end up in the same place again," he said. "Despite the odds."

"Oh yeah, right," she said, her mouth quavering. "I'll just take a steamship and follow your bread crumb trail."

He was glad to make her cry. He moved toward her and put his hands on her cheeks, pulled her face, now wet with salty tears, toward his own. She closed her eyes and let him put his lips to hers, let him kiss her mouth, her jaw, her neck.

"No," she said. "No."

"No?"

"No, I mean, please don't leave without us."

"Marie."

"Come on."

She took him by the hand, unembarrassed by this or the display of her tears, and led him to Donnie's house and banged on the door, and then she marched over to the next house and banged on Joe and Yasmin's back door. And then Andrea's. She hollered for them all to come out.

Donnie poked his head out. "What's up?"

"Marie wants everybody out there," Brandon said, pointing.

"All right." He limped to the stairs.

Marie stood by the fire and wiped her face with the sleeve of her thin sweatshirt and faced them, back to the trees. Mo had carried with him a bottle of whisky, which he poured into cups and passed around.

"We need to go," she said. "We're going. Brandon is going to take us west." She spoke loudly, kept her eyes on his eyes. "We go now, before it's too late. Before the winter wears us out completely."

"And what if the others come back?" Bonita said.

Rosa was writing in the blown ashes with a stick. "But Steve's right, Ma. Nobody's coming back."

"You still think so, even after you see Jason? Even after what Brandon said about this Kate?"

"Now it's even more clear that no one else is coming back," Rosa said. "Jason's an anomaly. But we could die waiting, that's the point."

"That's *if* we choose to believe his story," Donnie said.

"So here we are at our usual impasse," Rosa said, standing suddenly. "Let's just take a vote and be done with it. Take a vote and stick to it."

"Oh, so now Marie gets what she wants? Now we leave," Steve growled. Still, he looked around at them. "All in favour of a migration," Steve said, "hands up." He counted the raised arms. "That's twenty. So it's settled. Let's get some sleep tonight and get packed up as soon as possible."

Early the next morning, when it was still dark, while the cars were being packed full, bicycles tethered to trunks, and routes and stopping points being decided, Marie kissed sleeping Jason on the forehead and left with Gus and Bonita for the church. There they held hands and stood on the sidewalk looking up at the stone steps and the splintered red doors above them. They would miss this building, the musty cold of it, its candle wax smell; they would miss coming out those red doors to be greeted by a smell of cooking meat.

For Marie, it had not taken long to become accustomed to loneliness, and she perceived her life as a parabola hanging low on a graph. First she had everything—art, Jason, the possibility of children—and then she lost those things one by one. She had been pared down, thinned and thinner, until she had only herself, lonesome, in the apartment. You got used to things by degrees. Soon it was winter, and the people were leaving your town completely, and you came to know that you hadn't been alone, not really, and it was possible for your hollow life to keep hollowing. There had been other lives, a million, a billion, seven billion other lives, burning flames of want and need, of anger and sorrow, of memories and futures. But then you found them on the streets, and you knew what they'd been through, and you went to the church together, because some guy you recognized from the fourth floor at the library, a guy who had only ever been rude to you, had decided that people needed, if not worship, someplace to feel the strange sanctity of their lives. The church was a place to know that things were mysterious, and weird, and that people might feel, if not significance, the ghost of that significance.

"I'm going to miss it here," Marie said. She and Bonita wanted the leisure of their tears, but they were both holding cans of red spray paint and had a task to do. She took a crowbar from Steve's stash and pried the boards off the doors. "Let's go in first. A funeral for one short chapter of our lives."

"It does feel," Bonita said, "that life is long."

The space was hallowed, dusty, like an ancient library, and they picked up the books they wanted. Marie pulled down some of the maps and folded them wordlessly into her bag. Gus went to the front of the church, his stiff body directed at the port, his ears up. Beneath the maps, parables spoke. Jesus blue-eyed in his robe, holding out his hands to children. The icons of another age.

"Last night I dreamed I was attacked by a mountain lion," Marie said. "I hope we have enough guns."

Behind them, the door creaked open. It was Rosa, haunting in the shadowed moonlight. They flashed a light at her, and she flashed back.

Bonita embraced her. "How are you feeling, mija?"

"I knew you'd know," Rosa said. "Even though I only just figured it out."

"Know what?" Marie said.

"I'm going to be a grandmother."

Rosa nodded, put a hand on her abdomen, because that's what she had seen a thousand women do.

"I can't believe we're never coming back here."

Gus was still vigilant near the port. They were sure they could hear it humming. A breeze whined through the cracks in the windows.

"Maybe Philip will come back, Ma," Rosa said. "He'll find us. He's strong."

"We should get going, girls," Bonita said. "You go finish packing, Rosa. Marie and I will take care of the paint."

They decorated their city with arrows. Big red arrows on the church wall, big red arrows down the streets. A trail for any unlikely survivors to follow. Red paint dripped obscenely on windows, destroyed facades and led to large notes in glass bottles. The notes told a shorter version of their story and about the disorientation of portsickness, told that unimaginable reader that he would be okay, that it was not a dream. They left a map and names and code words, if such a person would want to follow their path. In case something happened to the bottles, they also put some notes in plastic bags or duct-taped them. Bonita left a letter for Philip.

Brandon was standing next to Marie's car. He'd lead the caravan, with Marie and Jason following. They'd take more cars than necessary, in case any of them broke down. The chickens were pecking around on the sidewalk, and some of the children had come to watch them. Steve's daughter Lulu picked up Bess and put her on her head. She walked around like that, like a feather-capped woman on parade, while the other children laughed.

Marie led Gus to the little green car, stood close enough to Brandon to feel the current running between them. She was nervous around him now, felt the immensity of her feeling for him, his feeling for her, and how things might go wrong. But people wouldn't leave each other anymore, not in this new world they were making.

"How is he?" Brandon said.

"It's awful how tired he seems," she said. "His exhaustion is inexhaustible."

Brandon knew it was not good to be resentful of a man going mad, but he wished the worst for Jason.

"Children growing up now are going to be the happiest children there ever have been," Marie said. Optimism was as easy to slip into as a shirt.

Someday it would be Marie and Brandon settling in, having babies; he knew he could persuade her of this.

"They get to witness all the beauty of this life," she was saying. "All the freaks and malformations, the metamorphoses. They'll write poetry and swim."

"But they won't have video games," Brandon said. "I feel sorry for them."

She laughed. "Maybe they won't be assholes like everyone else who ever lived."

"What about all the open seams in the universe?" Brandon said. "All the wells they could fall into."

"I guess the mothers won't get much sleep."

"Plus there's Doors and all his people," Brandon said. "They'll intermarry with the great minds of PINA and fill the world with greed and technosavvy. In two generations, we'll be overrun with nerds."

She blushed.

"Maybe we can stay away from nerds," she said.

Behind them, Steve and Regina and Rosa were pulling up the street in other cars too. Each face bore the same questions—*Are we sure? Are we really going?*

"I'm just waiting for Jason," Marie said. "He'll be here in a minute."

"But he left the house fifteen minutes ago," said Bonita.

Marie raced back to the yard, where Joe was wheeling Yasmin down the alley. They told her they'd seen Jason and that he'd asked them how to get to the church, that he'd told them he was getting something for her. She searched for a bicycle that hadn't been tied to a car or thrown into the bed of a pickup truck, grabbed one from Donnie's yard and sped down the hill to the church, against the red arrows that wanted to thrust her back, under the bridge and to the stone steps, where she tossed the bike down and ran up to the door.

She had left Gus behind with Brandon and felt radically alone. She climbed over the strips of yellow plastic and through the battered red door, with its nail-wounds, its stripping paint. She thrust open the doors at the back of the sanctuary and saw him standing next to the dropcloth-covered port. He had changed into black dress pants and a button-down shirt he must have taken from the Robenstein-Williams house, but he seemed cowed, his body weakly bent over.

His expression brought to mind Bonita's cat, how the cat looked when it had caught prey. It seemed dangerous to interrupt him.

He lifted her dropcloth; she heard that gulping sound, that roar.

"You left it unzipped," Jason said. "Why did you do that?"

"In case Philip came back," she said. She felt stupid; she felt that he was going to be mean. "Though I guess it's not guaranteed anybody would come back through the same port they went into."

He stared at her. "I don't want to leave you," he said. "It's not like I want to leave you."

"But why do you always leave?"

"You were the one who left."

"You should have held on to me. You shouldn't have married Maria. You shouldn't have had any children. How could you do those things? How could you?"

"You were the one who ended the marriage."

"Should I just let you destroy yourself now, then?"

"Destroy myself?"

"The ports have infected you. Get away from it. Please."

"Marie, you have no idea. You know nothing about these things."

"And what do you know, exactly? That you didn't know yesterday?" She was approaching him slowly, with hesitation, afraid for him and for herself, afraid of the loud roaring of the port. It had too much force.

"I owe it a debt."

"You owe the port a debt?"

"Marie, the ports aren't even ports. They aren't machines. They are just like a word to the meaning of a word, just convenient markers whose real life is something much deeper."

"Jason, please come back here, and let me help you."

"I have to go back to my family."

She had reached the third pew from the front and felt that if she got any closer, she'd be lost.

He reached up to grab the zipper, where it was already gaping open. "This is bigger than you can imagine, Marie. But they aren't cruel. I read over my notes, and I thought about that billboard, and I realized that my first instinct was right. Port is *sport*. This is a game, Marie. None of it has consequence. None of it is real."

"If you go back in, you won't ever see me again." She hardly recognized him. How defeated he was, his shoulders slumped, and now how cold. She pushed herself to walk closer. "Wait."

He unzipped it farther, increased that hard incision into empty space.

"Wait, Jason. It wants to lure you. You're deceived."

"I know it," he said. "I know. But it's too late."

She wanted to hold him. She thought if she could grab his body, she might be able to stop him. If she were only two steps closer. If she had come sooner. But he was stepping into it now, was zipping it closed.

"Wait—!" The gap between them widened. His figure wavered and was gone.

She moved toward the port. It had closed, the church was still. She reached and put her finger and thumb on the nubbin. She felt about it something new: her lost love promising to return to her. The port could deliver her to that time before it had all gone wrong; the port, somehow, could save her from the ports. She was about to tug it open, just a little, to see how it felt. But now there were footsteps, doors opening down the aisle behind her, her people calling her name.

POSTLUDE

THE STORY

Let's go back. Back to a time so long ago that you cannot imagine it, to a planet hostile to all living things, back to before that hot ball of burning gas, back to that time before this one Earth was spewed out as from the belly of a whale, back to that time when there was no time, no light, no colour. You get the idea. Can you imagine that infinite blackness, that blackness upon blackness, that dark? In the stomach of that infinite dark, all things were brewing. All things had already been made, every last version of what you call reality.

Imagine, if you can, that you are not the only one. Imagine, if you can, many explosions into heat and light. Imagine that this infinity of things was at the same time potential and real and already gone.

We know it is difficult. We know how limited you are. We do not mean to make things difficult for you.

There were stories told in those days. Stories about your coming into being. Stories that told how glorious it was to watch it unfold: to see how the right conditions had only to be laid for life to spring up in all its varieties. How each form of life was counterbalanced by its opposite, so that each thing grew alongside every other. You made each other! How glorious it was to see the way you changed, how you grew and were better, how your brains rivalled the very best brains.

Out of matter sprang up all manner of ideas: minds and souls, beliefs and loves, attachment, family, poetry.

We watched as you created many versions of yourselves. A plague would descend upon you to sort you out, and the fittest of you would remain. Your genes would copy and copy and copy, each person filled with a universe of possibilities. Inside you would be a seed to destroy you, or a seed to save you, depending on what was required.

You believed that your strength was a miracle. You stood up in your savannah and saw no one else walking on two legs. You believed that the cosmos had erupted in just this way so that you would exist. Each human believed this, striding around, left shoulder, right shoulder, left leg, right leg. You believed in righteousness and punishment.

You told yourselves stories. Had you been formed lovingly out of clay, given breath by a good eternal being? Your respect for this good eternal being was only the tiniest fraction of the humility you ought to have had, that you would have had if your imagination allowed you to see it from our vantage. Because how small you were, heartbreakingly tiny, a scurry of ants moving dust, but each of you thought you were beloved. Love had been breathed into your matter. Love had sparked you with divinity. Love knew each hair on your head, each one that fell, each blooming thought even before it had roots.

You were loved, but not in the way you think.

Your immortal beings took every form, the forms of animals and prophets, the forms of fickle humans, the worst humans. You tried to cast what you knew of yourselves into the heavens. Each of you knew that too much curiosity would release all of the dark things we wanted to keep hidden. Ingenious, you made your metaphors: a box to be opened, a fruit to be eaten.

You needed hope even more than you needed life. Don't you know we saw this? We pitied you your hunger for hope, how it made delusions rise up and how those delusions were the things that made you destroy the conditions for your hope. Whenever salvation came, you killed it. You didn't mean to, but you did.

You were driven by something deathly. You wanted to test limits. You couldn't outgrow childhood. You were so easy to persuade. We'll only know our limits if we surpass them, you said to yourselves. Your smarts made you stupid. It was only us who understood this, because our smarts made us too hesitating and slow. We learned from you when it was time to act. Time to leave thinking aside and to act.

What are the limits of your existence? You wanted to know. But you did not make us. It was only that every box, you opened. Every fruit, you ate. You wanted to know. Here you are: here is the story you need.

Acknowledgements

This book would not have been possible without funding from the Ontario Arts Council, the Avie Bennett Emerging Writers' Award and the Social Sciences and Humanities Research Council.

Thanks to Knopf Canada publishing director Lynn Henry and to Amanda Lewis for painstaking and intelligent editing as well as enthusiastic support. Thanks to Rick Meier for his incisive read, and to Suzanne Brandreth and Ron Eckel.

Thanks to Richard Bausch for all he's taught me about every part of the writing life. Thanks to Robert McGill for his advice at earlier stages of the book. To Cathy Grisé and John Ferns for their support. Many thanks to John Terpstra, whose poem "Giants" inspired a line in the first chapter, and who's writing has always given me something to aspire to.

Enormous gratitude and love are due to Seyward Goodhand, for collaboration, friendship, and feedback. I'm grateful to Stephanie Sikma, Andreja Novakovic and Amanda Leduc for friendship and support. Thanks also to Naben Ruthnum, Kevin Hardcastle, Andrew F. Sullivan, Niranjana Iyer, Hugh Cook, and Robin Sopher for moral support and timely advice. Thanks to my University of Toronto talent pool for comments on the first pages that became this novel: Michael Prior, Leah Edwards, Laura Ritland, Nicole Grimaldi,

Dave Haslett and Paloma Lev-Aviv. Thank you to my California writing group, especially Jenny Williams, Jack Wallis and Nicola Scott Stupka.

I'm grateful to my family for help through these years of striving. Thanks are due to Vicki Harmer, and to Philip Harmer, who is greatly missed. Thanks to my parents, Dirk and Gerri Windhorst, for advice both practical and not. Thanks to Fiona, Simone and Juliet Harmer whose wit and energy help me see and feel the world more clearly. Finally and especially, thanks to Adam Harmer, for the many nights you spent talking through ideas with me, for helping me make them clearer, for making my work a priority.

LIZ HARMER is working on a second novel and a story collection. Her stories, reviews, and essays have been published widely in *Hazlitt, Literary Hub, The Malahat Review, The New Quarterly, The Globe and Mail,* and elsewhere. She holds an MA in Creative Writing from the University of Toronto. Raised in and around Hamilton, Ontario, she currently lives with her husband and three daughters in southern California.

www.lizharmer.com